FALLING IN LOVE

With a valiant effort, Irene stayed at Ross's side while they skated farther down the canal. When he turned suddenly in front of her, she slammed against him, bringing them both down in a tumble of skirts and a tangle of legs.

"Oh! I'm so sorry! Are you hurt?" she said, trying to raise herself to her feet. But the attempt only made her slip and fall on top of him again.

With a cry of despair, she tried once more, but he quickly grabbed her and said, "I think it's better if I get up first."

Rolling over her with his nose inches from hers, he lay across her. The softness of her woman's body was apparent in spite of the heavy clothing she wore, and even if he'd tried, he couldn't have ignored the curves that lay beneath them.

Then her world reeled again as his lips pressed hers, searching, fulfilling. Lost to everything but the brush of his mustache and the strength of his hands, Irene succumbed to emotions she'd only dreamed about. But this wasn't a dream or a page from one of her novels. It was happening now, and it was real.

And she didn't want it ever to stop.

Other *Leisure* and *Love Spell* Books by
Melody Morgan:
JAUNCEY

MELODY MORGAN

ABIDING LOVE

LEISURE BOOKS **NEW YORK CITY**

To Carmen—without your inspiration, this book would never have happened. This one is yours. Love, Mom

A LEISURE BOOK®

August 1995

Published by

Dorchester Publishing Co., Inc.
276 Fifth Avenue
New York, NY 10001

Printed in the United States of America.

Acknowledgments

I'd like to thank the Grand Rapids Historical Society for publishing the two volumes of historical data including many wonderful old pictures. They were an invaluable aid in my research.

Also, a special thanks to John at the Ludwig Mill, a veritable fountain of historical information.

Another thank you goes to Jan P. at the Swanton Library, who knows my penchant for "old book" sales.

But my most heartfelt thanks goes to the proprietors of Grand Rapids, who have done a wonderful job of giving life to a lovely little historical town.

Thank you all!

Prologue

The church was filled to stifling capacity. Every friend and relative who lived within a decent distance had come to see the perfect couple joined in a perfect marriage. Love, honor, and money would be their foundation. Everyone had concurred on that point throughout the courtship.

Of one accord, all eyes turned to the back of the church as the lovely, dark-haired bride moved through the entrance to stand alone, silhouetted in the bright June sunshine. Her dress was of the finest imported silk, embroidered with tiny pearls and adorned with the most delicate lace. A unified feminine sigh could be heard echoing softly off the ceiling. Hardly a woman within the confines of the church could say she wasn't envious of Irene Barrett.

Irene looked out over the rows of smiles in an effort to find reality in this moment, but she couldn't focus on a single face. She couldn't recognize a single friend. Frantically, her eyes searched the front pews, where she knew her three sisters and her mother sat. With concentrated effort she was able to locate and identify the proud features of Winnie Barrett, who beamed happily back at her daughter.

Forced to look away, Irene swung her gaze toward the front of the church and had to steady herself.

Andrew was waiting. His self-assured stance and oh-so-charming smile tried to convince her that everything would be all right.

The organ struck a soft chord and the familiar wedding march vibrated through the air. Irene took a few halting steps forward as though an invisible string tugged her unwilling body toward the sophisticated man at the opposite end of the aisle. With each step, the soft rustle of her gown escalated into a deafening roar in her ears until she could hear none of the musical notes that floated toward her. The delicate scent of roses filled her nostrils, suffocating her. Hesitantly, she made her way past the pews until finally she stood beside the man who was to become her husband. For life.

Andrew reached for her cold hand with his warm one, his grasp supplicating. But her gaze was frozen on the minister who stood before them.

For life, she thought again as she swallowed hard against the lump forming in her throat.

The reverend smiled at her, then his words one by one surrounded her, enveloped her.

"Dearly beloved, we are gathered here this day to witness the joining of two wonderful people into marriage. A marriage that we all agree was made in heaven." He smiled at them with sincerity. "I'm surprised that the angels themselves haven't showed up for this event."

A reverent ripple of laughter flowed over the crowd in agreement.

Irene could feel the invisible push of those who watched just as she'd felt the invisible tug of Andrew drawing her down the aisle into marriage with him. But as the words of the reverend crept into her heart, she listened with a singleness of mind. Her mind.

"Marriage is many things," he went on. "Not just the everyday coming and going of two people, but the united coming and going of two people. United in their goals and purposes, united in their beliefs and, especially, united in their honesty and devotion to one another. And that's what we call . . . love."

Irene felt a stirring within her breast, an awakening.

"Do you, Irene Barrett, promise to love and cherish this man—"

"No," she whispered, interrupting him.

Aghast and bewildered, the reverend frowned as though he couldn't have heard her correctly—or maybe she hadn't really spoken. He paused, staring at her.

"No," she said again, a little stronger this time. "I can't." Then, with her heart thudding, she pulled her hand free from Andrew's grasp and turned away toward the open doors and sunshine.

As she half ran, half walked down the aisle, she heard those who had come to see her married gasp first, then whisper, and finally rise from their seats as though they could stop her. But she would not be stopped. Not now, not when she knew in her heart what her mind had been trying to tell her.

She hurried down the street, leaving behind the sound of rising voices. She did not look back for fear that someone might actually try to come after her and force her back to the church. At last she reached the safety of her picketed front yard, where she paused to catch her breath and glance behind her.

But nobody followed, not even Andrew.

Relieved, she crossed the small front yard, then stopped to lean heavily against a porch post. With the early summer sunshine pouring down on her head, she vowed never again to be bound by a relationship of which honesty and trust weren't the cornerstone. After all, that was the real basis for true love. And she would settle for nothing less.

Chapter One

Grand Rapids, Ohio—1879

". . . The tall, dark-eyed young man hurried past. He stopped suddenly in her path, turned, and his eyes met hers—those dark, laughing, magnetic eyes that few women had the power of resisting . . ."

Irene Barrett, alone in her upstairs bedroom, reclined comfortably with a dime novel in her hands. The glow from the single lamp beside her loveseat reflected on the well-worn page before her, and the romantic words charmed her now as they could not do in the bright light of day. Of course, she had more sense than to believe that such artificial, greater-than-life characters with their idyllic situations could ever exist. Experience had taught her well. Nevertheless, her heart begged for more.

With a restless sigh, she dropped the book against her breast and closed her eyes. If only there really were gallant men who would rescue ladies from their plights in life. She sighed again and momentarily considered her own particular plight before giving it a name: boredom.

Rising from her seat, she placed the book lovingly on the table and began to dress. This was her night to sit in front of the saloon to protest the behavior of the rowdies who frequented the many rough spots on Front Street. Needless to say, she never looked forward to it. But as the town's only spinster schoolteacher, indeed only spinster, she was expected to show her support. Just weeks ago they had not bothered to ask her to join them when they'd donned men's baggy pants and armed themselves with clubs before going on a saloon-smashing spree. Perhaps she might even have dared to go with them, if they'd asked, but they had already decided what her limits and expectations were. So that night she'd stayed home, pulled out the box hidden beneath her bed, and read her romantic novels.

But tonight she would sit before the saloon.

She dressed with the same care she might have taken to go to a dance. The skirt she chose was a warm burgundy, although some called it maroon, above which she wore a spotless white waist with a cameo brooch, topped by a matching burgundy jacket. Black piping accented the bottom of the skirt in large open loops, while the same design graced the jacket.

Her dark hair was done just as severely as when she stood before her class at the schoolhouse, with the exception of the softly rolled curls hidden beneath her large flower-adorned hat.

Irene lifted the hem of her skirt for a quick peek at the petticoat abundantly trimmed with pristine lace. She had applied the imported French lace herself only five years earlier as part of her trousseau. A trousseau she had never needed.

She gave herself one last look in the mirror, then blew out the lamp and made her way through the waning daylight down the narrow hall and the even narrower stairway. Her high-heeled shoes hardly made a sound as she walked lightly across the carpeted parlor and out the front door. There wasn't any need to lock it, since everyone in town looked upon her house as a sort of shrine to lost love, never to be desecrated by thieves, prowlers, or anyone who knew her. Or Andrew.

She stepped onto the newly laid boardwalk that barely extended to her end of town. Below the rocky cliff, located a mere road-width away from her front porch, the rushing water flowed and swirled over the shallow rapids of the Maumee River.

Across the river was the Miami and Erie Canal, stretching in the moonlight like a silvery ribbon. That same canal had brought birth and growth to old Gilead, as Grand Rapids had once been called, but it had also brought Irish immigrants bent on spending their hard-earned money in the saloons that prospered on both sides of the river. The Irish immigrants were gone now, along with their rioting drunken brawls, but the canal remained. And so did many of the saloons.

On she walked, crossing the Clover Leaf Division of the Nickel Plate Railroad tracks, then past the small, iron-fenced cemetery where Chief Te-Na-Beek slept in peace alongside the founders of Grand Rapids. She proceeded down a hill toward the brightly lit town, where numerous shops, liveries, and saloons lay nestled at the bottom of a ravine on the otherwise flat plain of northwest Ohio.

In spite of the raucous laughter spewing forth from the drinking establishments, she continued toward the rowdiest, where the matrons of the town would be gathering.

When she was within only a few doors of the Broken Keg Saloon, a sinking sensation started somewhere in the region of her stomach. A small knot of women stood in front of the solid wooden door, their hands clasped tightly around clubs raised awkwardly before them. With only a few lanterns hung outside to dispel the oncoming darkness, Irene had difficulty identifying each woman. Straining for a better look, she recognized Mrs. Wainwright and

Emma Gregg. But who were the men accompanying them?

Gradually, the distance between herself and the growing crowd of women lessened. And with shocking realization, she could plainly see that the short plump "man" was none other than the widow Clara Wilson dressed in her infamous baggy pants.

"Good evening, Miss Barrett," said Lucy Wainwright, her voice tight enough to suggest she'd been laced too strictly into her corset.

"Mrs. Wainwright," Irene returned, with a nod. Resolutely, she put down her dread, determined that she would not succumb to fright and return to the loneliness of her house and her novels.

Emma Gregg looked as skittish as a mouse in a barn full of cats.

"Hello, Emma," Irene said. Emma was the only married woman who might have a sliver of an idea of the sort of life Irene led. She, too, was twenty-six and a spinster—until a few weeks ago.

Emma turned small round eyes on Irene and squeaked out, "Hello."

"What is going on?" Irene whispered to the two women.

"I dare say that Clara has kept her word," answered Lucy Wainwright, her voice an inch tighter.

"Her word?" Irene asked.

Lucy and Emma nodded simultaneously while Emma clutched Irene's arm, drawing her near.

Just then Clara's voice rose above the murmuring group. "For the sake of the children, we cannot allow the devil's drink to continue to ruin our town!"

A shout of agreement went up around them.

Emma's grasp tightened on Irene's arm. "I'm so sorry I didn't warn you. But truly, I didn't believe she would actually go through with this again."

"Nor did I," added Lucy, shaking her head with quick, nervous movements.

"We shall meet the devil with force!" Clara shouted. "And not back down in the face of evil!" She brandished her club, which looked like a broken broom handle, and those who were armed did the same. "Forward, ladies! Do not be swayed by fear but press on! For the sake of the children!"

The crowd suddenly milled around Irene, Lucy, and Emma, sweeping them along like minnows in a flood. The door burst open, and the warm, smoky air surrounded each of them as they were forced inside the saloon by the women pushing from behind.

Irene heard the splintering glass before she could see anything but the backs of the women in front of her. She felt herself jostled and pushed from side to side, while all around her chairs scraped the wooden floor and tables were overturned. Through the ensuing melee she saw Clara sending glass after glass flying from the bar to land helter-skelter around the crowded room.

To her right, Irene watched while a woman clothed in a heavy jacket that reached to the tips of her fingers raised a club and brought it down on the back of a man.

"You said you were going to see your mother!" the woman yelled, raising the club again. "I should have known!"

The trapped husband crawled beneath a table. "I did!" he hollered back.

Then the tide turned once again, and Irene found herself mashed against the end of the bar. An elbow jabbed her in the ribs while a runaway husband trod on her toes. She clutched the raised edge of the bar to keep from being thrust to the floor. Her mind whirled and her eyes sought an exit from the turmoil and thunderous noise threatening to drown her.

A broken chair leg was suddenly forced into her free hand.

"Take this!" a woman screamed over the uproar.

Irene stared blankly at her. Was this Polly? Sweet-

16

natured, always smiling Polly?

"Don't just stand there!" Polly yelled. "Use it!"

When she didn't respond, Polly gripped the club over the top of Irene's unwilling hand. The wild-eyed woman pulled the club back sharply, stretching Irene's arm awkwardly, then swung wide and high. It sped by in a blurred arc, squarely on a collision course with the large mirror behind the bar. The impending crash resounded in Irene's ears even before the impact, and she closed her eyes, waiting for it to be over.

The weapon jolted her arm clear to her shoulder as the glass cracked and split. Her eyes popped open, and she and Polly watched as the shattered pieces fell to the floor, leaving nothing more than a bright spot in the exact shape of the mirror on the wall.

"Hallelujah!" Polly shouted with triumph and turned toward the chaotic room, disappearing into the midst of the rampaging women.

With the broken chair leg still in her hand, Irene stared at the shards of glass at her feet that still reflected bits of lamplight. Never in her life had she destroyed anything on purpose, not even something she didn't like. In a daze, she watched the hundreds of tiny sparkling lights suddenly dim as a pair of black boots crunched and ground the broken pieces of mirror into the wooden floor, halting less than a foot from the toes of her own shoes.

Irene glanced up the length of the man who stood before her, stopping when her brown eyes met his gray-blue ones. His cool gaze swept over her like a north wind from Canada in January, coming to rest on the club she held.

"Are mirrors your specialty?" he asked, his hostility as evident as the thick mustache brushing the top of his lip.

An overwhelming fear of this unknown man and an unquenchable anger at herself for being pulled into this situation suddenly gripped her.

Defensively, she stepped back two steps and, with every ounce of strength she possessed, swung her club.

Instantly, he lifted his arm and thwarted her attempt. Then, grasping the club tightly in one hand, he yanked it. Caught off guard, she hung on to her weapon and found herself flattened against his chest. His cold eyes bore into hers as his free hand came around her waist.

"Don't you know that *nice* ladies can get hurt in a place like this?" He spoke the words dangerously low, and she sensed the threat behind them.

Irene struggled to extricate herself from his hold and still retain the club. Even though her fear of him and her surroundings gave her added strength, she could not gain her freedom.

"Let me go!" She gritted the words out between her teeth.

"Let loose of the club and I'll let you go." The words, whispered close to her ear, sent a shiver down her spine.

Trapped, she knew she had no choice. Slowly, she released it. For a moment longer, he held her with her arms still helplessly pinned between them. Her heart pounded hard against her ribs, and her breath came in short gasps.

Around them the noise ebbed until, gradually, the room cleared of most of the women as well as some of the men, leaving behind broken bits of debris, like a shoreline after a storm.

"I think you'd better go," he said. "It looks like you're outnumbered."

Out of the corner of her eye, Irene searched for someone to offer her support. But it appeared that Emma and Lucy had gone.

Suddenly, he released her and she stepped back quickly to regain her balance.

"I suggest that you don't come back here again," he said. Then he cocked his head to one side and added, "I've got half a notion to let you spend the night in jail for disorderly conduct. Not to mention vandalism of my property."

Irene felt herself go white. Jail? What would the superintendent say about that? What would her mother say? If only she had stayed home. If only she were anywhere but standing in front of this man who threatened her with the unthinkable. Suddenly he represented all the people who had ever pushed or pulled her emotions.

Without thinking twice, she turned and jammed the heel of her shoe into the toe of his boot, nailing it to the floor. Then collecting as much of her dignity as was possible under the circumstances, she retreated, leaving him howling in pain.

Outside, her knees banged against each other so badly that she didn't dare stop to lean against one of the posts for a moment to rest and pull herself together. She had to get home where she would be safe and secure.

Irene hurried along the darkened boardwalk, unmindful of what had happened to the other women, and made her way up the hill toward her home.

On the other side of the river a canal packet boat sounded its strange, lonely horn.

Irene shuddered.

She quickened her steps past the cemetery and across the railroad tracks until she stood beside the neat picket fence surrounding her small front yard, where she came to a dead stop. Beyond the lace-curtained window of her parlor floated an ethereal light, bobbing and hovering until, finally, it stilled.

Reminding herself of the impossibility of ghosts, Irene clutched the gate of the fence tightly before pushing it open and proceeded with caution to the single step of her porch. With much trepidation, she crossed to the window, each footfall as silent as Old Te-Na-Beek's grave.

Who would dare to invade her home and privacy? she wondered, peeking through the tightly woven lace.

Inside, through the low flickering light of a small, nearly burned-up candle, she saw that everything was as she'd left it. Then her gaze fell on a small valise. Not many ghosts brought something as substantial as a carpet bag, she thought.

Forcibly stilling the quaking of her knees, she faced the windowless front door, then turned the knob. Slowly, she pushed it open.

Standing before her was a small boy and a young girl.

"Hello," the girl said, her voice timorous.

Irene wilted against the door frame with relief, her lopsided hat falling to the floor.

"We didn't mean to frighten you. We're sorry. We . . . we just got here. Your door was unlocked." She gestured helplessly toward the front door. "And Jonathan was getting scared," the girl finished in a rush.

"I was not!" cried out Jonathan, fervent indignation on his upturned face.

A quiet glare from the girl silenced him, although his chin jutted out in defiance.

"This is my brother Jonathan. My name's Lydia."

Irene pulled herself together.

"Are you alone?" she asked, glancing around at the dark corners of the room.

"Yes."

"Where are your parents?"

"Gone." Lydia stared down at her worn-out shoes.

Irene tried to comprehend the meaning behind that one word. Where had they gone? And just as important, where had these children come from? Their unkempt clothing would almost suggest that they were orphans who had wandered in from the streets. But Grand Rapids was a small town, and this was not a common occurrence.

"What do you mean, gone?" Irene asked softly.

"Our ma and pa died," Lydia replied, unblinking.

The events of the evening had taken their toll, and Irene felt a definite need to sit down. She made her way to the tapestry-covered settee and allowed her legs the luxury of giving way beneath her. The homemade candle the children had obviously brought with them sputtered, and the last of the tallow spilled onto her polished walnut table before plunging them into darkness.

20

A gasp from Jonathan belied his earlier bravado, and Lydia quietly shushed and soothed him.

Groping in the drawer of the stand for matches, Irene lit a lamp and the room brightened instantly. Then she lit another lamp, and the shadows fled to the corners.

Bravely, Jonathan moved two steps away from Lydia.

"Both of you sit here," Irene said, patting the space on the settee to her right. Once they were seated, she suggested, "Suppose you start at the beginning."

Lydia shrugged her shoulders. "There isn't much to tell. Our folks died about a month ago, and we come up the river looking for our aunt. But we ran out of money and the barge captain threw us off the boat."

Irene's mouth went slack with astonishment. What kind of heartless creature could do such a thing to a couple of obvious orphans? In one glance, she took in their poorly mended clothing and dishevelled appearance. She decided the man must have been an absolute dolt not to recognize that these children were in need of a place to stay—not to mention a warm bath and a hot meal.

Yawning, Jonathan leaned heavily against Lydia.

"Well, since I have two spare rooms upstairs, you'll spend the night here, and tomorrow we'll decide what to do next," Irene said.

"Are you sure?" Lydia asked, hope echoing in her voice. "I mean, we broke into your house and you don't even know us."

"First of all, you didn't break in, the door was unlocked as you said. Second, I know that you're Lydia and you're Jonathan," Irene nodded at each in turn, smiling. "And I'm Miss Barrett."

Smiling, Lydia replied, "We truly appreciate your kindness."

The next hour and a half consisted of Irene and Lydia working together to build a fire, heat bath water and almost forcibly subject Jonathan to a complete bath. Then it was Lydia's turn. After that, Irene fixed them warm milk and cold biscuits with jam. By the time everything had been tidied up again, Irene was totally exhausted.

Holding a lamp high, she led them upstairs to the two unused bedrooms, which were always made up as though a visiting friend would be arriving soon, but none ever did.

"This is where you'll stay, Lydia, and Jonathan will be at the front of the hall." Irene indicated the other door. "The one in between is my room."

"I want to stay with Lydia," Jonathan said staunchly.

Irene looked to Lydia for support in her decision.

"He's afraid," Lydia said.

"I am not!" he said, walking in the direction of the room appointed to him, his bare feet slowing down as he reached the limit of light from the lamp.

Lydia followed him, and Irene followed her.

Inside the room, Lydia pulled back the quilt and Jonathan climbed onto the high bed, where he sat, dwarfed by its size.

"I'll leave the door open," Lydia said. "Call me if you need anything."

When they walked away, he called out, "Where's the outhouse?"

"Behind the shed in back," Irene answered.

Satisfied, Jonathan pulled the covers up to his chin. Lydia patted the blankets and brushed the hair from his forehead. Then she leaned down to whisper in his ear. He smiled at her and closed his eyes.

Leaving him, they went back down the hall to Lydia's room and Irene stood in the doorway while she got into bed.

"We'll talk tomorrow," Irene said, her voice hushed. "Get a good night's sleep."

Sleepily, Lydia asked, "When does school begin in this town?"

"Next week."

But this had to be settled before then, Irene thought to

herself as she left Lydia and went inside her own room, closing the door.

Setting the lamp on the dresser, Irene stood before her mirror. She gasped in surprise at the absurd reflection staring back at her. The pins which she had carefully put in place earlier no longer securely anchored her nearly waist-length tresses. Long strands of hair not only hung down her neck but projected straight out from her head at crazy angles, while each and every hairpin dangled like so many uprooted fence posts on a string of wire. How absolutely ridiculous she must have looked to Lydia and Jonathan with her dignified manners and her bird's-nest hair! Indeed, she truly looked as if she had been to a saloon, not as a protester but as a patron.

It was too much. She felt herself traveling rapidly from one end of the spectrum of emotions to the other, and she could do nothing to save herself. Clapping a hand over her mouth to contain the overwhelming desire to laugh, she fell across her bed face-down while the events of the evening passed before her mind's eye.

First, at the saloon there had been the frightened, mousy Emma with her small brown eyes, and Lucy, whose tight corset made her look like a flattened pear. An uncontrollable, uncharacteristic giggle erupted as Irene visualized a mouse and a pear floating, swirling into the saloon to stop at the black-booted feet—

Rolling onto her back, she sobered instantly, thinking of her confrontation with the man who was obviously the new owner of the Broken Keg Saloon.

He had threatened her with jail! She shivered. Well, Irene, she chided herself, you could hardly expect to find a gallant man in a saloon of all places. Grimacing, she realized the words sounded as though they had come straight from her mother's mouth. Even so, she had to acknowledge the truth of the statement. Gallant men were certainly not to be found in saloons.

Although, she mused, he did have a mustache, and under different circumstances that would have been a qualifying factor. Even his cool gray-blue eyes and dark blond hair fit her description of a gallant man. But his actions and profession most certainly did not.

Then, with a sigh for what could never be and a shiver for what might have been, she prepared for bed. And for the first time in years, Irene Barrett went to bed without turning to her novels to dispel the boredom in her life.

Ross Hollister leaned against the bar cradling his injured foot in his hand while he watched the most beautiful woman he'd ever seen stalk away. He shook his head, thinking how unfortunate it was that it was his saloon she'd chosen to smash. And how foolish and dangerous it was for a woman to be in a saloon in the first place.

He limped to a chair, set it aright, and dropped onto the seat. And this was only his first night in town. He groaned.

The bartender walked around the room, setting up tables and crunching glass underfoot as he went. A few of the remaining men helped him stack the broken chairs near the back door.

"Don't let it bother you too much, Ross," the bartender said. "They get all riled up ever so often and come in to blow off a little steam."

Ross glanced around at the wreckage. "A little steam is one thing, Ben, but they seemed more like a runaway train on a downhill grade."

Ben grinned. "It ain't as bad as it looks. Your brother never knew the difference the last time it happened."

"Hey, Ross, whatever happened to your brother? Did he die or something and leave this place to you?" called a man from the opposite end of the bar.

Ross shook his head good-naturedly. "No. He just married a rich woman with big—" He held his hands out in front of his shirt. "Dollars."

Those within hearing distance hooted with laughter, and a few slapped him on the back.

Ross recognized the need to show them that the women's revelry would have little effect on business. "Give these boys another drink, Ben," he said, grinning. "On me."

Another round of howling approval rose from those who hadn't been run off. Ross raised his hand in acceptance of the thanks. He didn't mind being generous, especially if it created enough good will to keep them buying.

Actually, it appeared the attack on the saloon had increased business. The front door opened several times as curious patrons entered and ordered a beer.

Ross glanced around at the growing crowd in the small saloon. He had to give his brother credit; Harry sure knew how to pick the best business prospects, not to mention the right women. Of course, he personally wasn't looking for the right woman, or any woman as far as that went, but he didn't mind being the beneficiary of Harry's good fortune. At least for the time being.

He had arrived in town only that morning, traveling all the way from Black Hawk, Colorado, first by train and then by a lethargic canal packet he'd boarded at Cincinnati. When he'd stepped off the crowded little boat, everything had seemed so familiar, and yet not familiar at all. Undoubtedly, he'd been gone too long.

His decision to come back to Grand Rapids had taken all of two minutes. As soon as he'd finished reading Harry's letter telling about his marriage and the saloon he no longer needed, Ross knew this was his chance at a new beginning. He owed Harry a great deal for that. So after five years in prison, he was going home.

As the night wore on, money crossed the bar faster than water down a sluice in spite of the earlier trouble, or maybe even because of it.

Around midnight, Ross checked with Ben about closing procedures. Assured that he was not needed, Ross stepped outside and deeply inhaled the cold night air to clear his lungs of the stale smoke inside the saloon. Most of the town had long since folded up and put out their lights, leaving him to find his way in the dark. Cursing high-heeled boots, he hobbled along Front Street and headed up the hill to the old inn where he'd reserved a room.

The smell of dried maple leaves crushed beneath his feet and the wood smoke from chimneys brought back memories almost real enough to touch. Had it been sixteen or seventeen years since he'd been here? He wasn't sure. But it was good to be back, to remember the best times of his childhood. Strange, but he never would have believed he'd ever return.

Ross took long strides over the tracks, passing the few houses along the bluff on his way to the edge of town.

As a child he'd spent little time in Grand Rapids. Aunt Tilly had believed it wasn't a fitting place for young boys to go, and she'd kept Ross and Harry close to her side while she made her purchases, bribing them with store-bought hard candy. But with a few added years, he and Harry had made many trips to the river town on their own, some of which Aunt Tilly never found out about.

Now, with his hands stuffed into the pockets of his broadcloth trousers, he smiled at the memory. He hadn't thought of those times in years. He peered into the im-pinging darkness in the woods at the fringes of the town as though he could see all the way to its core, where her small, secure cabin had stood with its warm, friendly barn nearby. Were the buildings still there?

A gust of wind blew along the top of the limestone bluff, pushing at his back and forcing Ross to raise his collar. Winter wasn't far away.

Across the river no lights shone in the night to show where the mill sat on the bank between the river and the canal. The moon had disappeared behind a blanket of clouds, allowing the night to take over completely, except for one small light shining bravely in an upstairs window of the house he now passed.

* * *

Lydia lay in the large bed with the thick, warm woolen blanket and soft flannel-backed quilt pulled to her chin. She bounced ever so slightly just to test the mattress beneath her. It didn't make a sound, and it didn't bunch up around the edges of her body like the corn husk filling she was used to. And it smelled like Miss Barrett, clean and flowery. She stared hard into the darkness trying to make out the pictures and decorations on the walls, but the small amount of light reflected from the lamp in Jonathan's room down the hall scarcely made it through her door. She sighed and closed her eyes, deciding she would just have to wait until morning.

But worrisome thoughts of tomorrow and how she would deal with the things she'd told Miss Barrett—and more important the things she hadn't told—kept her awake. She rolled onto her side, burying her face into the feather-soft pillow. Lying to Miss Barrett hadn't been easy, but she'd really had no other choice. In a few more years, she'd be old enough to take care of herself and Jonathan; then she wouldn't need to lie anymore.

She climbed out of bed and padded down the hall to check on her brother. The lamp on a table at the front window burned low, casting a warm glow over Jonathan's well-scrubbed face. One arm lay flung out of the covers, exposed to the chill night air. Carefully, she moved it until she could tuck the warm blankets around him. His soft, rhythmic breathing told her he was sound asleep. Now she could blow out the lamp she'd promised him she'd light after Miss Barrett had closed her door.

Tiptoeing back through the dark, she felt her way along the papered wall. This hadn't been their destination, but perhaps they should change their plans. After all, would they ever find a home as nice as this or a lady as kind as Miss Barrett to take care of them?

Lydia climbed into the bed, her mind made up. This would be their home, one way or another. With that decided, she snuggled into the depth of the covers and went to sleep.

Chapter Two

Irene awoke to the smell of frying bacon and sat up with a start. Then the memory of the previous night's unusual events cascaded into her mind as if from a bursting dam. With a groan she lay back upon her pillow and closed her eyes to ward off an oncoming headache. She was not yet ready to deal with the decisions she'd have to make that day.

The slamming of the back door bolted her upright once again. With a deeply felt sigh, she threw off the covers and placed both feet on the floor, stepping into a dainty pair of soft-soled shoes and slipping a warm flannel wrapper over her finely embroidered cotton nightgown. A quick glance in the mirror before going downstairs told her that the braid she'd carefully plaited the night before still held every hair in place.

The smell of bacon grew stronger as she neared the kitchen doorway. Standing with her back to Irene, Lydia worked at the white enamel-trimmed cast-iron stove. Her dull blue dress didn't quite cover the tops of her shoes, showing an inch or so of sturdy black cotton stockings. A knotted string held back her long, limp hair so that it was kept tidily out of her way.

"Hurry up, Jonathan, put those plates on the table," Lydia said without turning around. "Miss Barrett will be up soon."

Irene held her breath as she watched Jonathan take three of her imported china plates from the cabinet and set them on the kitchen table. Lydia moved to the dry sink, where she lifted a small crystal vase containing water and a last lingering flower that had bloomed at the back door. She turned to set the vase on the linen-covered table when she spotted Irene in the doorway.

"Oh! Miss Barrett," Lydia said, staring in startled surprise. "I hope you don't mind. That is, about the vase and everything." She set the vase down and stood with her hands clasped in front of her, much as any student would during morning roll call.

"It's very lovely. I seldom take the time to add a flower to my table." Irene smiled, showing her sincerity. "And breakfast, too?"

"I just wanted you to know we can help around the house and we won't be any trouble to you at all."

Irene hardly knew what to say. She had yet to come up with a solution to their immediate problem. Of course, she would try to locate the children's next of kin; surely there had to be somebody somewhere who not only wanted them but missed them. In the meantime, she supposed they could stay with her.

"I fixed eggs and bacon," Lydia said, dishing out a portion onto each plate. "And I found the bread and sliced it thin." Lydia tried not to speak so quickly, but she wanted desperately to prove herself. Allowing a glance in the direction of Miss Barrett, she set a small dish of butter on the table.

Irene watched the young girl busy herself and heard the tremor in her voice. The security and love of her own childhood suddenly came back to overwhelm her, leaving an ache in her heart for these two children. Surely, she thought, an aunt or uncle or grandparent wondered where they might be and if they were all right. For their sakes, she would search until she found that family.

"Everything looks wonderful and smells delicious," Irene said.

"I couldn't find any coffee or I would have made some," Lydia offered.

"I usually drink tea, but we'll wait until later for that," Irene said.

Jonathan hadn't said a word since Irene made her presence known. He stood beside a chair, eyeing the plate where the aromatic bacon and eggs slowly cooled while they talked.

Pulling back her chair, Irene suggested, "I don't think we should let Lydia's cooking get cold, do you, Jonathan?"

He looked up at her, his eyes round and guarded. "No, ma'am." He, too, pulled his chair back, although with more eagerness, and plopped onto the seat. He glanced at Lydia to see if he could begin eating, then dug in.

Sitting across from Irene, Lydia buttered a piece of bread. She'd never been in such a fancy kitchen before. It had actually been fun to pump and carry water to the warm, cozy room. And she loved the pretty braided rugs that splashed color everywhere on the wooden floor. Nothing was out of place, not even in the small pantry off the side. She stared at the beautiful plate before her, thinking it was almost a shame to put food on it.

"You said you came up the canal?" Irene asked.

Brought out of her daze, Lydia nodded but offered no other information.

"Where did you live?" Irene asked.

"Kentucky." Lydia continued to stare with interest at the eggs on her plate before tasting them. "Do you raise chickens?" she asked.

Irene smiled. "No," she said, and decided to drop the questions for now.

When breakfast was over, Lydia pushed back her chair. "I'll do the dishes."

Irene looked down at her wrapper. "Perhaps I had better get dressed first," she said, rising from her seat. "I'll be down shortly to help you."

After Irene left the room, Lydia absently gnawed at the inside of her lip, wondering how long before Miss Barrett really started questioning her. Their only chance was to show they would help in every way. So she resolved to set to work immediately, knowing Miss Barrett wouldn't be sorry she let them stay.

"Jonathan, take this pail outside and fill it again," she said, thrusting a bucket at him. "And hurry." Then she cleared the table, shook the tablecloth outside, and poured hot water from a kettle into a dishpan. In a matter of minutes she had everything washed, dried, and ready to put away. Quickly she refilled the kettle from Jonathan's pail and placed it on the hot stove for brewing tea later.

A knock at the front door drew Lydia away from her task. She hurried through the dining room to the parlor, lightly touching the beautiful wooden furniture as she went.

When she opened the door, she smiled politely at the small brown-haired woman who stared back at her in surprise.

"Hello," Lydia said.

"Is . . . Miss Barrett home?" asked the woman distractedly. "I'm . . . Mrs. Gregg."

Pretending not to notice Mrs. Gregg's close scrutiny, Lydia nodded just as she heard Miss Barrett enter the parlor.

"I'm here, Emma. Won't you come in?"

Lydia stepped back, opening the door wide for Emma Gregg to enter. She watched as the two women stood facing each other, one short and slightly plump while the

31

other stood tall and elegantly graceful. "I didn't know you had a guest," Emma said, with a smile aimed in Lydia's direction.

"Actually, I have two. This is Lydia. Her brother Jonathan is in the kitchen." Irene sensed Emma's burning curiosity.

"I see."

But Irene knew she didn't see at all.

"I'll bring some tea if you'd like, Miss Barrett," Lydia said.

"That would be very nice, Lydia, but we can go into the kitchen to visit and I'll make the—" Irene felt a nudge against her arm, then saw Emma shake her head ever so slightly.

"Well, maybe you could bring us some tea," Irene said, taking the cue Emma gave her.

When Lydia left the room, Emma turned to Irene. "Is she a relative of yours?"

"No," Irene hedged.

Emma stared toward the kitchen. "Well, I can't say I'm surprised about that. She looks so poor," Emma whispered. "Where on earth did she come from? And how long will she stay?"

Irene feared how quickly talk could spread, and with school beginning next week she thought it wise not to put the children in an uncomfortable position before their classmates. But she really abhorred lying.

"They're only here temporarily," she answered, feeling good about not even having to stretch the truth.

"Temporarily? I don't understand."

"I can't explain now," Irene said, feeling good about that statement, too.

Emma's head lifted and her mouth formed "oh" as if she understood that Irene couldn't talk with the children so nearby.

"Well, truthfully," said Emma, "there's another reason I came to see you." She took Irene by the arm and led her to the settee, an air of confidentiality about her. They sat down and Emma leaned close.

"I wanted to explain about last night," she whispered. "You know how Clara is when she gets a notion in her head. Nobody can change it."

Irene listened, making no comment.

"But we—Lucy and I—didn't really think she would go through with it. Especially since she'd invited you to go along." Emma paused, fidgeting with the handkerchief she'd pulled from her sleeve. "I mean, you know how she is about . . . unmarried women."

Irene heard the unkind remark but refused to comment. She had no intention of disclosing her feelings on the matter. Besides, it would make little difference anyway. Clara did as Clara thought best.

"I suppose she had her reasons," Emma went on. "Unless she'd forgotten that she'd asked you to join in." The inflection of her voice made it sound more like an inquiry than a statement.

"Perhaps," Irene answered, unable to keep from bristling at being singled out so obviously.

"Well, I for one have no intention of ever joining in on anything even vaguely resembling the—the madhouse happenings of last night." Emma straightened, her small round eyes wide with repressed fear. "Did you see that man? What an awful person he must be! After all, he's from those gold fields out there in the mountains. You can imagine how uncivilized he is. At least I can imagine." Emma shivered visibly.

Irene knew first-hand just how uncivilized he actually was, and either Emma wasn't aware of her encounter or she was hoping Irene would tell her about it. But Irene kept silent.

"Clara said that man's brother almost never came to Grand Rapids. He just let the bartender run the business for him. Isn't it strange the way that man wants to be here in person? I say he's up to no good and wants to ruin the town just when things are getting so peaceable, too." She sighed and tucked the handkerchief back into her sleeve.

"What does Howard say about all this?" Irene knew him to be a level-headed businessman who might have a word to say about the situation.

"Oh, he just pooh-pooh's the things that Clara says and does. He said she needs to worry less about the business of others." Emma looked a little contrite. "I suppose I have to agree with that point."

So did Irene.

Emma shook her head. "Howard wasn't at all pleased about the doings of last night. Of course, I had to tell him all about it before some of his customers did. Thank goodness I could also tell him that we wouldn't be going to the saloon again for a while. Clara feels confident that we struck sufficiently hard enough to cause a problem for that man and he's probably packing his bags now."

Remembering those cold blue eyes, Irene doubted that was true.

"And if he isn't packing his bags, then Clara says he's up to something no good, even worse—"

The sound of teacups tinkling on a tray interrupted their conversation. Emma squirmed slightly on her seat.

Lydia carried the steaming, fragrant cups to a side table, handing each of the ladies a crisp linen napkin and a china cup with a saucer.

"Thank you, Lydia," Irene said, smiling. Where had Lydia observed such manners? she wondered. Then she caught a surreptitious glance from Emma toward Lydia and knew Emma wondered the same thing.

"I couldn't find a teapot or I would have brought it with me." Lydia straightened a lace scarf on the table and took the tray.

Irene watched as Lydia did her best to be seen favorably.

"Is there anything else you'd like?" she asked, her body almost leaning forward in her eagerness.

"No. Thank you."

Smiling, Lydia hurried off to the kitchen only to appear again a few minutes later, passing through the parlor and up the stairs.

"What an interesting child," Emma said. Then added, "Poor thing."

Irene decided to bring the subject back to the main reason for Emma's visit. "What sort of no good is he up to? Did Clara give you any ideas?"

"Well," Emma whispered, with one eye toward the stairs. "She heard that he might start a . . . a . . ." She paused as if she couldn't go on. "A . . . bawdy house," Emma finally finished, nearly choking on the words.

Irene felt a bolt of shock run between her shoulder blades. She was speechless.

"You're surprised, aren't you? So were we." Emma sat so close to the edge of her seat that she nearly fell off and had to squirm back a little.

"How can you be so sure?" Irene asked, her voice lowered in response to Emma's.

"Has Clara been wrong yet?" Emma didn't convey a gladness about this, but more of an inevitable dread of how right Clara had usually been.

It was true. Clara's insights had been remarkable in the past. Enough so that nearly every woman in town listened to her—and believed her. "How can he expect to get away with that? Surely, he knows the town would never stand for it," Irene said. But she remembered the town's history and the many saloons that still lingered. And she also remembered how callous and frightening the man was.

"Clara said, where he comes from those houses are common and he probably doesn't even consider what we think. It's just another opportunity to take money from our husbands."

Irene thought she could see the reason behind the ladies' fears now. They were afraid for their husbands' well-being, not just their money. But, she acknowledged, that was as it should be.

35

"What does Howard say?" Irene asked, deferring to Howard's sensible and logical mind again.

Emma blushed. "I haven't told him. How could I?"

Irene was amazed, although she hid it. She held the unshakable belief that a husband and wife should share everything without embarrassment.

"Perhaps you should mention it. Chances are he can put your mind at ease. I'm certain, if there was any truth to the matter, he would know."

Emma eyed her critically. She couldn't help but concur with everyone else that Irene had made a mistake five years ago when she'd turned away her chance of marriage to Andrew. And now here she sat, a single woman, giving advice to a married one. It rankled Emma no little that Irene thought she knew what a husband and wife ought or ought not to talk about.

"I do not believe that Howard would be any more comfortable discussing such matters with me than I am with him." Her small nose inched upward.

Emma's indignation seldom raised itself except in situations of high emotional intensity. This evidently was one of those situations. Irene reached out to touch Emma's hand in apology, but Emma pulled it back and the air thickened with unresolved hostility.

"I only meant," Irene began carefully, "that your husband might have obtained some information from a friend, or an acquaintance, that could settle the whole matter easily."

She watched with relief as Emma's hackles slowly drooped and she quickly went on. "We need to know for a fact what we're up against, don't you agree?"

Somewhat mollified, Emma nodded.

Irene patted Emma's hand, and this time she didn't withdraw it. Emma had been her friend from the moment Irene arrived in Grand Rapids all the way from Cincinnati. That had been six years earlier, when she'd accepted her first teaching position, and before she'd met Andrew. She truly didn't wish to alienate Emma for any reason.

"So what has Clara decided to do?" Irene asked, getting back to safer, more familiar ground.

"Well," Emma said, relaxing, "she isn't sure. But her advice is that we should double our efforts—at a later date, of course. After all, this is *our* town."

Would they actually go on another saloon-smashing spree? Irene fervently hoped not.

"Well, I really must go," Emma said, rising briskly and laying her napkin alongside the teacup. "Tell Lydia thank-you for the tea." At the door she turned to whisper, "I'll let you know if anything comes up."

They said their good-byes with their friendship safely mended although, Irene feared, somewhat frayed.

After she'd gone, Irene glanced around at the lovely room with its upholstered chairs, wooden tables, mirrors, and carpet. It was to have been her and Andrew's house, but now it was hers alone. Crossing the carpet, she put her hand on the newel post at the bottom of the stairs, feeling its smooth yet grainy surface. Time had healed the hurt and somewhat eased the pain of betrayal. Now there was nothing but a desperate loneliness that no one seemed to understand. Her friends had just the same as locked her up in this house, allowing her out only when they decided it was best for her. Everyone except Emma. And now she too, by silent consent, was locking Irene inside.

A movement at the top of the stairs drew her attention. Lydia came quietly down the stairs and stopped on a step that made them the same height.

"Has Mrs. Gregg gone?" she asked.

Irene nodded.

"I made all the beds and dusted the rooms. Is there anything else I can do?"

Irene decided that now was the time to talk to Lydia about her family, before she continued with the wrong assumption about living here permanently. And it was obvious that she hoped to stay.

37

"We need to talk, Lydia. Let's sit in the parlor."

Lydia followed, dread filling her and making her shoes too heavy to lift off the beautifully carpeted floor.

"I couldn't help noticing that you have lovely manners. Who taught them to you?"

Clasping her hands in her lap, Lydia sat as straight as a yardstick, trying to decide just how much truth to tell without divulging the wrong information.

"Would you tell me who?" Irene asked again, prodding gently.

Lydia bit her lip, not wanting to tell another lie, but unable to see any help for it. "Aunt Lenore." Then she hastily added, "But she wasn't my real aunt."

"Wasn't?"

"Yes, ma'am." Lydia bit her lip again. "She died."

"I'm truly sorry to hear that." Irene frowned. "Do you have any real family? I mean, surely there must be a cousin or an uncle . . ."

"Not that I know for certain," Lydia said, thinking at least that much was true.

This sort of questioning wasn't getting Irene anywhere, so she chose to look for facts.

"Where were you going when the captain put you off the barge?"

"Cleveland."

"And why were you going there? That's a very long way from here."

"I was hoping to find a home for us. I remember my mother once talked about an aunt in Cleveland, but I don't know if she's still there or if she's even alive." Lydia desperately appealed to this kind woman's heart and spoke softly of her greatest fear. "We don't want to live in no orphanage, Miss Barrett."

Taken aback, Irene was alarmed by the idea and reached out a comforting hand to the child. "Of course you don't!"

Lydia had just told more truth in the space of a few minutes than she had in the last few weeks. Not since her mother's death had she trusted anyone; but somehow she knew she could rely on Miss Barrett. She knew it in her soul. For the first time in months, a portion of her burden lifted and the relief she felt revealed itself with tears, hot brimming tears that burned her eyelids and scalded paths down her cheeks.

With her own soft heart aching, Irene watched her valiant attempt to stem the flow.

"Oh, child," she crooned, pulling her into the safe circle of her arms. She held Lydia close and let her cry, stroking the limp curls on her back. "Shhh. We'll work this out, you'll see. Don't worry anymore. Shhh."

Lydia wrapped her arms around Miss Barrett and cried as she had not allowed herself to cry since her mother's death. Someone cared, really cared. Whatever it took, she was determined to stay with this wonderful woman forever.

Finally, when the tears abated and the sobs became merely sniffles, Lydia lifted the hem of her apron and wiped her nose. She felt better than she had in a good long while.

"Now," Irene said, "I need some information if I'm to try locating your aunt. And you haven't told me your last name."

Brushing a stray lock over her shoulder, Lydia answered truthfully, "Our name is Jefferson, and I think my aunt's name is Sarah Jefferson."

"Good." Irene patted Lydia's clasped hands. She would not pry any longer and decided to end the questioning. "What do you say we cheer ourselves up by baking something wonderful?"

Lydia brushed back another lock of hair that slid over her forehead and nodded.

"I have some apples. We could make a pie or this delicious concoction of apples and cake that my mother taught my sisters and I to bake. Which one?"

A tremulous smile appeared. "The cake."

"Ah-ha, I take it that means you're adventurous." Irene laughed. "A girl after my own heart."

And she was.

They spent the remainder of the morning paring, sifting, measuring, and baking. Irene didn't ask any more questions, sensing Lydia's reluctance, as well as her relief and gratitude.

Soon the sweet smell of apples, spices, and cake floated throughout the big house along with the pungent but pleasant smell of wood smoke.

Jonathan, who had not been seen since breakfast, appeared as if by magic when the apple cake was done. A light noon meal, a piece of the cake, and he was on his way again, saying nothing to either Lydia or Irene. Since Lydia didn't seem to be concerned, Irene made no remark, but she thought Jonathan's silent behavior to be out of character for a boy his age.

Later that evening, after the baths were over, Irene saw the children to bed. Lydia explained Jonathan's fear of the dark, and Irene allowed the lamp to be left on in his room until after he fell asleep.

When she'd finally gone to her own room and prepared for bed, she had time to reflect on the happenings of the day. She still felt strangely disconnected from Emma in a way she hadn't before. Not even Emma's marriage to Howard had affected their friendship until now.

Remembering their talk, Irene thought about the man in the saloon. She could still feel his cold blue eyes staring mercilessly into hers. Indeed, this was a man who would do as he pleased regardless of the opinions of a town full of women. But she need not spend time worrying over his fate since she would have little to say on that subject. Clara rarely solicited her opinion on anything.

The smell of apples still lingered in the chill of the upstairs room, taking her back to her own secure, happy childhood. Her sisters Janie, Mary Ellen, and Rosie, along with their mother had had many wonderful hours in the kitchen. And probably they still did.

Irene stood before the large cherrywood secretary dominating one wall of her bedroom. The beautiful piece of furniture had been a wedding gift from her mother, having belonged to her father before his death. She never failed to think of Randolph Barrett when she sat before the polished desk with its multitude of pigeon holes and tiny drawers.

Pulling a piece of paper from a drawer, Irene removed the stopper from the ink bottle and dipped her pen. She needed to feel the touch of home right now, so she wrote a letter to her mother, telling only a little of what was going on in her life because very little usually did, and of course she omitted everything about the saloon and the children. After all, those were only momentary diversions in an otherwise ordinary life, she told herself.

When it was signed and sealed, she wrote another letter and addressed it to Lydia's aunt in Cleveland. Then she replaced the stopper on the ink bottle and cleaned the tip of her pen. She tidied up the already tidy desk, turned the lamp beside her loveseat a little lower, and pulled her box of novels from beneath the bed. Selecting the one she hadn't finished the night before, although she'd read it several times over, Irene tucked her feet under her as she sat on the loveseat. And once again she gave her heart to the gallant man who lived within the binding of her well-worn book.

Chapter Three

On this crisp October morning, Lydia danced and skipped circles around her teacher all the way to school, as if her new shoes were magic slippers. At last, Lydia thought, they would have a home and friends; finally, they were putting down roots. Her elation simply couldn't be contained. She danced along with the brilliant colors canopied overhead and carpeted beneath her feet, warmed with happiness inside, though her breath puffed visibly in the air before her. Occasionally she glanced back at Jonathan, who lagged several steps behind and smiled encouragingly at him.

Jonathan glared at his sister. He hated school and didn't understand what Lydia had to be so happy about. After all, they were living with the teacher! They probably would have to spend their entire evenings reciting their lessons. He paused long enough to kick a stone so hard it thumped on a nearby tree. With his hands jammed into his pockets as deep as they would go, he resumed his slow walk toward the large, two-story brick building looming before him.

Inside were two classrooms on the first floor. Jonathan tried not to breathe in the smell of chalk dust, waxed floors, and the other odors so peculiar to a schoolroom. It gave him a pain in the gut, as if he had eaten too many green apples. Reluctantly, he followed as Miss Barrett led the way through the door to her room.

Irene inhaled deeply the familiar scents of the tools of her trade and as always felt a satisfaction that nothing in life could compare to so far. Although she always left the room clean in the spring, with the desks and benches lined up and the slates neatly stacked, there was always some dusting to be done the day before school began. But yesterday, with Lydia's help, it had been finished in half the time and now all was ready.

As planned, Irene arrived at the schoolhouse precisely forty five minutes before the other children were expected. She wanted time to get the necessary admission papers filed for Lydia and Jonathan without the prying eyes of Clara Wilson looking over her shoulder. Actually, there was very little information to give other than their names and temporary address. But undoubtedly some explanations would be in order, and so far this past week, she'd managed to avoid Clara.

She set out a fresh bottle of ink along with her pen and the book in which she would write the names of the children while mentally deciding how to introduce Lydia and Jonathan.

Jonathan stood at the back of the room until several children had straggled in, then he made his way toward Lydia. She took his hand and he felt better. Most of the children stared at him, but nobody spoke. Finally, Miss Barrett rang a little bell on her desk and everyone ran to get a seat. Lydia wanted to sit in front, but Jonathan managed to tug her hand until they were a few rows farther back.

"Good morning, boys and girls," Irene said, smiling.

"Good morning, Miss Barrett," came the unrehearsed chorus.

"I see we have some new faces this year."

Jonathan slunk down in his seat as far as he could.

"Perhaps," Irene went on, "those who are returning students would like to help me welcome the others by standing and telling them your names. Let's begin with you, Mary."

Mary stood shyly and gave her name, then each child after her did the same until everyone but the newcomers had identified themselves.

"Now, let's find out who our new friends are. Would you please stand?"

Lydia stood up. Jonathan's heart pounded so hard that he thought for sure it would pop right out of his chest. To his dismay, Lydia pulled him to his feet.

"My name is Lydia Jefferson and this is my brother Jonathan," she said, her voice quavering.

Relief flooded Jonathan's entire body. He felt so thankful that he didn't have to speak, he could have hugged her right in front of everybody. After that the day was a blur of faces, names, and instructions. He sat for what seemed like hours and hours on the hard bench trying not to squirm. He daydreamed about walking along the river and pitching stones as far as he could and about the barges in the canal going to faraway places.

"Jonathan?"

Guiltily, Jonathan looked up at Miss Barrett, who had suddenly appeared by his seat.

"It's your turn, Jonathan," she said quietly.

His turn for what? he wondered fearfully. Panic-stricken, he glanced around the room, and to his horror everyone stared directly at him. Some even snickered behind their hands.

With a hammering heart and a queasy stomach, he edged from his seat, turning he ran as fast as his wobbly legs would carry him—down the hall, out the door, across the schoolyard, and along the street until he came to the hill above the river. He slipped and slid through the dying weeds, landing at the stony river's edge, where the shallow water burbled over big and small rocks.

"I'm never going back! Never, never, never!" he told himself out loud. He wanted to make it a promise, but he couldn't. Lydia would beg him to go back, and he knew he would. But, he consoled himself, he'd leave when he wanted to and he wouldn't go back until he felt like it. And right now he didn't feel like it.

Irene said good-bye to the last child, then glanced out the window one more time for a sign of Jonathan. She'd hoped that he would come back during recess and give her a chance to discover what had upset him. But he hadn't come back at all. Disappointed and worried, she'd sent Lydia ahead to look for him.

Gathering her things, Irene left the school and walked the two blocks home, hoping Jonathan would be there with Lydia.

When she came within sight of the house, she saw smoke coming from the kitchen chimney and Jonathan carrying wood from the woodpile to the back door. Stopping in her tracks, she closed her eyes briefly and heaved a sigh of relief.

What was she going to do in the weeks ahead to reach this child?

Ross squinted against the brilliant morning sun as he hefted the wooden cask onto his shoulder, then stepped from the barge to the landing with Ben right behind him. They were almost finished unloading the shipment that came in on the side-cut canal, a waterway that had been the true lifeline of Gilead and now Grand Rapids.

Nearby, a shaggy brown mule in harness rested one foot, eyes closed, ears twitching while the barge he'd pulled was being emptied of a portion of its cargo.

At the back door of the saloon, a little boy squatted on his haunches, watching the mule, then the procession of casks, and back to the mule again.

Ross had seen the boy a number of times hanging around the back by the canal. Until this morning he'd figured the boy's father was probably inside.

Memories of Harry and himself at that age flooded back; they too, had sat on back steps of saloons waiting for their father to make it rich at just one more game. Of course, he never did, but the boys waited patiently, night after night.

Inside the cool, dank interior of the storage room, Ross deposited the load from his shoulder to the waiting rack, then returned to the warmth of the sunny fall day. He leaned one shoulder against the door frame near the little boy while Ben took care of the business with the barge captain.

"Fine-looking animal, wouldn't you say?" Ross asked the boy.

The boy shrugged. "If you like mules."

"I like mules," Ross said, staring at the mule with great admiration.

The boy looked up at Ross. "Why?"

"When we'd stake a claim, they were our means of transportation for hauling supplies back into the mountains."

"What's a claim?" he asked, obvious skepticism in his bright eyes.

"Where I come from, a claim means this is your piece of ground to look for gold." Ross dropped his gaze from the mule to the boy.

"Gold?"

Ross nodded. "Yessir."

After a moment of silence the boy said quietly, "I ain't never seen gold."

"Well . . . What did you say your name is?" Ross asked.

"Jonathan."

Ross put out his hand. "Mine's Ross." They shook hands.

"Well, Jonathan, gold isn't anything like you'd expect it to be. It's not shiny like a gold watch or a lady's ring. It looks more like a rock when we find it."

Jonathan stood up. "A rock?" He was disappointed.

Ross nodded again.

"You got one I could see?" The skepticism returned.

Ross leaned over conspiratorially. "I do. But we'll have to wait until no one else is around." Ross winked at him.

Jonathan thought about that for a moment, then winked back.

"Now, I've got a question for you," Ross said. "Aren't boys your age supposed to be in school?"

Jonathan stuffed his hands into his trousers and hung his head. "Yes sir, but I don't like school." He knew it made Lydia hopping mad, but he ran away from school every chance he got. And he'd found the best times were usually when he asked permission to go to the outhouse. He was sorry to make Lydia so angry, but he just couldn't help it. School was nothing but a waste of good time, and besides, he just didn't like it.

"Me neither."

Quick as the release of a slingshot, Jonathan raised his head. "You don't?"

"Never did." Ross stared off across the canal toward the little island of trees in the middle of the Maumee rapids.

"My sister Lydia says I have to go so Miss Barrett will like us." His mouth pouted in disgust.

"Miss Barrett? Is she your teacher?" Ross asked, curious about the life of a little boy who hung around the back doors of saloons.

"Yeah, but it's worse than that. We've been living with her for weeks!"

Like Aunt Tilly, Ross thought, but his memories of her were the happiest of his life.

"Why don't you like her?" Ross asked.

"She's mean. And ugly," Jonathan said, sensing a sympathetic comrade in Ross. "I have to take a bath every night before I go to bed because she has these white, soft sheets. And I'm supposed to eat everything on my plate." Jonathan didn't think he should mention that he liked everything on his plate.

"That doesn't sound so mean to me. What does your sister say?"

"Oh, she wants me to do whatever Miss Barrett says so we can keep living there." Jonathan kicked at a stone. "She's ugly, too," he added again, just in case Ross had missed it the first time.

Ross immediately pictured a stern, well-endowed, gargantuan woman—the same woman he'd pictured when Aunt Tilly told stories about the swamp witch who lived in the bogs of the Black Swamp and would snatch any little boy who ventured out alone. He never went out alone after an evening of hearing those stories.

"Ugly, huh?" Ross mused aloud.

"And tall as a tree," Jonathan went on.

"How are you going to stay out of school forever?" Ross asked.

Jonathan shrugged. "Maybe I could run away on one of these barges." He stared at the long boat with the wide deck. A cabin, hunched low at the front end, resembled a tiny house just right for a boy to live in. And it probably didn't have any bath tub, either.

"But what about your sister?" Ross reminded him.

"Yeah." He kicked a stone viciously and watched as it bounced along the ground and dropped with a plunk into the canal.

Ross was thoughtful for a minute. "What if I have a talk with your teacher?"

Jonathan stared at Ross with a mixture of surprise and happiness. Then fear grabbed at his stomach, the same as it had when he and Lydia had run away. If Ross talked to Miss Barrett, he would know he'd made up those things about her, some of them anyway.

"Come on," Ross said, walking along the towpath. "Let's

have a talk with old Miss Barrett." Over his shoulder he called to Ben, "I'll be back later. We have some important business to take care of."

Ben waved him on.

Jonathan held back, not sure what he'd gotten himself into. Ross had been so nice, so easy to talk to. He swallowed the big lump forming in his throat.

"Come on, son. There's nothing to worry about." Ross waited.

Jonathan stared in amazement. Nobody had ever called him "son." Without another thought about the possible repercussions he might suffer from telling half truths, Jonathan hurried to catch up.

Together they walked toward the Clover Leaf Railroad, crested the ravine, and followed the tracks toward the two-story brick schoolhouse. The two of them stopped to stare at the imposing structure with its elongated windows, twin sets of double doors, and huge belltower presiding over all.

"Maybe I should do all the talking. What do you say?" Ross asked.

Jonathan nodded, a great tension building in his chest. They crossed the schoolyard, climbed the seven stone steps, and pushed open one of the heavy oak doors. The newness of the building still hung in the air, greeting their noses with the smell of freshly polished wooden floors and whitewashed walls.

Ross smiled at Jonathan in an attempt to bolster his courage, then opened the door Jonathan indicated as his classroom.

Jonathan stood close to Ross's side as every child turned to stare, some with large round eyes, others who giggled and pointed at them.

He wished now he had run away.

Ross stood stock-still as he stared at Miss Barrett. This woman was no Black Swamp witch, as Jonathan had led him to believe. This was a lovely, graceful woman who

49

undoubtedly would not appreciate his part in the truancy of her student.

He wished now he hadn't interfered.

Miss Barrett rose slowly from her seat at the desk on the elevated platform. She wore a blue dress so dark it appeared black at first. Her hair, pulled tightly back, was caught in a knot at the nape of her slender neck with only a fringe of curls to soften the look. She came around the corner of her desk and glided toward them.

Jonathan shrank back, hiding behind his newfound protector.

Reluctantly, Ross stood his ground. Then, with mild surprise, he realized that he had seen this woman before, in his saloon. *Well, I'll be damned,* he thought to himself, grinning. His eyes stole over her once more, finding little to compare this woman of obvious gentle breeding to the one who had wielded the club and smashed his mirror.

Irene was more than a little surprised to see Jonathan come through the door with a stranger, although something about the man seemed familiar. With little interest in the man, she focused her attention on the boy and walked toward him.

"Jonathan, where have you been?" she asked gently, leaning forward at the waist. "We've been worried about you."

Jonathan didn't reply, and he refused to look up from staring at his scuffed brown shoes.

She looked up at the mustached man standing defensively beside Jonathan. It was then that she knew why he looked so familiar. Her breath caught in her throat as once more she stood face to face with the new saloon owner. She fought unsuccessfully to keep the color from rising to her cheeks.

"He was at the canal with me, watching the barges unload." Ross placed his hand on Jonathan's blond head, hoping to transfer a measure of bravery to him. At the same time, he watched as full-blown recognition registered on Miss Barrett's now rosy face.

Aware of the on-looking students, Irene replied noncommittally, "I see."

"I thought I should bring Jonathan back," he went on.

"I'm glad you did," she said, her throat constricting so that the words were strained.

Jonathan looked up at Ross appealingly, and Ross squeezed his shoulder in reassurance.

"Maybe we could talk," he said to Irene. Then, lowering his voice, he added, "In private."

Irene felt sure she would die of mortification if anyone at all saw her talking to him in private or otherwise. But unable to see any way out of the situation gracefully, and especially in front of a room full of children, she acquiesced, motioning to Lydia who sat nearby.

Lydia slid across her seat and reached out a hand to the unwilling Jonathan, pulling him onto the bench beside her.

"We can stand in the hall," Irene said, stiffly.

Ross nodded, then followed behind her where it was difficult, if not impossible, to ignore the gentle sway of her bustled skirt.

Once they were in the hall, Irene held the door ajar so she could keep an eye on her students and still have a private conversation. She waited for him to speak first. Perhaps he had a clue that would help her understand Jonathan, she told herself, trying to justify why she had agreed to speak to him at all.

"I think I've been misled," Ross began, grinning a little sheepishly, "and maybe I should apologize for stepping in."

Glancing nervously at the only other classroom, across the hall from where they stood, Irene wanted to ask him to keep his voice low so as not to attract attention.

"Misled?" she asked, trying to concentrate on his words and not the other classroom door.

"Unless you happen to have a much older sister with warts on her nose," he replied.

He had her full attention now. "Precisely what did Jonathan tell you?" She noticed the mischievous twinkle in the depths of his gray-blue eyes.

"Well, let's just say that he and I see things a little differently."

"You mean, you don't see any warts on my nose but Jonathan does." Irene lifted one well-arched eyebrow, submerging her bruised feelings.

"There are definitely no warts. At least," he said, still grinning, "none that I can see."

Irene felt the uncustomary blush once again sneak up her collar as she nervously cleared her throat. She plucked a speck of invisible lint from the sleeve of her dress and dropped it to the floor.

"Well," she said, forcing herself to meet his gaze. "I appreciate your concern for Jonathan, and for bringing him to school, Mr. . . ."

"Hollister. Ross Hollister."

At that precise moment, the classroom door across the hall opened as if on cue, and Clara filled the doorway. She glared a warning at Irene and the back of Mr. Hollister, until he turned around. Then Clara's countenance turned from one of warning to one of horror. Momentarily, the shock held her transfixed.

"I—I really should get back to my class," Irene stammered. "Thank you again."

"No need." Ross shook his head.

Suddenly galvanized into action, Clara Wilson bent her arms at the elbows until they looked like chicken wings against her plump body and practically flew across the hall.

"What is the meaning of this?" Her voice was lowered with unutterable contempt.

To Irene's dismay, Ross turned to Clara and nodded,

bowing slightly at the waist. "Good morning, Mrs. Wilson."

"What are you doing here? This is a schoolhouse! There are children present," Clara said, her indignation flaring.

"Exactly my reason for being here," he said calmly. "But I'll let Miss Barrett explain it to you." He looked to Irene. "Before I go, I'd like to talk to Jonathan."

She glanced at Clara, who stood with her arms crossed over her ample bust, then at Ross Hollister, who seemed sincerely concerned about Jonathan.

"Of course," she said to Ross.

She watched as he re-entered her classroom and knelt down to speak to the child; she was surprised to see Jonathan respond without hostility. Then he rose and walked back toward her.

Smiling, he said, "Good day, ladies."

Irene watched as he walked away, his hatless head a dark gold when he opened the door to the brilliant sunshine. When he was gone, she pulled her thoughts back to the problem at hand and turned to Clara, who continued glaring at her.

"Do you know who that is?" Clara insisted rather than asked, her ire obviously in a fine state.

"Yes, I do." Irene answered, piqued by the ever-present will of someone else being imposed upon her own. She could not judge, think, or decide for herself without being told the correct way to go about it or even having the decision made for her. And more often it was the latter. Her mother had assumed the privilege years ago and never relinquished it, until Andrew took her place. And now there was Clara. When would her life ever be her own?

"Now, Irene, don't get in a dither." Clara placed a hand on Irene's arm, half as a warning, half as a placating gesture. "It's just that it wouldn't be proper for you to be seen talking to him. What if the superintendent came in?"

There was no point in discussing it further, she decided. Clara had already made up her mind what was best for her and nothing would change it.

"I should go back to my class," Irene said, trying to regain her composure.

Clara inclined her head in acknowledgment of Irene's change of attitude and walked back to her own classroom.

Turning away, Irene placed both of her cool hands against her cheeks, which burned with resentment.

Stepping inside the room, she was met by a high-pitched shriek from one of the girls. She took a deep breath to still her nerves and closed the door behind her.

Irene studied her students, trying to decide who had issued the scream. Then her eyes fell on blond little Mary Anderson, whose tears streamed down her cheeks, while behind her sat Jonathan with a belligerent smile on his face.

In the three weeks past, she had hoped to bring him out of his rancorous attitude toward her and everyone. Only Lydia seemed able to reach him. And now Ross Hollister. During her six years of teaching, she'd met several difficult children, but none so heartrending. He needed a family, of that she was sure.

Irene walked toward the front of the room, stopping beside Jonathan's seat, and lightly touched his shoulder. He flinched and drew away. She didn't press the matter.

Mary Anderson sat with her hand rubbing a spot on the back of her head, no longer crying. Apparently, her long braids had presented too much of a temptation for Jonathan, so she moved Mary to a vacant seat out of Jonathan's reach.

The day progressed without further incident, to Irene's relief and probably to her foresight in sending Lydia with Jonathan whenever he needed to go out back.

When the two-hundred-and-twenty-pound bell in the tower rang for dismissal, it didn't signify the end of her problems. On the contrary, it only presented a different set of problems to weigh heavily on her mind.

With a unified shout, the children jumped from their

seats and raced for the door, pouring into the hall like minnows from a bucket. Everyone, that is, except Lydia, who held a struggling Jonathan by the hand. Finally, he managed to loosen her grip and dash into the melee, mingling anonymously until he fled the building.

Irene watched him go, wishing she could do something for him. But it appeared that her only resource was to double her efforts to find their family. Tonight she would write another letter to mail the next day; perhaps the first one had been lost and that was why she hadn't heard anything.

"I'm sorry about Jonathan, Miss Barrett," Lydia said. "He isn't really bad. He's just mixed up."

"I know," Irene said as she straightened her desk and proceeded to collect the slates from the children's desks. Lydia picked up those on the opposite side of the room.

"The other boys teased him this morning about not having a pa," Lydia offered.

"Well, that's none of his fault," Irene said. "I don't know why some children enjoy hurting those who already hurt." The pain of rejection wasn't something to be explained, only experienced, and she knew it only too well herself.

Jonathan's legs couldn't seem to propel him fast enough. All day he'd sat on that hard wooden bench thinking about Ross and what he'd said. First, Ross had said Miss Barrett looked like a pretty nice teacher to him, but he paid little mind to that—after all, she didn't even want to keep him. She was just like all the rest. But then Ross said, "How about going fishing together sometime?" And with those words sounding over and over inside his head, like the clackety-clack of a train gaining speed, his feet fairly flew over the hard clay ground. He ran along the street, making a wide turn onto Front and down the hill into town where the canal butted up against the back of Ross's saloon. He dodged people, crates, barrels, and even a few dogs before he finally reached the back door.

To his disappointment, he found the warped, faded door shut. He stood pondering it, undecided about how to proceed. Lydia, not to mention Miss Barrett, would skin him the way a hunter did a wild rabbit if he actually went inside. But if he didn't, how would Ross know he was there? He couldn't take the chance of sitting outside the door all night and never seeing Ross, so with his heart buffeting his ribs, he turned the knob and pushed the door wide.

Although the sun shone brightly outside, darkness greeted him in the small back room, and a sweet, musty odor wafted past. He stared at the door to his left, then at the door straight ahead, where sounds of laughter and yelling mixed together in a sort of happy roar. Without a doubt, that had to be the right door. He pulled it open a crack, peeked inside, and skirted the deep, narrow room with his hands against the wall behind him.

But before he'd gotten far, someone hollered, "Hey, who's kid is that?" Then everyone near Jonathan got quiet and stared.

Bravely, he spoke up. "Where's Ross?"

"Hey, Ross! Why didn't you tell us you got a kid?"

They thought he was Ross's son. Jonathan puffed up with pride at the very thought.

Then, out of nowhere, Ross appeared in front of him, kneeling down. "What brings you here?" he asked, frowning.

Jonathan wasn't sure if Ross was angry or not since he wasn't smiling. He liked it better when Ross smiled. "I . . . I thought maybe . . . we could go fishing . . . like you said."

"Fishing?" Ross blinked in surprise, not only to find the boy in the saloon but that he expected him to drop everything and go that minute.

Jonathan tried to blend into the stained, partially torn wallpaper behind him, so great was his humiliation. Why did he think Ross would be any different than all the other grownups? They said one thing but did another. He slid backward along the wall toward the door where he'd entered.

"Whoa there, pal," Ross said, reaching out a hand and grabbing him by the shirt. "I didn't say I wouldn't go fishing. After all, I asked you first, didn't I?"

Jonathan eased up from pushing so hard against the wall when he heard Ross call him "pal."

"Does Miss Barrett or your sister know you're here?"

He started to nod his head, but changed his mind under Ross's heavy scrutiny and said, "No."

"Hmm. Just as I thought." Ross rubbed his mustache. "I think we'd better get permission. Don't you?"

Hating to agree, but seeing no way out, Jonathan nodded.

"I have to talk to Ben first, so you wait outside the back door. And don't let Mrs. Clara Wilson see you, or we'll both be in trouble." Ross winked.

Jonathan grinned. He knew no women went to the back doors of saloons, and the least likely of all would be someone like that stone-faced Mrs. Wilson from school.

Happiness once more lightened his heart and his feet as he ran from the building to wait on the landing where the barges were moored. Within minutes, Ross stood beside him, two fishing poles in his hand. "Ready?"

"Sure am!"

Together they walked along the side-cut canal, heading for Miss Barrett's house. From across the river near the mill, a canal boat blew its horn; out of habit, both the man and the boy looked in that direction.

When they reached her front door, they stopped and stared at each other.

"Should I do the asking?" Ross whispered.

"You like her better than I do," Jonathan whispered back.

Ross grinned and knocked on the door.

Irene opened it, her eyes wide with surprise.

"Hello, again, Miss Barrett."

She looked from Ross to Jonathan and back to Ross.

"We . . ." Ross put a hand on Jonathan's shoulder and went on, "wondered if we might have your permission to go fishing for a while."

"I . . . I don't know." Irene hesitated, looking from him to Jonathan. Was it wise to allow a friendship to blossom between this boy, her temporary charge, and this man of dubious reputation? No doubt the ladies who protested at the saloon would have an opinion about this. And it wouldn't take long for word to get around.

"We promise to be back before supper. As a matter of fact, we're just going across the bridge to sit on the bank by the mill." Ross turned to look across the river. "I believe you'll be able to see us from your front porch."

Irene took in the hopeful expression on Jonathan's up-turned face. Did she really have the heart to dash his hopes? So far she'd gotten nothing more than "yes, ma'am" and "no, ma'am" from him. Now he looked to her for approval. Could this be a start?

"Well, if you're back in time and if you're just going across the river," she said, not completely comfortable with her decision, "I . . . guess it would be all right."

"Good!" He turned to Jonathan and said, "What do you say, pal?"

"Let's go fishing!" And with that, Jonathan leaped down the single step as though there were at least three or four.

As they walked away, Irene had the compelling urge to call Jonathan back and tell Mr. Hollister he was unfit company for a young boy. But the unbounded joy so apparent in Jonathan was something she hadn't seen until now, and she knew she couldn't do it.

Alongside the mill, a canal packet boat sounded its horn and coasted to a bobbing halt before approaching Lock Number Nine of the Miami and Erie Canal. Passengers disembarked slowly with the aid of the captain.

Winnie Barrett extricated herself from the crowded,

cramped quarters she'd occupied for the past few days. She'd never spent a more miserable night and hoped never to repeat the mistake. The dust and noise of a stagecoach would have been preferable, and even the bumping and jolting would have allowed some movement to keep up one's circulation. As it was, she had little feeling left in one leg and feared she might not be able to step out of the boat without falling into the canal.

"Hope your trip was pleasant, ma'am," the captain said as he handed her out.

"Hope all you want, sir," was all she would say as she cast him a baleful glare.

Winnie Barrett saw to the loading of her bags, leaving nothing to chance, and refused a ride across the wagon bridge spanning the river. She let it be known to one and all that she would spend no more time in close quarters with anyone after that trip, then properly tipped the baggage man before setting out. Never had she felt so unkempt, wrinkled, and kinked-up in the legs and back as she did now. The walk was just what she needed to soothe her tight muscles and irritated nerves.

Glancing at the water below the bridge, she thought about how long it had been since she'd visited her daughter. More than a year, she concluded. Irene had come home for Christmas with a downcast spirit, and Winnie felt the familiar tug on the strings of a mother's heart, so she'd responded with a visit of her own. And now this last letter had tugged ever so gently, but just as surely, and she could not, would not rest until she knew Irene was truly all right. If only Irene had married Andrew when she'd had the chance. Then she would have been able to relax knowing that Andrew would take care of Irene. She held little hope that either Emma or Clara Wilson would be able to help or even understand Irene's needs. The Lord knew she herself was at a loss sometimes when it came to understanding Irene.

And that was the reason for this unannounced arrival.

She needed to see for herself that Irene was indeed all right, and she wanted no preparation to pretend that all was well, if in truth, it wasn't.

She charged ahead, anxious to see her daughter, barely aware of the boy and man who passed her, nodding a greeting.

Jonathan stared at the woman in the wrinkled dress with a frown etched deeply between her brows. After she hurried past them going in the opposite direction, he nudged Ross.

"She looks meaner than old Mrs. Wilson," he said. A few moments of silence passed, then he continued thoughtfully. "They're probably sisters."

Ross laughed. "Just so she isn't old Miss Barrett's sister, right?"

Jonathan stared at Ross. He didn't see any humor at all in those words. With his luck, she could very well be.

Ross laughed again and tousled his hair. "Cheer up. She's too old to be Miss Barrett's sister, and not nearly good-looking enough."

Ross was teasing him, he decided, and he returned the smile. He really liked Ross, especially the way he made a little boy feel good inside. And Jonathan hadn't felt this good inside for a long time.

Chapter Four

Winnie Barrett crossed Irene's porch and pushed the door open, tsk-tsking aloud about her daughter's habit of never locking it. This might be a small town, she thought, stepping inside and crossing to the parlor, but even so, one could never be too careful. She made a mental note to say so, again.

"Irene?" she called, poking her head inside the empty parlor. "Are you here?"

"Yes, ma'am, she is."

Winnie whirled, her hand braced against her chest where her heart gave one great thump before evening out again.

"Oh! Goodness gracious!" Winnie frowned. "Child, you oughten to frighten an old woman that way."

"I'm sorry. I thought you heard me."

"No. I most certainly did not." Winnie eyed the girl with an assessing glance, starting with the neatly braided hair on down the well-starched apron to the sturdy black shoes. "And who might you be?"

"I'm Lydia," she answered, smiling. "Who are you?"

Winnie's head moved a notch back on her spine while her eyes rounded in surprise at the girl's forwardness. "I'm—I'm Irene's mother."

"Pleased to meet you, Mrs. Barrett."

Somewhat mollified by the correctness of Lydia's manners, although still puzzled by her presence, Winnie half-heartedly returned the girl's smile. "Well, where is she?"

"In the kitchen," Lydia said, pointing in that direction.

Winnie held up her hand as if to say she didn't need directions and marched to the back of the house with Lydia right behind her.

Irene stood with her back to the door, working at the table.

"Who was it, Lydia?" she called over her shoulder.

"See for yourself," Winnie said.

Irene spun around, her hand to her heart. "Mother!"

"Yes, and a little worse for wear, I do declare," she said, brushing at the wrinkles in her clothing. "Don't just stand there with your mouth open wide enough to catch flies, give me a hug. And I don't want to hear anything about why didn't I write first. A mother has a right to show up unexpectedly now and then."

Irene embraced her mother and kissed her cheek. Winnie returned the hug, noticing that her daughter hadn't put on one ounce of weight. If anything, she was a little thinner.

"How did you get here? And why didn't you—"

"No, no. I told you not to ask me that."

Still in shock, Irene watched while her mother pulled the pearl-tipped hatpins from her hat. She wasn't sure if she was glad to see her or not. The timing certainly couldn't have been worse.

"I'll take your hat, Mrs. Barrett." Lydia extended her hand.

Winnie handed her the hat with the pins inserted, then patiently waited until Lydia left the room. With a look aimed directly at her daughter, she raised both eyebrows, obviously awaiting an explanation.

"It's a long story, Mother," Irene said, familiar with every unspoken word implied by the tilt of her mother's head or the lift of an eyebrow.

"Well, I've got plenty of time," Winnie returned, pulling out a chair and seating herself.

"I really don't think now is the—"

"I do." Her small chin jutted stubbornly.

With only a slight hesitation, Irene gave in and sat opposite her mother.

"The children are orphans. They're only staying here until I can locate a relative," Irene said calmly, hoping to allay Winnie's concerns.

"Children?" Winnie's eyes widened until Irene could almost count each eyelash surrounding the vivid blue eyes. "There are more?"

"Yes. Lydia's brother, Jonathan."

A silence filled the room and the familiar unspoken word, disapproval, hung like a frown.

"Irene, whatever are you doing taking in orphans?"

That uncomfortable and irritating feeling of inadequacy descended. Irene replied, "I didn't exactly go in search of orphans, Mother. They simply appeared."

"Appeared." Winnie looked skeptical. Once more silence settled on Irene. "Well, that does sound simple enough."

"I could hardly send them out into the night with no place to go, could I?" Irene went on defensively, wishing she didn't have to explain her every action and motive.

"Hardly." Then with an apparent change of heart, Winnie reached out for Irene's hand and held it gently. "I'm afraid we've gotten off to a bad start. What do you say we talk about this later, after I've rested and gotten settled in?"

Irene gladly conceded, although she knew that with a little more time her mother would probably have marshaled more tactics and strategies than a general going into battle.

Melody Morgan

Setting aside her preparations for supper, Irene and Lydia helped Winnie get the small traveling trunk and two sturdy valises upstairs, where a decision had to be made concerning who would sleep where. Finally, it was agreed upon that Winnie would take the front bedroom now occupied by Jonathan, and he would sleep on a cot in Lydia's room. The whole episode was so exhausting, on top of that tiring canal trip, that Winnie simply had to lie down before having tea.

Back in the kitchen, Irene made herself a pot of chamomile tea, which she was sure couldn't calm her nerves even if she drank the entire pot.

"I like your mother," Lydia said, lifting a lid and adding more wood to the cookstove. "I think she's funny."

Irene finished cutting up the potatoes and added them to the barely simmering beef soup. "I can assure you, she doesn't intend to be humorous."

Lydia glanced up. "I'm glad you told me. I wouldn't want to laugh and make her angry. I almost did when she called herself an old woman. She isn't at all an old woman, not like Mrs. Wilson is."

"Lydia," Irene scolded gently.

"Well, it's true. But I wouldn't say that to anyone but you. And Jonathan. He's terrified of Mrs. Wilson."

"She means well." Irene spoke aloud the words she'd been saying to herself for the last several years.

For the next few moments, they worked side by side with only the clink of dishes interrupting the silence as Lydia placed them on the table. Irene stirred the soup, thinking about her mother and feeling uneasy with her sudden appearance. Lydia lit a lamp to dispel the lengthening shadows, although outdoors the darkness had yet to come. Then the quiet was broken as the back door burst open.

"Lydia!" Jonathan yelled, rushing inside. "See what I caught!"

With the spoon poised over the cooking pot, Irene's

64

thoughts were jolted from her. Standing there proudly in front of Lydia, Jonathan held up a fish on the end of his fishing line. Behind him Ross Hollister stepped through the doorway like an exaggerated shadow.

"Evening, Miss Barrett. I hope he isn't too late for supper, but I didn't have the heart to make him quit until he'd caught his fish." Ross tousled Jonathan's hair. "And he sure got a fine one."

Staring at the occasional wiggle of the dying fish, Irene restrained herself from wrinkling her nose at the smell surrounding it.

"Yes, he did," she said at last. "And it's a big one, too."

"Big enough to eat!" Jonathan said with enthusiasm.

Lydia stepped forward. "Well, you'd better get it cleaned before it spoils."

Jonathan lifted suddenly somber eyes. "Could Ross eat it with us?" he asked quietly. "He helped me catch it."

Glancing up, Irene caught the surprise registered on Ross's face as he raised a hand, shaking his head. "Wait a minute, pal. You caught that fish all by yourself."

"But it's your pole."

"That doesn't mean I'd have caught that fish if I'd been holding it. Besides," he added with a wink, "I don't think it's polite to ask myself for dinner."

"You didn't. I did."

From the moment Ross Hollister stepped through her door, Irene had forced herself to respond calmly to his presence. She reminded herself that not once, but twice, he had gone out of his way to offer friendship to a small boy. And now that she saw him in a different environment and under different circumstances, she was surprised that he seemed so much less forbidding than when they'd first met. But how open-minded dared she be? After all, a man in his line of work could hardly expect his life to be an example for any child.

Yet it was easy to see that Jonathan had allowed Ross Hollister access to a part of himself reserved for no one but Lydia. In spite of all the reassuring things Irene had tried to do, she could not reach him.

In a fraction of a second, she weighed the consequences of having the saloon owner stay for dinner and Jonathan's disappointment if he didn't. And with a touch of defiance, she quelled the nagging worry over what her mother would undoubtedly say.

"I think Jonathan's right, Mr. Hollister. It's only fair that you should share Jonathan's fish."

Ross glanced from her to Jonathan and back at her again until she became uncomfortable and had to look away.

"She said it's all right," Jonathan appealed.

"Set another place, Lydia," Irene said, turning back to the now boiling soup. She pushed it to a cooler spot on the range, glad to have something that needed doing. If she allowed her mind to dwell on her decision too long, she would begin to regret it.

"Let's clean it, Ross. I'll bet it's gonna taste good."

"Sure thing," Ross answered.

After Lydia supplied them with the necessary pan and knife, the two disappeared out the back door. Irene brought out a heavy skillet and prepared to fry the fish. Within minutes they were back, and the smell of fish soon permeated the room.

Irene turned the fish in the hot skillet when one side had browned, all the while being fully aware of the presence of a man in her kitchen. Before tonight she hadn't noticed how small the room actually was, but now it felt confining and threatened to close in on her.

When Ross and Jonathan washed up at the basin and dried their hands, Irene walked around the other side of the table to avoid bumping into Ross when she hung up her apron. Unaware of her trip around the table, he stepped sideways away from the basin right into her path.

Quickly, Irene raised her hand to push at his shoulder in order to prevent him from treading on her toes. His head turned and their gazes collided.

"Excuse me," they each said at once.

"I was just trying to get out of your way," he went on apologetically.

At that moment, Winnie Barrett walked in, exclaiming, "What is that dreadful smell?"

A sinking sensation, not unlike what that unwitting fish must have felt when he took the bait on Jonathan's line, grabbed at Irene's stomach.

The lift of one eyebrow on her mother's face and the tilt of her head had the effect of a shouted word, and Irene hastily removed her hand from Ross's shoulder, then stepped behind the chair where Jonathan sat.

"Mother, this is Jonathan, Lydia's brother. And this is Ross Hollister. He was kind enough to take Jonathan fishing." Irene knew she'd left a lot unsaid, but she was sure saying more wouldn't improve the situation at all.

"I see." Winnie glanced apprehensively at the stove. "And we're all to share the bounty of this expedition? How nice."

The small table had a fifth chair crowded at one corner, which Jonathan quickly occupied in hopes that Ross would sit beside him. With a feeling of impending doom, he stared at the woman Miss Barrett said was her mother. He glanced at Ross, but Ross was looking at Miss Barrett.

Lydia saved Irene some embarrassment by taking the other seat next to Ross, which was normally Irene's.

When all were seated, the soup bowls filled, and a small portion of the single fish lay upon each dish, Winnie fastened a disbelieving stare on Jonathan's plate.

"Is something wrong, Mother?" Irene asked, almost fearful of the answer.

"Irene, you're not going to allow that child to eat that, are you? Those bones are extremely hazardous."

"I know how to eat fish," Jonathan said, his old defiance surfacing.

"Indeed," Winnie said, obviously taken aback.

Ross cleared his throat and everyone's attention riveted on his smiling face. "Ole Jonathan here is a veteran fisherman. You should have seen him cleaning this fish. Anyone who can clean a fish like that sure hadn't ought to have any trouble eating it." He winked at the boy and Jonathan smiled back.

Some of the tension in the air cleared, at least for Irene, and the meal proceeded on a less strained note. Everyone ate their fish, except for Winnie, who carefully pushed the dish aside and opted for the beef soup instead, unaware that her selection had been noticed by each of the others at the table.

When the meal was finished, Ross pushed his chair back.

"That's the best fish, and soup, I've had in a long time. And the first I've had sitting in someone's kitchen," he said, smiling at Irene.

"Really?" Winnie asked, her undivided attention resting on Ross.

"Yes, ma'am. The restaurant folks don't care too much to have their patrons underfoot while they're cooking," he replied, grinning.

"Then you don't have a home of your own?" Winnie continued.

"No. I live up at the old inn. At least for now."

"For now?"

Irene recognized when her mother was settling in for a long siege of questioning. She had done the same to Andrew and been well satisfied—or more truthfully, charmed. But Irene knew that these questions could only lead to disaster.

"Mother, I don't think we should detain Mr. Hollister. He's a busy man."

"Oh?" Winnie's gaze shifted from Irene back to Ross. "What do you do, sir?"

Irene held her breath.

"He unloads the barges," Jonathan piped in proudly before Ross could answer. "I watched him."

With a grateful heart, Irene released the breath held in her lungs.

"Actually, I own the Broken Keg Saloon in town," Ross answered. "But I unload barges, too," he said with a grin for Jonathan.

Winnie's back visibly stiffened, and her cool blue eyes suddenly froze over as she fixed him with a glacial stare across the crowded table.

"Saloon?" she croaked.

The embarrassment Irene experienced at that moment was close to actual physical pain. Not only for herself but, surprisingly, for Ross Hollister too. It was not easy to withstand Winnie Barrett's haughtiness when she brought the full impact of it down upon one's head, deserving or not.

"Yes, ma'am. But that's only been a recent occurrence. Actually, I'm a miner."

"Coal?" she asked, her voice brittle.

Ross shook his head. "Gold."

Irene slid a glance at her mother's profile. Even Lucy Wainwright's tight corsets couldn't improve Winnie's posture.

"Then are you here to stay, Mr. Hollister?" Winnie went on icily.

"Mother." Irene spoke softly, but the edge in her voice dropped the last syllable noticeably lower than the first.

Ross shrugged, appearing nonplussed by the verbal barrage. "I like Grand Rapids, but I haven't really decided."

He rose from his seat. "Well, your daughter is right, I do have to be going." To Irene he said, "Thank you for inviting me."

She nodded her head and politely answered, "You're welcome."

Jonathan jumped from his chair, grabbing Ross's coat. "Can we go fishing again?"

"Sure. I'll be kind of busy for a while but you can come down and watch me unload barges if you want."

"Okay." A mild disappointment sounded in Jonathan's voice.

Ross patted the boy's shoulder. "Well, I'd better be going. Thanks again."

When the door closed behind Ross, Irene self-consciously prepared the dishwater while Lydia quietly scraped plates and Jonathan escaped out the back door, voluntarily bringing in water and wood for the morning.

Winnie stood vigorously rolling up her sleeves.

"We'll do the dishes, Mother. Why don't you sit down and have a cup of tea? It's been a long day for you." Irene sent up a silent prayer, hoping to avoid a discussion of Ross Hollister.

"Thank you, dear, that does sound very nice," Winnie said, seating herself at the now cleared table. She took the offered cup of tea and smiled perceptively at her daughter, then lowered her voice, saying, "we'll talk about things later."

Cringing, Irene resigned herself to what was sure to come, then gave her attention to the dishes.

"Those canal boats might be wonderful means of transportation," Winnie went on, "if you're a crate of goods that is, but I don't believe I'll ever willingly set foot on one again. My backside will never be the same."

"You should have taken a train, Mother."

"If I'd known you had a . . . friend who could pick me up at the station in Toledo, I would have."

In exasperation, Irene turned around slowly. "He's not my friend, Mother, and you could have taken the train from Toledo to here."

Winnie noncommittally sipped her tea.

"And if you had written—" Irene began, annoyance creeping into her voice..

"Now, we've already discussed that," Winnie interrupted, setting her daughter straight once more.

Turning her back, Irene washed the last of the dishes with a little more splashing than was necessary. Never before had she been so truly irritated with her mother. She couldn't help thinking that if it had been Andrew sitting there, the conversation—not to mention the atmosphere—would have been entirely different. Everyone loved Andrew. But, she reminded herself, not everyone knew Andrew as well as she did.

Lydia hung her towel on a peg to dry. "I guess I'd better go find Jonathan and tell him he'll be sleeping in my room." And she disappeared through the back door just as her brother had twenty minutes earlier.

"How is school coming along?" Winnie asked pleasantly.

"Fine." Irene poured a cup of tea and forced herself to sit down across from her mother. Now that Lydia was out of hearing range, Winnie was bound to scrutinize every detail concerning the children and especially Ross Hollister. She prepared herself for the coming interrogation.

"And these children? How are you coming along with them?" Winnie stared over the edge of the china cup at her.

With a sigh, Irene set her cup down. "I've told you all there is to tell, Mother. The children let themselves in—"

"I've been meaning to talk to you about that unlocked door."

"—and I decided to let them stay while I locate a relative. So far there's been no word from anyone."

"And did the children arrive wearing new shoes and new clothing?" She arched an accusing eyebrow.

"No."

"I thought not." Winnie sat back in her chair, folding her hands in her lap. "Irene dear, I think you're becoming attached to these children, and you know that a single widow—"

"I'm not a widow, Mother!" Aghast, the words burst from Irene's mouth.

"I know. I meant to say single woman," she replied, her voice hushed with memories. "It's just that sometimes I

71

forget." Emotion clogged her throat momentarily. "It was all so perfect for you. I just don't understand why." Winnie's hand closed consolingly over Irene's where it lay clenched on the table.

"Andrew was such a wonderful man," Winnie went on.

"Andrew didn't die, Mother. He is alive and well. Somewhere." She didn't know where and furthermore, she no longer cared.

"I know. But he left you this beautiful house with all this lovely furniture as a testament of his love for you. Surely . . ."

But the rest of what she had to say fell on deaf ears as Irene stared into the bottom of her teacup. Yes, she thought to herself, he'd left her the house and the furniture, but what she'd never told anyone was that Andrew hadn't bought any of it. She had used the money left to her by her father. Some she had invested, but most of it was spent on the house and the furnishings. They had chosen everything together, buying only the best, keeping their secret so Andrew's pride wouldn't suffer.

She continued staring at the small heap of broken bits of tea leaves in her cup that so resembled her own crushed feelings when she discovered another of Andrew's secrets. And this one she would hide forever.

"I've made you sad. I'm sorry," Winnie said, and she truly was. Now was not the time, she conceded silently, to bring up her concern over the appearance of the saloon owner, Mr. Hollister. But eventually she would. It was a mother's duty to look out for her unmarried daughter, and she took that duty very seriously.

They sat thus for several minutes in silence. Then Winnie rose from her seat. "What do you say we pour another cup and go into the parlor? It sounds like Lydia is building a fire in the stove."

With cups in hand, they entered the parlor, which glowed softly with lamplight. Orange and yellow firelight shone brightly through the thin sheet of mica in the door of the ornate round stove. Brisk noises of crackling and snapping emanated from it, yet only a meager measure of heat penetrated the cool room.

"It won't take long," Lydia said, sweeping up the pieces of bark that had fallen on the floor.

Jonathan sat on a stool, staring into the flames, his mind obviously lingering on the events of the afternoon.

Winnie sat in a chair close to the edge of the heat. "Did Howard Gregg put up the stove for you this year?"

Irene nodded. "We didn't really need it until a few weeks ago. He offered to install it."

"He's such a reliable man," Winnie said. "Didn't you write that he'd married your friend Emma?"

"Yes. Almost two months ago."

Jonathan yawned wide, his face reddening with the warmth of the fire.

"Come on, Jonathan," Lydia said. "It's time to get ready for bed." She tugged at his arm and, without resisting, he followed her to the kitchen.

This unusual turn of events didn't escape Irene. There was a subtle change in the boy, and she was sure it was due to Ross Hollister.

"That girl's quite capable at most everything, isn't she?" Winnie asked, having observed Lydia closely all evening.

"Yes. She is."

Setting aside her cup, Winnie rose from her chair. "Well, I quite agree with her, it is definitely time for bed. I can't remember when I've been this tired."

Crossing the room, she bent and kissed her daughter's cheek. "It's really very good to be here."

Irene felt a constriction around her heart, not unlike the one she felt surrounding her life. Deep emotional childhood ties to this woman, her mother, jumbled together in confusion with these new feelings of responsibility and budding independence.

"It's good to have you here, Mother," she replied in a near whisper. "Sleep well."

Melody Morgan

When everyone had gone to bed and all was quiet, Irene rose from her seat before the dying fire. She checked the damper in both stoves and climbed the stairs to bed. After donning a warm gown, she pulled the box of novels from beneath her bed and selected one. Then she adjusted the lamp, crawled under a layer of quilts, and opened to a favorite page.

"The tall dark-eyed young man hurried past," she read silently. "He stopped suddenly in the path, turned, and his eyes met hers—those dark, laughing, magnetic eyes that few women even yet had the power of resisting. . . . "

Ross entered his room at the inn, closed the door firmly behind him, and locked it out of old habit. In the dark he sank onto the edge of the bed, tired to the bone.

After leaving Miss Barrett's, he'd gone to the saloon, where it seemed he'd broken up one fight after another. He and Ben had stayed late to clean up the mess, which had been almost as bad as the one the women had made a month or so ago.

He shrugged out of his coat and hung it on the back of a chair next to the bed, then pulled off his boots. The cold floor penetrated through the warmth of his socks to his feet. Without wasting any time, he divested himself of the rest of his clothing, dropping it on the floor, and crawled beneath the chilled covers.

His mind tiredly replayed the events of the day with each happening easily slipping by until he got to the part where Jonathan felt a tug on his fishing pole. The sparkle in the boy's eye left little doubt that this had been a high point in his young life.

Ross smiled remembering his own childhood fishing expeditions. He and Harry had managed to slip away on more than one occasion with a fishing pole after finishing chores or even during school days. Especially during school days, if he remembered correctly. He grinned in the dark.

He continued thinking about Jonathan, living in a houseful of women without a single man to show him how to bait a hook or gut a fish properly. It just didn't seem right. A boy needed someone to teach him what a woman couldn't. But he knew it wasn't wise to get too involved.

Like tonight, eating supper in the home of a bunch of strangers, and women to boot. He'd felt completely out of his element. Probably just the way Jonathan felt.

He smiled, remembering again Jonathan's description of Miss Barrett. Apparently, Jonathan wasn't the only one who had misjudged her. Ross remembered back to that night in the saloon, when it seemed that hell had marched in wearing skirts and high heels. He hadn't noticed her at first, not until he heard a screech and the splintering of glass. When he turned around, there she was, Miss Barrett the schoolteacher, holding a club and standing amidst the pieces of the only mirror the saloon sported. Of course, he hadn't realized she was the schoolteacher until later. And in spite of Jonathan's opinion, she was the prettiest schoolteacher he'd ever seen.

Tiredness crept over his body, while the warmth he generated became trapped by the heavy wool blankets, causing his eyelids to slide shut.

Hazily, his mind drifted back to winter days along the Maumee above the dam. He remembered how the ice got thick enough to skate on sometimes as early as Christmas, and even earlier on the canal where the water lay still. He remembered cutting holes in the ice like the Indians before them, and fishing until their fingers turned blue and numb.

Yep, he thought to himself just before dropping off to sleep, those are things a boy ought to know about.

Chapter Five

The new month of November had replaced the old one on Irene's calendar just a week earlier, and her mother was still there. So were the children and, with painful regularity, so was Ross Hollister.

The fishing expeditions had been abandoned with the advent of cold weather and several inches of snow, only to be replaced by rabbit hunting.

At first Irene had said no, believing the sport was too dangerous for such a young boy. But Jonathan had immediately resumed his defiant attitude toward her and school, forcing her to reconsider. The progress they'd made, while small, was at least better than this regression to running away from school and disappearing for hours. So when Ross had shown up a week ago and asked if Jonathan might accompany him on a hunting trip for just the afternoon, she had reluctantly agreed.

To be perfectly honest, her reasons for saying no in the first place hadn't been based solely on Jonathan's safety, but partially on her own feelings about Ross Hollister. His presence in her home, even though he never ventured past the kitchen, caused her some discomfort. After all, he did own a saloon, something her mother had never allowed her to forget since the evening she'd arrived.

And today was no exception.

"I suppose we'll be eating rabbit or some such wild thing. Again," Winnie said, sniffling slightly while she peeled the onions for the stew.

"You're catching a cold, Mother."

"It's only the onions," she replied. But a few moments later she sneezed.

"There now, you see? Onions don't make you sneeze," Irene said.

"Oh, posh. I'm fine. I'll let you know when I'm ready for a hot brick for my feet," Winnie said, sniffling again.

Knowing it was no use arguing with her, Irene took down the teapot from the shelf and brewed some comfrey tea.

"In case they come home empty-handed," Winnie began, a note of hopefulness in her voice, "do you have something else to put in the stew?" She sneezed again.

"We'll worry about that when the time comes." Irene pulled out a chair for her mother. "I want you to sit here and drink this."

Winnie looked as though she would object, then changed her mind and accepted the seat. She pulled a handkerchief from her sleeve just in time to catch the next sneeze.

"Oh, dear. Perhaps you should warm a brick," she said, sipping her tea. "I don't know what has come over me."

"I'm sure it's nothing to worry about, but it would be wise to prevent it from getting any worse." Irene took a couple of bricks from the pantry and set them on the stove to heat.

Lydia finished cutting up the onion and peeled some potatoes. Occasionally, she turned the bricks over until they were warmed through.

"If those bricks are ready, I'll go up to bed," Winnie said, her nose bright as a radish. "Lydia, would you mind carrying them for me?"

Wrapping them in a layer of towels, Lydia followed Winnie upstairs.

With winter coming on, most families expected at least one bout with a cold, so Irene wasn't too concerned. Undoubtedly her mother had just taken a chill, and a few days of bed rest was the perfect prescription.

The pleasant, sweet smell of cake filled the kitchen and Irene opened the oven door to stick a broom straw into the almost-baked cake to test its doneness. Not quite, she decided when the straw came out sticky. Carefully, she closed the door.

Lydia appeared in the doorway, inhaling deeply. "Mmmm. Sure smells good in here," she said.

Lydia had become an invaluable help in the kitchen, and everywhere else for that matter. Irene couldn't imagine how she would ever get along without her when the time came.

"How's Mother?"

"Under a pile of blankets so high all you can see is her red nose sticking out." Lydia grinned. "But she says the bricks are too hot and she's afraid they'll burn her feet. And she wants you to make her some tonic out of garlic and honey." Lydia screwed up her face and stuck out her tongue.

Irene laughed at her. "It's a favorite winter cure-all for Mother. Just make sure you don't catch what she's got."

Lydia looked aghast. "I won't!" Then she made a face again and shivered.

During the next hour the tonic was prepared, the cake came out of the oven, the stew bubbled cheerily, and Irene checked on Winnie, who slept, while outside the wind picked up, bringing a smattering of flakes against the kitchen window.

"I think I'll bring in some firewood," Lydia offered, pulling on her coat. "Who knows when Jonathan will be back. I'll get another pail of water, too."

But before she touched the doorknob, the door swung open, revealing a smiling Jonathan with Ross only a few steps behind. Suspended between them on a branch were four dead rabbits strung up by their hind legs.

Irene blanched at the sight.

"See what we got!" shouted Jonathan. "Four of 'em!"

"Yes," she managed to say, forcing a weak smile of approval.

Ross stepped back. "Maybe we'd better stay outside, Jonathan. We don't want to drip blood on Miss Barrett's floor."

"Oh, yeah, sorry," Jonathan said, backing out the door when the wind swirled snow into the room. "First we'll take off their heads and skins and—"

"Uh," Ross interrupted, glancing at Irene, "I'm not sure the ladies want to hear the details, pal."

Puzzled, Jonathan looked up at Ross. "Why not?"

Lydia spoke up with, "Because we're cooks, not hunters."

"Oh."

"Let's go before we let all the heat out of the kitchen," Ross urged.

Irene quickly handed him a pan and knife, averting her eyes like a shy schoolgirl and feeling foolish for doing so. Without a word Ross accepted the offered cleaning tools, his fingers accidentally brushing hers in the process. Since there was nothing more to be said, they headed for the shed out back. Lydia followed as far as the woodpile, filled her arms, and hurried back while Irene held the door for her.

"I think we may be in for some nasty weather," Irene said, trying to get her mind on something besides the upcoming meal that obviously would include Ross. Closing the door, she opened the woodbox. "If it really starts to snow with that wind, we may not being going out for a few days."

"Well," Lydia said, dropping the pile of wood into the box and shrugging her shoulders, "I guess we'll have plenty of rabbit to eat."

"Won't Mother be happy about that?" Irene replied.

"Maybe we could tell her it's chicken," Lydia said with a twinkle in her eye.

"She'd never believe it."

Before long Ross and Jonathan arrived with the meat ready for cooking. Irene took a few of the pieces and started them browning on the stove before adding them to the stew. Lydia packed the rest into a small covered crock to sit outside beneath a heavy metal tub, protected from animals.

The warmth in the kitchen forced Ross to remove his coat and hang it on the peg alongside Jonathan's as had become his custom after bringing in a mess of fish or a rabbit. If none had been caught, he stayed for only a few minutes, going over the events of their day before he left. He readily admitted that he was always sorry to arrive empty-handed.

But today had brought a bonus. And he welcomed the opportunity to spend more time in this homey little kitchen.

"Mmmm. It always smells great in here," he said, rubbing his cold hands together near the stove, feeling warm from the inside and knowing it had nothing to do with the fire.

"Sure does," Jonathan agreed, plopping down on a chair. "Did you make a cake?"

"Yes, I did," Irene answered. "I think it's your favorite." She glanced at Lydia for a verifying nod.

"My own rabbit and my favorite cake!" Jonathan said, beaming happily at everyone.

She lightly touched the top of Jonathan's head as she passed him to get the plates from the cupboard. He twisted in his seat to smile up at her, and something warm gripped her around the heart.

"I'm afraid the stew won't be ready for a while, Mr. Hollister," she said, setting four plates on the table.

"I don't mind," he replied, relaxing against the door frame out of her way. "It's much cozier here than in my room or down at the Keg." He smiled appreciatively. "And the food is a whole lot better, too."

She moved around the table in that same effortless manner he'd come to associate only with her, setting each dish in its assigned place. A crisp napkin lay neatly folded off to the side. Such a small thing, just an added special touch, yet it spoke loudly to him.

Feeling his eyes follow her every move, Irene nervously turned her back and reached for the flowered china teapot, placing it in the center of the table.

"Would you care for a cup of tea, Mr. Hollister?" she asked.

"Tea?" he asked with surprise. Then, catching himself, he replied, "No, thanks."

"Oh, I suppose you drink coffee." Andrew had always drunk tea with her, so she hadn't thought to ask.

He nodded.

"I'm sorry. I don't have any."

"That's all right," he said, brushing the air with a lifted hand.

Silence fell.

"Mother isn't feeling well," she explained, indicating the four dishes. "I think she's coming down with a cold."

"I'm sorry to hear that," he said politely.

"It's probably the weather," she went on, not really knowing what else to say, although her mother's health and the weather were probably boring subjects to this worldly man. Most of the time Jonathan did all the talking and the rest of them listened, but now he said very little while his hand propped up his chin. Irene glanced at him to check for signs of listlessness, a sure indication of an oncoming cold in a child.

"Looks like it could get worse," Ross offered, as the conversation lagged. He continued to stand near the cookstove, warming himself and observing her. Occasionally she stirred the stew, her face a little flushed from the heat, and she disappeared into the pantry a few times. It wasn't hard to tell that he made her nervous, and he wasn't even trying. She was nice to be around and he enjoyed her company, nervous or not.

Only the sounds of the bubbling stew filled the room, and the clink of the lifter contacting a stovelid when Irene added more firewood.

Acutely aware of Ross, Irene carelessly brushed against the cast-iron pot of stew with the outside edge of her hand. Immediately, she drew it back with a cry of pain. The stove lid clanged noisily onto the stove top and the lifter clattered to the floor. She stood back, staring at the angry red welt that appeared.

"Oh, Miss Barrett!" Lydia cried out. "I'll get some butter!"

"Wait," Ross said to Lydia. He quickly reached out to Irene, took her by the arm and pulled her out the back door to a snowbank. Quickly, he scooped up a handful of snow, and as the wind whipped around them, he applied the snow to her burn.

The cold air penetrated the thin fabric of Irene's dress and she shivered. Loosened tendrils of hair flapped across her face as she stared at the snow he compressed to her hand.

With his voice raised over the increasing wind, he said, "My Aunt Tilly taught me this."

Numbly, Irene nodded her head. "It was such a careless thing to do," she said, through her chattering teeth.

He felt the shudders run through her body and down her arm to where he held her by the wrist. "We need to get you back inside before you catch pneumonia." He grabbed another handful of snow and led her back to the house.

Once inside, he applied the snow, cupping his hand gently around hers as they stood side by side at the dry sink. Over his shoulder Ross said, "Lydia, get a shawl for Irene."

Irene glanced at him in surprise when he used her given name and brushed aside the warm feeling it gave her, trying not to think of his hand holding hers. Instead, she thought about how lucky she was that her mother hadn't witnessed the scene.

"I'm sorry to freeze you," he said as the melting snow dripped through his fingers and pinged into the the metal dishpan. "But you have to act fast." His smoky blue eyes peered into hers, frowning. "How does it feel?"

"Numb," she responded. Sort of the way she felt all over.

"It'll take more snow to keep it from blistering." Shaking the remaining snow from his hand, Ross grabbed for the dishpan. "Be right back."

Lydia draped a shawl around Irene's shoulders. Although she didn't really need it anymore, she didn't say so.

Through the kitchen window, she watched the bright red of his flannel shirt against the white snow in the deepening dusk. For five years she'd been a cautious person, holding back, watching, abiding in what she'd deemed safe. Now she felt that very caution slipping away like the melted snow between her fingers. She struggled to hold it in place.

Quickly, she reached for the nearest bowl on the table so that when Ross came back she could dip it full of snow and hold it herself.

Entering the door, he asked, "Is it beginning to burn?"

She hadn't really noticed the stinging until he mentioned it, but yes, it did burn. Irene filled her bowl and stuck her hand in it, getting immediate relief. She sat at her place at the table with the bowl of snow in her lap, her usual cautious reserve safely restored.

"Thank you. It feels much better," she said to Ross.

"What a resourceful person your aunt is."

"Was. She died quite some time ago."

"I'm sorry. Losing someone you care about is difficult."

Ross nodded. "But the memories are nice." And they were.

Lydia replaced the bowl Irene had taken with another, then stirred the stew and adjusted Irene's shawl as she passed behind her.

Throughout all this, Jonathan sat like a puppet, moving to see the activities but not saying a word.

"Jonathan?" Irene asked. "Where did you go this afternoon?"

From the corner of her eye, she saw Ross seat himself beside Jonathan and lean back comfortably with one arm resting on the edge of the table.

"Everywhere," Jonathan replied with a tired smile. He tried to hide a yawn. "We went out into the old swamp and found a log cabin that was almost falling down. Ross said he used to live there."

Irene swung her gaze toward Ross in surprise. "I didn't know you were from this area, Mr. Hollister. I thought you came from some place out west."

He nodded. "Colorado." Then he shrugged. "But I spent some boyhood days here in Grand Rapids. Things have changed a lot since then. I'm surprised the old cabin is still standing, and the barn too." A smile briefly lifted one side of his mouth, as though a private thought had suddenly occurred to him.

She would have liked to seize upon this new subject, but it was far too personal. It would be safer to go back to talking about the weather. But before she could say anything, Jonathan spoke up again.

"You should see it, Miss Barrett. The doors are falling off and the windows are gone, but the table is still there. Huh, Ross?"

"Yep. But that's about all," Ross said quietly.

"That's very sad," Irene said, thinking about all the childhood memories he must have.

"No, it's not sad," Jonathan interjected. "It's like an adventure. Ross said there used to be Indians around here, and we could probably find some of their arrowheads."

"That does sound like an adventure," Irene said, happy to have Jonathan take over the conversation once more.

"Maybe you and Lydia would like to go with us when we look for them." Jonathan sat up expectantly in his chair, his eyes bright with eagerness.

Until now Lydia hadn't said anything, but this was an opportunity that she obviously didn't want to pass up. "Could we, Mr. Hollister?" she asked.

Ross looked at Irene, then at Lydia and back at Irene. "I . . . Sure, if you don't mind traipsing around the woods."

"Well, I—" Irene began.

"We could dress warm," Lydia appealed.

Feeling caught in a very awkward situation, Irene hesitated. This would be even worse than letting Jonathan go hunting and fishing with Ross Hollister. And somehow it seemed more awkward than having him stay for an occasional supper with the children and her mother present. A warning signal went off in her head, telling her not to allow this to go any further than it already had.

"I'm not sure this is something for a lady to do, Jonathan," Ross said, sensing her reluctance. "It's pretty rough out there."

"Lydia could do it. She's tough. You should see how she can climb and run. I had an awful time trying to keep up when we were running aw—"

"Jonathan!" Lydia interrupted. "It isn't polite to brag." Jonathan shrugged. "Well, you can."

"I don't mind if Lydia comes along, if it's all right with Irene," Ross said, looking in her direction.

The uncustomary feeling of warmth, which was becoming very customary, glowed like a dying fire being fanned when he used her name again.

"I suppose, if she dressed warm, and if she wants to

go . . ." Irene said, glancing at Lydia's anxious face. "I suppose it would be all right."

"Of course, we'll have to wait until the snow is gone if we look for arrowheads," Ross said, bringing up the obvious.

Disappointment reflected on Jonathan's face and Lydia's, too.

Then Lydia brightened. "Why don't we take a picnic!"

"In the winter?" Irene asked.

"Why not?" Ross responded. "We could take some cold chicken, biscuits, and cake."

"Yeah, cake!" Jonathan echoed.

Feeling a little left out of this adventure, Irene allowed her worries and concerns of impropriety to slide. After all, how long had it been since she'd been on an outing?

"Won't you change your mind and come along, Irene?" Ross asked, sincerity plainly visible in his blue eyes.

Beneath the table where she held the bowl on her lap, Irene plunged her hand into the now-melted snow. Its coolness had a stabilizing effect on her emotions.

Then, taking a moment to consider the looks on the children's faces, she replied, "Well, I suppose it might be fun."

"Hurrah!" Jonathan yelled. "We're going to have an adventure!"

"You're going to do what!" Winnie couldn't believe her ears. She let the pillow she was fluffing fall onto her lap, then sat motionless beneath a mound of quilts. "Tell me again. I must be going daft because I thought you said you were going on a picnic with the children and Mr. Hollister."

"You will never go daft, Mother, and you know it. You heard me correctly." More than a little provoked, Irene placed a tray with biscuits, cups for tea, and the ever-present garlic-and-honey tonic on the table beside the bed.

"Irene, you can't be serious." Winnie allowed her aching body to fall back on the rest of the pillows propped against the high headboard. "That man is the owner of a saloon! And it's the dead of winter!" She released an exaggerated, exasperated sigh. "This would never have happened if I'd been at supper last night."

Irene stared at her mother in disbelief. "And why is that?" she asked.

"Well, for one thing, he might not have had the nerve to ask, and for another, I would have put my foot down and said no."

Her mouth dropping open, Irene continued to stare.

"And now that we're on the subject," Winnie went on, unaware of her daughter's expression, "I really think you ought to refuse to allow him to stay for meals. It just isn't proper."

Defensively, Irene tried casting aside her own guilty feelings of impropriety. For once she wanted to see things in a different perspective, one that her mother never used. But even in her anger, it was difficult to disagree with the truth of Winnie's words. The situation was improper and she knew it.

"You know how people talk," Winnie went on, seeing that she was gaining the advantage in this discussion. "Not that I care a fig for the thoughts of gossips. But there's your teaching position to be considered. Have you thought of that?"

Irene sank into the chair beside the bed. Yes, she most certainly had. And she was concerned about word getting to the superintendent. She loved teaching, and she loved this town. If she couldn't teach here, she would have to go elsewhere or live in Cincinnati with her mother. Was it worth the risk?

"There, there." Winnie reached over and patted Irene's folded hands. "This is really for the best. After all, you're only encouraging the man by allowing him to return day after day."

Irene glanced up in surprise. "He comes to see Jonathan,

Mother, and that's the only reason I've consented to his visits."

Winnie stared long and hard into her daughter's eyes. "Is that what you believe?"

A touch of defiance flickered in Irene's return gaze. "Of course!"

Winnie looked away. "Maybe so."

"There's no maybe about it. They don't need me to go fishing or hunt rabbits or arrowheads or go on a picnic!"

"Then why are you going?" Winnie asked quietly.

Stopped dead in her thoughts by the abrupt question, Irene paused, searching for an answer. Why was she going? Obviously not to please her mother, and she didn't care about pleasing Ross Hollister in spite of her mother's opinion. It was Jonathan she hoped to please, to reach out to with care and understanding.

"For Jonathan," she said simply and truthfully.

"For Jonathan," her mother repeated.

Irene tried to decipher her mother's meaning, but for once she couldn't.

"Well," Winnie said, with an overly dramatic wave of her hand, "do what you must. But just remember, I warned you."

Irene hoped that meant it would be the last time for this particular discussion. Even so, the warning lay heavily upon her conscience.

Chapter Six

Saturday morning finally arrived. Irene and Lydia fried chicken, baked biscuits, and made an apple cake. The sun gave its consent to their outing by warming the air and adding a startling brilliance to the crusted snow until they could hardly bear to look at it.

Jonathan dashed into the kitchen at least ten times, if Irene counted correctly, asking if the picnic was ready and when would Ross be there. And each time Irene answered the same: It was almost ready, and no, she didn't know when Mr. Hollister would arrive.

Lydia hummed and Irene picked up the tune, joining her as they prepared a basket of napkins, plates, and food.

The day had a lighthearted feel even though it had barely begun. Irene couldn't remember when she'd last experienced such exhilaration. Even Winnie's foreboding silence during the previous week couldn't dampen her spirits, and when it had, all she had to do was look at Jonathan's smiling face.

The hamper was packed by ten o'clock, and not five

minutes later, Jonathan ran through the house and out the back door, shouting, "He's here! He's here!"

Irene slipped her coat on over the simplest day dress she could find in her wardrobe. She'd chosen it partially for comfort but also so her mother couldn't say she'd fancied-up for Mr. Hollister. Beneath the deep blue dress she wore an extra petticoat, since it didn't require a bustle, and breathed a welcome sigh of relief to leave the binding corset behind, something her mother didn't need to know. Two pairs of stockings made her boots a little snug, but warmer. An old-fashioned bonnet replaced her usual modish one for added warmth and a sun shield for her eyes.

She glanced approvingly at Lydia, who likewise had dressed suitably for the occasion.

"I feel like a pioneer," Lydia said, laughing.

The infectious spirit caught Irene as she laughed too. "So do I."

Ross stepped inside the back door with Jonathan, who was about as jumpy as a frog.

"Everyone ready?" Ross asked.

"Everyone except Jonathan," Lydia replied, trying to hold him still long enough to get him into his coat and scarf, which he promptly pulled off.

"I'm not wearing no silly scarf around my neck. How can I go on an adventure dragging that?" He scowled up at Lydia. "Ross ain't wearing one. He's just got his hat on."

Irene found herself looking at Ross's hat. It was black and battered, as though he'd used it to fan fires or beat the dust out of it against his thigh. Until the weather turned cold, he hadn't even worn a hat, but the crumpled brim said this one was an old favorite. Her eyes moved down to his heavy, hip-length wool coat, unbuttoned from top to bottom, showing the familiar bright red shirt beneath.

"Is this the picnic?" he asked, lifting the hamper and gauging its weight. "Feels mighty heavy. Do you suppose we'll be able to eat all this?" He winked at Jonathan.

"Sure! An adventure will make us real hungry."

"I hope so," Irene said, feeling happier than she had in a long time.

"Come on, let's go!" Jonathan urged, heading out the door. "We're wasting time just standing here talking."

Ross smiled at Irene. "I guess he's right," he said, waiting for her and Lydia to go ahead of him.

Lydia dashed out the door, her long brown curls floating out behind in her attempt to catch up to her brother. "Wait, Jonathan! Wait for me!"

Standing together on the back porch with the glare of the sun all around, Irene turned to smile at Ross. And when the door clicked shut, she purposely left her worries closed inside. Today nothing would interfere with the pure and simple pleasure of a picnic in the woods. Nothing.

"I'm afraid I couldn't get a four-seater. I hope you don't mind a wagon. Actually, for the place we're going I'm not sure a buggy would be a good idea," Ross said with an apologetic smile.

"Well, I guess this will be a real adventure then," Irene said, smiling back. "I've never ridden in a wagon."

Ross stared in disbelief. "You're joking. Right?"

Irene laughed. "No, really, I'm serious."

"Well, you are about to take the ride of your life," he said, grasping her by the elbow and steering her in the direction of the waiting wagon.

In front of her house stood an old wagon hitched to two horses of reasonable sturdiness. The back was piled and overflowing with straw, leaving a trail, she was sure, from the livery to her front door. From beneath the straw came the sound of giggles.

"It's Jonathan," Lydia said, whispering loudly, her body covered to her shoulders in fluffy, clean straw. "He's hiding."

"Here I am!" he said, leaping to his feet.

"Good thing," Ross replied. "We're just about ready to leave."

He handed Irene up the spokes of the wheels with a few

instructions as to where to place her feet, then climbed in on the other side.

"As you can see," he said with a bounce on the seat, "it's well sprung." When it barely budged, he bounced harder, making Irene hold on to the edge of her seat, laughing.

"You've really never ridden in a wagon before?" he asked again.

"No," she said, smiling at his puzzled frown.

"Hmm. Well, the best advice I can give is to hang on tight." And with that he slapped the reins.

They jolted over the rutted road with the clip-clop of the horses' hooves on the frozen ground echoing in the still winter air. Irene held tight—at least she tried, but the jerky movements over the uneven ground combined with the barely sprung seat did little to help her keep steady.

An occasional deeper rut brought howls of laughter from a bouncing Jonathan and an "ouch!" from Lydia.

"It could be worse," Ross said to Irene, inclining his head toward the back.

"Not much," Irene laughed, clutching the edge of her seat. She was laughing too much, feeling too good, and thoroughly enjoying every minute of it.

They bounced along the river road east of town, then south for a few miles before turning off. Few wagons went this route, so the road smoothed out as they followed the little-used trail.

"You and Jonathan walked all this way?" Irene asked.

"No," Ross replied. "We took a more direct path through the woods." He glanced at her with a twinkle in his winter-blue eyes. "But I didn't think you wanted that much of an adventure."

"You're right about that. This is quite enough."

She turned to look at the children stretched out on the straw, soaking up the warmth of the sun on this windless day. Facing front once more, she stole a sidelong glance at Ross's profile. He had a strong chin—decisive she'd call it, not at all stubborn or belligerent. Another peek at him brought her attention to his mouth beneath his thick mustache. It seemed as though a smile perpetually lurked at the corners, not a smile contrived to charm but an honest one, full of fun. Without warning, he turned his head and caught her studying him. Embarrassed beyond words, she jerked her eyes away, but not before she saw the mischievous glint in his eye.

"Do I have straw sticking out of my hat or something?" he asked, grinning.

She blushed and glanced quickly at his hat, then away. "No," she answered as innocently as she could, keeping her sight centered on the ears of the horses.

"Then what?" he insisted, trying to hold her gaze.

"Nothing. Really." She gave him only the quickest glance with the briefest of smiles. The way she'd been staring, he would think she was like the giddy young girls at the school, and the last thing she needed was for him to get the wrong impression of her.

Still grinning, Ross shrugged his shoulders and turned his attention away from her rosy cheeks to the trail beneath them.

Here the snow wasn't deep, but it was untouched, muffling the sound of the horses' hooves. The wagon creaked less without the jolting ruts, and Irene became more aware of the silence in the deepening woods. The sycamore and elm of the wetter lands gave way to the taller trees of the higher ground where they now rode. An occasional woodpecker rapped out a steady tattoo on a branch of deadwood overhead.

"When I was a boy like Jonathan, there used to be bears and what everyone called panthers roaming these woods," Ross said.

"Bears?" Irene repeated, a shiver running up her spine.

"And mountain lions," he added. "But from what I hear, the bears disappeared about ten years ago. And as far as the mountain lions are concerned, I never did see one around here. We just heard stories about them."

93

"Ten years ago isn't very long," Irene said, unable to control her eyes from searching the distant trees. "Did you ever see a bear?"

"Yep. Harry and I used to hide in the trees waiting for them to walk by. When one finally did, it scared us to death." He laughed at the memory, a warm, rich sound. "But that never stopped us. We'd just do it again."

"Harry?"

"My brother."

"Oh." She'd forgotten the stories about the brother who had previously owned the saloon.

"There it is," Ross announced.

Peering through the thickset trees to a large clearing in the distance, Irene saw a small log cabin amidst a bramble of brushy undergrowth and a moderate-sized barn with broken fences surrounding it.

Poking his head between their shoulders, Jonathan shouted, "There it is! Hey, Lydia, look!"

In a few minutes they pulled into the clearing between the cabin and the barn. Ross climbed down, but not before Jonathan jumped from the back of the wagon and started running toward the cabin. Lydia hopped out and followed.

While holding onto the seat, Irene grasped Ross's extended hand with her free one, climbing gingerly over the side of the wagon onto the wheel spoke.

"Be careful," he warned.

To her dismay, her skirts became tangled with her petticoats, and she couldn't free her foot to take another step down. She tried desperately to shake her foot loose but couldn't.

"I'm caught," she said, struggling. "I can't seem—"

"Here, let me help." Ross reached his other hand up through the layers of petticoats until he found her ankle and guided it out of the tangle of material and onto the next spoke.

The touch of his hand made Irene catch her breath. Even Andrew, her fiance, had never touched her ankle. Yet here was this man doing just that as though it was an everyday occurrence. She wondered if for him it was, and her cheeks flamed.

Once she stood solidly on the ground, she busied herself with brushing her skirts until the cool air took the heat from her face.

"Just one adventure after another," he said cheerily.

Her hand stopped in mid-brush. Did he mean the climb down the wheel or her foot tangled in her skirts? she wondered, afraid of risking a look at his face.

When she finally did glance up, he smiled and asked, "Ready?"

She simply nodded and let him lead her by the elbow to where the children ran in and out of the cabin's open front door. Beside the opening, a plank door hung at an odd angle to the rest of the building by one rusty hinge. Irene peeked inside. Only two windows and a broken place in the roof dispelled the gloom lurking within. A blackened stone fireplace dominated one end of the room, while a small partial loft hovered over the other.

"Kind of small, huh?" Ross asked, gazing at the open rafters then down the narrow width of the one-room cabin.

"Yes. But it looks as if it must have been cozy," she replied.

"It was." Swiftly, the memories returned as Ross stared at the sagging loft, where a supporting timber had shifted. "Harry and I slept up there. We always felt safe, sort of like when we hid in the trees from the bears."

Jonathan stood beneath the loft. "Where's the ladder, Ross? The one you said you used to climb on to get up there. Huh?" He searched through the pile of debris that must have been brought in by small animals making nests, but found nothing.

"Gone, I suppose. Besides it isn't safe anymore," Ross answered.

"Could we build a fire with some of this wood?" Jona-

95

than asked. "I'll bet Miss Barrett is getting cold."

"I'm all right, Jonathan, but thank you anyway." Irene smiled at him, genuinely pleased with his show of chivalry.

"Could we eat now?" Jonathan asked. "That was a long ride."

"Sounds good to me," Ross answered.

They returned to the wagon, where Lydia already sat on the lowered tailgate, swinging her feet. "It's so peaceful and quiet out here," she said.

Ross lifted the hamper over the side of the wagon and brought it to the back. "It sure is," he said, looking around, wondering who owned the property now. A feeling of home settled over him, stronger than the memories he'd carried, surprising him more than a little.

"I'll bet when the Indians were here it wasn't so quiet and peaceful," Jonathan said, his eyes alight with excitement. "There were probably Indians hiding behind every tree just waiting to shoot someone."

Ross laughed. "Not when I lived here."

Disappointed, Jonathan stared at Ross. "Really? I thought you said—"

"I don't mean to disappoint you, son, but the Indians were pretty well gone by then. I'm afraid things were more civilized than that. We had regular chores to do, like milking the cows and feeding the chickens. The only things we looked out for were the bears and the panthers, but no Indians."

"Oh." Silently, Jonathan accepted the chicken Irene handed to him.

"Sit up here, Miss Barrett," Lydia coaxed, patting the straw beside her. "It's warmer for your feet than standing in the snow."

The tailgate was almost as high as Irene's waist, and though Irene would dearly have loved to get up out of the snow, she shook her head.

Sensing her hesitation, Ross asked, "Why not?"

But before she could answer, he grasped her by the waist and sat her up beside Lydia.

"Oh!" she exclaimed in surprise. But when she was seated, she truthfully admitted, "Well, this *is* warmer."

Jonathan giggled at the sight of his teacher being lifted off the ground. She looked so funny with her black boots hanging out from under her skirts, dangling off the end of the wagon that way.

Smothering her own giggle behind her hand, Lydia saw the rise of color in Miss Barrett's cheeks and the huge smile on Mr. Hollister's face.

Irene mumbled a thank-you and quickly busied herself with the hamper lying open between herself and Lydia. "Would anyone care for bread?" she asked. Glancing up, she found Ross's eyes resting on her with that persistent twinkle, his lips curled into a ready half-smile. More ill at ease than before, she hastily turned away.

Bringing plates appeared to have been a mistake, since they all ate with their fingers, using the bright red napkins she'd packed. It was something she would remember for the . . . She caught herself. She wouldn't think about if there would be a next time.

"Cake?" she asked, lifting the already sliced pieces from the basket.

"I do!" Jonathan cried.

"Me, too," Lydia said, wiggling around to look inside.

"I think I'll just have another piece of that chicken," Ross said, standing so close to her knees that she didn't dare move. "I'll save the cake for the ride home."

Irene couldn't look up. Instead, she put some in a napkin for each of the children and handed it to them. Then she chose a chicken leg for Ross and gave it to him.

He accepted the chicken with a polite nod and moved to lean against the sideboard of the wagon near her shoulder. Sensing that she was uncomfortable with his closeness, he then moved to a tree and squatted down on his haunches.

"How long did you live here, Mr. Hollister?" Irene asked, not wholly for the sake of conversation.

Ross tossed the clean bone into the woods and rose, walking back to the wagon. She handed him a napkin, which he momentarily glanced at before wiping his mouth.

"Not as long as I would have liked. My father was a drifter, a gambler really, so we never stayed in one place for very long." Ross peeked into the basket and rummaged for another leg. "Until Aunt Tilly decided enough was enough. Then she'd insist he bring us to stay with her a while so we'd know what real family life was like."

"So this place has special memories for you, then." Irene watched as he looked over at the old cabin and the clearing that wasn't very clear anymore. "How nice of you to share it with us," she said quietly.

He pivoted to look at her, his hat sitting at the back of his head, his sandy hair turned golden in the sun.

"My pleasure." And he meant it. Her company alone was a pleasure and he didn't mind admitting it. Seldom had the opportunity arisen for him to spend time with a real lady, certainly not in the last five years. It was easy to see that Irene was a woman with roots, a family, a home where meals were eaten at certain times of the day and baths were taken regularly whether little boys liked them or not.

She glanced away from his perusal of her face, feeling the need to shift the subject to safer territory.

"Jonathan," she began, "is this where you said you caught those rabbits last week?"

"Yep," he answered, mimicking Ross's usual response. "Right over there. You want to see it closer?"

"I certainly do. How about you, Lydia?"

Lydia jumped off the wagon with a springy bounce. "I'm ready."

Contemplating the same jump, Irene bit her lip apprehensively. Sure as the world, she'd probably sprain her ankle—or worse. She looked up in time to see Ross wink at Lydia before he stepped to her aid.

"I didn't think you had enough nerve," he said, grinning. Then he whisked her down and set her gently on her feet.

"Am I suppose to take that as a challenge, Mr. Hollister?" She tipped her head sideways and arched both brows at him.

"Only if you think it's necessary." He threw her a beaming smile.

She didn't respond, but mulled his words over in her mind. Did he think her life was without challenges? Hardly. Perhaps she never took chances, but why should she? Only gamblers took chances, and she was sure they lost as often as they won, and probably more.

They followed some distance behind Jonathan and Lydia, who dashed through the underbrush away from the cabin. Occasionally, Jonathan would run back to Lydia, make a few circles around her, then run on again.

As Ross walked beside Irene with a small stretch between them, he wondered about her. An unmarried, very attractive woman who took in two orphans in a town full of capable families. She seemed perfectly content to handle the responsibility on her own, in spite of her mother's apparent disapproval. He suspected that the care she gave went beyond the obvious things she'd done for them, like food, shelter, and new clothes.

With a sidelong glance, he saw her smile at Jonathan's antics. And he liked the easy warmth of that smile. A fleeting thought crossed his mind as he stared at her mouth. Had anyone ever kissed her? Why hadn't she ever married? His only answer to that was, either every man in town was already married, which he doubted, or they had the eyesight of a ground mole in sunshine.

Finally, Jonathan came to a halt, jumping excitedly in one place, allowing the rest of them to catch up, although Irene suspected she was the one holding up Ross's progress.

"Right here," Jonathan called. "This is where they lived, in a nest under the leaves and dirt."

They all stood in silence looking at the place. Irene felt a little sad, and the look on Lydia's face echoed her own feelings. Then like a shot, a blur of brown fur raced from the hole across the snow, dodging each tree as though it knew the path well.

Irene shrieked with surprise, and Lydia leaped back. Jonathan yelled with delight, and Ross hooted with laughter.

"Did ya see that!"

"Oh! Oh, I certainly did!" Irene laughed, her heart pumping.

"He nearly ran across my feet!" Lydia cried almost as excited as her brother.

Ross's laughter dwindled to chuckles. "I saw his nose barely sticking out just before he took off."

Laughing, Irene tried to glare at him with pretended irritation. "That's not fair! You were prepared."

He shrugged. "Hunter's instinct, I guess."

"Instinct indeed!" she replied, smiling up at him when she sat down on a fallen log. "I'd say it's more like a mischievous spirit."

His only answer was a wide grin.

Jonathan climbed on the log and walked its length, back and forth. Soon Lydia joined him.

"I think we should be getting back," Irene said, squinting up at the mid-afternoon sun. She knew her mother would worry if they were gone too long.

"Yep. It's quite a ride back, and it won't be as warm this time of day," Ross agreed.

They retraced their path to the wagon and everybody climbed aboard with little trouble, including Irene, who concentrated on each step she took up the spokes of the wheel. When everyone was settled, Ross snapped the reins and clicked to the horses, encouraging them to head out of the peaceful, silent woods.

It wasn't until they reached the river road and turned west toward home that Irene spoke. "This has been a wonderful day. Thank you for taking us."

"My pleasure, ma'am," he said with an exaggerated drawl, raising his hat slightly to make her laugh.

The wagon jolted and bounced along the rutted road once more. With the sun full on their faces, it cast shadows behind them to where Jonathan and Lydia huddled together in the not-so-fluffy straw.

Unable to help herself, Irene's smile lingered. The day had truly been wonderful. She couldn't remember how long it had been since she'd laughed and had such a good time. How sorry she was to have the day come to an end. Slowly they neared town, passing the bridge to the right and on the left the old inn with its broad porch and tall white columns.

Shortly, they pulled up at her front porch.

"Whoa, there," Ross said, bringing the two sedate horses to a halt. "Well, here you are, safe and sound at your front door. None the worse for wear, I hope."

"Not at all, Mr. Hollister," she replied, unable to stop smiling.

He turned in his seat to face her, leaning his forearm on his thigh. "Call me Ross," he said quietly.

Flustered, she stammered, "I —uh, I don't think that's a good idea."

"Your mother wouldn't approve. Right?" He gave her a half grin.

"Well, it's not just that. I really don't think I know you well enough and—"

"You're not sure you want to, is that it?"

Her face burned with embarrassment. "Please."

Ross studied the cracked and scarred reins in his hands, knowing that if she knew his past there would be little if any chance she'd even speak to him, let alone take a ride in the country. He looked over at her, but she kept her head down. "I'm sorry. I didn't mean to embarrass you."

101

Forcing herself to look at him, she replied, "I did have a lovely adventure today, but I think we should let it go at that."

He nodded his head, then climbed out of the wagon.

Irene hurried to get down before he could assist her, but she wasn't quick enough or adept enough to manage it. With her eyes averted, she reluctantly accepted his hand. At least this time she didn't tangle herself in her own clothing. He released her as soon as she stood safely on the ground, for which she was grateful since her mother very likely would be watching.

Jonathan and Lydia swung the hamper between them after they climbed out of the wagon and headed for the house.

"Thanks, Mr. Hollister," Lydia called. "We had a great time!"

"Don't mention it." Ross lifted his hand in farewell.

"See you later, Ross!"

Irene followed the children onto the porch. She turned and, with a small wave of thanks, sent him a smile, then watched him clatter up the spokes. He whistled once and the horses moved on. With her feelings in a jumble, she closed the door behind them.

Glancing into the parlor, she drew in her breath sharply. There on the settee beside her mother sat Clara Wilson. Instantly, her body reacted with ice-cold prickles, much like what a child feels when he's caught telling a lie.

"Good afternoon, Irene," Clara said, her words dripping with accusations.

"Hello, Clara," she replied as evenly as the prickles would allow. She shooed the children off to the kitchen to safety.

Winnie sat sipping her tea, looking for all the world like an innocent bystander, but Irene wondered just how innocent she really was. Somehow she couldn't help but believe that Winnie had called in reinforcements.

"Is there more tea, Mother?"

"Yes, dear, there's plenty. I'll get you a cup."

Irene lifted her hand to stay her mother before she could rise. "That's all right, I'll get it myself. Excuse me." She needed a little time to gather her wits about her before the coming confrontation.

In the kitchen, Lydia stared at her with wide eyes while Irene removed her coat, gloves, and bonnet, then found a cup and saucer. She smiled with more reassurance than she felt, and patted Lydia's arm.

"Everything will be all right," she said quietly, then reluctantly returned to the parlor.

Far from being collected, but hoping it didn't show, she poured her tea and sat opposite the two women.

"What brings you out today?" Irene asked Clara, with a fleeting glare for her mother.

"You know me, I'm not going to beat around the bush, Irene." She settled deeper into the cushioned settee. "There's been talk and a lot of it. I'm sure I don't need to tell you about what."

Winnie raised both eyebrows and dipped her chin slightly before sipping her tea once more.

Irene ignored her.

"About the children?" Irene knew she was baiting Clara, but she couldn't help herself.

"No." Clara frowned.

Winnie took another sip.

"About what then?"

"Not what. Who." Nearly beside herself, Clara practically shouted, dragging out each word. "And that who is one Mr. Hollister, the saloon owner—in case you've forgotten."

"I haven't."

"Good. Because I have it on very good authority that the superintendent is not at all pleased with your socializing with that man. You have a standard to set for the children, all children. And if you're not careful, you'll lose your position."

103

Irene felt as though the floor were shifting beneath her feet. She loved teaching. She couldn't imagine what else she would do. There wasn't anything else she wanted to do. With the delicate cup held tightly in her hands, her earlier defiance slowly slipped away like the warmth of the setting sun.

"I can see that you understand now." Clara raised herself from her seat and placed her cup on the tray. "There's one more thing before I go. I think it's important for you to show your support for our cause a little more openly, Irene. You have neglected to take your turn sitting in front of the saloon."

Irene's head shot up, her attention focused on Clara's every word.

"We cannot give up our fight to close down each and every saloon in town. Even if it means using force once again."

Her mouth went dry. She couldn't do that. Jonathan would never understand.

"I'll be in touch with you later. Don't get up. I'll see myself out." And with a briskly spoken "good day" she left, closing the door firmly behind her.

"Irene?" Winnie stared at her quizzically. "What did she mean about using force and sitting in front of a saloon?" A slow dawning changed her puzzled frown to a look of horror. "You're not one of those saloon smashers!" The tea cup and saucer slowly rolled from her hands down the front of her skirt, tinkling and cracking as they hit the floor. "No, Irene, no!"

"Yes, Mother, yes." And she rose from her seat and climbed the stairs to her room.

Chapter Seven

Winnie Barrett took to her bed with the worst case of the vapors she'd ever experienced and stayed there until the next morning. When Lydia knocked on her door to see how she was doing, Winnie sent her away.

What was a mother to do? she asked herself with a groan. If only Andrew were still in town. If only the two of them hadn't had a falling out, or whatever it had been, then she wouldn't have to worry about Irene. And oh, how she worried about Irene!

Sitting up, she punched her pillow several times, more vehemently than necessary, to rearrange the feathers; then she tried to relax against them.

Why couldn't Irene have been as fortunate as her sisters?

A sigh of thankfulness escaped her when she thought of Janie, Mary Ellen, and Rosie, married to husbands who took such good care of them. Oh, Randolph would have been so proud of their choices! Remembering the lovely parlor weddings—three years in a row—that she'd put on for her daughters momentarily eased the worry on her mind. Everything had been so beautiful, so absolutely perfect. There had been roses in abundance, and she'd brought out her best china and crystal, of course. And music had floated throughout the house and even out the open windows from the small group of musicians she'd hired.

She sighed again.

But Irene! What had the girl gotten herself into? And Clara Wilson, too, for that matter. Hmph! She should have suspected that Clara, with her crisp, clipped talk and always minding other people's business, would be up to something like this. Truth to tell, she'd never really cared much for Clara, and now she knew why. Smashing saloons! Why, it positively sent shudders throughout her whole body. Not that she condoned drinking by any means. But vandalism?

Winnie rolled over and tossed the covers back, swinging her legs over the side of the bed, her vapors long forgotten.

No daughter of hers was going into any saloon and breaking the law. No sir, not as long as there was breath in her frail body.

She bustled around the room barely noticing the chilled air or the cold floor, dressing herself while several plans formed in her head. There was no way on God's green earth that she would stand by and let Clara Wilson ruin her daughter's life any more than she would tolerate that roaming saloon owner spending another evening in this house.

With the bed made up and the room straightened in record time, she hustled down to the kitchen, her mind alive with the details of her plans.

Irene awoke with a heaviness on her shoulders that couldn't have weighed less than the trunk her mother had brought with her.

Sunday morning, she thought, and grimaced. She felt

far from charitable or Christian. Suppressing a groan, she pushed back the cocoon-like warmth of the covers, stepped into the cold morning air, and shivered. A double layer of goosebumps coated her arms and legs while she dressed. Tossing a shawl around herself, she hurried down to the kitchen to build a fire.

Inside the doorway Irene stopped as she saw her mother remove a shawl from a peg and wrap it around her shoulders. Reluctantly, she moved into the kitchen. She had hoped to have a little time to herself before having to deal with her mother's advice and admonitions. And truthfully, she was in no mood to listen to either.

Mechanically, Irene shook down the ashes in the range from the night before, laid the kindling in the small fire box, and tried to adjust to Winnie's presence. Striking a match, she lit the kindling. A weak fire struggled against the cold cast iron of the stove. Quickly she opened the damper to encourage the brave little flames, but the burst of draft extinguished it.

With a sigh of exasperation, she battled her inability to focus on the simplest task of the morning. Instead, her mind concentrated on the problem of Ross Hollister.

She struck another match.

Why had he ever come to town in the first place?

Once again she lit the kindling, now charred and smoking, then fidgeted with the damper. The minutes ticked by while Clara's words forced their way into her thoughts just as they had into her dreams.

She could lose her teaching job!

Or she could alienate Jonathan forever.

Winnie filled the teakettle while watching her daughter over one shoulder and feeling the added coolness emanating from Irene's stiff, straight back. There was little she could say. They simply didn't agree on this situation and there was nothing she could do about it. Frustrated and a little irritated with her daughter's stubbornness, she plunked the kettle on the stove.

Now more than ever, Winnie's mind was made up. She sat at the table, patiently waiting for the water to boil for tea.

The morning stretched endlessly for Irene. Everyone seemed to be upset or nervous. Winnie said nothing. Lydia sidestepped to keep out of their way, obviously sensing the tension between them. And Jonathan pouted, saying he didn't want to go to church. When Lydia quelled him with a look, he defiantly re-stated his opinion.

Finally, they were ready and out the door.

The sun was as bright today as it had been the day before, making the walkways slushy.

All wore solemn expressions, but for different reasons.

Lydia worried over Miss Barrett and what she would do about Mrs. Wilson's threat. She'd heard every word clear back to the kitchen and disliked Mrs. Wilson even more than before. And poor Mr. Hollister! He was so nice. But nobody seemed to like him except Jonathan, herself and, she thought, Miss Barrett. Actually, she hoped Miss Barrett liked him a lot. Maybe being a saloon owner wasn't the best thing in the world to be, but he hadn't exactly bought the saloon. Even Mrs. Gregg had admitted that Mr. Hollister's brother was the one who'd done that. Oh, she'd heard most of the things people said, and she didn't believe anyone was being very fair to him. Not fair at all.

Ordinarily, Jonathan would have loved running through the wonderfully wet, sloshy snow, but not this morning. He didn't exactly hate going to church. At least it didn't last as long as school, and he only had to pretend to listen, but he did have to dress up more. Even worse, he wouldn't see Ross.

Irene glanced at Jonathan walking ahead of her all dressed in his Sunday best. The brown pants and matching jacket fitted him nicely, and with the little string tie he looked like a miniature grownup. He was a fine boy in need of a firm, loving hand. Watching him, she grappled with the idea of telling him he could never see Ross again.

How would he react? She could barely bring herself to think about it.

With a little more spring in her step than she would have anticipated being possible, Winnie marched along beside her daughter. Her plan was complete. Now all she had to do was set it in motion. She could barely refrain from humming a tune, so she struck up a conversation.

"Irene, have you seen Emma Gregg lately? Or that fine husband of hers?"

"Not since last Sunday. Why?"

"No reason. It's just that I always did think a lot of Howard Gregg. I don't mind admitting that I'd hoped if you were interested in another man it might be him."

"Mother!" Irene came to a dead halt. "He's a married man!"

"I know that. I meant before Emma came along."

"Emma didn't come along, as you put it, she was always there. They belong together." And Irene sincerely meant it.

"Mmmm. I suppose you're right. Anyway, I guess that's water under the bridge." When Irene continued to stand, still gaping, Winnie tugged pleasantly on her arm and resumed walking.

They rounded a corner and climbed the hill to the Presbyterian Church, which overlooked the town below. There were a number of other churches in Grand Rapids, but since Irene had been raised Presbyterian, and so had Andrew, it was only natural that this was where they attended.

Inside, all four took their seats halfway up the aisle on the right-hand side. Rays of light beamed through the tall windows. Irene inhaled deeply, feeling the first moment of peace since Clara had come to call. Glancing to her left, she nodded to the parents of some of her students. Then Emma and Howard made their way into the pew ahead, sitting directly in front of Irene.

Everyone rose and the singing began.

The familiarity of the hymns washed over Irene, and she put from her mind the hard decisions she was forced to make. Later she would have to think about them, but for now she accepted the reprieve.

Ross stood in the cold, narrow room above the saloon, looking out the only window facing Front Street. From this vantage point, his eye caught the crowds of people emerging from the different churches up on the hill. He watched as they made their way through melting snowbanks, going in varied directions, sometimes in lines, sometimes three abreast or two by two. All separate yet drawn together in one purpose.

After a while he found himself following the progress of a set of two-by-two's. Something about the gliding walk of the tall woman drew his attention. She reminded him of Irene with her hat, the tilt of her head and . . . He smiled. Only Irene could walk like that. No wonder he'd picked her out of such a large group of people.

Ever since the night she'd smashed his mirror and then his big toe, she'd been on his mind. He'd wondered even then about her involvement with a temperance group, since she was obviously out of place in their midst. And now that he'd gotten to know her a little better, he felt sure her presence in the saloon had not been her idea.

He continued watching until they moved from view, blocked by a series of houses, then appeared again. Concealed, he was able to observe them unabashedly as they descended the hill and turned onto Front Street.

After yesterday's trip to the woods, he found he couldn't quit thinking about her, with her quiet, reserved ways that she wore like a protective shawl and movements that were careful and studied as though she'd thought each one out before carrying it through. Then there was her concern about the kids, especially Jonathan. But more than any of those things was the loneliness. He sensed it, recognized it because he lived with it too.

Suddenly, out of nowhere, a group of young boys dashed along the street, making a wide berth around Irene, her mother, and the children. Their laughter and calls of hello greeted Ross's ears even at this distance. On their shoulders they each carried a pair of skating blades.

Skating. On the canal.

From the recesses of his memory flashed a vivid picture of himself and Harry playing tag on the ice, accompanied by a crowd of townspeople, young and not so young, sliding, gliding, and slipping along the glistening surface of the frozen waterway.

Why hadn't he thought of that before?

Turning, he quickly crossed the room with its unfinished walls and clutter of empty crates. Two steps at a time, he descended the back stairs, hoping Irene and the children wouldn't get too far up the street before he could reach them. He strode through the saloon, crossed the street, and arrived on the boardwalk seconds before their path crossed his.

"Good morning, Mrs. Barrett," he said to the older woman, touching the brim of his hat. Then, giving Irene his full attention, he smiled and nodded. "Irene."

Winnie stiffly allowed a slight return nod of her head, although she barely glanced at him, obviously wishing Irene would do the same. Her posture told him she was not pleased to be standing on the same street with him.

With unleashed glee, Jonathan bounced around while chanting, "Ross! Ross!"

But it was Irene's response that interested him most.

"Good morning, Mr. Hollister." Her voice was distant, cool.

He decided to pay no attention to that; after all, her mother stood close by with disapproval sticking out all over like the quills of a porcupine. "Do you mind if I walk with you?" he asked.

A small gasp escaped Winnie, and she cast a furtive glance around her.

"Yeah! Sure, Ross! Come with us!" Jonathan yelled, even though the still air surrounding them held nothing but awkward silence.

Winnie cleared her throat. "If you'll excuse me, I believe I'll drop by Clara's for a visit."

Irene shot her a look of warning.

"I won't be long." With a quelling look of her own, Winnie added, "Don't you be either." Then she turned and walked away.

Ross watched the play of emotions on Irene's pinkening face—surprise, repressed anger, then controlled composure.

As if there hadn't been any interruptions, he asked again, "Do you mind?"

She saw a glimmer of a twinkle in his gray-blue eyes. Was he offering a challenge to her? Did she dare accept it? Should she accept it?

"If you'd like," she answered noncommittally, then proceeded walking past the businesses whose closed signs hung in the windows.

Jonathan wedged himself between them, happy to have Ross along. "What're we gonna do today, Ross?" he asked.

"Funny that you should ask," he began, staring down at the boy, "because I happen to have something in mind." He looked over at Irene, whose eyes never left the snow-covered road before them, giving him the opportunity to study her profile. He liked what he saw—her smooth cheekbones, not too high, a perfect nose, and especially her proud chin.

"What? What have you got in mind?" Jonathan tugged on his coat sleeve.

"Skating."

At that, Irene turned to stare at him.

"Do you skate?" he asked.

She stopped walking. "Skate?" she answered, as if she'd never heard the word before.

He nodded, his face in the semi-shadow of his hat. "On

112

the canal. I thought maybe we could go across the river this afternoon."

Irene scrutinized his expression. "You're serious, aren't you?" She tried to picture this man, who always wore a cowboy hat and boots, on skates. A smile twitched at the corner of her mouth. He was such a surprise. She'd never met a man like him before.

"Why not?"

Her light laughter filled the air. "I really don't skate very well, Mr. Hollister. As a matter of fact, I haven't been on skates since I was Lydia's age."

Ross grinned, pleased that he'd made her laugh. "So?"

She laughed again. She couldn't explain why except that the idea was so preposterous.

"What about skates?" Lydia asked.

"Yeah. We don't have any," Jonathan added, suddenly downhearted.

Without taking his eyes off Irene, Ross ruffled Jonathan's hair and replied, "We'll find some." To her he said, "What do you say?"

She didn't know what to say. It was tempting; it was also a little frightening. But it did sound like fun.

Fun. It was a new word in her personal vocabulary, and Ross was the man who had introduced it. Now wasn't the time to analyze it, but he added exhilaration to her life, made her feel younger and lighter of heart than she ever had before.

"Where will we find skates?" she asked, realizing that she'd just said yes.

"Leave that to me," he answered, beginning to walk in the opposite direction. "I'll stop by your house around two o'clock. Okay?"

She nodded, still smiling.

The children and Irene hurried through the noon meal, barely noticing when a disgruntled Winnie entered the kitchen through the back door. Nobody mentioned their plans for the afternoon. Not even Jonathan.

In record time, the dishes were washed and put away, the wood box was filled, and a fresh bucket of water was brought in. Then Irene saw to the selection of warm outer wear for each of them. In her wardrobe, in a hat box with cedar-wood chips, was a beautiful muff that she'd used as a girl. It was perfect for Lydia.

Stroking it as though it was alive, Lydia felt its deep silky fur. "Oh, Miss Barrett! I've never held anything so . . . so . . ." Unable to come up with an appropriate word, she put her hands into the tunneled ends, enjoying the texture and the fit.

"It's yours. I want you to have it."

"Mine?" Lydia asked, disbelieving.

"Yes."

Without warning, Lydia threw her arms around Irene, hugging her tight.

"I love it. Thank you!" *And I love you, too,* she thought. Her throat constricted and she had to work her chin to keep from crying. This was going to be the most wonderful day, and she didn't want to ruin it by bawling like a baby.

Holding her close, Irene enjoyed the heartfelt embrace. Gently, she patted Lydia's back and said, "It must be about two o'clock. Are we ready?"

Smiling, Lydia nodded and led the way.

Downstairs, Winnie sat near the stove knitting a pair of mittens for Jonathan. She'd muttered more than once that she figured he must be giving them away at the rate he lost them.

When all three tromped through the parlor apparently dressed for a blizzard, she laid down her needles. "Where are you going?"

"You don't want to know, Mother." Irene pulled on her warmest mittens, a pair Winnie had recently knitted, and with her back to her mother, glanced through the curtained window.

"Let's go," Irene said to Jonathan and Lydia as she held

the front door open. Turning to her mother before following the children, she said, "We'll be back before dark."

After the door clicked behind them, Winnie dashed from her seat to the window. She watched as Ross Hollister waited at the front gate and held it open, then parceled out skates to everyone except Irene. But she didn't miss the two pairs on his shoulder.

Frowning, Winnie puckered her mouth in irritation. What was a mother to do with such a willful daughter? She had half a mind to tell the superintendent herself before Clara could.

And that was another problem.

She had hoped to talk some sense into that waspish woman and make her realize that it wasn't decent for any woman to go into a saloon for any reason. Instead, Clara had practically threatened her! Or at least, Irene's job had been threatened. Nevertheless, Winnie had given her a good what-for before she left, gaining a little satisfaction from that much.

Poking her nose between the curtains, Winnie surveyed the foursome crossing the bridge, with Irene walking beside that man, nearly flaunting her association with him for the whole town to see, including the superintendent.

A glorious sun dangled in a flawless blue sky, its radiance like that of a many-faceted gem, no matter that the cold air dispersed the warmth of it long before it reached them. Beneath their feet the bridge carried the vibrancy of other feet heading to and from the canal.

Cheerful sounds of friends hallooing to one another greeted the foursome as they neared the opposite bank of the Maumee. The swooshing and scraping of skate blades filled the air, bringing a measure of anticipation to all of them.

Ross led the way to a fallen log that had been dragged to the edge of the ice.

"All right, are we ready for this?" he asked to all in general, but he looked at Irene.

With more apprehension than she'd expected to feel, she took her seat on the log. She watched those already on skates slicing along, expertly cutting circles and figure eights or, even more daring, gliding backwards.

"Who's first?" Ross asked, smiling.

"Me!" Jonathan volunteered.

Ross helped him on with his skates and walked him to the rock-hard canal. Jonathan clung to Ross's coat while he made an awkward circle around him. Then, bravely, he set off on his own, both feet rigidly held close together. After a yard or two, he turned to smile and wave, promptly falling on his bottom.

Lydia let out a squeal of delight, clapping her hands over her mouth.

"Your turn," Ross said to her.

Giggling, Lydia shrugged and let Ross help with her skates, then lead her onto the ice. She waved her arms for balance, bending first front, then back, but managing to stay on her feet for a whole three minutes.

Irene bit her lip and watched with building anxiety. Yet she couldn't keep a smile off her face to save her soul.

Standing with his weight mostly on one foot, Ross turned to her. He pushed his hat to the back of his head and studied her expression. She squinted up at him through the brilliant sunshine.

"Well?" he asked, grinning.

"I don't know about this," she answered half-heartedly.

He knelt down in front of her and grasped her by the ankle. "I do," he said, then proceeded to put her skates on.

Irene forced herself not to blush at his touch.

When he'd finished with her blades, he dropped onto the log beside her and put on his own. Then he laid his hat on the end of the log. "It's been years since I've done this," he said.

"What?" Irene gaped at him in surprise. "I thought you

must be—well, fairly good, since you suggested it." While still safely seated, she tested the slippery snow, running her blades back and forth. Immediately, her anxiety turned to dread.

As he stood, offering his hand, she stared at it, strong and squarish, with long fingers and callouses on the palm. It crossed her mind that some of the callouses were fresh, probably from splitting wood at the saloon.

"Well?" he asked, bending his fingers in a let's-go attitude.

Glancing up, she took in the way the sun danced on his blond-brown hair and even his mustache. He was a very handsome man, she decided. And she wondered why he'd never married.

Smiling, yet unsure of what she was letting herself in for, she placed her mittened hand in his bare one. When he grasped her by the elbow for added support, she tentatively moved her right foot.

"It's really been a long time," she said, laughing. "I'm not—"

"Think positive," he admonished. "And don't look down at your feet. Sort of like dancing."

Dancing? She couldn't remember when she'd last done that either.

He guided her to the edge of the ice and stopped.

"Wait here while I test my legs," he said, turning her loose.

At his sudden absence, she groped the air, reaching for him.

Fearfully, she clutched his arm, thinking she had definitely made a mistake.

"What, no balance?" he teased. Then he steadied her and eased away from the bank alone and onto the canal. In a short time, he had executed a few turns and skated back to her.

Irene pierced him with a look. "How long did you say it's been?"

He shrugged innocently. "Guess my feet remember real good."

Just then Jonathan came whizzing by, neither foot in motion, but propelled from behind by a school friend.

"Hey, Miss Barrett! Look!" he called, his arms out-flung. "It's easy! Just let Ross push you around." Then he was gone from earshot.

Ross skated to her side, took her by the elbow and one mittened hand, and gently pulled her onto the ice. He heard her sharp intake of breath at the same time that he felt the stiffness of her body when her arm clamped his hand tightly against her side.

"You're less likely to fall if you relax," he said close to her ear.

"Not exactly like dancing," she responded drily.

He laughed, saying, "I guess you're right."

She attempted to move her feet, but nearly lost her balance and gave it up.

"Let me do all the work," he said. "I'll just lead you around until you get the feel of it."

Without venturing far from the log, they moved together across the ice, making wide turns at the ends of their imaginary circle. After a while she relaxed somewhat; then he changed direction and she had to gain her balance all over again.

"You're sure you wouldn't like me to push you like Jonathan's friend?" he asked, grinning.

"I'm sure." She smiled up at him. Perhaps it was the crisp air and sunshine, along with the mingling of carefree voices surrounding them, but she couldn't remember when she'd felt so light of heart.

After a few moments Ross spoke, tentatively asking, "Your mother doesn't like me very much, does she?"

With a small shrug of her shoulder, Irene replied, "There are times Mother doesn't like anybody very much."

Ross chuckled, his voice low, almost shy. "Well, I suppose I can understand." His expression sobered, and with

118

a tinge of regret he said, "I guess she doesn't think I'm proper company for you and the children." And undoubtedly, if Irene knew his past, she would never consent to seeing him again.

Sensing a feeling of inadequacy that he hadn't shown before, Irene looked up at him and spoke softly. "I'm not my mother, Ross. And I think you're very good company." Irene's cheeks grew uncomfortably pink with her disclosure. For the first time, she admitted that she enjoyed his company for her own sake, not just the children's.

Surprised, he gazed at her. "Thank you. You don't know how much that means." With a devilish grin he added, "And it's about time you called me Ross."

Embarrassed, yet warmly pleased with his reply, Irene could only return his smile.

Skating nearby, Lydia proudly displayed the muff Irene had given her for all to see. Happiness glowed inside her until she felt sure she appeared as bright as the sun to everyone who saw her. She glanced at Miss Barrett clinging to Ross Hollister, and an added burst of gladness filled her. She liked Ross almost as much as she liked Miss Barrett. If only . . .

"Hey, Lydia, what are you thinking about?" Carrie whispered with a knowing smile. "I'll bet you're thinking about Miss Barrett and her beau."

"So what if I am?" Lydia didn't like Carrie's tone of voice.

"My mother says he's not a good choice for a schoolteacher." She shrugged. "Everybody says that."

"What do they know?" Lydia came to a halt, nearly falling over.

Carrie looked at her in surprise. "Well, don't get so mad. I'm only telling you what everyone thinks."

"You don't know what *everyone* thinks. Nobody does." She tried to skate away, out of earshot of Miss Barrett.

Carrie followed. "I'm sorry, Lydia, I didn't mean to make you mad." After a pause, she added. "I like your muff."

Turning, Lydia watched her closely. "You do?"

Carrie nodded. "Could I put my hands in it once?"

Lydia hesitated, hating to part with it even for a minute. "I suppose." Then she added, "Miss Barrett gave it to me."

Slipping one hand inside, Carrie smoothed the fur with the other. "It's beautiful."

"I know." Lydia glanced once more at Miss Barrett, who now skated alone with Ross close beside her.

Carrie reluctantly handed the muff back. "Well, I've got to go. I see my mother coming across the bridge to get me." She stared at Lydia, who was older by a year. "You really aren't mad at me?"

After a deliberate pause, Lydia answered, "No."

Smiling, Carrie said, "Good. I'll see you in school tomorrow." For good measure, she waved and called out, " 'Bye, Miss Barrett!"

Irene lifted her hand, still maintaining her balance, and waved at Carrie. With Ross beside her, she skated to where Lydia stood watching her friend remove her skates.

"You skate very well, Carrie," Irene complimented her.

"Thank you, ma'am."

Polly Anderson crossed the snow-covered towpath and kept a distance of about ten feet between herself and the canal. "Are you ready?" she asked Carrie, with only a narrow smile for Irene and none for Ross.

"Yes." Carrie gathered her skates together, waved goodbye at Lydia again, and followed her mother up the hill toward the bridge.

Irene knew it was a small thing, but it was such an obvious rebuff. She tried to keep Polly's unspoken words from settling on her mind, refusing to let them ruin an otherwise lovely afternoon. But she couldn't.

Sensing her injured feelings, Ross tugged her elbow. "How about another turn around the dance floor?"

She glanced up at him and forced a smile. "It's getting late."

Ross gazed into her hazel eyes. "Wasn't that Polly Anderson?" he asked quietly.

"Yes."

"It isn't much wonder she feels like she does. Her husband comes into the saloon so regularly that he has a reserved table, chair, and mug."

"I know. Everyone knows."

"But?" he prodded, realizing this was something they ought to talk about. At the same time he wasn't sure that they could. After all, their friendship was only beginning.

"I really should be getting the children home. It'll be time to start supper, and I don't like to leave everything for Mother to do."

He regretted that she hadn't offered him an invitation.

"Well, if you insist." He helped her up the bank and off with her skates. "I'll go round up Jonathan."

Lydia skated to the edge of the ice near Irene. "Are we leaving?"

"Yes, dear. We really should be getting back." Irene felt as much as saw the disappointment in her eyes. "But you can come back with Jonathan another time."

"What about you? Won't you come with us?"

Irene looked out over the heads of the skaters in search of Ross and Jonathan. "We'll see," she said absently to Lydia.

Walking back across the bridge, their faces ruddy from the winter air and their skates slung over their shoulders, the children chattered about the fun they'd had.

Irene cast a glance at Ross who carried her skates as well as his own, his slow stride matched to theirs. A small frown caused one eye to squint a little while a new tenseness appeared in the tightening of his jaw. She knew his thoughts were like her own. Ignoring the situation wouldn't make it go away for either of them.

The clank of blade occasionally hitting blade sounded like low, off-key chimes, a melancholy sound that echoed her own feelings.

Chapter Fight

Irene prepared for school as she always did, with her hair neatly pulled back and knotted, a dress of somber hue but well-cut, and an eagerness to meet the challenge of teaching fresh young minds.

With Lydia and Jonathan beside her bundled from nose to toes, she hurried to the schoolhouse through the stinging air. With silent agreement, nobody spoke since it was far too cold for unnecessary chatter.

Inside, the warmth of the classroom suffused their clothing and allowed their tense muscles to relax in the welcome heat. Once again Irene felt grateful to Mr. Atkinson from the livery, who'd been hired to get the fires going early. It was an added benefit of teaching in the new building over the one-room school she'd started in six years ago.

After the children arrived, taking the usual time to quiet them, she began with a lesson in arithmetic. She believed mornings to be the best time for this subject, since her students' attention wavered less than in the afternoons.

But on this day it was her mind that wandered.

More than once her head filled with daydreams, causing her eyes to search the vast, cloudless sky beyond the windows of her classroom. Each time her thoughts followed the same path to the same destination. Ross Hollister.

Several times during the times-table recitations, when the monotone voices blended into a litany, Irene found herself thinking of the gallant men in her romantic novels. And each time he wore a lopsided grin beneath his sandy brown mustache and a twinkle in his gray-blue eyes. With little or no effort, she would call up those visions throughout the day. Once he rowed a boat on a gentle stream while she trailed a finger in the clear water, causing v-shaped ripples to follow in their wake. With her eyes averted, she could feel him watching her. Then she'd turn and catch him staring, his eyes smiling.

She shook herself and blinked several times to erase the daydream from her mind. But as if it were drawn on a poor piece of slate, the image remained, leaving her to ponder her situation with mixed feelings of frustration and enchantment.

The day wore on until, finally, the bell tolled its end. The children departed amidst a flurry of coats, scarfs, and calls for lost mittens. When she'd collected her own coat and mittens, she glanced up to find not only Lydia waiting for her but Jonathan as well. Gladness warmed her. Usually he ran off before the last echo of the bell ended. But not today.

"Are we ready?" Irene asked, smiling down at Jonathan.

He slipped his hand in hers and nodded.

Her heart swelled at this first sign of acceptance. It had been a long time coming. She didn't question why now, but simply enjoyed the feel of his small hand seeking companionship in hers.

Walking home, Irene allowed the comfort of their presence to steal over her, and her attachment to the children became obvious. She hadn't meant for that to happen; she hadn't even realized there had been a gap in her life until now. Her only intention had been to provide them with food and shelter until relatives could be located, but so far, there hadn't been a reply to any of her letters. And now she wasn't sure she wanted any replies, as unfair as she knew that was to the children.

Ahead, she watched the spiraling plume of smoke rise from the kitchen chimney. Supper would be ready, along with a dessert meant to heal any broken bonds between mother and daughter, not to mention making allies of the children. Irene stifled a smile with the shake of her head. Lately, her mother had broken so many of her own rules on the correct way to raise children. Then, as if to declare her rules proper and true, Jonathan had thrown up a very rich chocolate cake with chocolate fudge icing the night before.

"What do you suppose she cooked for us?" Lydia asked, casting a wary glance at the back door before climbing the steps.

"I'm not eating any more cake," Jonathan spoke testily. "I don't care how good it looks."

"Don't worry. Mother realizes that rich desserts aren't healthy." Then, under her breath, Irene said, "She was just a little desperate yesterday."

Inside, the smell of a hearty ham-and-potato soup greeted them, but not a sign of anything resembling dessert. Relieved, Jonathan hung up his coat.

"I made bread this morning," Winnie said, turning to the group huddled near the back entrance where the pegs for coats protruded from the wall. "Would anyone like a piece?"

"That's sounds good, Mother." Irene removed a cup and saucer from the cupboard for tea.

Jonathan plopped down on a chair. "Could I have some jelly with it?"

Winnie stood over him with one hand on her hip, considering. "Do you think you can keep it down?" she asked.

"Mother." Irene stopped pouring the tea in mid stream to stare at her.

"Well, I just thought I ought to ask after last night."

Irene continued staring. There was no doubt who was at fault for that. "There's a big difference between bread with jelly and chocolate cake, as you well know." She finished pouring the tea and sat at the table.

Ignoring her daughter's remark, Winnie cut four slices of bread and buttered them, adding elderberry jelly to Jonathan's.

"A letter from Janie came today," Winnie began. "She had good news. There's going to be an addition to their family."

A small sting of jealousy pierced Irene. A child. Janie would have a child to hold and love—and keep. Then a rush of guilt forced aside those feelings, and she spoke from her heart. "That's wonderful," she said quietly. "I imagine they're excited."

"Nervous is more like it."

Irene sensed there was more to come. "Did she say anything else?" she asked, sipping her tea.

"Actually, yes." Winnie fiddled with the knife alongside her plate. "They want me to come and stay with them when the time comes." She glanced up, giving Irene a meaningful stare. "But I'm not sure I'll be able to leave by then."

"Of course you will. There's nothing more important than being present at the birth of your first grandchild."

"Except watching over your own children."

The two women locked gazes, one imploring for understanding, the other doing the same for different reasons.

"I'm fine, Mother. I have been since the day I moved to Grand Rapids. You have nothing to worry about." Inwardly, she asked for the chance to make her own decisions and to be treated with the respect she felt she deserved when she did make them.

"I have cause to worry, Irene, and I can't go gallivanting

125

off until I know you're all right."

With eyes as big as saucers and ears to match, Lydia and Jonathan watched the stand-off. Neither had expected to witness the conflict that existed between the two women. Jonathan, who wasn't sure what it was all about but suspected it had something to do with his presence in the house, decided he didn't want to witness anything and rushed from the room. Lydia, who was sure they were talking about Ross Hollister and Mrs. Wilson's dislike of saloons, had no intention of missing anything. So she sat as still as an owl in the night, unblinking, glued to her perch.

"Janie is the one who needs you now," Irene reminded her.

"She has her husband, and he's a good man."

The words were like an accusation, leaving Irene heartsore. Her mother didn't believe she could possibly make a decision on her own, a good sensible decision. She believed, as did most of the town, that she'd made a wrong choice when she'd let Andrew go. Poor Irene.

"Irene, you're a dreamer with your head in the clouds. You've read so many books, you believe in them. You need to keep both feet on the ground. Be sensible. Stop staring off into meadows that don't exist."

Even though spoken gently, the words hit Irene with the impact that only the truth could hold. She had spent most of her day dreaming of faraway, nonexistent meadows and languorous boat rides, of a man who didn't suit life in a small town. But she refused to acknowledge this aloud and defiantly lifted her chin.

"I'm a grown woman and I'll make my own decisions." Then she added, "Without consulting anyone." Rising from her chair, Irene stalked from the room, barely hearing her mother's exasperated sigh.

Winnie watched her daughter leave, unable to call her back. What was the use? She hardly knew how to deal with this side of Irene, a side she'd never seen before the disaster of the "almost" wedding. Frustrated, she poured another cup of tea.

From her end of the table, Lydia spoke softly, "Why don't you like Mr. Hollister?"

Startled, Winnie glanced up. She'd forgotten about the girl's presence.

"Why?" Winnie repeated Lydia's question.

"Don't you think he's a nice man?"

"Hmph! Hardly." Winnie fiddled with her knife again.

"I think," Lydia began thoughtfully, "that sometimes you have to look real close at a person before you can judge them. The things they do and say don't always tell all there is to know. It's sort of like people who act ornery on the outside, but have good hearts on the inside. Or like people who tell lies and really want to tell the truth and they hope someone cares enough to find out why they tell lies. It's just that things get locked up inside and it's hard to let them out."

Winnie listened to the young girl's words. Any other time she would probably have agreed, but this situation affected someone too dear to her heart, and she would not allow herself to be swayed by "maybe's."

"But," Winnie said, rising, "sometimes all you need to know is what you see." She stirred the thick soup, set a trivet on the coolest part of the stove, and placed the pot on it. Then, in an attempt to dismiss the subject, she announced, "The soup's ready. Call your brother and Irene."

The meal passed in stilted silence, which had become the way of most of their meals recently. Afterward, when the table was cleared and the dishes done, not a word had been spoken.

Seated around the parlor stove, the evening seemed interminably long, just as the winter stretching before Irene seemed unending. Her head ached so badly with the decisions she needed to make that she couldn't concentrate on her lessons for tomorrow.

"I think it's time for bed," she said to Jonathan and Lydia as much as to herself.

Without complaint, the children readied for bed.

"I believe I'll sit up and knit for a while," Winnie said. "I'll tend the stoves before going up."

"All right, Mother."

Irene followed Jonathan to Lydia's room, where a lamp was left glowing until he fell asleep. She pulled the blankets up to his chin and brushed his hair back from his forehead. He smiled and she smiled back.

"Can we go skating next Saturday?" he asked.

"We'll see," she answered, unwilling to make any decision at this time. "Get some sleep."

He snuggled down and closed his eyes.

In the bigger bed beside his, Lydia motioned Irene to sit on the edge near her.

"Don't be sad, Miss Barrett. It'll all work out. You'll see."

Looking into the earnest face of her charge, Irene replied, "I hope so, Lydia." Then she tucked the blankets warmly around her. "Good night."

"Good night." Lydia watched Miss Barrett's slender form disappear through the open doorway, thinking that somehow, some way, everything had to turn out all right. It just had to!

Clara Wilson turned down the only lamp burning in her house. Her policy of never using more of anything than was necessary applied to every aspect of her life.

She laid down the bible she'd been reading and pinched the bridge of her nose in an attempt to ease the strain in her eyes. But it didn't help. It was more than eye strain and she knew it.

With considerable effort, she managed to hoist herself from the chair. Then, reaching for the lamp, her eyes rested on the tintype of her late husband which stood propped against a neat stack of school books.

"Oh, Thaddeus," she said, bringing the picture closer to

her face. "There's so much to be done."

Oftentimes she would speak to him as though he were with her. Somehow it eased the loneliness—and the guilt.

Replacing the old picture, she carried the lamp through the house while she locked her doors and checked the windows.

After negotiating the narrow staircase and crossing the tiny hall to her bedroom, she blew out the lamp. In the privacy of the dark room she removed her black bombazine dress and hung it beside all the other dresses exactly like it. Every move was executed with as much precision and efficiency as if they were carried out in the bright light of day. After donning a plain flannel gown, she slid between the cold sheets to ponder and plan.

First, she pondered Irene. Such an attractive, bright young woman, but obviously not bright enough to stay away from the wiles of Ross Hollister. And no wonder, with a mother like Winnie Barrett. Clara had assessed the stuffy, socially conscious woman in one glance as caring more about what others thought than what they did.

Tucking the covers tightly to her bulk in an effort to get warmer, Clara released an exasperated sigh. Saving Irene from herself, Ross Hollister, and that mother of hers could turn out to be more of a task than a woman her age ought to take on. She sighed again. But she cared about Irene, and she despised Ross Hollister, while Mrs. Winnie Barrett simply irritated her.

She remembered the day Winnie had arrived on her doorstep strutting like a banty rooster and gaining entry, then demanding that Clara stay out of Irene's affairs. It had been all she could do to keep from taking her broom from behind the door and sweeping the little woman from her porch. If she truly cared about her daughter, the thoughtless woman would see they could accomplish more by working together than threatening each other. In actuality, Clara had not threatened but merely warned. If the superintendent found out, Irene would lose her position, and that man was not worth it.

Finally warmth surrounded her, but anger kept her from sleeping.

She needed a plan. One that would help Irene as well as rid the town of that evil drink. She could not—no, would not—rest until she found a way to achieve that end. It was her mission. One she had accepted a long time ago.

Chapter Nine

Lydia walked the distance to the general store with a mittened hand protectively covering her coat pocket. With her mind so thoroughly occupied, she hardly gave a thought to the snow crowding the tops of her boots. Familiar, yet scarcely heard, were the sounds of jangling horse harnesses and creaking wagons surrounding her as she plodded on.

Thoughtfully, she patted her pocket.

This was the third letter she'd posted for Miss Barrett since they'd arrived. Pulling off her mitten, she withdrew this last one from its sheltered place. The neat handwriting, so perfect with its beautiful flourishes, reminded her of Miss Barrett. Carefully, she returned the letter to her pocket.

Inside Mr. Gregg's store, she made her way to the section where the mail was sorted and put into wooden cubicles. She stopped at the window.

"Hello there, young miss. Have you come for Miss Barrett's mail?" the postmaster asked, winking at her.

"Yes, sir." She allowed the letter to remain hidden for a while longer.

"Well, it just so happens I've got something for you."

Lydia's heart ground to a halt. Would this be the one from her aunt? Silently, she prayed that it wouldn't be.

"Here you go. And it's all the way from Buffalo, New York. Imagine that." He winked again good-naturedly.

Lydia accepted the letter with a feeling of dread. She tried to smile a thank-you, since her throat felt so tight that it wouldn't let any words pass through.

She forced herself to look at the return address for the name of the sender.

S. Jefferson Blakely.

Something painful spread from her stomach and radiated toward the outward reaches of her suddenly cold body. Numbly, she tucked the letter inside her pocket, alongside the one she was to have mailed, and walked from the store.

Outside, a leaden sky dropped great feathery flakes of snow around her, and like a veil it curtained her from those who passed by.

She couldn't go home yet. Not until she decided what to do.

Wandering up the hill, she followed the railroad tracks until she stood before the school. How could she leave? For the first time in her life she'd made friends, real friends. She and Jonathan belonged here with them, with this wonderful little town, and especially with Miss Barrett.

Behind the building, rows of long rope swings hung listless, drawing her to them. She brushed the snow from the wooden seat and sat down, her arms looped around the ropes, her hands folded in her lap.

In the hush of a Saturday schoolyard, she stared absently at the beautiful blue mittens Winnie Barrett had made for her while her mind, in a state of confusion, desperately sought an answer.

It wasn't fair, she thought. None of it was fair.

She'd tried so hard to make things right for Jonathan and herself since their mother had died. When nothing else worked, she'd lied, taken what wasn't theirs, and even run away to protect her brother.

And now this.

Pulling both letters from her pocket, she compared the handwriting on each. The one from her aunt contained small, carefully spaced lettering as though she held tightly to what was hers. Lydia knew she must be stingy and probably didn't understand children at all, or even like them.

What choice did she really have? Only one.

Lydia removed her mittens and slipped a finger under the edge of the envelope, her heart deafening in her ears. Slowly, she tore the paper until the letter lay exposed under her gaze.

This was wrong. She knew it. Guilt pounded in her chest as she watched the snowflakes melt on the letter, making inky blotches.

There could be no turning back, just as there had been no turning back when they'd escaped the orphanage. And knowing she couldn't explain her actions to Miss Barrett or bear to see the mistrust in her eyes forever after, she vowed never to tell a living soul about this transgression. Nevertheless, it was the only answer.

Fiercely, she clutched both letters in her fists. Then one at a time she tore them up and stuffed them into her pocket, hidden until she could burn the tiny pieces in the kitchen stove.

Sitting very still with the gray light of day shadowing her, enveloping her, a new burden lowered, resting heavily upon her young shoulders. Without trying to justify her deed, she simply accepted the weight as necessary.

Then, slipping on her mittens, she left the swing and the empty schoolyard behind, taking the long way home.

* * *

Melody Morgan

Monday morning dawned bright and sunny. And for once Jonathan looked forward to going to school. He rushed through his usual chores with less foot-dragging and more enthusiasm, even drawing a few words of praise from Mrs. Barrett, who he suspected didn't really like him.

But today he didn't care.

"My, my! What's this?" Winnie exclaimed. "A second bucket of water when the first one is only half empty?"

"Yes, ma'am," he answered brightly.

"Hmm. Are you expecting an extra cookie after school, perhaps?" she prodded.

"No, ma'am." And in spite of his earlier indifference, he puffed up a little at her words.

"Well, I believe hard work should always be rewarded," she said. "So you can count on that cookie. Maybe two."

He smiled, unable to hold it back.

With his chores finished, he sat down to a bowl of oatmeal, not exactly his favorite kind of breakfast. He preferred eggs and bacon. But today it was acceptable. And the funny thing was, he wasn't just sure why.

On the way to school, he hopped and skipped circles around Miss Barrett, and once in a while around Lydia, too. With each turn he studied his teacher as he had never done before. If he didn't think about her as his boss in school, he guessed he'd have to say she was kind of pretty. She had a special smile that seemed to make her brown eyes sparkle, and that's when he liked her best.

When they arrived at the school, he held the door open.

"Why, thank you, Jonathan," Irene said. "What a gentleman you are."

He puffed up a little more.

Inside the classroom, he hung up his coat, giving extra care to make sure it wouldn't come off the peg as soon as he turned his back, then went to his bench and patiently waited for school to begin.

A few times he noticed Miss Barrett watching him, but she didn't say anything.

When all the children arrived and the bell became silent, Jonathan forced himself to give his full attention to the lesson. He even volunteered a few answers.

The entire day became one happy blur, and still he didn't know why. But that was all right; he didn't have to figure it out to enjoy it.

At the end of the day, he dashed for the door, unable to allow David Peters to be the first one through it again. This time the victory was his, and he raced down the hall toward the second victory. He felt untouchable, soaring ahead with David close behind, yet not close enough to beat him into the bright sunshine beyond the open front doors. Practically flying down the steps, he felt a tug from behind on his coattails, but he shrugged it off and kept on going until both feet landed firmly on the ground.

"I won!" he yelled, thrilled with the ending of a perfect day.

"You cheated! You got up before the bell started ringing. Cheater! Cheater! Cheater!" David chanted.

"I did not!"

"Did too!"

"You're just a poor loser," Jonathan said with a wave of his hand.

"Am not!" David leaned over Jonathan with the advantage of an inch and a half in height.

"You must be 'cause I didn't cheat. Just ask Miss Barrett."

David snorted in disgust. "Her? Why would I believe her? She's just a—a—" He searched his mind for the word he'd heard his mother use when she talked to their neighbor about his teacher. "A hussy!"

Jonathan had no idea what that meant, but he didn't like the way David said it and he didn't like the way his eyes squinted when he said it or even the way his mouth curled around the word.

"You take that back!" Jonathan yelled.

With a threatening push on Jonathan's coat front, David said quietly, "Make me."

At that point Jonathan didn't care if David was an inch and a half taller or that he knew big words, he was angry. So angry that he pulled back his small fist and whammed it into David's stomach.

Surprised but ready, David slugged him back, not once but twice.

Jonathan wrapped his arms around David in an attempt to throw him off balance, but it was he who ended up on the ground with David sitting on him, punching his face.

Within seconds, an older boy had lifted David by the collar of his coat, allowing Jonathan to suck air into his lungs. The cold snow seeped into his coat sleeves and around his pant legs. But the humiliation of the beating burned him inside and out.

"That's enough fighting, you two," said the older boy, still holding David by the scruff of his neck. "Get up," he said to Jonathan.

Jonathan scrambled to his feet. The crowd around them had grown, and all eyes fastened on him.

"You both better hightail it before Mrs. Wilson hears about this," the boy went on.

Jonathan didn't need to be told twice.

With every ounce of strength left in him, he ran for home. Slipping and sliding in the snow, he sped across the schoolyard as if pursued. But not in fear of Mrs. Wilson—he just needed to escape the mocking faces staring at him. The one who'd lost the fight.

When he reached the small ravine behind his home, he tripped and tumbled a short distance down the hill like a dark snowball. Righting himself, and feeling less threatened when he spotted the smoke rising from the kitchen chimney, he continued on. His pace was a little slower and his spirits a lot lower.

Instead of going to the back door, Jonathan went behind the shed to sit on a rock, his back to the wooden boards.

Why had that rotten David Peters ruined his perfect day? And why did he want to call Miss Barrett awful names? What had she done that was so bad?

He leaned his head against the shed and closed his eyes. Thinking made his head hurt, so he just sat there with the pale sun hanging low in the sky, casting almost no warmth on his sore face.

He wasn't sure how long he'd been there when he heard Lydia's voice and Miss Barrett's laughter.

With a sigh of resignation, he stood up. Either he had to run away again or he had to go out and meet them. And since he shivered with the cold already, he decided to get it over with and go in where it was warm.

He walked around the end of the shed past a dense growth of wild grape vines and stood in the road, waiting.

Irene saw the dejected droop of the little boy's head and shoulders. As she came closer, the bruises on his face stood out like measles on a baby. Her step quickened until she could grasp him by the shoulders.

"Jonathan!" She lightly touched the bruised spot on his cheek. "What happened to you? Who did this?"

Jonathan screwed up his mouth and worked his chin in an effort to keep from crying. It didn't really hurt all that much, but the care and concern on her face had a strange effect on his emotions. If he said one word, he'd break down and cry like a baby.

Kneeling in the snow until her face was at his level, Irene surveyed the damage. His nose didn't appear swollen, so she felt sure it hadn't been broken. But by morning one eye would be a bright purple.

"Tell her, Jonathan," Lydia entreated. "Who hit you?"

He glanced at his sister, then at Miss Barrett. Did she really care? She looked as though she did.

"David," he finally answered.

"David Peters?" Irene asked. She'd never considered David a violent child. "Why?"

Would she think he started it? "Because," he replied.

137

Lydia peered into his eyes. "Tell us why, Jonathan. Did you say something to make him mad?"

"No! He did! He called Miss Barrett a hussy and I got so mad I hit him. Then he knocked me down." It was all still so fresh that he started crying. He couldn't help it.

Irene rocked back slightly on her heels when he uttered the word "hussy," and a small gasp escaped her. That wasn't a child's word. Neither boy probably even realized what they'd said, but Irene knew its import. People were talking.

Gathering her wits about her, she held Jonathan close to comfort him. "Let's go inside where it's warm," she said softly to camouflage her shaking voice. "You're shivering."

He clung to her skirts as she put her arm protectively around his small shoulders.

As they walked through the back door, Winnie gasped at the sight of Jonathan's bruises. "Lord in Heaven!" She shot a questioning look at Irene.

"There was a fight at the school," she said simply.

"Well, I can see that, for goodness sake." Bending down she scrutinized Jonathan's face, touching it here and there for reassurance that there were no broken bones. "Umm."

Straightening, Winnie fixed her daughter with a stare. "I believe we can remedy those scrapes, but the bruises will take some time."

Irene had the uncanny feeling that her mother had just looked into Jonathan's eyes and read the entire sequence of events. With every intention of avoiding the coming questions, she busied herself helping Jonathan off with his coat. Then she removed her own.

"If only I had my herb bag with me . . ." Winnie began, frowning over the misfortune of leaving it at home. But how was she to know when she left Cincinnati that there would be children at Irene's house? And scrapping children at that.

With a cloth and warm water, Irene cleansed Jonathan's face, encouraging him to hold on just a little longer whenever he winced at her ministrations.

Over Jonathan's head, Winnie asked, "Are you going to tell me what happened?"

"This is hardly the time, Mother." She continued dabbing gently without lifting her eyes from her work.

"I'd say it's exactly the right time."

Irene leveled a look at her mother. She would not discuss this now and subject the children to further evidence of her difficulty in agreeing with her mother on anything.

"All right," Winnie said, her tone placating.

With that settled, Irene returned to caring for Jonathan. He sat completely still with his eyes closed, no longer flinching when she touched him.

She bit her lip, thinking of how he'd defended her honor. It was her fault this had happened. If she hadn't been so stubborn, she would have seen where her behavior was leading. But no, she'd allowed her better judgment to be clouded by a romantic heart and a contest of wills with her mother.

And Jonathan had been the one to pay.

Perhaps Lydia would feel the repercussions next.

No, she vowed silently, she would not allow that to happen. Nor would she allow anyone else to make her decisions for her. This was her life, and she would make the choices from now on.

Chapter Ten

Thanksgiving had come and gone, leaving Christmas only weeks away. Normally, this time of early winter held nothing but cheer and warm thoughts of home for Irene.

But not this year.

She had tried convincing Winnie to spend the holidays with Janie or Mary Ellen or Rosie, to no avail.

Winnie wasn't budging. And she made that quite clear.

Even so, life moved along on a fairly even keel, with Irene's days filled with teaching and preparations for the Christmas play, while her evenings were spent keeping Jonathan busy.

Not seeing Ross had caused a few complaints at first, but the cold weather hadn't exactly been conducive for any of them to be out and about anyway. But as the days and weekends passed, Jonathan began pressuring Irene with questions—questions she felt hard-put to answer.

How could a little boy understand the difficulties adults placed upon each other, not to mention on children? So instead of being completely honest, she evaded the issue by saying that Ross was probably too busy.

Occupying Lydia's time had been easily remedied. Winnie decided the girl ought to know her stitches and set about giving Lydia lessons on plain muslin. Next she could work on pillow slips, if she improved. She turned out to be an avid pupil, and Winnie took more pleasure in the lessons than she'd anticipated.

But Jonathan proved to be another matter.

Drills in arithmetic and selected readings were hardly substitutes for an evening with Ross.

Tonight happened to be such an evening.

With her patience dwindling, Irene put down the book she'd been reading aloud. Jonathan lumped himself in the corner of the settee, pulling at a loose thread on his shirt front.

"Jonathan, you're not listening," she said quietly.

"I know." He puckered his lips, showing his boredom.

Winnie tossed a quick glance his way as her fingers flew through her stitching. "If you'd sit up straight, your ears might work better."

With skepticism in his eyes, he looked to Irene for verification of that statement, but she only smiled. He went back to pulling the thread.

Outside the wind increased, setting up a fierce howling around the corners of the house and making the wood in the parlor stove suddenly burst into a spasm of energetic snapping and crackling. Everyone sat at attention for a few moments, then resumed what they'd been doing.

"It sounds like a cold one tonight," Winnie said, tucking her skirt closer around her.

"Yes, it certainly does," Irene answered, her head tilted to listen to the pounding of the wind.

Lydia laid aside her work and added a few chunks of wood to the stove.

Then the pounding began again. And again.

Winnie laid her mending in her lap and looked to Irene. "I believe someone . . ." she began.

But Irene was already up and on her way to the back of the house, where a lamp burned low on the kitchen table. Within seconds the others followed, peering over and around her as she opened the kitchen door to reveal Ross with the wind tearing at his hat. Frigid air rushed into the room, swirling around Irene's skirts.

"I'm sorry to bother you, but—"

"Oh! Come in, come in!" Irene called, stepping aside and closing the door as soon as he'd entered.

"Thanks," he said, smiling his gratitude. "It's worse out there than I expected when I left the saloon." His ears were so damn cold he feared they might fall off. He cupped a gloved hand over the left one in a futile effort to warm it.

"Here. Take off your coat and gloves." Irene extended her hand to take them. "Stand by the stove and get warm." She hung the coat on a peg, laid the gloves on the table, and lifted a lid to stoke up the dying fire.

When he held his hands over the stove, Irene saw that they were red in spite of the gloves he'd worn, almost as red as the tips of his ears.

Sidling up beside Ross, Jonathan said, "I'll bet it's cold enough to freeze to death out there."

Ross shuddered. "You're right about that." To Irene he said, "I hate to disturb you like this, but I wasn't sure I could make it to the inn without losing a few toes and fingers." He grinned to lighten his words a little, but he knew it was true. As it was, there wasn't much feeling left in his little toes now. He tried wiggling them to get some circulation going.

"You're not disturbing us," Irene replied, looking up at him as she dropped a piece of wood into the stove. She left the lid off so the heat could come directly into the room instead of going up the chimney.

"Well, I wasn't sure . . ."

Irene glanced away, poking at the wood and sending tiny sparks up into the room. She knew his unsaid words referred to her avoidance of him over the past few weeks.

When Ross had passed the house in daytime, she'd made sure Jonathan was busy elsewhere. And twice she'd changed her mind about going to town, just so their paths wouldn't cross.

Winnie cleared her throat. "I guess I'll make some tea since you've got that fire hot enough to burn the house down."

"Ross doesn't drink tea, Mother."

Winnie stared first at Irene, then at Ross. "Well, we haven't got anything stronger."

Irene's face reddened. "I only meant he drinks coffee, not tea."

With a polite shuffle of his frozen feet, Ross interjected, "Actually, a hot cup of anything sounds pretty good right now."

Winnie lifted a knowing eyebrow at Irene and plunked the kettle down on the stove.

"I'll get the cups," Irene said, turning, but Lydia already had them set out. Instead, she turned up the lamp and sat at the table, her eyes suddenly fastened on the back of Ross's dark brown shirt. His shoulders were straight and wide, as though strong enough to carry any burden placed there. He still wore his hat, the same one he always did, with the battered brim slightly curled up on one side. Then he turned, surprising her, and she averted her gaze.

"This sure feels great." He rubbed his hands together behind his back near the heat. Watching her, he said, "Thanks again."

Jonathan dragged a chair over to Ross. "Gee, we're sure glad you stopped. We wouldn't want you to freeze to death out there, would we, Miss Barrett?"

"No. No, of course we wouldn't," she replied, feeling more uncomfortable now than the first time he'd come to her kitchen door almost two months ago.

With his presence so completely filling the room, her decision to keep a permanent distance between them wavered. The smell of wet wool from his coat hung in the air, along with a hint of shaving cologne, familiar because of him yet unlike any that Andrew had worn. With a concentrated effort, she forced a vision of Jonathan's bruised face to flash through her memory, reminding herself of the reason for her decision to avoid Ross in the first place.

Yet she could no more disregard Ross than the sturdy, warm, cast-iron stove behind him.

Winnie bustled around the kitchen and around Ross as though he were an inanimate object, preparing the tea and replacing the lid on the stove.

"It's hot enough in here," she declared, restoring the lifter to its place with a clang. Then she poured a cup of barely steeped tea and indicated that he could sit down now.

"Thank you," he said, wrapping his hands as well as he could around the small china cup.

"Is it snowing hard, Ross?" Jonathan asked, leaning on the back of Ross's chair.

"Not yet. Just mostly wind." He took a long sip. "A north wind that will likely bring a lot of snow."

"Me 'n Lydia ain't never seen so much snow before. Have we, Lydia?"

With her gaze narrowed, Lydia replied, "Have never seen."

"That's what I said."

"No, you didn't." Lydia didn't look away.

Puzzled and a little irate, Jonathan raised his voice. "I did, too!"

Intercepting, Irene spoke up, "We'll talk about it later, Jonathan. Lydia, would you see if there's any cake left?"

"None for me," Ross said, raising his hand. "I'll be on my way as soon as I finish this." He directed a smile at Irene. "I think I've thawed out enough to make it just fine." He gulped down the last of the hot tea and rose from his chair.

"How come you have to go?" Jonathan asked.

"The longer I stay, the longer I want to stay." His glance met Irene's.

She blushed; he didn't.

"Well, that's all right. I want you to stay a long time," Jonathan said, sticking to Ross like a burr in a sock.

Smiling, Ross pulled on his coat, then ruffled Jonathan's hair. "I have to get going before it gets any worse out there, pal."

At the door, Ross turned. His eyes held Irene's. "I appreciate your sharing the warmth of your kitchen." He tipped his head. "Good night."

With her emotions in a tumult, Irene watched the door close behind him.

"Hmmph! I suppose he thinks we're some kind of way station, where he can just come and go as he pleases," Winnie said with a flip of her hand.

Irene had the definite urge to roll her eyes heavenward, but refrained. Instead, she began getting Jonathan ready for bed.

"Cold!" Winnie went on. "I'm sure it must be colder in the mountains where he says he mines gold. Hmmph! What does he do out there when he needs to get warm?"

Irene poured a bucket of warm water from the reservoir into the round tub in front of the stove. "I'm sure I don't know, Mother."

"I'll bet I do!" Winnie muttered under her breath as she left the kitchen.

Too busy with nighttime chores to allow her emotions to surface, Irene set them aside until later, when she could scrutinize them in private. Perhaps then she wouldn't feel so vulnerable.

The next day, Ross stood in the upstairs room over the saloon with a smattering of snow pellets clinking against the only window. Even though he was inside, his breath hung frosty in the air. Outside, the cloud-filtered light made little impression in the dim attic, even though it was two o'clock in the afternoon.

Surrounding him lay a legacy of clutter, most of it unusable. Dozens of broken crates, pictures of nudes in broken frames, ropes, and an old round heating stove with a cracked door lay stacked or in piles around the room.

Glancing around, he visualized a warm stove, a large bed, and a table with a lamp. It was all he would really need.

After last night's walk in the cold, he'd come to a decision; he'd had enough of living at the inn. As he crossed the attic room toward the rear and descended the stairs to the back of the saloon, he figured that with Howard's help he could be moved in within a few weeks. He decided to pay a visit to the mercantile.

Inside the store, Ross looked down a long, dimly lit aisle with a counter on one side and fabrics, sewing notions, and other household goods on the other.

"Howard?" Ross called, leaning over the counter.

Howard poked his head around the doorway of the adjoining room, which held an assortment of small farm implements and hardware.

"Hello, Ross," he answered, smiling warmly. "Just tidying up a bit since not many folks are out and about in this weather." He brushed his hands on his apron. "What can I do for you?"

"Well, I've been thinking for quite some time about—"

"Howard?" Emma Cregg called from the back of the store. "Howard? Are you here?" She rounded a corner and walked down the long aisle when she saw the silhouette of the two men against the large glass windows. With just a few more steps, she clearly made out the face of Ross Hollister.

"Oh, excuse me," she said to her husband. "I didn't know you were busy."

Ross removed his battered hat. "Mrs. Gregg." He nodded.

Emma returned the nod with an almost imperceptible smile and moved to stand beside her husband's elbow, grasping it safely with one hand.

Patting her hand protectively, Howard gave her his attention.

"I only came by to get a little thread for the dress I'm working on," she said shyly, turning to a counter display of sewing paraphernalia. "Don't let me interrupt."

Howard looked at Ross, encouraging him to continue.

"Well, I was thinking about getting some bedroom furniture for the room over the saloon. Nothing fancy, just serviceable. And a good heating stove."

Shocked, Emma dropped the tin she'd been fingering, blessing her stars that the lid hadn't come off. She stooped to pick it up, trying to hide her crimson cheeks. Mortified, her ears burned with the blatant advertising of Mr. Hollister's new line of business, and right there in her presence! So Clara hadn't been wrong after all.

Quickly, she replaced the tin, grabbed the wrong color of thread, and rushed out the door without even a farewell to Howard.

Heading east, she started up the hill toward the railroad tracks, then made a right turn. Continuing on, she passed her own street barely aware that she skirted the piles of dung almost hidden in the snow. She didn't stop until reaching Clara's front door, where she pounded unceremoniously before it opened.

Out of breath from her brisk walk, Emma could do nothing but fan the air in front of her in an attempt to communicate.

Clara whisked her inside, closing the door perfunctorily behind her. "For heaven's sake, Emma, what is it?"

"I—I—We—We—"

"Sit down over here," Clara said, pulling her to a straight-backed wooden chair. "Would a glass of water help?"

Emma nodded, trying to slow down her breathing. Be

calm, she told herself over and over while Clara disappeared into the kitchen. Just be calm!

When Clara returned, Emma had better control of herself. She sipped from the glass.

"Now. What has gotten you so excited, Emma Gregg?" Clara asked, depositing herself on the edge of a very plain settee.

"Mr. Hollister." She had to say this slowly or she would certainly lose control again. "I heard him say he wants to put beds in the room above the saloon." She waited for Clara's response.

Clara's face hardened and her eyes narrowed to tiny slits.

"And a heating stove," Emma added quietly, almost sorry she'd brought the news. Never had she gotten such a reaction from Clara.

"He won't get away with this," she said with deadly intent while rising from her seat. She tugged on the bodice of her black dress as if adjusting a military uniform. "It's time."

"For what?" Emma squeaked, wishing with all her heart she'd never overheard that conversation.

Clara pierced her with a look. "For what? Isn't it obvious?"

Not to Emma it wasn't, but she didn't say so.

"A meeting. Here. Tonight." Clara began pacing, her plans forming, sharpening with each and every step. "You pass the word along to Polly, Lucy, and Irene. I'll tell the others."

Gathering her wits about her, Emma rose. Polly, Lucy, and Irene; she repeated the names over in her mind. "I will." So with her knees nearly knocking together, she left Clara's house with her mission clearly imprinted on her brain.

First, she would go to Irene's, then to Polly's and Lucy's.

Walking through Irene's open picketed gate, Emma's mind rushed ahead to the probable events being planned by Clara. There was little doubt that another smashing spree was on the agenda of tonight's meeting.

"Oh dear, oh dear," she mumbled. After the last time, she'd promised herself she would never get involved in anything like that again. She'd also promised Howard.

With a worried sigh, she knocked on Irene's front door. Another knock and the door opened to reveal Winnie Barrett.

Still very agitated, Emma could hardly keep her voice from quavering. "Hello, Mrs. Barrett, is Irene home yet?"

"Yes, she's upstairs resting, but would you like to come in anyway?"

"No. No, thank you. I have some business to attend to. But perhaps you could give her a message."

"Of course," Winnie replied. "Are you sure you wouldn't like to come in? We could have tea."

Emma flashed what she hoped was a friendly smile, shaking her head. "Thank you. Some other time. Just tell Irene there's a meeting at Clara's tonight. She'll understand."

"A saloon meeting?" Winnie asked, carefully surveying the nervous woman before her.

"Yes." Emma glanced away, biting her lip. "Would you tell her?"

Winnie smiled sweetly. "Of course. Now you run along to your business and don't worry about a thing." She continued holding the door open while watching the young woman make her way across the porch and down the street, barely aware of the sharp December wind.

Easing the door closed, Winnie stood with one hand fiercely clutching the doorknob. Her temper flared with irritation at Clara, that meddlesome woman! She paced the parlor floor, her stomach churning, her blood racing. Coming to a halt, she stamped her foot on the soft carpet.

It was time! How fortunate she had a plan ready. Glancing up the stairs, she knew the first thing to do was to keep Irene home tonight. That would be easy. She had no intention of telling her about the meeting. And if Emma Gregg had any sense, which she doubted, she'd stay at home with her husband.

Irene lay on her bed with a quilt thrown over her, mulling over the possible solutions to her many problems. All day long between lessons, and even during them, she'd considered what the alternatives were and which ones she could bear to live with.

There were the children. Before they'd arrived, her life had been simple, but lonely. Until now she'd had nothing but a beautiful house full of beautiful things, and no one to share them.

And of course, she must consider her teaching, which now hinged on her willingness to participate in protesting at the saloon and her lack of association with Ross Hollister. Which in turn related directly to Jonathan's well-being

She'd made little headway with him on her own. Not until she'd accompanied them to the woods had she seen a change in him. Acceptance? Was that the word for it? And later, when they'd gone skating, he'd opened up even more until, finally, one day after school, he'd placed his small hand in hers.

And if she ended the friendship between Jonathan and Ross, how would he react?

She already knew the answer to that before she'd asked the question. He would run away. Just as they'd done, she suspected, before arriving on her doorstep.

Forcing all those worries aside, she wondered about a man like Ross and why had he befriended a small boy. It wasn't in character for a man who catered to a saloon clientele. But lately she'd been having trouble remembering that he did indeed make his living with drink. Instead, she thought about the laughter he brought and the contentment she felt when he came to call. These were new things in her life and in her usually silent home.

Until now, she'd kept to her determination to shield herself from the company of men, to protect her heart from the pain of betrayal. But somehow, with the arrival of the children, there had also appeared a small fissure in that determination.

When had she ever been so tossed about with such turbulent emotions? Not since Andrew, she acknowledged silently, and her last-minute decision to stop their wedding. The comparison did little to ease her mind.

From downstairs she could hear the sound of voices drifting up, but the closed door to her room muffled them. With a sigh, she threw off the quilt and rose to check her hair in the mirror before going down. Small frown lines creased her brow, and she smoothed them with a fingertip, wishing it were that easy to remove the worries that caused them.

When she stepped into the hall, the house was silent. She glanced out of the window facing town in time to see the hurrying figure of Emma Gregg being swept along by the wind.

Once downstairs she found her mother pacing the floor, a storm brewing in her determined features.

Suddenly aware of Irene's presence, Winnie halted.

"Was that Emma you were speaking to, Mother?"

Winnie forced herself to breathe calmly in an attempt to control her initial angry reaction. "Yes. Yes, it was."

With suspicion, Irene eyed her mother's agitated state. "What did she want? I was only lying down. I would have gotten up."

Unable to come up with a plausible answer that hid the truth, Winnie hedged for time. "She wanted to see you."

"Did she say why?"

"Not at first." Winnie turned to the cherry-wood table she'd been dusting before Emma knocked. Carefully, she ran her rag around the curved edges, which had the feel of glass.

"Mother," Irene said firmly, determined to get to the bot-

151

tom of this. "What did she want?"

Winnie braced herself for the coming confrontation. She'd tried—oh, how she tried—to ward it off, but now she stood ready to fight for her daughter's future.

"There's to be another meeting tonight at Clara's." Winnie's chin lifted stubbornly. "Irene, I forbid you to go."

Irene felt as though she'd been slapped in the face, not once but twice. Her heart sank at the news of the meeting. Then it raced when her mother uttered her command.

In a hushed voice, Irene demanded, "You forbid me?"

"Yes."

With a full three feet between them, it seemed to each woman that they stood nose to nose, staring, unflinching.

Never had Irene felt so angry!

Never had Winnie been so determined!

"You cannot forbid me like a naughty child."

"Then don't act like one."

"You're forgetting whose house you're in," Irene reminded her.

"No, I'm not." Then, with emphasis, she added, "You are."

Hurt by her mother's words, Irene gasped. Along with everyone else in the town, Winnie believed that the house had belonged to Andrew, and that only through his love and generosity had he allowed her to keep it after she had so heartlessly left him standing at the altar.

But that was far from the truth, although no one would ever know. Irene had vowed never to publicize what had actually happened, since that would also mean public humiliation for her. So she bore the secret of her rejection silently.

And now, the ghost of that lost love loomed between her and her mother, becoming as palpable as the furniture surrounding her and as stifling as the dust in Winnie's rag.

Without another word, Irene turned on her heel. Nothing good could come of this continued stand-off; she would do as she saw fit, regardless of her mother's wishes.

Or maybe in spite of them. She would go to her room and make her plans in private, although her mother would undoubtedly think she went to sulk. Let her, Irene thought, as she slammed the bedroom door.

Whether she'd wanted to attend the meeting at Clara's or not, her decision was made. She was going.

Chapter Eleven

Sitting on one of Clara's stiff, straight chairs, Irene surveyed the over-filled parlor. By the looks she'd received from Polly Anderson and a few others, she felt as conspicuously present as Emma was absent.

Of all the women in the room, Irene was the only one who had little cause to be a part of this meeting. She'd come strictly for the sake of her teaching position—and perhaps to prove her own independence.

Ringing a small bell, Clara called, "This meeting will now come to order." With a quelling stare, she quieted those who continued talking.

Silence encircled the group of women.

"Something of great importance has been brought to my attention, and I feel it my duty to pass this along to you." She studied the face of each woman, finding strain, anxiety, even anger on some. "We all know about the new saloon owner, Mr. Hollister—"

A few titters interrupted her while several women cast side-long glances at Irene.

"—and his defiance, along with the other saloon owners, in continuing to remain open for business. But now he's gone a step further than the others, just as I had predicted he would."

Once more silence girdled the room.

Clara's pause held everyone captive. "He's opening a brothel."

The entire group inhaled with one great gasp.

"That's absurd!" Irene said, coming out of her chair. "Mr. Hollister would never do such a thing."

All attention swerved to Irene. Appalled, they gaped at her, some with their mouths open, others with an I-told-you-so look on their faces.

"It's the truth," Clara said firmly.

"Well, I don't believe it."

"What makes you so sure it can't be true?" Clara prodded.

Uncomfortable with the subject matter, Irene stared straight at Clara and nobody else. "He's too kind to children to be a man who'd do such a thing."

"We can hardly judge what a man will do by his kindness to children," Clara replied. "Many of those who frequent bawdy houses have families and profess to love their wives and children."

Irene could not comprehend the idea of Ross, who had taken her and the children on an adventure in the woods and skating on the canal, in the business of selling the favors of women.

"If a man will drink and sell drink, why is it so inconceivable that he would bring fallen women to our town and sell the wares of the flesh?" Clara's eyes peered into Irene's, and her harsh voice softened. "You haven't forgotten that he comes from the wild part of our country, where these goings-on are common place. Have you?"

Unable to dispute most of what Clara said, Irene felt her defense slipping, although she clung stubbornly to her belief.

155

"If that's the way you feel, Irene Barrett," spoke Polly Anderson, her chin raised haughtily, "then perhaps our children have been incorrectly placed in your care."

A murmur of agreement rose up around her.

Clara rang the little bell once more. "This meeting has not been called to discuss Irene." She impaled each one with her gaze.

A disquieting silence followed, as though all were reserving judgment on that statement.

Taking her seat, Irene vowed to hold her tongue. Now was neither the time nor the place for a discussion of her beliefs about Ross Hollister.

"We are here," Clara went on, "to prevent this venture from ever taking place. We must consider the lives of our children." She would like to have added "and the souls of our husbands," but could not bring herself to do so.

This time Polly stood up. "Are you proposing we go back to singing and praying before the saloon? That's hardly gotten us anywhere," she said with a hearty dose of disdain. "Signing promises won't work with a man like Ross Hollister."

"I'm afraid you're right," Clara said. "This last bit of news verifies the fact that he's a man who needs to be dealt a severe blow."

Irene held her breath, waiting, like every other woman in the stuffy little parlor. She'd thought she was willing to do her part, to do what was right for the town and, she admitted, to keep her job. But this wasn't fair. It smelled of vigilante justice, when the accused had no opportunity to defend himself.

"We will not only attack his saloon," Clara began, her eyes roving over the mesmerized group, "but we'll roll his barrels out into the street and demolish them before his eyes. Afterwards, Mr. Hollister will barely be able to scrape enough cash together to get out of town."

Peripherally, Irene saw the satisfied smirk on Polly's

face as her head turned toward Irene, her chin tilted. Irene ignored her.

"Are there any questions?" Clara asked.

"Have you decided when?" Polly stood in her eagerness to hear the answer.

"Friday evening. That gives us four days to assign every woman a specific job. We'll have another meeting the night before. I want all of you to be here." Clara imprinted her words on the brains of each woman by staring into each face. "We will adjourn."

The ladies retired to the small kitchen, where Clara served tea, giving everyone an opportunity to voice her feelings about the coming Friday night. Irene politely sipped her tea, but her growing anxiety would hardly allow her to swallow it. At the first opportunity, she tried to slip away.

"Wait, Irene," Clara called to her just as she pulled on her coat. Then she added quietly, "I'd like to have a private word with you. Stay until the others are gone."

Slipping off the coat once more, Irene refilled her cup and found a seat in a corner of the parlor. The voices of her friends and neighbors filled the rooms, but no one spoke to her. Undoubtedly, they considered her a spy, infiltrating their ranks, and gave her a wide berth. And, truthfully, she felt like a spy. At least her views were enough different from theirs that she might have been one, which only added to her discomfort.

Finally, the crowd dispersed, Polly being the last one to leave.

Clara closed the door.

"Irene," she began, taking a seat opposite the young woman, "I know this is difficult for you. But perhaps you haven't considered everything."

Looking at the older woman, Irene replied, "You mean my position at school and in the community."

"No. I'm talking about *you*." Seeing Irene bristle at the mention of her personal life, Clara searched for a way to

157

say her piece as carefully as possible. She wasn't used to worrying about the feelings of others, having treated everyone the same in her quest for decency and honesty, finding little if any of those qualities in most other human beings. But Irene was different.

"I want you to think about what I'm going to say before you make a reply." Clara fingered a seam in her plain black dress. "What do you plan to do about the children? Are you going to keep them? Raising a family is difficult enough with two parents, let alone a single woman who must work. Have you thought about what would be best for them?"

"Actually, that's being taken care of. I've been searching for their aunt, who will undoubtedly want them." A stab of regret pierced her heart at the words, and she wished they weren't true.

"I see." Clara fingered the seam again. "And Ross Hollister? What about him?"

Irene didn't answer. She forced her features into a look of composure and control, giving nothing away.

"Irene, do you suppose a man who lives by drink can ever live without it? What would he do to support a family? Could he support a family?"

"I really don't think—" Irene started to rise.

"No, wait." Clara stayed her with a hand. "He won't stay in town long. That kind never does. He'll go from town to town, dissatisfied with life but unable to change." Then softly she said, "Could you live like that? Be honest with yourself."

Sitting the teacup on the plain, sturdy table beside her, Irene let Clara's words sink in. Could she?

Clumsily, Clara patted Irene's folded hands. "You think about it."

Without answering, Irene rose and drew on her coat. At the door she turned. "Good night, Clara."

"Good night." Clara caught herself just in time, before she'd added "dear."

Outside, a brilliant moon shone in a winter sky so clear that it appeared more blue than black. Far above her head, a million stars winked and blinked in a sparkling display, while beneath her feet the packed snow crunched noisily with every step.

Irene pulled her coat tighter.

Clara's words had served to remind her of just how alone she really was, and how lonely she would be.

"Mr. Hollister," Winnie began, "I'm here to do you a favor."

Ross sat at the table across from the older woman and raised his brow, questioning her remark. She'd practically accosted him in the lobby of the inn when he'd come down from his room on his way to town. And now, in the semi-privacy of an off-side little table, she presented her case. He'd bet a week's worth of liquor that it had something to do with Irene.

"I suppose you know I don't exactly approve of your business nor do I approve of your . . . consistent appearance at my daughter's home."

He guessed she meant well and he liked her spunk, but he questioned her authority.

"Does Irene feel the same way? I mean, about my . . . appearances at her home?" He already knew Irene didn't much like his saloon; he had the bill for one very large mirror to prove it.

"She hasn't put it in so many words, but as her mother, I know what's best for my daughter," she said, her shoulders squared and her chin leveled.

And obviously she damn well meant to see that her notions were carried out. He suddenly understood Irene's hesitancy.

"How does this turn into a favor for me?" he asked, wondering about her scheme and feeling sure that Irene had no idea what she might be up to.

Winnie glanced around secretively before leaning forward, both hands on the table. Ross leaned forward, too, bracing his forearms on the edge.

"There was a meeting the other night, and I can tell you for a fact that you are about to be attacked again." Winnie sat up straight, waiting for that bit of information to register.

Ross frowned. Could she be right? It had been months since the women of the town had paid him a visit. He thought, or rather hoped, they'd gotten it out of their systems. Apparently not.

"Believe me. I know what I'm saying." Winnie assuaged a small sliver of guilt for having eavesdropped on Emma and Irene only last night, justifying her actions as the rights of a mother. "Of course, you must realize I'm not in favor of vandalism of any sort. I feel that with this information, I can prevent you from incurring any property damage and save Irene from embarrassment." She pierced him with her gaze. "Is it a deal?"

Relaxing back in his chair, Ross studied her. Perhaps he'd misjudged Irene after all. He'd really believed she'd been there the first time against her will. Yet, here was her mother saying she would accompany the raiders again.

"How do you propose to save Irene from embarrassment?"

Without the flicker of an eyelash, she replied, "Two ways. One, she's running the risk of being incarcerated if the local constabulary decides to get involved."

"You mean, if I press charges."

"Exactly. I choose to see that prospect eliminated—with your help. And two, she's also running the risk of losing her teaching position if you continue to call at the house."

"So I should stay away. Is that the deal?" he regarded her with a mixture of wry humor at her ability to scheme and irritation that she could very well stop him from seeing Irene again.

"Precisely."

"When is this raid to take place?"

"Ahhh," she said quietly tapping her finger on the table. "First you must agree to my terms." She threw him a self-satisfied smile.

Still frowning, he said, "I need some time to think about this."

Winnie gathered her gloves and pulled them on. "Don't take too long, Mr. Hollister." Rising from her seat, she waited for him to stand. "Time is your enemy. Good day."

"Good day," he mumbled to her retreating back. Of all the conniving . . . He should have known. How could he be so surprised when she'd treated him like a leper from the first? Slamming his battered hat on his head, he headed for the door.

He needed a drink.

Outside the sun glared, reflecting off the snow and ice on the river below. Marching ahead of him, Mrs. Barrett's efficient little steps took her all the way to the picketed gate, where she turned in. With long, angry strides he passed the house in time to hear the click of the latch.

Meddling woman, he thought. Then he considered some of the things she'd said. Irene could lose her job. He supposed she could; he hadn't thought about it. But wasn't it her decision to make? To tell him to stay away?

He thought back to the day in the woods at Tilly's cabin and how pleasant it had been for him, and he'd thought it had been for her too. And the day they'd gone skating, she seemed to enjoy herself. And he believed that hadn't happened very often. Now he knew why. If there ever had been any suitors, they probably hadn't lasted long, which would explain why a woman like Irene still wasn't married. Ross shoved open the front door to the saloon, nearly knocking over a man who could hardly stand as it was.

"Excuse me," Ross muttered on his way to the bar. He picked up a bottle of whiskey, glancing around the room, then changed his mind. Drinking never solved anything. One quick look told him that.

In the dim interior sat men of all ages, some laughing,

161

most hanging over their glasses, looking for answers they'd never find.

"Hell." He walked through the saloon, dodging tables and chairs, then out the back door to stand on the banks of the silent, wintry canal. With his hands jammed in his pockets, he followed the waterway west toward the dam at the head of the rapids.

Cold air hit him squarely in the face but did little to clear his thoughts.

If he disregarded Mrs. Barrett's attempt to protect her daughter, what would the outcome be? His saloon would be smashed again, and he would continue to see Irene when he wanted. But would that lead to her losing her teaching job? Very likely. Then again, would she even consent to seeing him? The way she'd avoided him lately, his prospects of seeing her at all were slim. But slim was better than none.

But more importantly, should he continue spending time with her? He could feel himself becoming more and more involved in her life each time they'd been together. Was that wise? For him or for her? He didn't know the answer to that; he only knew he enjoyed being with her. She made him feel as though life could be good again, that he could put the past behind and start over.

Irene walked home from school beside Lydia, who chattered away about the things she and her friends had discussed. With one ear listening, she nodded at the appropriate times, but her mind lingered on the more serious matter of resolving her predicament. That was how she'd come to view the matter of Ross versus Clara, because that's what it boiled down to in the end.

"What's wrong, Miss Barrett?" Lydia asked quietly, keeping step with her teacher who was so much more than just her teacher.

"Hmm?" Irene glanced at her, her eyes focusing on the present, coming from some place far away.

"Something's bothering you." It was as plain as the red tip of her nose that Miss Barrett was unhappy. And she bet she knew why. "Do you want to talk about it?"

Irene smiled. She wanted more than anything to talk to someone about it, but there wasn't a person in town who seemed to understand—not Clara, not even Emma, and certainly not her mother. She studied Lydia's trusting eyes, which mirrored her heartfelt feelings. With a sudden flood of warmth, Irene reached her arm around Lydia's shoulder and squeezed her tightly.

"Don't worry about me," she said in her most reassuring voice. "I just have a few things to work out, that's all."

They walked in step together for a while, crunching the cold, packed snow beneath their shoes while heavy clouds scudded across the sun.

"I know what Mrs. Wilson wants you to do," Lydia said hesitantly. "I don't think you should do it."

Bringing both of them to halt, Irene asked softly, "Why not?"

"Because I think it would hurt Mr. Hollister's feelings."

Digesting this bit of advice, Irene peered into the small, upturned face, wondering how one so young could be so wise.

"Feelings are important," Lydia went on, her voice as hushed as the snow beginning to fall lightly around them. "Sometimes more important than anything else in the world."

Suddenly needing to comfort this child, Irene wrapped both arms around her and held her close. Surprisingly, it worked both ways, because Irene in turn felt comforted. When she released Lydia, she smiled and said, "I'll keep that in mind."

They walked on in companionable silence, the wood smoke from nearby chimneys filling the heavy air. A fresh layer of snow drifted down gently like feathers from heavenly pillows, covering the older, less-than-white snow.

Irene contemplated the steady snowfall, each flake unwavering in its destination. If only she could be as single-minded, instead of considering all the possibilities before her.

They arrived at the back door, greeted by the smells of cinnamon buns, baking bread, and spicy beef stew. Winnie had tried every wile known to motherhood to patch the rift in their cooling relationship, yet at the same time she let it be known that she would never give in. Irene shook her head sadly at their stalemate.

Once inside, Lydia unwrapped herself and hung up her things while her stomach rumbled loudly. She loved the warmth and smells of this kitchen, where laughter and happiness had once abounded. But lately there had been only the smells and little of the happiness.

"Oh, Mrs. Barrett!" Lydia sniffed the air dramatically. "Your cinnamon buns are the best!" She poked a finger into the center of one, where the icing was soft and gooey, then popped her finger into her mouth. "Mmmm!" she groaned in ecstasy. "Do I have to wait?"

"Of course you do. You'll ruin your appetite if you eat those sweets now."

"Your cooking could never ruin my appetite."

Winnie secretly smiled, pleased with the young girl's extravagant praise. Lydia's honesty and straightforwardness had gradually warmed her heart, eventually thawing the indifference she'd tried to hold in place.

"Where's Jonathan?" Irene asked, hanging her coat on a peg.

"He's been here and gone. But he'll be back. I made him promise." Winnie stirred the stew, keeping her eyes on the boiling pot.

"He won't want to miss out on those buns—that's why he'll be back," said Lydia. She took the dishes from the cupboard and set the table, as had been her custom since she'd come into the house.

"Maybe so." Turning to her daughter, Winnie asked, "Would you like some tea? I made your favorite. Mint."

Irene refused to allow herself to be swallowed by the guilt her mother tried heaping on her. She'd seen Winnie use these same tactics on a number of people over the years, but until now she'd never been the victim. It was a most uncomfortable position.

"Yes, thank you," she answered politely, but with an obvious cool reserve. Irene retrieved a cup and saucer, placing them on the table, but before she could move to get the teapot, Winnie was there pouring it for her. Stubbornly, Irene steadied her resolve, refusing to let it be shaken.

"How did your day go?" Winnie asked, turning back to the stove and the stew.

"Fine." But she offered nothing more in order to hold firm.

Finally, Winnie gave up trying. Obviously, she couldn't win her daughter over to her way of thinking. She could only hope Ross Hollister wouldn't take too long to make up his mind. The saloon bashing was only three days away. Glancing over her shoulder at Irene, she prayed that she wouldn't go through with it.

Ross sat at the rear of the saloon nervously drumming his fingers on the table, watching the front door, wondering if tonight was the night. He'd thought long and hard about his decision, even losing sleep over it, but his mind was definitely made up. He would not agree to Winnie Barrett's "deal." Come hell or high water, he'd just have to handle the situation, whatever happened. Somehow, deep in his gut, he knew there was more riding on this than the physical condition of his business. But he refused to label it or even think too seriously about it.

His fingers thrummed the table in a rhythm that matched the jumping of his nerves. Three days had passed. Tonight was the night; he could feel it.

*   *   *

Irene tried tying the tape of her petticoat around her waist for the third time. Her hands shook so badly that she could do little more than secure a knot.

You shouldn't be doing this, she told herself. Jonathan won't understand. Ross won't understand.

Dropping the dark-blue dress over her head, she pulled it into place, tugging it here and there until it lay correctly. With ice-cold fingers, she worked at each of the buttons down the front of the bodice.

She glanced at the clock on her bureau.

Thirty minutes.

A few stray strands of hair escaped from the tight, thick knot at the nape of her neck. She tucked them in. With a few finishing touches to her white collar and placing the most insignificant hat she owned on her head, she sat on the bed to wait.

The clock tick-tocked loudly, but not as loudly as the beating of her heart.

Why do you want to do this? she questioned herself. *Can you really walk into that saloon brandishing a club? Then walk right up to Ross, who has done so much to help Jonathan, and break his mirror or his bottles or anything?*

Agitated beyond endurance, Irene vaulted from the bed and paced the floor.

She glanced at the clock again.

Twenty minutes.

But she had to consider her job, her place in this town, her future. The children were only temporarily in her charge, a brief although welcome respite from the tedium of her life. With a wrench of her heart, she recognized it only as a postponement, just as Clara had warned her. Logically, she tried to deal with it as such and prepare herself for the return to her old life.

Like it or not, the children weren't a part of her future, and without them, there would be no Ross Hollister to be concerned about.

Still, she was not convinced that Clara was completely

right in thinking that vandalism was the best way to handle the problem.

Ten minutes.

Darkness had settled. The lamp from the bureau cast a weak shadow of her figure on the floor before her. She rose from the bed. Each step was a burden, a decision in the making, as she crossed the hall and descended the stairs.

Without a word or even establishing eye contact with Winnie, who sat still as a stone with embroidery in hand, Irene walked through the parlor. The house nearly reverberated with waves of disapproval, so palpable was her mother's opposition. Irene knew she would never understand. In the kitchen she put on her coat and slipped out the back door.

Chapter Twelve

The sound of hymns and the light of a few flickering candles greeted Irene before she could make out the faces of the women standing in front of the Broken Keg Saloon. Soft soprano voices melded into a unified melody, signifying their oneness in this cause.

Irene joined the ranks of the chorus in the street, whose job was to divert the attention of those inside. Blending into the group, her skirts pressed against those nearby. With an effort, she forced the familiar words from her lips while her eyes fastened on the door to Ross's saloon.

With her mind rebelling and her heart racing, she felt the cold hardness of a wooden club slip into her hand. She looked to see who had pushed the object into her grasp, insisting that her fingers hold it tight.

"Hide this in the folds of your skirt," Polly demanded, her eyes bright in the candlelight, daring Irene to refuse.

Irene thrust it back. "I don't want it."

Polly clenched her teeth and snatched at the club, but said nothing.

Turning toward the door once more, Irene waited, staring, thinking. Saloons were an injustice to society, but that didn't mean everyone in the saloon was a wicked person, in spite of Clara's opinion. Surely, Polly's husband could not be completely wicked, or why would she have married him in the first place? And Ross? No, he definitely wasn't a wicked person. She'd seen his kind heart in action with Jonathan and felt his sensitivity to her predicament.

And yet, he did own the Broken Keg. In all honesty, she couldn't condone that. In fact, she'd tried to ignore it, hoping . . .

Hoping what? she wondered.

A series of screams rent the air simultaneously with the splintering of wood from the rear of the saloon. The voices surrounding Irene lifted higher until the melody could no longer be heard and only the words filled the air.

But even that didn't shut out the sounds of destruction.

Polly brushed past Irene, stepping quickly through the crush of women until she stood on the boardwalk, looking over their heads.

"Are we ready?" she yelled, holding her club high in the air.

A soft murmur flowed through the crowd.

Timidly, a voice spoke from the back. "Clara said we were to wait out front for her."

With fists resting on her hips, Polly glared into the soft candlelight before her. "Our sisters need our help! Should we wait out here like a flock of lambs and stand idly by while they do our work?" Her eyes roamed over the group of women. "I say no!"

More screeching reached their ears, but this time it was accompanied by the low roar of angry male voices. Each woman turned her head to search the face next to her for the guilt building in her own breast.

"Well?" Polly called out. "Are you with me?"

A few women started moving toward her, but others held back, still unsure.

Polly pointed an accusing finger. "Where is your husband tonight, Ida? At home with his children?"

Ida dropped her head and slowly made her way forward. "And you . . ." she pointed into the crowd once more and three other women came to the front.

In amazement, Irene watched as everyone followed Polly's orders. She felt herself jostled and tugged along. She planted both feet firmly, refusing to be swept into the tide of the coming maelstrom. She was not of the same mind as the others. Her reasons for being here were childish. She'd thought she would make her own decisions and not let her mother coerce her. And here she stood, in a group of nearly militant women trying to drag her into a saloon fight.

Reaching out, Polly grabbed Irene's hand with a grip Irene could not break.

"Irene Barrett, you *are* going in there. And you *will* show that man you mean business!" Polly clamped her teeth together in determination.

"No!" Irene struggled to free herself, but the surrounding crowd pushed against her in their effort to gain entrance through the front door. Once again, she was swept into the saloon by the pulling and pushing of the others. "No!"

Inside, chaos had already taken hold. A bottle flung through the air crashed at her feet, spraying her skirts with its sickening sweet contents and broken bits of glass. She stepped around the puddle only to be bumped and butted into a row of chairs. Unable to keep her balance, she toppled a teetering table and bounced into a chair which slid into the wall.

The noise of splintering glass, screeching women, and howling men was deafening.

Glancing around, she saw the faces of strangers. Not all the customers lived in Grand Rapids; some were travelers, others hauled goods along the river by wagon.

Suddenly, an unshaven face loomed over her, its bleary,

bloodshot eyes peering into hers. He smiled crookedly at her while the bottle of whiskey he held tipped slightly, spilling into her lap.

Gripping the arms of the chair, Irene pressed back until the wooden spindles imprinted themselves in her skin and her corset cut off her breath. The brim of the small hat she wore became trapped between her head and the wall, flattening the ring of dried flowers until they were no more than dust.

"Now ain't you a purty thing," he said, his words slurring together while his whiskey breath warmed her cheek.

Irene twisted her head away, feeling the painful pull of the hatpins in her hair. She thrust her hands against his loathsome shirt in a desperate attempt to be free.

"Get away." The words, barely a whisper, caught in her throat.

Clumsily, he grasped her hands and pinned them to his chest. "How about a little kiss?"

Around them the conflict grew in noise and intensity. Frantically, she realized that this one small incident was but a ripple in a stormy sea. Nobody would hear her if she screamed. Panicked, she tried shrinking into her chair, hoping to gain enough clearance to land a well-placed kick on her assailant.

Then suddenly he was gone, lifted from her like a heavy sack of soured whiskey mash.

"Leave her alone." Ross held the drunken man by his shirt, anger clearly etched in the lines around his mouth. Then, just as quickly, he released the man, forcing him to stumble to regain his balance. He teetered momentarily, mumbling under his breath, then made his way along the wall toward the front entrance.

Dazed, Irene watched the entire episode as though it were a play and she was the only one to see it. Gradually, as her fear subsided, the ringing in her ears dimmed to a low hum. She stared up at Ross, more grateful than words could say, and just then she had no words at all.

171

"What the hell are you doing here?" His voice was harsh from anger and fear of what could happen to her, and he knew better than most exactly what could happen. Ross reached out and grabbed her by the hand, uncharitably pulling her to a standing position.

Stunned, Irene wobbled on her feet.

"You shouldn't be here." He thrust an arm in a semi-circle to include the entire scene being played out behind him.

She didn't like his tone of voice, and she didn't like what he said. She was sick and tired of being told what to do, how to do it, and when she could do it.

"I don't like your tone of voice," she bristled.

"How can you even hear my tone of voice!" he yelled. Pulling her by the arm, he said, "Come on! You're going home where you belong." He glanced around the saloon, muttering, "Damn women!"

Stubbornly, she held her ground by grasping the chair. "Release me," she warned.

Ross faced her. "All right. Have it your way." In one swift movement, he leaned down and hoisted her over his shoulder.

What breath she had left instantly whooshed from her body. Her arms dangled down his back as her corset cut into her ribs. She tried to struggle, but his arm locked behind her knees, holding her securely.

"Put me down," she wheezed.

"Not until we get out of here."

Mortified, Irene pounded on his back, her cheeks flaming with embarrassment and the sudden rush of blood to her head. So much for her kind thoughts about Ross Hollister, she decided. Oh, how right Clara was!

Outside, the brisk air slapped her in the face, bracing her. She levered herself upward until the blood flowed naturally; she sighed with the relief of it.

"Mr. Hollister!" The words bounced out of her mouth

with each jolting step he took. "I insist you put me down this instant."

"Not until I get you home." He kept walking as though she weighed no more than a keg of liquor. "And I've already told you to call me Ross."

Losing her grip on keeping herself somewhat upright, she found herself once more facing his back, upside down.

"How do I hate thee," she mumbled into the rough wool of his jacket. "Just let me count the ways!"

"What's that?"

"I said, put me down. I can barely . . . breathe."

He stopped, considering her obvious discomfort. "Only if you'll promise to do as you're told."

His words seared her. "No!" she replied.

"Then we'll go on." He started up the hill.

If only she could cry, but there wasn't enough air in her lungs to afford such a luxury.

Occasional patches of silver moonlight filtered through the dark sky, lighting up their surroundings and casting their shadows against the white snow. She forced herself not to look at their ridiculous silhouettes.

"I can't believe you're doing this," she gasped.

"And I can't believe you're setting this kind of an example for the children."

"Me!" she sputtered. "What about you, running that saloon!" He was being unfair and impossible. She struggled against his grip, hoping to force him to set her down.

"Hold still! It's slippery enough walking in the snow without you squirming around." He crossed the tracks. "We're almost there."

In one last attempt, noting they'd just walked through the gate in her front yard, she said, "This is uncalled for."

In desperation she struggled once more, and her poor insignificant little hat fell onto the porch. Giving as much of a sigh as her cramped position would allow, she resigned herself to the upcoming confrontation with her mother.

Without knocking, Ross burst into the house, his anger still smoldering. Unceremoniously, he dropped her to her feet.

Winnie and the children sat in stunned surprise, like figures etched in ice.

"Mrs. Barrett. Here is your daughter safe and sound." He turned to Irene. "I suggest you stay at home where you're needed. Good night." Then he stomped out the door, slamming it behind him.

"So he brought you home," Winnie said, a smug smile hovering at the corners of her mouth. A grudging admiration for the man wheedled its way into her thoughts.

Irene blinked when the door banged shut.

"Oh, no you don't, Mr. Hollister," she said, her voice barely above a whisper. Now that she stood on both feet and had plenty of air in her lungs, she had a few things to say. He wasn't getting away so easily.

She yanked the door open just in time to see him slam the fragile picket fence gate behind him.

"Mr. Hollister!" Without waiting for him to stop, Irene closed the door, crossed the porch where her hat lay, and hurried down the walk. Angry puffs of breath showed white in the cold air before her.

Ross halted and turned to meet her head on. The full moon escaped the clutches of the dark, scudding clouds, and he saw clearly the lines of determination in her beautiful face—the same face that had been haunting his dreams for weeks.

"I believe you owe me an apology." Now that she stood directly in front of him, she felt her bravado slip. The set of his jaw made him look positively fierce.

"I'm supposed to apologize when you're the one who's busting up my saloon?" He raised his eyebrows in disbelief.

"I didn't break anything. But you—you nearly broke my ribs. I hardly think your behavior—" It suddenly seemed absurd to accuse him of ungentlemanly behavior when

174

she'd willingly been a part of that rioting scene at the saloon, exposing an unlady-like behavior herself. And she still would be if he hadn't carted her off. But some new-found defiance reared up and wouldn't allow her to give in.

"Go on," he prodded, still scowling.

"You had no right to handle me in such a fashion."

She stood close enough so that Ross could smell the fragrance of roses. Her heavy hair tumbled about her head in disarray, while the thick knot hung over one shoulder. He saw her shiver, but she refused to pull her coat closed.

Expelling a long, exasperated breath, he pushed his hat back on his head and stared at her. Then he tugged her coat closed and fastened one button.

"You're right," he said. "I'm sorry. It's just that when I heard you were coming, and then I saw you there with the rest . . ."

Even in the dark she could see his blue-gray eyes and thought about sunny summer days and picnics along the river. But there wasn't any humor in those eyes as there had been that day in the woods or when they'd skated on the canal. Now he stared earnestly at her.

"Irene . . ."

Dappled moonlight crossed her face, hiding any signs of her feelings. He tried again. "Irene, I worry about you and the children."

"Worry?" she asked, puzzled. "Why?"

"Don't you understand? Those children respect you and look up to you. If you go off breaking up saloons, how will that affect them?"

"At least we're dealing with the real issue. Saloons!" she said. It was because of that saloon that her mother, Clara, and Polly were after her. Until now, her life had been simple! She used to be able to come and go as she pleased, causing barely a ripple in the grapevine. But now everybody worried about her!

She forced herself to keep calm, but her voice shook

anyway. "You have no need to be concerned. I'm quite capable of taking care of myself."

"Really? What about that drunk leering down the front of your dress? Were you going to take care of him?" He didn't want to be angry with her, but she wasn't being sensible.

A slow shudder passed along her spine as she remembered the disgusting man.

Taking her silence for agreement, he stepped forward, placing both hands on her arms. "I just don't want to see you get hurt. I care about you." He pulled her closer.

Irene swallowed hard, her anger extinguished by this new, unfamiliar feeling. Andrew had never held her so tightly, nor had he ever looked so intense. Ross's hands branded two spots on her upper arms, burning through the fabric of her coat and jacket. Then the shadow of his hat descended and she swallowed again.

Tentatively, he touched his lips to hers. When she didn't back away, he slipped both arms around her, cradling her against his chest. She tasted as sweet as she smelled.

Her hands lay still, pinned between them, and her breath hovered in her lungs, trapped. She couldn't seem to expel the air, and her head lightened while her right hand tremulously clutched her left.

Ross lifted his head, smiling into her eyes. "It's all right to breathe, you know," he said, grinning.

She exhaled explosively. Her heart pounded her ribs as his smile slowly faded, the intensity returning.

With one finger beneath her chin, he kissed her lightly, once, twice. But the third time, he wrapped his arms around her, pressing her tight until her knees weakened and she felt grateful for the hold he had on her. She tried to concentrate on breathing, but the butterflies in her stomach were such a distraction. Then his hand came up behind her head and, instinctively, she raised her arms to circle his neck, forgetting all about whether she breathed or not.

Lost. The word murmured through her mind. That's how she felt. Beautifully, wondrously lost. Suspended in time like the ladies and the gallant men of her novels who lived where only love abounded.

Ross cradled her slender figure as the contours of their bodies melded. His fingers lightly touched her neck where he felt her quickened pulse match the thudding of his own heart. Never had he been so affected by a woman.

Gently, he pulled back.

"You're so beautiful, Irene," he said in a voice rich with emotion.

She would have blushed, but all the blood in her body was busy pounding in her ears. Their noses were so close that they almost touched, and his warm breath brushed her lips when he spoke. Barely able to stand, her arms hung listlessly over his shoulders.

"I suppose that's the customary thing to say after . . . after . . . well, after kissing a woman," she whispered.

"I suppose it is," he grinned. "But that doesn't mean it isn't true."

"Then I suppose I should thank you," she said.

"For the kiss?"

"No. For the compliment."

He played with a lock of her hair, wrapping it loosely around his finger. "Why? Didn't you like the kiss?" His gaze locked with hers.

"Well, I . . . yes. I mean . . ." Flustered, she lowered her eyes until they fastened on the soft brush of his mustache. "Should we be discussing this?" she whispered.

"Why not?" he asked with a grin, looking over her shoulder. "Nobody's listening."

She smiled. He had such a way of making her feel at ease. And it did seem as though most of the time she was looking over her shoulder, wondering what someone would say or think about everything she ever did.

"At least, not at the moment." He gave a small jerk of

his head toward the saloon. "They're all back there making splinters out of my saloon."

It was a sharp reminder that quickly brought her back to reality. She slid her arms down until he caught her wrists against his chest.

"Irene," he said, feeling her pull away from him.

"I should go in. Mother will be wondering . . ." She tugged lightly to get free, reminding herself that once before she'd succumbed to the charming wiles of a man only to be betrayed and heartbroken.

"Wondering? Does that bother you? What your mother and Clara and the others think?"

He held her firmly. A chilling light wind brought the pungent smell of woodsmoke to her nostrils, clearing her head.

"I really don't want to discuss this." She pulled harder, freeing her hands.

"Were you at the saloon that first night because you wanted to be there or because you were expected to be there?" Frowning, he jammed his hands into his pockets. "And what about tonight?"

"I don't think it is any of your business."

"I think it is."

With surprise and anger, she stared at him through the dimming moonlight. "Why is it that everything I do seems to be everyone's business! I am perfectly capable of taking care of myself!"

"Then why don't you?" he said just a little more sharply than he'd intended.

"I will! If everyone, including you, would give me half a chance."

"I'm willing to give you more than half a chance," he said softly.

"Of course you are! That's why you bodily hauled me out of there tonight."

Ross's jaw tightened. "I told you, that drunk was leering down the front of your dress. What was I supposed to do?"

"I don't believe the only way to save me was to forcibly remove me from the premises!" With that, she turned on her heel and stalked back to the house.

"That's exactly what I'd like to do to every one of those women!" he yelled at her back.

Irene slammed the door with as much force as she could put into it.

Ross whacked his hat against his thigh in agitation. He stared at the darkened porch, then at the lamplit window of the parlor. Maybe she was angry and maybe she would never speak to him again, but he wasn't sorry for a word he'd said. Like it or not, she needed to hear it.

The sound of screams coming from the saloon brought his attention to the current problem. The clamor echoed along Front Street like a knee-high fog. Resolutely, he made his way back, crunching through the snow.

When he arrived at the front door of the Broken Keg, he was greeted by Ben, who escorted two unwilling ladies into the street. Behind him came another man with two more ladies in tow. The shrieking was deafening.

Ben motioned to Ross with his head. "We can't be toleratin' this," he yelled over the noise. "We'll be out of glasses—ow!" Ben released his hold on her arm to rub his shin. His captive smiled smugly at hitting her mark.

Within five minutes the men had emptied the saloon of all the women, including Clara Wilson. They thronged noisily around the men barricading the door, but they weren't as insistent as before. They had wreaked enough havoc to satisfy them.

"You women go on home now," Ben said, shooing them like a flock of chickens. "You've had your fun, so go on."

Ross scanned the crowd of women until his eyes came to rest on Clara Wilson. She stared long and hard at him, her eyes unflinching. It was impossible to miss the threat they held. And he wondered if the reason was the saloon or Irene.

Chapter Thirteen

Bright moonlight slipped into Irene's room like an intruder, its searching bluish-white light prodding into the recesses of her thoughts. Then, just as quickly, the light disappeared behind heavily layered clouds, hiding the objects in her room from view.

Wide awake, Irene lay staring at the dark ceiling, her heart heavy and her mind full. With her emotions going up and down like a schoolyard see-saw, she went over each happening of the evening from the buffeting of her body at the saloon to the tender caress in front of her home.

And on the same see-saw, she heard once again the words Ross had said, "Irene, I worry about you and the children. . . . I can't believe you're setting this kind of an example for the children. . . . I heard you were coming. . . . "

Then her own words, "I'm perfectly capable of taking care of myself!" And his answer, "Then why don't you?" It echoed in her mind. Why don't you? Why don't you? Why don't you?

Instantly, she rolled over, burying her face in her pillow. She tried—oh, how she tried! If it weren't for that saloon . . . She pounded the pillow with her fist in the most unlady-like fashion. It was all because of that dratted saloon that her life had become miserable. She punched the pillow again.

And Ross. He was as much, or more, at fault than anything.

Squeezing her eyes shut, she willed herself not to remember the warmth of his embrace, the concern in his voice when he told her he cared, and she especially didn't want to remember the touch and taste of his lips on hers.

But oh, she did.

In her memory, his fingers grazed her chin and cheek while her heartbeat escalated. Slowly, with her face still buried in her pillow, her fist unclenched and her eyes relaxed. Then, almost as if it were real, she felt the panic rise in her breast as his lips touched hers. Breathless.

Suffocating, she lifted her head from the pillow to see the room bathed once more in moonlight. Snuggling down into the warmth, she closed her eyes, inviting sleep while her thoughts lingered over the warm memory.

But Ross's other words intruded into her brain: "I heard you were coming."

With a gasp she sat up. He'd known all about it! He'd known she'd be there even though the meeting at Clara's had been a secret. How had he heard? Then she remembered the smug look on her mother's face and the I-told-you-so look she'd flung at Irene upon her return to the house tonight. She had almost overlooked both the statement and its implication.

Ambushed by her own mother! Of all the insufferable things she'd been through, this was the most humiliating.

Angrily, she flung back the covers and, mindless of the penetrating cold, stormed from her room on bare feet. Without a knock or even asking permission to enter, Irene burst in upon the sleeping Winnie.

"Mother." Irene stood over the bed, her body shaking more from anger than from cold. "Wake up," she said, none too gently.

"What is it?" Winnie asked, blinking the sleep from her eyes.

"Did you or did you not tell Ross Hollister that there would be a protest at the saloon tonight and that I would be there?"

Winnie sat up, leaning back against the headboard and pulling the blankets around her. "Irene, you'll catch your death running around with nothing on but your gown."

"Never mind that. Did you or didn't you?" She crossed her arms in irritation.

"As a matter of—"

"Mother! How could you?" Irene cried, flopping her arms against her sides.

"Well, I thought if he know, then he—"

"Then he could haul me out bottom-up in front of the whole town just to humiliate me! Is that right?"

"The whole town?" Winnie frowned in the moonlit room. "Really, dear, I think you're exag—"

"Why did you do it?" Irene paced the floor near the bed, stamping her foot once for emphasis.

"I didn't tell him so he could . . . Did you say bottom-up?" Winnie sat straighter. "Oh, Irene, the fix you've gotten yourself into this time."

"Me? I didn't ask Clara Wilson to start protesting against the saloons or ask to be included. I don't need anyone to manage my life for me. Not even you!" She dropped into a chair in the shadows, cocooning her feet under her gown.

"Irene, what has gotten into you?" Winnie swung her legs over the edge of the bed. "This just isn't like you."

"This just isn't like me? Well, what is like me, Mother? How should I behave? What should I say?"

Suddenly tired, Irene shook her head. Why did she feel so confused when it was all so very clear? Obviously, everyone wanted to control her life, but it was her life and she should make the decisions. What was so difficult about that?

Everything.

Curling her toes against the cold floor, Winnie walked to stand beside her daughter, laying a hand on the dark head. "You're tired. You need to get some rest. We can talk about this in the morning," she said gently.

Looking up at her mother, Irene knew it would be useless to press the issue. Sighing, she replied, "I suppose you're right." When she rose from the chair, Winnie put an arm around her waist, ushering her to the door.

"Good night, dear," she said softly.

Without answering, Irene walked back to her room.

Ross swept up a pile of glass, twinkling in the bright morning sun that spilled through the open door of the saloon.

"Heard you had a ruckus in here last night."

Glancing up, he saw Howard leaning against the door jamb.

With a wry half-smile, Ross nodded. "I've seen vigilante parties that were friendlier." He propped the broom against the wall. "Come on in, Howard. How about some coffee?"

"Sure." Howard stepped around the broken glass and followed Ross to one of the few tables with four legs. Then he searched for a chair stable enough to sit on while Ross brought out two mugs of steaming coffee.

With a salute of his own mug, Ross sat gingerly on a nearby chair, testing it for strength. "Here's to women," he said with a frown.

Howard lifted his cup in agreement, although he figured his toast was more sincere.

"What brings you here?" Ross took a swallow of coffee. Right from the beginning, he'd liked Howard. He was honest, straightforward, and didn't mind having an opinion that differed from others.

Howard set his cup down and looked around. "Curiosity."

Ross nodded. "I suspect half the town will be by here today. That's why I left the door open. No sense making them miserable with wondering." Sarcasm crept into his every word, but he didn't care. "You think they've had their fill yet?"

"I hope so. At least I know Emma won't be a part of it anymore."

"She wasn't here last night if that's what you're wondering about."

Howard shook his head. "No. She was home last night with me. She has no interest in vandalism for any reason. Especially now." He grinned proudly. "She's expecting."

Setting his cup down first, Ross reached across the table and clapped him hard on the back. "Congratulations! You're a lucky man, Howard." And he meant that.

"I know. Sometimes . . . well, I can hardly believe it myself."

They sat in silence for a few moments, Howard contemplating the fullness of life ahead of him and Ross feeling the emptiness of the future stretch out before him.

"Are you going to clean up and get back in business?" Howard asked.

"I don't know." He took another swallow of coffee and wished he could ward off any more questions he didn't have answers for.

"This isn't the best line of business, you know."

Squinting one eye at his friend, Ross asked, "Did Clara send you here?"

With a deep chuckle, Howard answered, "No."

Finishing his coffee, Ross leaned back in the rickety chair.

"I guess I was just thinking about your gold mine. It must be doing all right. How long have you been mining?"

Ross glanced at Howard before answering. Should he tell the whole story or just skirt the issue? He'd hoped to get a fresh start and leave the past behind, but could he do that honestly? He guessed he'd have to try.

"Jeff and I have been bustin' rock for about seven years." He shrugged. "It pays enough, but I doubt if we'll get rich. 'Course, don't tell Jeff I said that. He's damn sure we'll be stinking rich every time he swings that pick." Ross smiled. "I'm afraid he's got the fever. I suppose he'll be heading on to better places if this one doesn't pan out."

"You sound as though you never caught the fever." Howard drained his cup then sat back with interest to wait for Ross's answer.

Shaking his head, Ross said, "Not really."

"So why are you wasting your time with mining?"

Surprised at Howard's perception, Ross answered truthfully, "I don't know. I guess there hasn't been anything better come along."

Changing the subject, Ross asked, "How well do you know my brother?"

"In business only. Harry sold me that piece of ground with a cabin on it."

"Tilly's place?"

"I believe that's what Harry called it, too." Idly, Howard turned the mug in a circle on the table. "He sold it to buy this saloon. But I don't know what I'm going to do with it, since it's all grown to brush and the cabin needs repair."

"Sure does. I was out there in the fall with Irene."

Howard glanced up.

"I didn't know it belonged to you. Or anyone for that matter."

"Irene?" Howard asked, surprise in his voice.

"Yes. Why, does that surprise you?" Ross asked.

"It doesn't. Exactly."

"Exactly?" Ross prodded.

"Well, it's just that since Andrew left town, she's pretty much kept to her house."

"Who the hell is Andrew?"

"Her fiance and my ex-business partner," he replied drily.

Leaning his arms on the table, Ross bent forward. "Fiance?"

"Don't look so surprised. Irene's a good-looking woman, in case you hadn't noticed." He threw Ross a good-natured smile.

"Why didn't they get married?"

"That's a mystery that even Emma doesn't know the answer to."

"Mystery?" Ross prodded again.

Nodding, Howard went on. "Actually, they almost did get married. Got clear to the altar, then she said no and turned and ran. People haven't stopped talking about it yet."

Ross couldn't picture it. Irene standing before the whole town and saying no. What could have made her do it?

"That was five years ago. When he left, they must have agreed that she'd keep the house he'd bought for them. But that's pure speculation on my part. I only know that Andrew borrowed a great deal of money from me before catching a train to who knows where. After that, Irene bought out his share of our business."

"You mean, she's your business partner?"

Howard nodded. "But it's an investment-type business for her, since she's not involved in the store. Not like Andrew was. Thank God."

Sitting back in his seat, Ross stared vacantly at Howard. "Holy . . ." He'd wondered how she could afford a house like that on a teacher's salary. And the clothes she wore were always of a fine quality. "Well, I'll be."

Stretching back in his own seat, Howard said, "She has everything she'll ever need. Almost."

Not hearing the "almost," Ross spoke his thoughts. "It's a wonder Harry wasn't after her. He has a nose for money, especially where women are concerned."

"Wouldn't have mattered if he was. Irene hasn't taken

up with a man since Andrew. And, truthfully, I can't remember anyone before Andrew either." Watching Ross carefully, he added, "She's a lovely woman."

"I know," he said thoughtfully, staring into his empty coffee mug. Then he looked up. "But she's pretty hard to understand."

"Not really."

"Then explain to me why she lets people like Clara Wilson talk her into doing things like this"—he glanced around the broken saloon—"when she doesn't want to."

Shrugging, Howard replied, "Seems to me she's the kind of person who tries to avoid conflict. You know, the kind of conflict that goes on inside of you."

He did know. From the beginning, he could see she only wanted life to run smoothly, bending when she needed to bend to make it so. He wondered if life had been smooth for her when Andrew was around.

"What would Andrew have said about the saloon protests?"

Howard replied, "He wouldn't have tolerated it. Andrew had a way of controlling situations. And particularly people, if he could. You know, in a charming sort of way," he added with a hint of sarcasm in his voice. "It worked pretty well in business. Unfortunately, he didn't confine his charm to business only, if you catch my meaning."

Ross did catch his meaning. Andrew had been two-timing Irene, and she'd found him out. That was all Ross needed to know to decide he didn't like Andrew and it would be best if they never met.

"Then maybe giving her the house was his way of controlling Irene even after he'd gone?" Ross suggested.

"That's very likely, knowing Andrew as I did." Then to be fair, Howard added, "I suppose he loved her. He just had a strange way of showing it."

"And then," Howard went on, "there's Mrs. Barrett. Who, I'm sure, means just as well."

"Sounds like too many well-meaning people to me."

"Without a doubt."

Pushing away from the table, Howard stood. "I'd better get back to the store. Emma will be wondering where I've gone." He walked to the doorway and turned. "Of course, when I tell her I was here, she'll be full of questions." He smiled and shook his head, lifting his hand in farewell. Then suddenly remembering his reason for coming, he stopped. "I almost forgot. That furniture you ordered should be in day after tomorrow. You know, for your . . ." He pointed a finger at the ceiling, grinning. "Brothel. And by the way, when do these women start arriving?"

Perplexed, Ross only stared at him. Then it dawned.

"Is that what this was all about?" he shouted angrily, his arm flung out to encompass the destruction surrounding him. "An upstairs whorehouse?"

Still grinning, Howard said, "I'm afraid so."

"Who started that rumor?"

"That's the one thing I haven't heard." Once again he raised his hand in farewell. "I'd better be going."

After Howard had gone, Ross sat staring at the open doorway and at the snow piled outside in the street. The fresh winter air crept in and settled around him in spite of the warm sunshine slanting over the threshold.

So tongues were wagging because they thought he was planning a brothel. Had Irene heard the same thing? Undoubtedly. Clara would certainly have seen to it that she did. Well, let them worry. He didn't give a damn what they said or what they thought. Scraping back his chair, he strode to the doorway and grabbed the broom. He'd mind his business, and they could mind theirs. From now on, he'd hire someone to stand guard at both doors if necessary to keep the do-gooders out.

Clenching his jaw, Ross pushed the broom harder, creating a dust storm.

As for Irene, it was high time she looked them all in the eye and thumbed her nose. And he was just the man to help her do it, whether she knew it or not.

For several days Irene avoided everyone. At school she avoided Clara as much as possible, speaking only when others were present. She avoided Emma entirely, feeling somehow that she'd been abandoned by her once-close friend. And of course, she refused to even talk to Winnie, the root of her embarrassment, if not her entire problem. Instead, she concentrated on preparing her lessons and devoted a good amount of time to planning the Christmas pageant.

Staying busy soothed her. And it kept her thoughts from straying to Ross.

With less than a week until Christmas, she immersed herself in the Christmas play. Mary and Joseph knew their parts well, as did the sheep, the crown, and the stars in the night sky. Even so, the dress rehearsal scheduled for that evening had Irene in a high state of anxiousness.

She tugged her gloves snugly into place, going over in her mind for the thirtieth time the order in which the children would enter the stage. The stars first, then the angels. She wished they had a proper stage with a curtain, but there was no help for it but to use the raised platform where her desk sat. At least the classroom was bigger than the one she'd had before the new school was built, so she'd have plenty of seating for parents.

"Are we ready to go?" she asked, looking at Lydia and Jonathan.

Both faces smiled eagerly back. "Yes," they answered, costumes in their hands.

Irene had been more than a little surprised at Jonathan's willing participation. She'd allowed the children to choose the minor parts they preferred to play, hoping that would infuse some enthusiasm. For the most part it had worked. Especially for Jonathan, who chose to be a star. Lightly, she brushed at his straight brown hair, an amused smile creeping to the corners of her lips when she remembered his reply to her question of why did he choose a star. Very seriously, he'd answered that he'd always wondered what it would be like to hang above the world and see everything happening at one time. And he figured the stars could see as much as an angel without having so much work to do.

Smiling broadly, Jonathan said, "I'm ready."

As usual, Jonathan was out the door first, leading the way through the frosty night. He raced down the hill, then up the other side, slipping and falling occasionally but enjoying every minute of it.

Beside Irene, Lydia walked sedately, mindful of the slippery spots.

"Are you nervous?" she asked Irene.

"Yes. I suppose I am," she answered tilting her head to look at the intuitive girl. "But I don't know why." She smiled and put an arm around Lydia's shoulder to give her a quick squeeze. "All of you have done such a fine job, and I'm sure it will go smoothly."

"I think so too."

And it did. The homemade gowns were short enough that the angels didn't trip and their wire halos didn't fall. The sheep were peacefully herded to the right side of the stage away from the cows without a single scuffle, while the stars carefully stood on chairs looking over the wooden crate that served as a manger. And Mary and Joseph spoke their lines with almost no prompting from Irene.

With a sigh of relief, Irene applauded to signal "the end." A few parents standing around the perimeter of the room, waiting to walk the children home, clapped in appreciation also.

"You sure have a way with kids." Ross's hushed voice came from directly behind her.

Before her eyes, the room suddenly reeled and the din from two dozen children held restrained for too long filled her ears. Dazed, she turned to see him, hat in hand, smiling with that same mischievous twinkle in his gray-blue eyes.

"I heard you were having a rehearsal tonight, and I thought you might need some help moving chairs," he said, still grinning.

"I—I—well, no. But thank you, anyway." She felt the stares of several women searing her.

"Well," he shrugged, "since I'm already here I might as well be useful." He scanned the small group of fathers in attendance, calling to one he knew. Not in the least embarrassed, the man nodded and ambled over to join Ross. "Give me a hand, Ira."

"Sure thing, Ross."

They hoisted the heavy desk up onto the platform, but Irene turned her attention to helping the children with difficult buttons and scarves that wouldn't stay tied. Her hands shook, and she bit her lip in an effort to concentrate on each small task before her. Why had he come? Her mind echoed the words until she was sure that everyone could hear them. Was he trying to humiliate her even further?

In a blur, the faces of a few mothers passed near her, uttering their farewells while most of the others simply left without a word of good-bye.

Then he was there beside her holding her coat.

Awkwardly, she pushed her arm into the sleeve, trying not to get close to him. While avoiding looking at him, she glanced around the now empty room, once more restored to its original classroom arrangement. A sort of peace descended on her.

"I'll walk you home."

Turning to look at him now, she saw that the twinkle was gone, replaced by something else. A challenge. And she remembered her own words spoken to him and to her mother—"I'm perfectly capable of taking care of myself . . . I don't need anyone to manage my life for me."

Especially Ross Hollister.

"No, thank you just the same. I can walk with the children." She yanked her gloves on, refusing to meet his gaze.

"They're gone," he said, walking to the lamp that burned on the desk.

"Gone?" she repeated. Then the room suddenly plunged into darkness. Slowly, she made her way along the wall to the doorway, not waiting for her eyes to adjust to the moonlight coming in through the windows. She bumped into the edge of a desk and the sound grated in the still, dark room.

"Wait," Ross called to her. But she kept going.

Out in the hall, Irene felt her way toward the main entrance. She could hear Ross crashing into desks in his haste to follow her, uttering a few unintelligible oaths.

Once her hand grasped the cold metal of the doorknob, she pulled the door open. Thankfully, the moon shone bright enough to reflect light off the snow, giving the impression of illumination from the ground instead of the sky. At least she would be able to see herself home without bumbling along in the dark. She hurried down the stone steps.

Ross made his way down the pitch-black hall to the door, wishing he had the eyes of a cat or at least the agility of one. When he reached the door, he pulled it open and closed it behind him, all in one swift, smooth movement. Through the dappled moonlight he spied her moving under the bare maple trees across the schoolyard. He took the steps quickly and with sure-footedness and sprinted though the crusted snow until he reached her side.

"I said I'll walk you home," he repeated his earlier offer, but it sounded more like a command even to his own ears.

Ignoring him, she continued on her way.

In silence, they followed the descent and incline of the ravine to her back door—she with her back ramrod-stiff and he with his jaw clenched.

At the door she faced him. "You see? It wasn't necessary for you to walk with me."

Thrill to the most sensual, adventure-filled Historical Romances on the market today...

FROM ▊ *LEISURE BOOKS*

As a home subscriber to Leisure Romance Book Club, you'll enjoy the best in today's BRAND-NEW Historical Romance fiction. For over twenty-five years, Leisure Books has brought you the award-winning, high-quality authors you know and love to read. Each Leisure Historical Romance will sweep you away to a world of high adventure...and intimate romance. Discover for yourself all the passion and excitement millions of readers thrill to each and every month.

Save $5.⁰⁰ Each Time You Buy!

Each month, the Leisure Romance Book Club brings you four brand-new titles from Leisure Books, America's foremost publisher of Historical Romances. EACH PACKAGE WILL SAVE YOU $5.00 FROM THE BOOKSTORE PRICE! And you'll never miss a new title with our convenient home delivery service.

Here's how we do it. Each package will carry a FREE 10-DAY EXAMINATION privilege. At the end of that time, if you decide to keep your books, simply pay the low invoice price of $16.96, no shipping or handling charges added. HOME DELIVERY IS ALWAYS FREE. With today's top Historical Romance novels selling for $5.99 and higher, our price SAVES YOU $5.00 with each shipment.

AND YOUR FIRST FOUR-BOOK SHIPMENT IS TOTALLY FREE!
IT'S A BARGAIN YOU CAN'T BEAT! A Super $21.96 Value!

▊ LEISURE BOOKS A Division of Dorchester Publishing Co., Inc.

GET YOUR 4 FREE BOOKS NOW — A $21.96 Value!

Mail the Free Book Certificate Today!

Leisure Romance Book Club
65 Commerce Road
Stamford CT 06902-4563

"I never said it was. I did it because I wanted to, not because I had to." He grasped her gently by the shoulders, leaning toward her.

Her heart pounding, Irene turned her head away. When he released her, she stared through the darkness beneath the brim of his hat to where she knew his cool blue eyes sought hers.

Then, remembering the humiliation she'd suffered at his hands just days earlier and again tonight, she said, "I told you before, I can take care of myself."

Quietly, he replied, "To whose satisfaction? Yours or theirs?"

Her mouth opened with a gasp of surprise. "I don't believe I owe you that explanation, Mr. Hollister."

"No. But you do owe it to yourself." Then he tipped his hat and turned on his heel, leaving her to stand alone in her quandary.

Chapter Fourteen

The next day passed in a blur for Irene—a blur of last lessons, a suddenly ill Joseph, and a desperate search for his replacement. Allen Dickson, who had also wanted the part, was selected. Irene knew it was impossible for him to memorize every word of his lines in such a short time, even though there weren't many. She would have to prompt him through the entire play.

Sending Lydia and Jonathan home for their supper, she stayed behind, too nervous to eat anyway, arranging benches. Her desk had been set up along the side of the room for cookies and fruit punch, which would be brought by several of the mothers. Her own lovely china dishes were already filled with the assorted cookies she and Lydia had made.

She glanced around, pleased with what she saw. Taking a deep breath, she sat on a bench and willed her nerves into submission. Each year it was the same; she was always anxious and hopeful that everything would go well. But this year she was even more so. She knew from many of the looks sent her way by the parents that she walked a fine line between their world and Ross's, and they were waiting to see which way she would fall.

And tonight Mr. Walker, the superintendent, would be there.

She took another deep breath, rose from her seat, checked the watch pinned to her dress, and paced the wooden floor.

Surely, Ross wouldn't show up to further embarrass her. She prayed not—oh, she certainly prayed not!—though after last night she couldn't be positive he wouldn't come. She'd heard clearly the challenge in his words, had been hearing it over and over ever since. But she would not succumb to his tactics, which bordered very closely to a threat as far as she was concerned. And that threat had her worried.

"Good evening, Miss Barrett," said Mr. Walker, entering briskly through the open classroom door, his military bearing an echo of his army background.

Irene jumped guiltily, but didn't waste a second composing herself. "Good evening, Mr. Walker."

"I see everything is ready," he boomed, surveying the room. "You always were an efficient teacher, one we could be proud of."

The absence of a smile did little to bring the compliment home, but Irene politely answered, "Thank you."

Without waiting to be asked, Mr. Walker helped himself to the cookies beneath the napkins. "You're a very good cook, too," he said appreciatively, eating one cookie and holding another.

"Thank you," she said again, wishing someone else would arrive. Would he take this opportunity to bring up the subject of Ross Hollister?

While munching the second cookie, he walked around the room inspecting window sills for dust. Finding none, he returned to the cookie dishes.

Unable to bear the silence, Irene spoke, "I'm sorry I can't

offer you any punch. But Mrs. Dickson should be bringing it soon."

Nodding, he brushed the crumbs from the front of his suit. "I always look forward to her punch."

As though waiting for that introduction, Mrs. Dickson could be heard in the outer hall giving instructions to her husband.

"Do be careful, Mr. Dickson. Please don't spill it!" she reprimanded him.

"I'm being careful," he replied patiently.

Mrs. Dickson hustled in ahead of her husband, leading the way as though he'd never find it without her. "Set it down right here before you drop it."

"I'm not going to drop it." Instead of doing as his wife instructed, he poured the contents of the heavy crock into the waiting bowl. When he'd filled it, he placed the crock on the floor where the desk and the wall met.

Mrs. Dickson looked as though she would wilt from relief.

"I really hated to bring that heavy thing, but it was all I had to carry it in," she said to Irene. Then, without giving her a chance to respond, she turned to Mr. Walker. "Good evening, sir. I suppose Miss Barrett told you that Allen will be playing the part of Joseph tonight?"

"We hadn't gotten around to it yet." He glanced at Irene as if to say they hadn't gotten around to several other things either.

"Well, let me tell you," Mrs. Dickson went on, "Allen has been working very hard on memorizing his lines. I don't believe he will let you down, Miss Barrett." She smiled proudly.

"I'm sure he'll do his best and we'll all be proud," Irene answered.

Then the other parents, along with their children, began streaming in. Each child already wore his or her costume; some ducked their heads self-consciously while others chatted nervously with the children around them.

Suddenly having plenty to do, Irene left the refreshment table to the capable hands of Mrs. Dickson, who gladly informed everyone bringing cookies that her son had the leading part.

Keeping one eye always on the door in case Ross appeared, Irene organized the stars, cows, and sheep to one side of the platform stage while the shepherds, Mary, and Joseph stood at the other side. Then, after a brief welcome to the audience, she took her place in an offside chair where she could easily prompt those who needed it. Before sitting, she perused the crowd quickly for a glimpse of Ross, but to her relief he was not there.

With her back to everyone, Irene focused on the written play laying in her lap and the participants before her. She blocked from her mind as best she could that her audience contained many who disapproved of the way she led her life, including her mother sitting front and center.

Whether the children took their cue of nervousness from her or not, she couldn't be sure, but from the beginning everything went wrong. A few of the sheep jostled a cow, and a scuffle ensued but was quickly contained by a nearby star. Unfortunately, the star lost her balance and fell, unhurt, from her chair. Irene jumped up to aid the little girl and stand her securely on her perch once more. After a few deep chuckles subsided, the play continued.

Allen Dickson proved to be a very apt pupil, surprising her as well as his mother by learning not only his lines but most of Mary's as well. Showing almost no restraint, he prompted Mary nearly every time she had a line until finally, provoked beyond measure, she landed a well-aimed punch to his stomach.

At that moment, Irene called an intermission while she and the two mothers attended to the behavior of Mary and Joseph.

When the play resumed, things went much better even though Mary sent threatening looks toward Joseph, who in turn eyed her warily. At the end of the program, they all took their bows before a smiling, well-entertained audience.

Afterward, Irene gratefully took a cup of punch poured by Mrs. Dickson and mingled with the crowd, accepting congratulations spiced with a few words of advice. Smiling politely, she listened with one ear, all the while skimming the sea of faces apprehensively for one possible latecomer.

Sidling up to Irene, Winnie whispered, "Looking for someone?"

With a sudden twist of her head, Irene briefly glared at her mother before seeking friendlier company. She didn't like being watched, nor did she like being reminded of her own vacillating emotions. But as usual, her mother perceived her every nuance of feeling almost before she herself was aware of it.

In her flight across the room, she was intercepted by Mr. Walker.

"Miss Barrett, I just want to say what a fine job you and the children have done." He gave a slight shrug of his shoulders. "In spite of a few unexpected events. Congratulations." He paused, a long pause heavy with meaning. "I know we can always count on you."

Irene heard quite clearly his emphasis on the word *always*. She also caught the full brunt of what he hadn't said; it would have been impossible to misunderstand. Her actions were under scrutiny and her position hung in the balance. She'd realized that as soon as he'd entered her classroom, and now it was in the open between the two of them, no longer hearsay from Clara.

"Now, if you'll excuse me," he went on, "I must be getting home."

She was dismissed. A flush of anger climbed from her collar to her cheeks.

He nodded smartly, made his way through the thinning group, found his coat, and departed.

Watching him go, Irene felt a fierce need to be alone,

but that would be impossible until every last person had gone. The strain and tension built within her until she could barely smile.

After an interminably long time, the last set of parents left. Only Winnie, Lydia, and Jonathan stayed behind. Thanks to some of the men, the desk and benches had been returned to their normal places, and she remembered that the last time it had been Ross who'd performed the task.

"Well," Winnie said, buttoning her coat. "Are we ready?"

Irene nodded.

"Just think. No school for a while and Christmas is only two days away."

"I'm too tired to get excited right now," Lydia said behind a yawn. "But I will be tomorrow."

"Me, too," agreed Jonathan.

Silently, Irene added her hopeful agreement.

Ross pounded the nail home and added one last hit for good measure. Sitting back on his haunches, the hammer across his thigh, he surveyed the almost-finished room. It wasn't anything fancy, just rough sawn boards across the rafters and side walls. He'd added a partition to make the attic room smaller, so he could heat it fairly well with the round stove he'd purchased. Rubbing his cold hands against the sides of his trousers to create a little friction for heat, he turned to Ben, who had been helping him.

"What do you say we go downstairs and get warm?"

"Sounds good to me. I hit my thumb a while ago and didn't even feel it."

Chuckling, Ross clapped him on the back. "I know what you mean."

It was early in the day and they had closed up for the holidays, since it was Christmas Eve, telling everyone he wouldn't be open tomorrow and they should all stay home with their families. There had been a little grumbling but most of his customers looked guilty, not saying a word.

Ross made a pot of coffee, motioning Ben to have a seat at a table. "Got any family around these parts?"

"Nope. Never did get married. Just a brother over in Indiana," Ben answered.

"Me neither. Just Harry, wherever he is." He sat down to wait for the coffee to boil. "But this town feels like home as much now as it did before." He grinned. "In spite of the occasional ruckus raised in here."

Ben shook his head in disgust. "What d'ya suppose ever got them women to thinkin' you'd open a whorehouse upstairs?" he said, pointing at the ceiling.

Ross shrugged. "Rumors and fear, I guess."

"You're mighty understandin' considerin' how much damage they managed to inflict on the business." He looked around at the mended tables and chairs. "Serve 'em right if you did bring in a few doves." Ben smiled. "Some from Denver, maybe? I hear they're somethin'."

"Then they'd probably burn the place down. No thank you, not if I'm going to live here."

"Hell, they'd like to burn it down anyway."

They sat in thoughtful silence, each contemplating what he would do if such an event happened.

Shaking himself free of the morbid thought, Ross asked, "What kind of plans do you have for Christmas?"

"Thought I'd put a hole in the ice and do a little fishin' above the dam a ways. How 'bout you?"

"I haven't even noticed Christmas for years. I guess not having a family does that to a fellow." He got up and poured the coffee into two mugs. "Maybe I'll join you on the ice."

"Plenty of room," Ben said, swirling the hot coffee until the floating grounds coagulated into the center. He sat the cup down and waited for them to sink. "I thought maybe you'd get an invite from the teacher."

"I doubt it. But I'm not going to let that stop me." Ross leaned his chair back, balancing it on two rickety legs.

Ben liked his boss. He wasn't afraid of much, was kind

to little kids, and he sent people away from his business because he believed they should stay home with their families. Yep, he plain-out admired the man. "What about her mama? I hear she's a tough one."

"Tough?" Ross grinned. "Just smart."

Swigging his coffee, Ben watched Ross over the brim of his cup. Nope, he decided, this man didn't let anything stand in his way once his mind was made up. He could see it as plain as day in the confident set of his jaw.

"What do you know about this Andrew fellow that Irene was supposed to marry?" Ross asked.

"Not much. 'Course there wasn't much to know. Either you liked him or you didn't," Ben answered.

"Doesn't sound as though you cared for him."

Ben shrugged. "Hard to care about a dandy. Seemed to think he was better than anybody else if you could see beyond that shining smile of his. Except for Mr. Barrett, I doubt if he had any real true friends. Never saw him actually help a fella out if he needed it. 'Course, there was Howard, but I never got the impression they were much more than partners." Ben pushed his empty cup aside. "Even Howard come in once in a while for a drink. But that was before he got married," he finished with a grin. "Guess you can't hold that against a man."

"No, I guess not." Ross brought his chair down on all fours with a thud. "Well, I suppose we'd better get back to work if we're going to get it finished before Christmas."

"Sure enough."

The two men walked to the stairs. In a friendly gesture, Ross thumped Ben on the back. "I can't tell you how much I appreciate your help."

"Don't mind at all. What else would I be doing?"

"Fishing maybe?"

Ben stopped. "Hmm. You got a point there."

They worked together with only the sound of hammers pinging against nails while the smell of freshly cut wood added a clean smell to an otherwise musty attic. By five o'clock they had the walls finished.

Surveying the neatly enclosed room, the framed window and double paneled door, Ross experienced a surprising amount of satisfaction at the results of his handiwork. He barely noticed the soft new callouses appearing on his hands and fingers where the old ones had faded. He simply felt good.

Next, they carried in the bed from the unfinished side of the attic and set it up, placing a warm feather mattress on top.

Staring at the bed, Ben asked, "Are you sure you won't reconsider about those doves from Denver?"

Ross only laughed at the forlorn look on Ben's face.

They struggled with the heavy iron stove until, finally, it stood along a sidewall where a hole awaited the pipe for the chimney.

"What do you say we try it out?" Ross asked, gathering up some scraps of leftover pieces of siding.

"Sounds good to me."

With a little patience and a lot of coaxing, the small fire soon turned into a roaring hot one.

"Better shut down that damper or we'll burn ourselves out with no help from the women of this town," Ben said, rotating the arm connected to the flap inside the chimney.

Sitting on the edge of his new bed, Ross stared at the flames through the glass in the door of the stove, barely listening to Ben's words. He'd move out of the inn tonight, he decided, and with the pile of blankets he'd bought from the mercantile he'd be as cozy as two butterflies in a cocoon. Well, almost.

"Guess I'll be getting on over to my place," said Ben. "Unless you need some help bringing your things down here."

Shaking his head, Ross said, "No, thanks. All I've got are a couple of valises." He stood. "Thanks again for your help."

"Don't mention it." Ben walked to the door. "I'll be on the ice in the morning."

"I'll be there, but I have something to do first."

"Got anything to do with the teacher?" Ben asked with a grin.

Ross smiled. "Yep."

Irene wrapped the porcelain doll with soft flannel and tucked it into the small wooden cradle she'd had specially made. Thoughtfully, she stroked the long brown curls that were so much like Lydia's, wondering if she'd made a mistake. Perhaps Lydia would think she was too old to play with dolls, and maybe she was. But Lydia had carried too much responsibility for a girl so young and for such a long time that Irene believed she needed the chance to be a child with childhood fantasies, if only for a while. And if she herself hadn't been able to resist the beautiful doll, how could Lydia resist it? Irene hoped she couldn't.

Buying for Jonathan had taken longer. His interests centered only around hunting and fishing, and even though she knew he would dearly love to have his own hunting knife, she couldn't bring herself to buy one. Instead, she bought the best fishing pole in the mercantile. The next day she returned to buy a game board with checkers for winter evenings, when he was usually so bored.

Casting a glance toward the stairs, sensing the restrained excitement generated by the two wide-awake children upstairs, Irene placed all the gifts near the richly decorated Christmas tree.

Earlier that day, when Howard had brought them the tree, the entire house had instantly filled with the scent of woodsy pine. Lydia and Jonathan had been entranced, if not spellbound. Unlike her usual talkative self, Lydia became quiet, even pensive. But Jonathan had more than made up for her silence with hundreds of questions about where the tree came from, what they would put on it, how they would reach the tip of it, if any squirrels still lived in it. Most of her answers satisfied him until he asked if Ross would be coming to Christmas dinner along with Mr. and Mrs. Gregg. She had been unprepared for his reply to her simple "no." Quietly, with his head turned to one side, he'd asked, "Why? Aren't you friends anymore?"

Stumped for an answer, she searched his small face and found only bewilderment. Sitting on the edge of the settee so they were at eye level, she took his hand.

"Jonathan," she began, but hardly knew how to go on. "It isn't that we aren't friends anymore as much as we shouldn't be friends."

"Why not? Did he say something bad to you?"

"No," she answered honestly. "It isn't anything he's said."

"Did he do something wrong?" He squinted his eyes, trying to understand the way that grownups thought and why they made everything so complicated.

"Let's just say that he and I really have nothing in common, and friends need things in common so they can talk." She smiled weakly at her lame attempt to justify her actions. "Do you understand?"

Shaking his head, he replied, "No."

How could she tell him that it was improper for her, a schoolteacher, to spend a family holiday with a saloon keeper? The implication would be far too obvious to the townspeople, as well as the superintendent, even if it weren't obvious to a small boy.

And in spite of the challenging words that Ross Hollister had spoken several nights ago, she had to consider the impropriety of having him sit at their Christmas dinner table. Jonathan would simply have to accept a final "no" as her answer.

She stood back now looking at the beautiful tree with its strings of popcorn and tiny bows of ribbons. As wonderful as it was to be able to share the holiday with the children and her mother, there was still an emptiness within her—that same emptiness that drew her to the novels beneath her bed. But now, even they didn't fill the need. And without intentionally doing so, her mind settled on the memory of Ross Hollister standing before her in the moonlight, his arms holding her close to his heart.

Giving a shake of her head to dispel the thought, she chided herself. "Such a foolish romantic heart, Irene. Mother was right."

And with that, she blew out the lamp and went to bed.

Chapter Fifteen

Christmas morning brought snow from the heavy, overcast sky, but neither Jonathan nor Lydia even noticed as
they scurried around getting dressed.

"Let's wake her up," Jonathan whispered while the two
of them stood outside Irene's door.

"All right," Lydia agreed, her whole body trembling with
excitement. "Miss Barrett?" she called through the closed
door as she knocked gently. "Are you up?"

"She won't hear you if all you're gonna do is whisper,"
he whispered to his sister in exasperation.

"Well, I'm not going to bang on the door!" Lydia said,
raising her voice slightly.

Jonathan eyed her with irritation. They'd never have
Christmas if he left it to her.

Suddenly, the door opened. "Good morning, you two,"
Irene said smiling. "It's barely daylight. You could have
stayed in bed a little while longer."

"We couldn't sleep," Jonathan answered, anticipation
shining in his eyes.

Placing her arms around their shoulders, Irene led them to the stairs. "Neither could I. I suppose we might as well go down and build a fire."

"Oh, no you don't," called Winnie emerging from her room. "Not without me."

Once downstairs, with the frigid air surrounding them, Jonathan and Lydia stood transfixed, staring at the gifts beneath the tree.

"My, but it's cold in here!" Winnie said, shaking down the ashes in the parlor stove. Quickly, she laid pieces of kindling and lit them.

Wrapping her shawl closer, Irene watched the children. Jonathan's eyes sparkled as he stepped closer to the tree. Lydia didn't move. She just stood there with wide eyes, staring at the doll in the cradle.

"Isn't it ever going to get warm in here?" Winnie complained, fiddling with the damper.

"I don't suppose there's any chance of having breakfast first . . ." Irene teased.

Jonathan turned toward her, hopeful. "Do we have to?"

Smiling, Irene answered, "No. Breakfast can wait." She moved to the tree and lifted a long narrow package wrapped in brown paper. "This is for you, Jonathan."

Without reserve, he tore the paper away to reveal the fishing pole. He'd hoped that was what was inside. "My own fishin' pole! Now Ross won't have to let me use his all the time." He studied it and touched it lovingly.

"Lydia?" Irene bit her lip, wondering if she'd insulted her by giving her a child's toy. Perhaps the doll had been a mistake.

As if released from a trance, Lydia turned to Irene. Never in her life had Christmas been this beautiful. She wanted to say her thoughts aloud, but they stuck in her throat. Bending to lift the fragile doll from the cradle, the remnants of her childhood surrounded her and she held the doll close. For a long time, she'd hoped for a home where she'd be cared for, instead of carrying the burden of caring for others. As she stared down at the lace-and-satin-dressed doll cradled in her arms, a new kind of serenity enveloped her. The doll signified to her that someone did care, very much. With a small movement, she brushed away the tear that trickled down her cheek.

"Do you like her?" Irene asked, softly.

Glancing up, Lydia nodded. "I love her." Smiling, she added, "Thank you."

With a quiet sigh of relief, Irene pulled another brown package from under the tree and handed it to Jonathan.

Laying his fishing pole aside, he took the gift. "Thank you." Opening it, he found the wooden game board and pieces.

"We'll have all winter to challenge each other," Irene said.

"You'll have to teach me. I don't know how to play. Is it hard?" He touched the wooden squares, thinking it would certainly be better than doing homework, no matter how hard it was.

"Not really," Irene replied. "We'll try it out later when Mr. and Mrs. Gregg arrive."

After that, they all handed out the gifts they had made or bought.

Winnie gave matching mittens and scarves to each of them, and even Jonathan appreciated their bright colors and warmth. Lydia gave Winnie and Irene handkerchiefs that she had meticulously embroidered, and a pair of socks that took her forever to knit went to Jonathan.

Now it was Jonathan's turn. Excited but shy, he produced from his pocket a small, well-polished rock that he gave to Irene. "I found this along the river," he began. "I thought maybe you could use it to hold the papers down on your desk when the wind blows in the door."

Irene took the rock, studying the distinct layers, admiring its polished surface. "Thank you, Jonathan. It's a wonderful, thoughtful gift." She leaned over and kissed his cheek.

Ducking his head, he moved on to Lydia. "I found this in the woods when me and Ross went hunting." He reached into his pocket and placed an arrowhead in her palm. "I saved it until Christmas to give it to you."

"Oh, Jonathan!" she exclaimed, turning it over and over. "Thank you. It will always remind me of the adventure we had at the cabin."

Turning to Winnie, he reached inside his pocket once more.

"Ross said this would bring good luck to anyone who has it," he said as he dropped a soft, silky rabbit's foot into her hand.

Forcing herself to accept the gift without showing her queasiness, Winnie smiled and responded, "Thank you, Jonathan."

Irene looked around and felt a warmth she had not known before. The children brought her a measure of happiness she hadn't expected. By direct contrast, she was also keenly aware of the emptiness deep within her being. And lately she had come to realize that even Andrew hadn't filled that emptiness. Then, with a shake of her head to dispel her gloomy thoughts, she reminded herself that they had guests coming.

"I suppose," she said, heading for the kitchen, "we'd better get that turkey in the oven, or we'll be eating it for dinner tomorrow!"

"You're absolutely right," Winnie replied, rising from her seat. "You children pick up those papers."

Irene brought the turkey from the ice-cold pantry and prepared it, while the stove burst to life under Winnie's capable hands. Lydia placed three pies on the side table in the seldom-used dining room and six of the eight places available were set with Irene's china.

In a short time, the house radiated warmth from the kitchen to the parlor, where Jonathan had taken an armload of wood. There was an excitement in the air that only

Christmas could bring, and none of them was exempt from feeling it.

Later, when the smell of turkey was strong in the air, a knock at the back door brought Irene from the pantry, dusting her floured hands on her apron. She opened the door, expecting to find Howard and Emma arriving early, but instead found Ross Hollister burdened with an armful of packages.

Surprise and shock coursed through her body. She wanted to send him away immediately, remembering their last encounter when he walked her home after rehearsal, yet at the same time she wanted to invite him in.

"Merry Christmas," he said, looking at her and relishing what he saw.

Stepping aside in invitation, she answered, "Merry Christmas to you." She untied her apron strings behind her, then changed her mind and tied them again. Flustered and confused by his appearance at her door, she waited for him to make the next move. But as usual Jonathan saved the moment for both of them.

"Ross!" Jonathan cried gleefully. "Boy, are we glad you came. This makes Christmas just perfect!" Out of the corner of his eye, he glanced at Irene, hoping she wouldn't send Ross away.

"I'm real glad to be here too, pal," he said softly.

Ross held Irene's gaze even though he spoke to Jonathan, and she knew he meant to include her in his statement. She didn't know whether to blush or be angry, and the heightening pink in her cheeks could be evidence of either.

"What've you got there, Ross?" Jonathan asked, bouncing around on his toes.

"This is Christmas, isn't it?" Ross teased.

"Sure it is!"

"Maybe you could lead the way to the tree so I can set these things down." He continued to look at Irene, but she knew he was actually speaking to Jonathan. Whatever he had in mind was already set in motion, and there was little she could do to stop it.

"This way. Can you see?" Jonathan asked, trying to see Ross over the top of his load.

"You bet I can." Ross forced himself to look away from Irene and followed the boy through the house to the parlor, where a cheery fire crackled and popped.

Irene, with a grumbling Winnie trailing behind her, followed in single file right after Lydia, who could barely contain her rising excitement.

"That sure is one nice tree," Ross commented as he placed his packages on the floor, then turned to Irene.

"Howard brought it," she offered. "He gets one for me when he gets his."

Ross wondered if Andrew had ever cut down his own tree and taken her with him just to enjoy her company on a special occasion. He knew he would.

Looking at his gifts wrapped in paper, Irene said, "You really shouldn't have."

With a shrug he replied, "I just thought this is the time of year to put behind us any differences we have. And I'd hoped you wouldn't be able to turn away a man bearing gifts."

His genuine smile, combined with the mischievous twinkle in his eyes, made her smile in return.

"That's a start," he said, glad to see she didn't plan on throwing him out. But he wasn't so sure about her mother, who stood glowering behind her.

With a timid tug on Ross's coat, Jonathan asked, "Are these for us?"

"Yep. I wouldn't let Christmas pass by without bringing something for a special boy and girl." Ross squatted down on his haunches and reached for a package.

Seeing him like that, in her parlor before her tree, did something to Irene. She felt the emptiness within her suddenly ebb, and for the first time she was willing to admit that his presence wasn't foreign, but welcome.

"Let's see . . ." Ross began, pulling a long, narrow package from the pile. "This is for you." And he handed it to Jonathan.

Hiding a smile behind her hand, Irene recognized the shape of the package as a fishing pole.

Jonathan tore the paper away to reveal another fishing pole. "Oh, boy! Two of 'em! Now I can ask Bobby to go with me. He doesn't have one."

Ross looked up at Irene, who'd been watching with amusement. "Did you already give him one?" he asked, a half smile lingering at one side of his mouth.

She nodded.

"Well, he doesn't seem disappointed," Ross replied.

"Heck, no!" Jonathan answered. "This is great!"

Searching to the bottom, Ross pulled out a small package and handed it to Lydia.

She accepted the gift with a quiet "thank you." Inside was a rainbow of ribbons for her hair. "They're beautiful. I've never had so many before." Impulsively, she kissed his cheek.

Pleased that he'd made the right choice, he winked at her. Then he reached for one of the two remaining packages, handing it to Winnie.

Caught somewhat off guard, Winnie sputtered, trying to say nice things while deep in her heart her misgivings about him hadn't changed. She untied the string, letting the paper fall away to reveal a beautiful shawl the color of a summer sky.

Truly at a loss for words now, she wrapped it around her, mindful of the dusty apron she still wore. "I . . . I don't know what to say. . . . "

"If you like it, that's all that matters," Ross said, watching while the war within her was reflected in her eyes.

"I do. Very much. Thank you." She could see plainly now that his appearance on this day stated very clearly what his intentions were toward Irene. And try as she might, she couldn't help but draw a contrast between Ross and

Andrew, with the saloon keeper at a distinct disadvantage. Her loyalty still belonged to Andrew.

Ross brought the last package to Irene and placed it on the settee beside her. "It was a little awkward to wrap," he apologized, sitting near her but separated by the gift.

She stared at the odd shape, puzzled.

"Open it," he urged.

As she pulled the paper off, she found the smallest coffee grinder she'd ever seen, and it was accompanied by a tin of coffee beans and a coffeepot.

"I thought maybe you'd like to offer your guests coffee now and then," he said with a twinkle in his eyes. "And one more thing . . ." He reached inside his pocket and took out another package, handing it to her. "I hope you like it."

Not knowing what to say or do from the moment Ross had arrived at her door, she quietly accepted the flat, rectangular gift. Inside the plain paper wrap was a book of poems by Elizabeth Barrett Browning. Irene's heart practically flipped over in her chest. This was her favorite reading by far. She looked up into Ross's face. How could he have known? Even Andrew hadn't guessed.

"Howard told me how much you like books, so I chose this one because it has your name on it. Barrett." He watched her expectantly for some sign of approval. He'd read some of the poetry, and while most of it wasn't in a style he easily understood, he did realize that it was basically poetry of the heart. Would Irene be offended or embarrassed by such a gift?

"It's beautiful," she said softly. "This is a favorite of mine. Thank you."

Winnie had some difficulty in keeping her eyes from rolling toward heaven for help. He had appealed to that part of Irene that was always off on a dream cloud, and she had to admit it had probably gained him favor, at least from Irene.

"You didn't have to . . ." she began, indicating with her

hand all the gifts he'd brought.

"I wanted to," he replied simply. And even with her mother and the children sitting around, he couldn't take his eyes off her face.

She squirmed slightly on her seat, uncomfortable with his searching look. "Well . . ." She tried to think of something to say to get past this awkward moment. "It was very nice of you to think of us."

A knock at the front door interrupted any further conversation, and Irene gratefully opened the door to Howard and Emma. A round of greetings and a handshake between the two men changed the somber tone to a lively one. Irene took their coats and hung them on the pegs behind the door.

"We're a little early," Emma said, "but I thought maybe I could help with dinner. And I brought a cake."

Winnie took the cake, sniffing it appreciatively. "Smells wonderful.

"Sure smells like the ladies cooked us a fine dinner, huh, Ross?" he said with a wink.

An embarrassed silence fell over the group.

"I, uh . . ." Ross began.

"Mr. Hollister just dropped by," Winnie interjected.

"And so, of course, we invited him to dinner," Irene finished, sending a glare of defiance at her mother. This was her home and she could invite whomever she wished, regardless of what her mother or Emma or anyone else thought!

"Well, it sure will be nice to have another man around. I sort of felt outnumbered, if you know what I mean," Howard said, smiling.

Emma was too shocked to say anything.

After that, the women went to the kitchen and busied themselves with preparing and serving a delicious meal, while the men retired to the parlor to talk and wait.

Lydia added another setting to the table, secretly glad that Irene had insisted that Ross was staying, although she would never voice her feelings in the face of such obvious disapproval by Winnie and Emma. It was plain to see that Winnie refused to talk, even to her. And Emma, with her eyes still wide in disbelief, couldn't seem to talk if she wanted to. Silly women, Lydia thought. They acted as though Ross was a bank robber, when he was actually a very nice man with deep feelings for Irene. Couldn't they see that?

Still bristling, Irene spoke to both women, ignoring their disapproval of Ross's presence at the dinner table.

"Would you make the gravy, Mother? And Emma, would you ask Howard if he'd carry the turkey to the table?"

When Emma had left the room, Irene heard her mother mumble, "I'm surprised she didn't ask the saloon owner to do it." Then she stirred the gravy hard enough to make the spoon ring against the side of the pan.

In a short time, everyone was seated and Howard had carved the turkey, releasing even more of the spicy aroma. Plates were passed and compliments were given.

"I suppose Christmas has been good for the mercantile?" Ross asked Howard, ladling gravy over his potatoes and stuffing.

Nodding, Howard replied, "This year was better than last for some reason."

"I got two fishin' poles," Jonathan offered, smiling.

Laughing, Howard said, "Maybe that's why."

"Next year you'll be doing some extra shopping," Ross said to Howard, including Emma with a glance. "Congratulations again."

Three forks suddenly suspended in mid-path. Emma's eyes widened once more while Winnie and Irene simultaneously turned their heads to stare at her, then at Howard.

Unaware of the consternation of the three women, Howard replied with a proud look, "Yes, I guess we will."

"Emma?" Irene asked, trying to hide the small hurt she felt that Emma hadn't confided in her.

Winnie pressed her knee into Irene's. "The children," she whispered behind her napkin.

Irene ignored her. "I'm so happy for you," she said quietly to Emma. And she was. But she was suddenly reminded of the vast differences in their lives. Emma was in love and married and expecting her first child. They really had very little in common anymore. No wonder she'd kept the news to herself.

Turning a bright pink, Emma smiled and forced out a "thank you."

"I thought I saw some pie," Jonathan interjected.

"And maybe some coffee to go with it?" Howard asked with a knowing grin.

Winnie, still balking at the entire scene got up to cut the pies. Irene happily escaped to the kitchen to grind the coffee.

"I think I'll give her hand," Ross said, pushing back his chair.

Winnie threw a glaring look over her shoulder at his back just as he disappeared through the doorway.

Ross found Irene in the pantry, her hands stilled against the pie safe, her head slightly bowed in thought.

"I'm sorry . . ." he began.

Startled, she faced him.

". . . about everything," he finished quietly. "I only intended to drop by to bring the gifts."

Uncertain about her feelings, she shook her head. "No. It isn't you. I . . . Sometimes . . . Mother . . ."

"Sometimes your mother is a pain in the—uh, neck?"

She nodded with a half smile on her lips. "Sometimes, yes."

He shrugged. "If nobody else minds, you shouldn't either." He gave her a warm grin and leaned a shoulder against the door frame of the small pantry. "I don't mind."

"It isn't just mother." He looked so at ease and comfortable standing there, as though he had all day to listen to her problems when in fact he was one of her problems.

216

Actually, he was her main problem.

"It's me, right?"

"Ross—I mean, Mr. Hollister, I have to return to my guests with the coffee, and I haven't even ground it yet."

"Here, I'll help you."

In the confines of the pantry, it was impossible for two people to move without touching. With her back against the shelf, he faced her, reaching around her for the grinder. A flowery scent lifted from her hair to his nostrils and mixed with the tangy odor of dried herbs and spices that hung by strings at the ends of the shelves. Held as if spellbound, he gazed into the warm depths of her honey-brown eyes until she looked away. He was tempted to kiss her again, long and sweet. But he reminded himself of her guests just a room away and promised himself that at another time he would, when neither of them was fettered by the presence of others.

"Where's the tin of beans?" he asked, still close enough that he could almost feel her breath on his neck.

"Over there . . . behind you."

He stepped aside, allowing her the opportunity to breathe and move a little distance from him. She took hold of her emotions as best she could with him standing so close. "I'll grind them," she offered. "It can't be too difficult."

Once more he leaned against the door jamb.

In a short while she had ground enough beans; looking up, she waited for him to leave the pantry so she could do the same.

He continued to stand in the way, his gaze fixed on her face.

"You're beautiful," he said. And he meant it. He'd never seen a more beautiful woman in his life.

Surprised at his remark, she returned his stare. Andrew had said similar words and she had believed them, but she heard a sincerity in Ross's voice that she'd never heard in Andrew's. Suddenly, she felt beautiful, as though a glow suffused her inside and out, bringing a warmth she hadn't known before. This was certainly like no moment she'd ever shared with Andrew—so personal, so intimate and so honest that it held her mesmerized.

The clanking of the coffeepot lid broke the spell.

"Are we going to have to eat the whole pie before we get any coffee?" Winnie called from the kitchen.

"Excuse me," Irene said, squeezing past Ross.

As he watched her perform the task of making coffee, he decided it was about time she escaped from her daily duties and from the watchful eye of her mother, even for a short while.

And although it wouldn't be easy, he had an idea about how to achieve this that he was sure would work.

Chapter Sixteen

After restlessly walking the kitchen, Irene decided to make herself a cup of hot milk. Perhaps then she'd be able to sleep. She moved about the warm room, getting a pan, pouring the milk, turning down the damper, and stirring the milk to keep it from scorching as though this was a nightly occurrence. Thankfully, it wasn't. Only lately, since Christmas actually, had this restlessness gripped her. Each night she'd gone to bed only to toss and turn, unable even to keep her eyes closed until finally she fell asleep. But tonight her thoughts plagued her so thoroughly that she hadn't even attempted going upstairs, knowing sleep was impossible.

With the damper partially closed, the stove cooled, giving off an occasional cracking sound as the cast iron contracted. In a matter of minutes, the milk was hot and she poured it into a stoneware mug. Holding it between both hands, she sipped it. This was not her favorite drink, but she took it like medicine, grimacing only slightly.

Another cracking sound emanated from somewhere,

but hardly paying attention, she assumed it was the cooling stove. Then it came again. Alert now, she realized that it sounded more like tapping, and it echoed softly in the room. Glancing at the window, she saw a small flickering light beyond the glass. Straining to see what it could be, she rose from her chair to peer outside for a better look.

There, standing ankle-deep in the cold snow, was Ross. She hurried to the door and opened it.

He met her at the door, a finger to his blue lips and a smile lurking in his eyes. "Sh-h-h!" he said, tiptoeing inside. "I thought you'd never see me!" he whispered.

"What are you doing?" she whispered back.

"Waiting for you to let me in." He hugged his body as close to the stove as he dared.

Opening the damper, she frowned at him. "But what were you doing waiting out there in the dark like some kind of thief?"

He peeled his gloves from his hands and carefully laid them on the table, then stretched his hands over the warmth of the stove.

"I thought we'd go ice skating," he answered with a shiver. "After I warm up a little."

Incredulously, she stared at him. "Ice skating? It's practically the middle of the night!"

"Sh-h-h! I don't want to take your mother with us. I only want you to go." He smiled at her wickedly. "Are you scared?"

"Of what?" she asked, forcing her voice to stay low. She recognized the challenge he offered, just as she'd recognized it the night he walked her home.

And she would accept the challenge; he could see it in the warm bronze of her eyes.

"I don't have any skates," she said as the rising excitement of doing the forbidden seeped into her bones, almost making her shake.

Ross shrugged casually. "Nothing to worry about. There

are two pair outside. Waiting." He raised his eyebrows. "Ready?"

Irene bit her lip, but was unable to hold back the smile. This was just the thing for her restlessness, not the mug of tasteless warmed milk. Without hesitation, she nodded her answer.

He helped her on with her coat and the mittens and scarf that Winnie had knitted for her. In a short time she was bundled for a midnight skate on the canal. Quietly, Ross closed the door behind them, picked up the skates he'd laid in the snow, and pulled her along in his hurry to get her away before she changed her mind.

With her free mittened hand clasped over her racing heart, Irene had difficulty resisting the urge to laugh aloud. This was the best, and certainly the most daring, adventure she'd ever entered upon! The exhilaration was almost more than she could bear as they dashed along the snowbanks and over the bridge. Only the clinking of the skates in Ross's hand and the rush of their breathing filled the cold night air.

When they reached the canal, staying upstream from the mill, Ross pulled Irene behind a tree, where they flattened their backs against the rough bark.

"Do you think anyone saw us?" he asked, out of breath.

Laughing, she responded, "No. I can't imagine anyone else being up this time of night."

"Me neither." After a minute he confessed, "I waited three nights in a row for you."

"You what?" Her tone implied disbelief, but inside she felt warmly flattered.

"I finally decided that you probably never stayed up late. I figured I'd have to throw stones at your bedroom window, but I wasn't sure which one it was." Turning his head, he smiled at her. "I almost gave up."

"I'm glad you didn't. I feel just as Jonathan must have when he skipped school to go fishing."

Ross shook his head. "No, that's an entirely different

221

feeling. Do you want to try it sometime?" he asked seriously.

She laughed again. "Me? Skip school to go fishing? What would the children think? What would the superintendent say?"

He shrugged. "Would it matter?"

"Of course, it would!" But she didn't want to talk about reality. Not on an ice-covered canal in the small hours of a winter morning, when reality and fantasy hovered so close together that they could easily be intertwined. "Are we going to skate or are we going to talk?" she asked.

He pondered the options for a moment. "Skate."

Aided by only a meager light from a sheltered moon, they found a log nearby. Irene sat while Ross helped her on with her skates. After he fastened on his, he pulled her to her feet until they stood toe to toe while his gloved hand held her mittened one.

"Are you steady?" he asked, feeling her tremble. "Here. Give me both of your hands."

She offered the other one, and he took it in a strong, secure grip, pulling her closer until the only thing between them was the bulkiness of their coats.

While her heart hammered loudly, not at all muffled by the layers of warm clothing, his hat tipped toward her, and she closed her eyes. Waiting.

The kiss was gentle, almost asking if she was in agreement with him. Her only answer was compliance as she leaned against him, liking the clean soapy smell of him as it mixed with the cold air.

Slowly, he deepened the kiss, searching now, no longer asking. Compelled to draw her closer, he wrapped both arms around her, nearly crushing her to him.

Weakening, her knees began to give and her palms, overly warm inside her mittens, became moist so that it was impossible to grasp the sides of his coat. In an almost dream-like state, she gave herself over to the wonderful feelings dancing through her body. This was similar to the last time he'd kissed her, yet inexplicably better.

All too soon, the kiss ended and she stood shaken in its aftermath.

"I thought we came here to skate," she said, her voice a hoarse whisper.

"That was part of it." He relaxed his arms around her so that they rested at the back of her waist, not at all ready to let her go.

"And this was the other part?"

"Yes, but I hadn't planned on this part coming first," he replied with a grin she could barely make out in the darkness. "But I don't mind if you don't," he teased.

She reached up to touch his thick mustache, but the silkiness of it was kept from her fingers by the heavy yarn of her mitten. "And if I should agree to skip school with you, would you have a two-part plan for that, too?" she asked, enjoying his lightheartedness.

"That would be telling."

"Mmm. I see," she replied, tracing the firm line of his jaw. "And should I believe that we would actually go fishing if I skipped school?"

He smiled at her. "Are you asking if we really are going to skate tonight?"

Blushing but answering bravely, she replied, "Yes."

"That was part of the plan." He dropped his hands from her waist to grasp her elbows. Moving backward, he gently pulled her onto the ice, stumbling a little over a twig in his path. He managed to catch his balance without upsetting both of them.

"Oh! Oh!" Irene cried in alarm. "Are you all right?"

"Just a little clumsy, I guess. But don't worry, I'll keep us both on our feet. Ready?"

"I don't know . . . it *is* awfully dark." She peered through the dim shadows. The snow along the banks cast some illumination across the darker, solidly frozen canal.

"Are you afraid?" he challenged.

No, she thought, not as long as she was with him. Shaking her head, she replied, "No."

They made a few circles around the ice near the log where they'd sat with their skates. Feeling less afraid and more sure on her feet, she embarked on her own, making a wide turn and skating back toward Ross who stood still, watching and waiting.

Laughing, she said, "I don't know how to stop." And she would have skated past him except that he reached out and grabbed her hand, surprising her. He swung her in a tight circle, until she begged him to stop.

"I'm getting dizzy!"

He pulled her to him, braking her skates with his. "Me too."

Dropping her head to his chest to restore her equilibrium, she smiled at the pleasure of feeling his arms surround her once more.

"Better?" he asked.

"Mmm. Yes," she replied softly.

"Cold?"

"No, not really." She wiggled her toes, wishing she'd worn another pair of stockings.

He lifted her chin with one finger and stared long into her eyes. "What does 'not really' mean?" Then he touched the tip of her cold nose.

"Well, maybe just a little."

"Some exercise will help that." And he tugged her along after him. Letting go of her hand, he said, "Can you keep up?"

With a valiant effort, she stayed at his side while they skated farther down the canal. When he turned suddenly in front of her, she was unprepared and slammed against him, bringing them both down in a tumble of skirts and a tangle of legs. He had taken the worst of it and lay flat on his back with her staring into his face.

"Oh! I'm so sorry! Are you hurt?" she said, trying to raise herself to her feet. But the attempt only made her slip and fall on him again.

"Ooof!" he grunted.

With a cry of despair, she tried once more, but he quickly grabbed her and said, "I think it's better if I get up first." Rolling her over with his nose inches from hers, he lay across her. The softness of her woman's body was apparent in spite of the heavy clothing she wore, and even if he'd tried, he couldn't have ignored the curves that lay beneath him.

Irene inhaled sharply as Ross's hand crept along her side, subsiding only when he reached her chin. The pressure of his body on hers brought a forbidden tingle of excitement and she hoped that he would kiss her once more.

Hidden by the darkness and the banks of the canal, they lay upon the ice, aware only of the heat building within them.

"This isn't as easy as I thought it would be," he said, his voice vibrant with emotion.

"No," she whispered her agreement, "it isn't." Then her world reeled again as his lips pressed hers, searching, fulfilling. Unbidden, the thought came to her that it had never been like this with Andrew and it would not be like this with anyone but Ross.

Bracing himself on one elbow so as not to hurt her, he cradled her head in his other hand while his mouth plundered hers. She was so soft, so willing, so right.

Lost to everything but the brush of his mustache and the strength of his hands, Irene succumbed to emotions she'd only dreamed about. But this wasn't a dream or a page from one of her novels. It was happening now, and it was real.

And she didn't want it ever to stop.

Using more control than he'd believed he was capable of, Ross lifted his head and forced his thoughts to take a different route. With an impatient sigh, he rolled away onto his back, staring up at a patch of stars revealed by a passing cloud. The cold ice beneath his bare head helped clear his mind.

Reaching over, he grasped her hand.

She lay there, chilled on the outside but glowing on the inside, sprawled upon the ice, wondering how they must look to any brave winter bird sitting on a lofty perch. The image brought to mind the snow angels that children made by lying in the snow to make an imprint of their bodies. She smiled. Two grown adults acting like children. Well, not exactly.

"Ross?"

"Hmm?" he answered, still holding her hand.

"Are you getting cold?"

"No. Are you?" He turned to look at her.

She rolled her head against the ice. "No."

"I suppose we'd better get up," he said, not moving.

"Mmm. I wonder what people would say . . ."

"If they saw us?" he asked, then went on without waiting for her answer. "I guess they would be wagging their heads, not to mention their tongues, about us being out here this time of night. Alone. They'd probably drop in a dead faint if they had seen us a minute ago. Especially Mrs. Wilson." He rolled on his side toward her. "Does that bother you?"

She considered his words for a moment, knowing that she needed to be truthful, with him and with herself. "Well, I do have to consider my teaching position. I like teaching. Very much. It isn't just a job for me. It gives me a sense of . . ." She searched her mind for the right word. "Fulfillment." Looking away from him, she said, "Now I really sound like an old-maid school teacher."

Using his teeth, he removed the glove from his hand and touched her chin with his bare finger. "I'd hardly call you an old maid, Irene Barrett."

She couldn't make a reply; her breath had become lodged in her throat.

Leaning down, he kissed her lightly. "And if anyone says you are, they're lying." He kissed the tip of her cold nose, then pushed himself up and off the ice. "I guess we should be going in before we turn into icicles," he said, standing.

He helped her to her feet and brushed the bits of crushed ice from her damp skirts. Skating hand in hand, they found the log along the bank and removed their skates.

"Thank you for asking me to come," Irene said. "But I'm sorry I knocked you down."

Grinning at her, he replied, "I'm not."

Now that the magical evening was almost over, she was a little embarrassed at his reference to the kisses they'd shared. She wondered how she'd feel in the bright light of the morning.

He extended his hand and she took it; together they walked along the canal and across the bridge. His thoughts weren't far from the same vein as hers, wondering how it would be if they could spend nearly all of their time together. Only hers also wondered what others would think. Especially Clara and the superintendent.

At her back door, he took her by the shoulders and pulled her into his arms. After gazing long into her eyes, he leaned down and kissed her one last time, then backed away.

"Good night," he said.

"Good night," she replied, then turned to go.

Inside, she leaned against the door, holding the leftover warmth from being in his arms close to her heart for a little while longer. This night had been a moment in time she'd never forget, even if he left town.

And he very well could. Clara had warned her that men like Ross weren't the staying kind. And somewhere in her heart, she knew that was what she feared. What if he did go? Well, she certainly had no hold on him, just as she had no hold on Jonathan and Lydia. All she really had was her teaching and this town.

On another street, standing in an upstairs bedroom without benefit of lamp or candle and looking out the window through the bare trees was Clara Wilson. There was no mistaking the dark figure of a man leaving Irene's back door. Without a lamp burning in the whole Barrett house, what was a woman to think?

Chapter Seventeen

Clara Wilson whisked the simple black hat from her head and placed it on the peg inside the classroom door; beside it she hung her coat. Leaving the door to the hallway open, she briskly walked to the platform at the front of the room, intending not to miss the first opportunity of seeing Irene enter the building.

Today had not come soon enough.

She fiddled with her pen and ink bottle, always with one eye toward the hall, then organized her already neat desk.

With this new year she'd had hopes of a new beginning for Irene, but after what she'd seen a few nights earlier she just couldn't be sure of that now. Tapping a finger restlessly, she thought about that awful Ross Hollister, who was obviously trying to ruin Irene's life. On top of that, he seemed intent on flaunting in Clara's face the fact that she'd been misinformed about the incident concerning the bordello by continuing on with business as usual. It had been difficult to hold her eyes steady whenever she'd confronted any of the women from the meetings, but somehow she'd managed. Even so, there was no denying they had lost the battle, and the bitterness of that defeat lay like gall on her tongue.

Clara had purposely waited until today, being the first day of school, to present her advice, having decided against going to the younger woman's home. What she had to say was best said on the premises of Irene's vocation; perhaps then the warning would take better root. She certainly hoped so.

Out in the hall, the heavy entrance door opened, then clicked shut. Clara narrowed her gaze as she stared across her room to the dimly lit hallway, where the voices of Irene's charges echoed in the nearly empty building.

And that was another problem. The children. Couldn't Irene see that a woman of her position in the community and the school had an example to set? Granted, caring for an orphaned boy and girl was a commendable deed, but it was hardly up to Irene to carry that burden alone if there were any family members living. And she couldn't help wondering just how much effort had been made to locate that family.

"Irene!" she called, bustling to the doorway. "Irene!"

With her hand on her own classroom door, Irene stopped, a feeling of dread washing over her. Had Clara heard about Christmas dinner? Had Emma told her that too?

Speaking to Lydia, she said, "You may get the slates ready to pass around. I'll be right back."

Before even taking off her outer garments, she crossed the hall to Clara's room, trying to prepare herself for whatever advice was to come her way.

"Good morning, Clara," she said stiffly, meeting the older woman's gaze.

Clara motioned her inside, ignoring her standoffish demeanor, and closed the door behind her. "You know I don't hold much with beating around the bush, and time is limited anyway. So I'll just be plain-spoken."

Irene found herself bracing her back, much the way a cat does when it readies itself for a fight. Anticipating an attack on her dinner guest, she formulated her defense in her mind. After all, if she chose to invite whomever she wanted, that should be her business and hers alone. Whether the guest was an orphan or a store owner or even a saloon owner, that should be of no interest to anyone but herself. With her back sufficiently stiffened, she felt ready to do battle.

"I guess I'm at a loss as to how to begin," Clara said, clasping her hands together. "Except to say I'm disappointed in you, Irene. I never expected such behavior out of a lady like yourself."

"Disappointed?" she returned, bristling at Clara's choice of words at having Ross over for dinner. "I hardly think you should concern yourself with the company I choose to eat with."

Puzzled, Clara frowned at her. "I'm talking about two nights ago when I saw Mr. Hollister leave your back door." She paused for effect. "After midnight."

Completely taken by surprise, Irene stepped away from Clara.

"What?" Irene asked. Then she knew. Somehow Clara had seen Ross leave her back door after they'd been skating. Had she been spying on her? Well, she had no right! Nobody did!

"I couldn't believe you'd do such a thing," Clara went on. "I . . . I still can't believe it."

Finally finding her tongue, Irene asked, "And just what did you see that you can't believe?"

Shocked, Clara replied, "Must you force me to say it?"

Irene silently stood her ground.

Wishing that Irene had somehow brought forth a logical explanation for Mr. Hollister's presence, Clara let out a sigh of regret before going on, "If I saw you, then it's likely that others have seen you. What if this should get back to Mr. Walker?"

"Perhaps I should tell him to mind his own business! Really, Clara, what are you suggesting?"

"I'm not suggesting anything. I only know what I saw, and it looks as though you have put yourself in a very compromising position," Clara finished with her chin jutting stubbornly.

"Apparently, you and the people of this town have little faith in me." Irene had begun to see their attitudes in a new light. It wasn't her good name they were interested in; evidently they considered her to be of a weak character, unable to make sane, stable decisions.

"Faith has nothing to do with it when you're dealing with a man like Ross Hollister. He's the one who can't be trusted. And your future is at stake, not only as a teacher, but as a woman. People will talk and rumors will spread until Mr. Walker is certain to hear them."

If that happened, she would undoubtedly lose her position. Clara or Polly or a number of other women would gladly do their duty by informing the superintendent of her wayward ways.

"He isn't worth it, Irene. No man involved with drink is." In desperation, she added, "I know what can happen. It happened to me."

Irene had heard the gossip about Clara's first husband. It was no secret she'd been married twice, first to a canal man who had hauled her in and out of every canal town along the river. He died young and left her with a bitter heart, so they said. Then she'd married Thaddeus Wilson, and she'd seen to it that he was no imbiber. After his death, she went back to teaching, then made it her personal crusade to stop men, young or old, from drinking.

"I suppose you know about my Thaddeus. He was a kind man, but a drinking one. I chose not to see his only downfall, and it killed him. He drank quietly when I wasn't around, thinking I wouldn't know, but I did." She wrung her hands absently. "If I had stood up to his drinking, maybe I could have helped him and he would be alive to-

day." She looked up at Irene. "I only want to save you from
that kind of torment. A man who lives by drink can live
no other way."

Something inside Irene agreed with her. But was Ross
like that? She couldn't believe he was. Saloon keeping
wasn't the only thing he'd done in his life; it was a new
thing. Would he be willing to give it up? And did she have
the right to expect him to?

"I think you have the wrong impression, Clara. Mr. Hollister and I have never spoken of commitment. But even
so, I have to say in his defense that he isn't a bad person.
I think you as well as the others have misjudged him."
Whether anyone approved or not, she had opinions of her
own and she intended to voice them.

"I'm sorry you feel that way. I had hoped to turn you
from a path similar to the one I trod, but I see that isn't
possible, so let me give you something else to consider. If
you allow yourself to become . . . entangled . . . with this
man, you will be setting yourself up for a fall when he
decides to be on his way again. And mark my words, when
the spring thaw comes, he will be on his way. That kind
always are." With that, she turned away from Irene, dis-
missing her.

Feeling more subdued than she'd anticipated when the
confrontation began, Irene returned to her classroom. Clara's words settled in her heart, pricking her conscience.
There was truth in what she'd said, but did it apply to
Ross? Then she thought about his leaving in the spring,
and she felt sure he would go. Without a doubt he had
other ventures that would need tending to, and she could
hardly expect to be more than a diversion to him while he
was here.

As her day progressed, Irene considered more of Clara's
warnings than she wanted to. There was no doubting that
Ross had no roots or that he would likely be moving on.
For the first time in her life, she was glad spring was a long
time away.

* * *

Ross sat opposite Howard in the small room that served as the mercantile office. Obviously, it lacked the organization of a woman's touch.

"So you want me to sell you the cabin?" Howard leaned forward in his chair. "May I ask what prompted this idea?" he asked, grinning.

"Well, I'm not sure myself except that's where I spent the best years of my childhood," Ross answered with a shrug. "But I didn't exactly want to buy it."

Howard raised his eyebrows in surprise. "I'm supposed to give it to you?"

Laughing, Ross shook his head. "No, I didn't mean that either. I'd like to trade the Broken Keg."

With mild surprise on his face, Howard replied, "Emma would divorce me with Clara's blessings." Relaxing back in his chair, he replied, "Sorry, Ross."

"Well, I thought maybe you could abolish the saloon and get on the good side of every woman in town, then expand your mercantile or use it for storage." With a wicked half smile, he added, "I'm sure you'd be Clara's hero then."

"Becoming Clara Wilson's hero isn't the quest of my life. But staying out of her path is." He tapped a finger on a pile of papers. "Let me think about it. I could use the storage space and being right on the canal couldn't hurt anything." Then, considering the other side of the deal, he said, "You realize that the cabin and the barn are in pretty bad shape, don't you?"

Nodding his head, Ross answered, "Yep, but not beyond repair."

"Somehow, I feel as though I'd be getting the best part of the bargain," Howard said.

"Just what I like, a man who thinks he's taking advantage of a friend." He smiled.

"Well, I wouldn't go that far. There is a lot of land that goes with the cabin. Of course, I know it hasn't been farmed in years and the woods have taken over most of it."

"Sounds to me like it could be an even-up trade," Ross said.

Howard nodded, "Could be."

"I'm sure one of the other saloons would be glad to buy the supplies—that is, what's left of them."

Leveling Ross a hard look, Howard said, "How would you live? I mean, you need food and a place to stay, and that cabin sure isn't livable."

"I've got that partner in Black Hawk who's itching to buy me out. So I thought come spring I'd head on back to settle up. In the meantime, I've got enough set by to tide me over. And I thought maybe you'd let me continue living over the saloon. I'd be glad to trade some work for the cost of rent."

Howard eyed him thoughtfully. "Sounds to me as though you've been thinking about this for some time. Any reason in particular?" he prodded.

"Not any I care to discuss," he answered with a grin, tipping his hat back on his head.

"Okay, okay. Just thought I'd ask." Then, considering another tactic, he said, "You know, Emma has a pretty lively imagination. She'll be doing some wondering on her own and probably come to a few conclusions, too." He raised a hand in a helpless gesture. "Hard to say how far it could get around town."

"Well, if you're worried about it," Ross replied, "don't tell her until the deal is done."

Smiling and nodding, Howard said, "Okay, okay. I guess you'll tell when you're ready."

Ross simply smiled in return.

Later that evening in his room over the saloon, Ross stretched out on the bed. Listening to the crackling fire in the nearby stove, he considered what moves he'd have to make to settle up with Jeff concerning the mine. He didn't see how he could make this transaction over the distance of so many miles. No, he decided, this would mean a trip west, but that could wait until spring, after the crops were in. In the meantime, he'd write to Jeff and let him know what he intended to do.

A round of laughter from below interrupted his thoughts, bringing him back to the present. He was sure Howard would take him up on the deal and that gave him a satisfied feeling. Being in the saloon business wasn't for him, any more than mining had been. Those years in prison had taught him lessons about enjoying life and appreciating even the simplest things—especially freedom.

The freedom to choose what time you got up and what time you went to bed, to choose to go outdoors or to come in, and to choose to live life to the fullest. It was that very thing he most wanted Irene to understand. Her prison had been built by her friends and family, but she had the right to choose to unlock that door and free herself.

For Ross, freedom was beginning to take shape in the form of Tilly's small farm. There he could spend all of his time doing exactly what he wanted to do, with plenty of fresh air and sunshine and enough hard work to make a man tired to the bone. But all of it would be satisfying. Very satisfying.

First he would have the job of clearing the land and fixing the barn for animals. It would be a grueling task, but he looked forward to it. He'd need some horses and a wagon to begin with, then some supplies for rebuilding the barn. The cabin would need a little restoring before he could move in, but that would be temporary since he intended to build a big white farmhouse with a big front porch.

Downstairs, the sounds of the revelers subsided and finally quieted as the last of the customers wound up the night and headed for home. He heard the door shut for the last time as Ben closed up. Outside his only window, layers of large flakes of snow built up along the wooden edges of the panes suggesting that a new, heavy wet snow would blanket the old by morning.

Ross threw a couple of chunks of wood into the stove then undressed for bed. It felt good to be putting down roots, real roots, and making plans for a future. No, he told himself, it felt more than good, it felt great.

With her eyes closed, Irene relived once more that magical night on the ice. How wonderfully free she'd felt! Free to be herself without the imposed restrictions of her mother, her neighbors, and even the old pain of Andrew's betrayal.

Andrew, who had held her in reserve while he pursued at least one other woman, who would never have lain on the ice with her or kissed her with such honest abandon. No, the Andrew she knew would have clicked his tongue at her unbecoming behavior while his own he kept hidden.

But Ross encouraged her with his humor, his unexpected arrivals and—she warmed at the thought—his touch. He more than encouraged her, he filled her with hope. She enjoyed his unabashed approach to life that seemed so daring and exciting in contrast to her own.

Only during the night, when she was alone in her room like this, did she dare review these events, taking them out one by one, examining each and testing her feelings about them. She knew she must be honest with herself before she could be honest with anyone else. And to do that, she had to think and re-think not only with her mind but also with these wonderful new emotions.

Logic told her that a relationship of any kind with a man of Ross's background was unthinkable and out of the question. But, her emotions countered, that was Clara's way of thinking and she should try harder to think for herself. Considering another angle, logic pointed out that tempting herself with emotions that were unfamiliar could lead to dangerous situations. But she cast that thought aside, realizing that Andrew had instilled that fear within her to keep her in safe bounds.

Finally, she decided that there was no clear-cut right or

wrong, good or bad, black or white, just gray areas in between holding her transfixed, as if she were seeing them for the first time in her life. Ross, with his kind heart, loving touches, and warm kisses was definitely a gray area. She could see no bad in him, although she did not believe in saloons or the havoc they wreaked in people's lives.

Well, she didn't have to be logical tonight. She would allow her emotions full swing and simply savor the aftereffects of Ross's presence. After all, it had been a magical winter night, and spring was a long time off.

Lydia lay wide awake listening to Jonathan's soft, even breathing coming from the cot along the wall. She wished she could sleep so soundly, but she hadn't been able to do that for weeks. Each night she worried if the next day would be the day another letter would arrive from her aunt; then all her lies would be exposed and her dreams shattered.

Turning her head, she stared at the window where fat wet flakes of snow brushed against the pane. She loved the snow and the fresh whiteness it brought to everything, covering the bare limbs and dead grass.

She snuggled beneath the covers, dreading the thought of having to leave this house and Miss Barrett. How she'd grown to love Grand Rapids! And of course, there were her friends at the school whom she would miss and all the wonderful things they liked to do. She thought about spring so far away and wished with all her heart that she would be here then to see the river free of ice once more. She wondered what sort of flowers bloomed along the banks, what sort of berries she could gather—that was, if she still lived here in the spring.

A small tear leaked from the corner of her eye and stained the perfectly ironed pillow slip beneath her head. How she wished spring would hurry up so she wouldn't have to wonder about all these things before her aunt came to take her away.

Chapter Eighteen

Even for late January, the morning had a bone-chilling coldness to it. Frost covered the window panes in every room of the house so that it was nearly impossible to see anything but the daylight that shone through.

Jonathan sat at the breakfast table with his cheek barely propped up with one fist.

"Eat your eggs, Jonathan," Irene said, pouring milk into his glass.

His only answer was a cough and a wheeze.

The ominous sound of a cold made Irene look closer at him. "Are you feeling all right?" she asked, laying her hand on his forehead.

"He coughed like that all night," Lydia said.

"Hmm. And he's feverish, too," Irene said thoughtfully.

Winnie left her post at the hot stove to check his condition for herself. "No doubt about it," she said, heading for the pantry. "I'll make the honey and garlic."

"Don't want any," Jonathan spoke up, then started to cough.

"I'd say it's too late to say no," Winnie called over her shoulder, gathering the paraphernalia for her favorite medicinal concoction. "Little boys who take off their mittens to make snowballs should think about what will happen if they go bare-handed. And by the way, where is your scarf?"

"Don't know."

"Well, I'll make you another one," she said standing beside him. "Now open up." She held the spoonful of medicine ready.

"Don't want any," he repeated.

Lydia patted his hand sympathetically, secretly glad she didn't have to swallow the awful-smelling stuff. "She only wants to make you better."

"No." He sat staring straight ahead, with his hand still holding up his head, not budging an inch.

"It doesn't really taste so bad," Lydia whispered to him. "I was only joking when I told you that."

He turned to look at her. "Then you take it."

Lydia glanced at Winnie, who turned expectantly toward her. Swallowing hard, Lydia replied, "All right, I will. If you promise to take it, too."

Jonathan stared at his sister, thinking hard. If she could do it, he could do it. He nodded.

As the saliva ran inside her mouth, Lydia bravely opened up to the spoon, forcing herself not to flinch as it slid down her throat.

With admiring eyes, Jonathan watched her face. If she could do it, he could do it, he told himself again. So he opened his mouth to take the pungent dose. Unwillingly, his eyes squeezed shut and his teeth gritted together.

"Ugh!" he groaned.

"You'll get used to it," Winnie said.

But he seriously doubted it.

Irene pulled him gently from his chair, feeling his face once more. "No school today for you. Let's get you back to bed."

This time he offered no resistance, but followed docilely alongside her. At one time he would have loved getting out of school, even if it meant taking that horrible medicine, but he liked school pretty good now and kind of hated missing it.

"Will you tell Danny that I'm sick?" he asked her as she tucked him into Lydia's bed.

"Yes. I'm sure he'll miss playing with you at recess."

"Will he be able to come over and see me after school?"

She pulled the covers up to his chin. "Well, I'm not sure that's such a good idea. What if he catches your cold and then has to miss school just when you're getting better?"

"Oh. Yeah, I didn't think of that. Just tell him to send a note instead."

"I will," she answered, brushing his thick brown hair back from his face.

"Miss Barrett?"

"Hmm?"

"I never told you this, but I like living in your house. A lot." He tried to smile, but he was too tired and hot. "I think you're a pretty good teacher, too." His eyes drifted shut.

"Thank you, Jonathan. That means a lot to me," she said softly. Frowning at the flush on his cheeks, she laid her hand against their bright pinkness. It's probably just a cold, she told herself, nothing to worry about. All children come down with one at least once during the winter. Still, she wouldn't rest easy until that fever was gone.

Downstairs, Lydia wiped the last dish as Irene walked into the kitchen. "How is he?"

Irene could see the concern on her face and forced herself to sound positive. "It's just a cold, I'm sure. A day in bed will make all the difference."

"Jonathan never gets sick," Lydia said. "But when he does . . . Well, he always worried Mama."

It was the first reference Lydia had made to her mother, and for some reason it gave Irene an odd catch in her chest, a sort of prick almost like a wound. But she forced the feeling aside.

"We'll check on him at noon," she said. "He'll be all right with Mother to look after him."

Lydia nodded and pulled on her coat.

All morning, neither of them could help thinking about Jonathan, wondering if he was better and maybe even giving Winnie a hard time. At least they hoped that was how it was.

At noon they hurried home to see for themselves.

Winnie met them at the back door. "Irene, I think we should get the doctor. That child is burning up, and nothing I do seems to help." She wrung her hands. "I wish I had my bag of herbs."

Irene pulled off her coat and hung it over a chair. Turning to Lydia, she said calmly, "You know where Doctor Stephens' office is, don't you?"

Wide-eyed, Lydia nodded.

"If he isn't there, you know where his house is, right?" She nodded again.

"Good girl." Irene smiled reassuringly. "Everything is going to be all right. We'll just have the doctor take a look at him and make sure it's only a cold."

"Irene," Winnie began, "I think that boy has pneumonia." She wrung her hands again.

Without a word, Lydia dashed out the back door.

Fear clutched Irene's heart. Pneumonia. Children died from pneumonia, and there was so little they could do to stop it.

"We don't know that, Mother," she replied, forcing herself to remain calm. "We'll wait for the doctor to decide." With that, she turned and went upstairs, a prayer forming on her lips.

Lydia ran as fast as the snowy streets would allow her. The bursts of her frosty breaths could not keep up and trailed behind, only to disappear.

"Oh, please," she whispered, hoping God would hear. "Don't let Jonathan die." He was all she had left. *Don't let me lose him, too!*

She tried not to remember how feverish her mother had been or how bad she'd coughed. She tried to think only about how fast she must run to get the doctor and concentrated on not falling down and delaying her mission. Hurry, hurry, she told herself.

With her head more down than up, she didn't see the man who had just come out of the livery stable, and with a solid thump she slammed into his chest.

"Oh!" she cried.

"Whoa there!" he said, grabbing her by the shoulders. "Lydia! Is that you?"

"Ross?" She looked at his familiar, kind face and, like a dam bursting with the pressure, she released a torrent of tears.

"What's wrong? Tell me," he insisted, peering into her tear-streaked face. "Is it Irene? Jonathan?"

Nodding her head she said, "He's sick. I'm—I'm going for the doctor." She tried to get a hold of herself, but she was so afraid. Mama had died of pneumonia, and she just couldn't lose Jonathan, too!

Ross's instant relief that nothing was wrong with Irene was quickly replaced with worry for Jonathan.

"I'll go with you."

They found Doc Stephens at home having lunch. In a matter of minutes he had his coat on, tucking his scarf around his throat. When they arrived at the back door, they were greeted by a very nervous Winnie.

"Oh, I'm so glad Lydia found you, Doctor," Winnie said. "Hello, Mr. Hollister." She took their coats. "I was just making some tea for Irene. Would you like some later?"

Both men declined.

"Follow me," she said and led the way up to the room where Jonathan lay in a feverish sleep.

Irene heard them coming and was relieved that Lydia

had found the doctor home. Sitting on the edge of the bed, she smoothed the covers under Jonathan's chin, then touched his hot, dry cheek. He looked so small in the big bed with its thick comforter—so vulnerable, too. Rising, she turned to speak her thankfulness when she saw Ross standing there beside the doctor.

Her first instinct was to go to him and wrap her arms around him for comfort, but of course she didn't. Instead, she allowed a measure of relief to wash over her at just having him near at a time when she needed his comfort.

Without saying a word, she stepped aside and Doctor Stephens took her place. He laid a hand on Jonathan's brow, then pulled back the covers. Jonathan flinched at the sudden cold but didn't open his eyes. While the doctor checked him over, Irene stood with the others in tense silence.

Ross moved to stand beside her, his hand slipping into hers, gripping it with reassurance. She didn't dare look at him for fear of dissolving into tears, but she was grateful he'd come, so very grateful.

At the foot of the bed, Winnie stood with an arm around Lydia's shoulders.

Turning from his patient, the doctor scanned the worried faces surrounding him. "He's a very sick boy, which you already knew or you wouldn't have sent for me." He took a bottle of medicine from his bag. "I have no doubt he's come down with pneumonia."

Lydia's body went rigid, and she forced herself not to burst into tears again. Later, she promised herself, later when she was alone.

"But," the doctor went on, "he's young and strong, and with the proper care as well as a few prayers—well, I think he's got a good chance of throwing a few more snowballs before winter is over. Now I'm not saying this isn't serious—it is. Very serious. But like I said, with the proper care, which should come easily in this household"—he smiled at Winnie, Irene, and Lydia—"he should improve.

I'll leave this medicine for you to give to him. Whether he likes it or not, understand?"

They all nodded.

"Good. Now, I believe I'll have that tea, Mrs. Barrett. It smelled like mint. Am I right?" With a twinkle in his blue eyes, he added, "Did you know that mint is wonderful for a cold?"

With one last look of concern toward Jonathan, Winnie led the doctor out of the room. "Yes, I've always believed in the powers of the plant. Doctor, perhaps you could tell me if you've used garlic and honey as a tonic and what results have you had?"

Their voices slowly ebbed until their words were indistinguishable.

"Is he going to— Lydia sniffled and wiped at her nose. "Is he?" She moved to the bedside, wanting to be closer to her brother.

"Whatever we have to do to help him get better, we'll do," Irene told her.

"I'll stay up all night with him," Lydia promised.

"We'll take turns," Irene replied. With a catch in her throat, she watched as Lydia crawled up on the bed, tucking her feet under her.

Ross leaned over the sleeping boy and brushed the hair from his face. Then, leading Irene by the hand toward the door, he stepped into the hall and pulled her into his arms. She went willingly, allowing him to cradle her while he rubbed her shoulders and felt the tension in her back.

"He'll be all right," he whispered into her hair. "You'll see."

With her eyes closed, she accepted his soothing ministrations. How wonderful to be held so securely by his strong arms, to share her emotions in this unspoken way.

"I'll stay if you want me to," he offered, hoping she'd take him up on it but not wanting to push.

Oh, yes, she did want him to stay! To stay forever like this, holding her, helping her keep strong for Lydia and

245

Jonathan! But she knew she couldn't expect that of him, even though for once she didn't give a tinker's damn what the people of this town thought.

Pulling away, she looked up at him. "Thank you, but I'll be all right, and there are three of us to look after him."

"I'll stop by again later. If that's okay with you."

Smiling, she nodded. "That would be fine. Maybe by then he'll be a little better." She knew that was wishful thinking, but at least it was positive thinking.

Grasping her by the shoulders, he bent and kissed her forehead, lingering over the scent of her closeness. "If you need anything, anything at all, will you promise to send Lydia for me?"

She nodded, her forehead rolling against his chin. "I promise."

He backed away then, slowly dropping his arms to his sides, hating to let her go. "If you need anything . . ."

"I promise," she repeated.

He nodded, then turned to go.

Irene went back to stand beside the bed, where she could hear Jonathan's labored breathing. How could he have gotten so bad so quickly? she wondered. Had he been sick for a while and she just didn't notice since she was so wrapped up in her own emotions?

She pulled up a chair and sat close to the bed. She might be a teacher, and a good one too, but she wasn't a mother. Maybe she didn't have the instinct for it. Surely, if she did, Jonathan wouldn't be so sick right now.

Before he left, she asked Doctor Stephens to drop by the school to say that she wouldn't be in for the remainder of the day. Her class would have to be incorporated into Clara's, which would please neither Clara nor Irene's students, but there was simply nothing else she could do. Perhaps by tomorrow Jonathan would show some sign of improvement. She prayed so.

For the rest of the day, Lydia and Irene kept their vigil, bathing Jonathan's hot forehead with cool cloths. Winnie prepared chicken broth and made bread, occasionally leaving her duties to check on Jonathan or bring a cup of tea for Irene and warm milk for Lydia.

Later Winnie came quietly into the room, lit a lamp, and slipped an extra shawl around Irene's shoulders, then coaxed Lydia off the bed. "You need to get some rest," she said softly to the girl. "We don't want you coming down with it, too."

"I'd rather stay here," she insisted.

"Mother's right," Irene said. "I want you to put on a warm gown and climb into my bed. If there's any change, I promise to wake you." Irene tucked a wisp of hair behind Lydia's ear. "All right?"

"I won't sleep. I know I won't," she replied reluctantly.

"Well, at least try to rest. And stay warm."

"I don't have to go to school tomorrow, do I?"

"Of course not. I'll be staying home, too."

"All right," Lydia said, giving in. "But if you want me to sit up while you sleep, I will."

"We'll all take turns," Winnie said. "So come along."

With a backward glance, Lydia followed Winnie out of the room.

Irene watched Jonathan's shallow breathing, herself taking deeper breaths in an attempt to help him. Glancing at the clock on the nightstand, she saw that the next dose of medicine wasn't due for another thirty minutes. She wished the time would hurry. Anxiety forced her to touch his fevered brow for the tenth time in twice as many minutes. She wrung out the cloth in the washbasin and applied it. If only he was well enough to run, slam the back door, shout for Lydia, even pout and complain about having to go to school. If only . . .

"It's nearly time for his medicine," Winnie spoke softly from behind Irene.

"I know. If only it would take hold quickly."

"I'm keeping the fires going downstairs so that it won't be nearly so cold in here."

Irene nodded while she bathed his bright pink cheeks again.

"Mother, if anything happens to him . . ." Her throat closed, choking off the unbearable words.

"Now we won't think such things," Winnie said, patting her shoulder in understanding. "He's a strong boy, and we'll do whatever it takes to see to it that he gets well."

Another glance at the clock said it was time for Jonathan's medicine. Irene sat on the edge of the bed, supporting his head and shoulders in a raised position while Winnie spooned the proper dosage into him. He coughed a little and opened his too-bright eyes, then lay back on the pillow.

"Are you thirsty?" Irene asked.

He nodded.

She poured a glass from the pitcher on the table and held it for him to drink. Then he closed his eyes and drifted off.

"I know it's good for him to sleep," Irene said.

"Best thing for him."

"But I'm concerned when I can't talk to him."

"I know just what you mean," Winnie said. "When Janie had pneumonia, I had the hardest time keeping myself from waking her up every few minutes just to ask how she was feeling. Of course, your father was there and he was a great help, assuring me that she would be fine and to let her rest. I did, and she was. Jonathan will be fine, too." She rested her hand on her daughter's arm.

"Thanks, Mother," she replied, squeezing her mother's hand. "I'd forgotten Janie was so ill when she was young. You'd certainly never know it now." She smiled, thinking of her younger sister.

"Why don't you go down and make us a pot of mint tea while I sit here for a while," Winnie suggested. "You probably need to straighten out a few of your muscles before you get cramped."

"All right." Irene left the room, stopping downstairs in

the parlor to add another chunk of wood to the fire. In the kitchen she put on the kettle and prepared the tea for the teapot. It was going to be a long night and probably the first of many.

Carrying the tray upstairs, she wondered what she would do about her students at school. She couldn't continue having Clara crowd them into her room. The only thing she could do was to contact Mr. Walker; perhaps he could take over for her as he'd done for one of the other teachers. Hopefully it would only be for a few days. Surely Jonathan would be showing some signs of improving by then. She prayed he would.

She placed the tea tray on the stand and poured two cups.

"That smells wonderful," Winnie said, accepting the cup Irene offered her. "You know, I think Dr. Stephens is a very modern man. He's so open-minded that you just can't help but trust him."

"That's because he didn't disapprove of your herbal remedies."

"That, too. And he doesn't seem to have the gloomy approach so many doctors have. I like him."

"I think Jonathan will like him, too." Irene pulled up another chair alongside her mother's.

"Before this is all said and done, Jonathan will undoubtedly have Dr. Stephens promising to take him fishing in the spring," Winnie said, with a bit of hopefulness in her voice.

As he had Ross, Irene thought, which brought another problem to mind.

"Mother," Irene began, feeling as though she needed to clear the air between them on this subject, "I've decided not to participate in the temperance meetings anymore."

Setting her cup down in the saucer on her lap, Winnie stared at her daughter with relief. "You don't know how glad I am to hear you say that."

"Clara will be furious."

"Let her."

"I have to make my own choices."

"You certainly have that right. Everybody does."

Irene knew there was more to be said, but not now. Not when she was so worried about Jonathan. She set aside her half-empty cup and leaned over the bed.

"He seems to be sleeping soundly," Irene whispered, noticing his even, although shallow, breathing.

"It's the medicine."

He looked so small and vulnerable tucked beneath the comforter that way. Even his hands were hidden from view.

"Have you heard anything from the children's aunt?" Winnie asked.

"No, nothing. I suppose I should send another letter. Maybe I'm not sending it to the right place. Lydia wasn't sure of the woman's location. Anything could have happened to the ones I've sent."

"Yes, I suppose you should." Her feelings weren't as set about that as they once had been.

Jonathan coughed, a dry, wheezing sound, and both women turned their attention to him. Irene looked at the clock, wishing the time away until they could give him more medicine.

Winnie laid her hand on his forehead. "I believe I'll go down and check the fires," she said, gathering up the cups.

When she'd gone, Irene took her place beside the bed, pulling the shawl she wore closer to her. Although the room was chilled, it wasn't cold and she knew Jonathan was plenty warm beneath the comforter even without the fever. She supposed it was her nervousness that caused her to shiver.

She glanced at the clock again. Eleven-thirty and she wasn't the least bit sleepy—tired and tense maybe, but not sleepy.

The creak of a stair tread was common enough, but this time it was louder than usual, making Irene turn to see who it was. Within a few seconds, Ross stood at the door. Her heart quickened at the sight of him.

"Your mother said it was all right to come up. How is he?"

Rising from her seat, she faced him. "The same, I think." She took a step away from the bed. "What do you think?"

He quietly crossed the room to stand beside her and stared down at the motionless boy, who had never been motionless during the whole time Ross had known him.

"No change. Yet." He turned his gaze to her. "He'll be better tomorrow. You'll see."

It helped hearing him say that, and it gave her more than hope; it gave her a little peace. Something about his presence did that to her; she'd sensed it—no, felt it—before. When they were on the adventure in the woods, she'd had a feeling of security and solidity just being with him. And again, when they'd gone ice-skating alone, she'd felt free, but even better than that she'd felt protected, cared for in a way she'd never experienced with Andrew.

"Has he complained about the medicine yet?" he asked, leaning down to touch Jonathan's face.

"No. He hardly seems aware that we're giving it to him."

Then he turned to her. "How are you holding up?"

"Me? I'm all right. I'm just worried. I can't seem to help it. I only want him to get better. Soon."

To her surprise, he gathered her in his arms and held her. She tucked her head beneath his chin, closing her eyes, then relaxed against him. Under other circumstances she would have reveled in the feel of him, the smell of him. But now she simply welcomed his strength and support. They stayed like that for several long minutes with the quiet thud of his heart soft and steady in her ear.

Irene was the first to break the pose.

"He'd be so glad to know you're here," she said, reluctantly moving away. "You know he talks about you all the time."

251

Ross smiled. "I'll bet that gets kind of old after a little while."

She smiled back, apologetically. "Well, I'll admit I was a little jealous."

"You have no need to be. He likes it here and he likes you."

Nodding, she replied, "He said the same thing today. He even said I was a good teacher."

"I'd be willing to bet you're the best," he said, softly. "If you had been my teacher, I might not have skipped out to go fishing so often."

"That's very nice of you to say that."

"I mean it," he replied with an earnestness that made her look at him. "And a whole lot more."

His gray-blue eyes had the warmth of a summer sky, and she felt as drawn to him as any flower would be to the sun. The intensity of his gaze held her transfixed while she tried to discern his thoughts. Neither moved nor spoke.

Winnie stood in the doorway, knowing they were unaware of her presence. She sensed rather than saw what was transpiring between them, and being uneasy with it she rustled her skirts and cleared her throat to break the spell. She had enough worrying on her hands with Jonathan, and this was the last thing she intended to get into with Irene. At least for now it was.

"Any improvement?" she asked, as though she hadn't witnessed anything out of the ordinary.

"No," Irene replied, turning to Jonathan once more.

Winnie took the chair Irene had vacated, pulling her shawl around her and settling in like a brood hen.

Unable to miss the message she was sending him, Ross stepped away from the bed and Irene. "I guess I'll be going. You need your rest."

"I'll walk you out," Irene offered, leading the way toward the door.

When they were downstairs in the kitchen, Irene turned to Ross.

252

"I should apologize for Mother."

"No, that's all right. At least she's straightforward in her own way." He grinned.

"Well, would you like a cup of coffee before you go?" she asked. "I haven't exactly had a lot of practice at making it, but if you're willing to let me experiment on you, I'll give it another try."

"Sounds good," he replied. "I'll give you a hand."

She got out the beans and the little grinder, while he offered suggestions on the length of time to grind them and how much to put into the pot.

"That much is easy to remember," she said. "It's the boiling time I'm not sure about."

He stood beside the stove, enjoying the warmth of her company. "Well, there's no doubt about it, time is important." The time he'd been spending with her had come to be very important.

She walked around the table in the soft glow of the lamp to the cupboard, from which she removed a stoneware mug. Smiling, she lifted the mug and said, "I thought you might be more comfortable drinking from this instead of a china cup."

He knew immediately that she'd bought it just for him and couldn't help being pleased. Grinning sheepishly, he replied, "Did I look that obvious?"

"No, not really. I just suspected it." Turning her attention toward the boiling pot, she asked, "Is that long enough?"

Ross nodded, so she pushed it to the cooler part of the stove. The pleasant aroma filled the room. It would be so easy to get used to this, he thought. But what would her reaction be if he told her about his past? Would she be so willing to serve him coffee if she knew the truth about him? Not likely, he decided. His being a saloon owner had been a big enough obstacle to overcome, and he wasn't sure it had actually been overcome so much as temporarily overlooked. No, if he told her now, it would break these new-found feelings and he didn't want that to happen—not yet, maybe not ever.

As he took the filled mug from her hand, their eyes met through the steamy vapors. He held her gaze as long as she let him, until finally she drew away and seated herself at the table.

"I hope there'll be a change for the better by morning," she said, returning to what was uppermost in their minds. "If only the medicine would take effect."

He pulled out a chair and sat across from her. "He's a tough little fellow. You can't deny that."

"And thank goodness for it."

After that they sat in silence; everything seemingly had been said, and neither could think of anything else to say.

Ross took a sip of his coffee while he continued to watch her. Unaware, she thoughtfully traced an ironed crease in the table cloth.

"Well, I'm keeping you from Jonathan," he said, gulping down the last of it.

"Mother would let me know immediately if there was a change."

"I'd better be going anyway." He rose and took his hat from the peg where he usually hung it. "Remember, if you need anything, just send for me."

"I will," Irene replied.

"I'll drop by sometime tomorrow."

She nodded. "Good night. And thank you for coming by."

"Good night," he said. Then he was gone. But his presence lingered, giving Irene a measure of comfort.

Once upstairs, she went directly to Jonathan's bedside.

"I'll take the first watch," Winnie said. "I'll wake you when I need some rest."

"Are you sure?"

"Positive."

"Well, I guess I am tired." She leaned down and kissed her mother's cheek. "Good night."

Irene undressed in the dark and climbed in beside Lydia, who stirred, then became wide awake.

"How's Jonathan?" she asked.

"The same, dear. Go back to sleep."

"I don't think I can. Is Mrs. Barrett with him?"

"Yes."

"I think I'll sit up with her a while," she said, scooting from the bed.

"Take a blanket to keep yourself warm."

"I will."

Alone, Irene closed her eyes. It was important that she get some rest, she told herself, if she was going to be any help to Jonathan or her mother. And after only a few minutes, she drifted off.

The next few days were a repetition of the first except that those who watched over Jonathan and cared for him had become more quiet and somber-eyed. At Winnie's suggestion, they began a process of patting Jonathan's back after he'd been roused for his medicine in an attempt to help "loosen his lungs." She said it was what she'd done for Janie, and she didn't see how it could hurt anything. It had made good sense then, and it made good sense now. Neither Irene nor the doctor disagreed.

Ross came to call, sometimes twice a day, and Dr. Stephens stopped by every morning, but he could only tell them what they could already see: there was no improvement.

Then, on the evening of the fourth day, Jonathan's fever dropped and the tight cough gave way to a loose, productive one.

Irene stood at the stove, stirring a pot of vegetable soup. She and her mother agreed that it was important to keep nourishing food in Jonathan's body. Surprisingly, they had agreed on several things lately. She ladled a small amount into a dish just as Lydia burst into the room.

"It's down!" she all but shouted at Irene. "The fever broke!"

Quickly setting aside the dish, Irene replied, "Thank God," and hurried along behind Lydia, who had already turned and dashed from the room.

Upstairs, Irene rushed to the bedside, where Winnie was sitting holding Jonathan's hand.

Leaning over, she pressed her lips against his now cool forehead, saying a silent prayer of thanks. Moving away, she said to him, "How are you feeling?"

"I'm hungry," he said, his voice weak.

"Well, what would you like?" she asked, willing to give him just about anything.

"Something besides soup," he replied.

Irene and Lydia laughed, and even Winnie couldn't help smiling.

"How about soup for now with some biscuits, and tomorrow we'll make something you can sink your teeth into?"

He nodded. "I'm too tired to chew much anyway."

"I'll be right back," she said, touching his face once more just to feel its coolness.

As she was leaving the room, she heard Lydia say, "Oh, Jonathan, you gave us a real scare. I'm so glad you're getting better."

And she agreed. Never had she felt such a depth of fear. She'd fought against the sickening worry that gripped her heart, knowing deep inside that this child could be taken from her. It was too easy to believe in the worst, and she'd tried so hard not to, harder than she'd even realized until now. As she descended the stairs, her legs shook with her relief.

By the time she got to the kitchen, the previous days of worry took their toll, and standing in the doorway she leaned her forehead against the framework. Unable to stem the tide, she allowed the tears to flow. What would she have done if something, the unthinkable, had happened? Thank God, oh, thank God, he was beginning to improve!

A knock at the back door escaped her awareness, so wrapped up was she in the overwhelming release. When the door opened, she wasn't startled, but glad to see Ross's face. Quietly, she walked toward him.

"What is it? Has he gotten worse?" Tension showed in the lines around his mouth. The worry had gotten the best of him, too.

"No," she said, and walked into his waiting arms. The comfort and security of his embrace cushioned her tumultuous feelings and eased the anxiety that had built up within her for so long. Even longer than Jonathan's illness, she now realized.

"What then?"

Without raising her head she spoke into the coolness of his jacket, "The fever broke."

Barely intelligible, her words caused his eyes to close in thankfulness. "I was beginning to worry that maybe he wouldn't make it." Tightening his hold on her, he rubbed the tenseness out of her back and shoulders.

"I know," she said, the tears once more flowing. It felt so wonderful to have his strong arms hold her like this. So wonderful.

"I've been worried about you, too," he said, kissing the soft curling hair at her temples.

She lifted her face to his, needing more than just being held and stroked. He lowered his lips and gently touched hers. The warmth of his kiss spread like warm honey in the sunshine. Then he deepened the kiss, igniting her from within, and a desire such as she'd never experienced overtook her. It carried her to a peak that she could not seem to climb, nor could she leave it. Her arms stole around his neck and she felt the pressure of his body against hers, molding and melding. A small groan emanated from him, sending shivers down her spine, a chill which soon warmed and heated in her rising passion. Never had she been brought to this height before, and never was the soonest she wanted to leave it.

Breaking their bond, Ross traced the line of her jaw to the tender spot at the curve of her neck. His breathing was as erratic as hers, and he wondered who would have the will to bring them under control. She was a treasure, and he feared that if he let her go he might not be allowed to sample it again. If she knew his past, the truth . . .

"Irene," he said, suddenly able to get a grip on his escalating emotions with the sobering thought that she really knew nothing about him.

She lay limp in his arms, relaxed to the point of wilting. "Hmm?" she responded.

"If your mother should see us . . ."

"She'd see two adults doing what adults do."

"She'd be very angry with me."

"I'd tell her it was my idea."

"Then she'd be angry with you."

"I don't care," she said with emphasis, smiling. And she meant it.

He kissed her lightly. "I don't want to be the cause of any more trouble between you and your mother. Especially not now, with this good news about Jonathan."

"It is wonderful, isn't it?" she replied, moving back in the circle of his arms. "Do you want to go up and see him?"

"You don't have to ask twice," he said, following her.

Inside the bedroom, Lydia was telling Jonathan about all the friends who had asked about him. Her chatter could be heard to the foot of the stairs. When Ross entered with Irene, she turned happily to him to give the same good news he'd already heard.

"Hello, pal," he said to Jonathan, who still looked peaked.

"I'm feeling a little better today, Ross," he said, but looked as though he wished he felt a whole lot better. A sudden coughing spasm gripped him.

Winnie jumped to his aid, as did Lydia. When he was

comfortable again, he smiled weakly at everyone.

"Well, I've been thinking," Ross began, "maybe when the weather warms up and you're feeling like your old self, we could take a picnic out to a little rocky creek just east of here. What do you say?"

With drooping eyes, he nodded. "I'd like that." Then he closed his eyes, thinking about how nice it would be when the sun warmed everything up and he could spend some time at the river. A picnic would be nice; then everyone could go and have fun. Even Mrs. Barrett.

Chapter Nineteen

On an unusually warm late-March day, Ross rested with his weight braced against the handle of the axe he'd been swinging all morning. Mopping his brow, he squinted across the now-open barnyard. Gone was the brush that had crowded the barn, as well as several good-sized trees that had threatened its stone foundation.

An immeasurable amount of satisfaction filled him as he surveyed the work he'd accomplished over the last two months. He didn't know whether to attribute it to being on the farm where he'd spent the best years of his youth or whether it was simply the freedom.

The freedom to do as he pleased when he pleased and how he pleased. The freedom to feel the warm sun on his back doing work he enjoyed—and he did enjoy it, more than he'd ever expected he might. All the years he'd spent living the life of a rover, gambler, and miner, had been wasted. He could see that now. Actually, he'd seen that during those years in prison, when he'd had all the time in the world to reflect on his past, the good and the bad.

But he'd never expected to return to his roots like this and feel this kind of exhilaration. Now more than ever, he was glad he'd made the deal with Howard.

He scanned the surrounding area, where several cords of dead wood stood neatly stacked between trees not too distant from the cabin. The green wood was stacked separately so it could season for next year. The barn stood solid once more, with a good tin roof that should last a lifetime, thanks to Howard's and Ben's help. Sometime during the coming summer he planned to add a coat of red paint.

In the meantime, he needed to build a new chicken house, since the old one had long since fallen to decay with the help of small woodland critters. It wouldn't take long, nor would it take much lumber, although he wasn't exactly ready to fill it with hens. He had little need for that many eggs.

And then there was the old cabin.

He'd given that the least attention, thinking it would be replaced by the end of the year with a large frame house, once he sold his share of the mine. But then, he didn't exactly need a house that big for just himself, so maybe the cabin should be repaired to make do until he was ready for the house. And with the time for field work approaching fast, it seemed inappropriate to spend time on anything else.

Laying aside the axe, he walked toward the cabin, eyeing the roof critically and checking the exterior for soundness. It seemed plenty stable; no shifting had taken place. Minor repairs should have it livable in a relatively short time. It would be good enough for him; he'd certainly lived in far worse. And even though Howard seemed in no hurry to take over the saloon, he knew he would eventually need a place to live.

Pushing the hanging door aside, it nearly fell beneath his weight. Stepping inside reminded him of the day in early winter when he'd brought Irene and the kids out for a picnic. She had seemed as eager as Jonathan and Lydia to be free of the confines of her house. He'd seen the anticipation in her eyes each time the wagon had turned a bend in the road and especially when they'd entered the clearing where the cabin stood. There was little doubt in his mind that she'd never ventured this far from town before.

Leaving the cabin, he walked into the sunshine once more. He picked up the axe and returned to the work at hand. With each swing and jarring thud as the axe bit into the trunk of the tree, he felt a notch closer to being a new person, or maybe just the person he'd always been but didn't know how to find. Time after time, he swung the axe, feeling the rhythm as his hand slid down the handle and swung again. Perspiration popped, cleansing away the old as he prepared for the new. At last the tree gave way and slowly crashed through nearby branches until it hit the ground accompanied by various snaps and crunches.

He wiped his brow with the sleeve of his shirt. No longer did this sort of strenuous work cause his muscles to ache as they had at first. Now it just felt good.

Propping his boot up on the fallen tree, he wondered what Irene would think of the changes. Perhaps he'd ask her and the kids out again, maybe when they took their picnic to the creek as they'd promised Jonathan.

With that pleasant thought in mind, he went back to work.

Irene stood in the empty classroom, summoning the courage to do what she'd said she would, but it was one thing to say it and another to go through with it. Clara could be a formidable opponent when she set her mind to it, and there was little doubt how her mind would be set on this issue.

She'd sent Lydia and Jonathan on ahead so she could approach Clara alone, since there was no telling what might be said after she stated her position. It was best if she dealt with this by herself.

Taking a deep breath, she crossed the hall and waited outside Clara's door, assuming that neutral territory would be the wiser choice.

She didn't have to wait long.

"Hello, Irene. Are you waiting to see me?" Clara asked, closing the classroom door behind her. She was an imposing figure in her black-as-night dress, hat, and coat.

"Yes, I am." But the rest of the words stuck in her mouth. Actually, she was having a hard time forming them in her head.

"Well, go ahead." Then, becoming aware that Irene was extremely uncomfortable, she asked, "Is something wrong?"

"No, not wrong, it's just that . . ." Telling herself that a promise was a promise, she forged ahead. "I won't be participating in the meetings or the saloon sittings anymore, Clara."

Taken aback by the statement, almost as though it had been a physical blow, Clara felt sure she must have misunderstood. Certainly she hadn't said she would no longer participate . . . had she?

"Would you repeat yourself, please?" Clara demanded, pulling herself up to her full height.

Refusing to cower, Irene said, "I won't be at the meetings or the saloon anymore, Clara."

Eyeing her speculatively, Clara wondered where this decision had come from.

"And pray tell, why not?" she challenged.

"I have to think about the children—"

"Children who are not yours," she reprimanded.

"Nevertheless, they are under my care and therefore I must consider their feelings."

"Feelings? Feelings! Really, Irene, what do feelings have to do with the health and well-being of the families of our town? You seem to have forgotten the very reason for our meetings. The children. All children. As a teacher, it is

263

your bounden duty to care for all children, not just a selected few."

"I'm not so sure that what we do as a group has a positive effect on any children," Irene stated in a clear tone.

Shocked, Clara sucked in her breath. "How can you say that?"

"Dressing like men and causing destruction to another's property is hardly a good example to set."

"It is when you're defeating those who sell drink!" Then realization dawned as Clara suddenly became aware of who it was that had undoubtedly put Irene up to this refusal. Ross Hollister.

"I believe I understand," Clara went on, a new hardness in her eyes. "I'm sure you wouldn't be so quick to defend saloons if left to make your own decisions."

"This is my decision."

"I think not. It's very plain to see that you have been swayed against your better judgment. And in spite of my warnings, you did not guard yourself against the persuasiveness of Mr. Hollister." In a lower voice, she added, "I told you this would happen."

Forcing herself not to blush at the memory of being in Ross's arms and therefore look the part of a guilty person, Irene lifted her chin and stared Clara directly in the eye. "I'm sorry you don't believe me."

"Oh, I believe you think this is your idea. And I believe your intentions are the best. But I also know that you're making a mistake. Not one, but two."

"I'm also sorry you feel that way. I had thought that if I were honest, you would at least try to be understanding of my feelings."

"There's that word again! Feelings!" Nearly irate, Clara glared at her. "What have feelings got to do with the condition of the soul?"

Irene had never witnessed Clara like this before. She wished now that she had stated her piece, then turned and left. But it was too late to undo what had already been done.

"I'm not changing my mind, Clara, no matter how hard you lecture me. I'm a grown woman capable of making up my own mind. I think it's high time everyone knew it." With that said, she pulled on her coat and turned to go.

"You'll rue the day you made this choice," Clara said to her retreating back. When the big front doors had closed behind Irene, Clara said again, sadly, "You'll rue the day."

With a deep-felt sigh, she walked the length of the hall. Her age had somehow crept up on her, and she felt it now more than ever. She reached for the door, but before her hand touched the coldness of it, the familiar pain, dull and heavy, gripped her chest, and she gasped for breath. Slowly she inhaled, while she carefully clung to each little bit of air that she was able to draw into her lungs. With her eyes closed and perspiration accumulating on every part of her body, she leaned heavily against the door, waiting for the frightening moment to pass. Then gradually, the grip of pain lessened and she could at last breathe more normally.

Time was wasting, and she had so much to do. She would need to give herself a little better care so she would live long enough to carry out all her plans. Not for herself—no never for herself—but for the good of others, and somehow for Thaddeus, whom she'd failed.

With her gait a little slower, she walked the short distance home.

"Did you tell her?" Winnie prodded the moment Irene walked through the door.

"Yes." She pulled off her coat and gloves.

"And?"

"She didn't like it."

"Well, I figured that much," Winnie said with a huff and poured a cup of tea for each of them. "What I want to know is her reply."

265

"I'm tired, Mother. Do we have to go over it right now?"

"Irene," she said, putting the teapot down with a gentle clink, "that woman has been an irritation to me and to you for a number of years. Are you going to deny me the details of her comeuppance?"

"I'm afraid so. At least for now." She sipped the aromatic brew. "Thank you for the tea, Mother. It's just what I need."

Relenting a little in the face of her daughter's apparent tiredness, she changed the subject. Somewhat.

"Have you seen Mr. Hollister lately?"

"You know very well when the last time was that I saw him." Irene remembered two evenings ago when he'd stopped just to visit, as had become his habit since Jonathan's illness, and they sat in the kitchen talking of spring picnics and fishing.

"Well, I just thought maybe he'd stopped by the school or . . . something."

"You can rest easy. There's no 'or something' to wonder about."

As much as she hated to admit it, Winnie didn't totally disagree with Clara. Even though they would never see eye to eye on the saloon situation, they both were on the same track when it came to Ross Hollister. How could she not be? After all, who wanted her daughter spending any time with a saloon owner-gambler-gold-miner? He was hardly the catch of the day and certainly nothing to write to her other daughters about. But first things first, and getting Irene out of the saloon definitely came first. She could at least be happy for that much. For now.

"It certainly was a beautiful day," Winnie went on, hoping to turn the conversation to a lighter note.

"Yes. I believe winter is finally fading." Irene sipped her tea, not wholly relaxed, waiting for the real reason behind this apparently benign maneuver.

"It won't be long before things begin to turn green and

the flowers start to sprout. I suppose back in Cincinnati that's already happening."

"I suppose it is."

"The gardener has undoubtedly started pruning some of the shrubs around the east side of the house. The girls—that is Mary Ellen and Rosie—said they would look after things."

"Mother," Irene said, setting down her cup. "I can tell you're getting homesick. You've been here for five months, and with Janie's baby due in a few months, maybe you should be considering going back home."

Releasing a sigh, Winnie admitted, "I do miss everything a little bit."

"Everything here is fine. There's nothing to worry about. Jonathan is as good as ever, and I've made a firm decision not to go to any temperance meetings. Doesn't that put your mind more at ease?" she asked.

"Well, yes, it does."

"You've been away from home too long. The girls are undoubtedly wondering if I'm going to keep you up here forever," she said with a smile. "And your first grandchild will be born soon. Then you can fuss over him and spoil him for a change."

Winnie sent a sharp look toward Irene. "I never spoiled you. Or the girls."

"And what about the fussed-over part?" she teased.

"That's what mothers do best. It's part of the job."

Irene held back her normal response: since Jonathan's illness she understood more than she had before. To a point.

"I'm old enough to take care of myself, Mother," she said. "Or bear the consequences if need be."

Winnie understood what her daughter was telling her, although she didn't completely agree. Some consequences could be impossible to bear, and she only wanted to spare Irene those. In that sense, she and Clara were definitely in agreement.

"Well, at least think about it."

After a moment of thought, Winnie replied, "I will."

Irene rose from her seat, glad that the idea had been planted. It would be much easier to get on with her life if her mother would return to her own. Not that things hadn't improved lately. They had. But two women under the same roof with different viewpoints were bound to clash again and again.

"Where are Jonathan and Lydia?" she asked over her shoulder as she went into the pantry to retrieve the coffee grinder and some beans.

"You can guess where Jonathan is—at the river with his little friend, what's-his-name. And Lydia is up in her room."

Frowning, Irene placed the beans in the grinder. "Is she feeling all right?"

"She's very quiet, but other than that she seems fine."

"I thought she appeared a little distant today, but I thought she was just bored. I'd better check on her later."

Winnie eyed the ground coffee. "Expecting company?"

"Oh, not really. I just thought I'd have some ready in case Ross dropped by after supper. And besides, I sort of like the smell when it's freshly ground. Don't you?" she asked, smiling.

"Hmph. Your father drank it sometimes, but I never took a liking to it, smell or taste." She went to the stove, where a pot of noodles simmered in beef broth. Removing a pan of biscuits from the oven, she tried to ignore the aroma of the coffee.

When Irene finished her small chore and stored everything away, she decided to look in on Lydia. She didn't like to see her so listless and inattentive when she was usually so vibrant. Something was bothering her.

The door was open and Irene could see that Lydia, curled up warmly in a ball, was staring intently at an object across the room.

Tapping lightly against the door frame, she asked, "May I come in?"

"Sure." Lydia looked up and forced a smile.

Entering the room, she said, "You look sort of sad. Is everything all right?"

"I guess I'm just tired."

"Of what?"

She shrugged. "Waiting for spring, I guess."

Irene sat on the edge of the bed. "Well, it won't be long now. I saw a robin on my way home from school, and you know what that means, don't you?"

She nodded. "But I'll bet he was alone. All the smart ones stayed behind."

Irene smiled and gently smoothed the curls back from Lydia's face. "Before long we'll be able to open the windows and put the parlor stove back in storage."

"I can't wait." But she sounded as if she didn't believe it would ever happen.

Still smiling, Irene remembered the impatience of youth. How hard it was to wait for everything—summertime, wearing longer dresses, putting up one's hair like a young woman, and hoping for the attentions of a favorite boy.

"Irene!" her mother called up the stairway. "You've got company. I'll get the coffeepot out."

"Ross is here," Lydia said, smiling genuinely now. "I could've told just by her voice, even if she hadn't mentioned the coffeepot."

"You're right. Me, too." Rising from the bed, Irene asked, "You'll come down, won't you? Just so he'll know that not everyone disapproves of his visits."

Sitting up, she asked with a wide-eyed, almost worried look, "You don't mind that he comes, do you, Miss Barrett?"

"Of course not. Are you coming?"

"In a little bit."

After hesitating a moment, Irene nodded, then left the room.

Lydia brushed a strand of hair over her shoulder. When spring finally arrived, would she and Jonathan still be there? Would they get to go on the picnics that Miss Barrett and Ross talked about? Would they take more adventures into the woods, looking for arrowheads and rabbit holes, then stretch out in the sun just enjoying the day as well as each other's company?

Scooting off the bed, she couldn't rid herself of the fear and worry that maybe her Aunt Sarah would still come for them even though she'd destroyed nearly every letter she was supposed to mail. What if that one had gotten through? What if Miss Barrett had mailed some herself? Or even Mrs. Barrett?

She could hardly bear to think about it. Yet with spring getting closer, it was all she could think about.

Chapter Twenty

Gathering the last of her things from the desk and putting them in the drawer, Irene surveyed the empty classroom while listening to the shouts and laughter coming through the open windows. Only moments ago the bell had rung and everyone had fled the room as though it was on fire, leaving her alone with her thoughts.

With just one day to go before early spring dismissal, Irene didn't know who was happier—the children or her— which was a surprise. Usually she dreaded the end of the year, when the summer loomed before her devoid of . . . companionship. Yes, she admitted, her students had been her companions, her distraction from the solitary life she'd led.

But that was before Lydia and Jonathan.

And Ross.

Now she, like the children, yearned for hot summer days to spend out of doors doing the many things that everyone loved to do, such as fishing, picnicking, and riding into the country. And cool summer nights for walking along the river, where the rocks protruded from the shallow water and fish could be heard jumping in deeper places.

As soon as school was out, they had great plans to enjoy each and every day. Jonathan had already spent his fair share of time at the river fishing with his friend and his new poles. Sometimes Ross went with him, but more often than not Ross was difficult to find.

Lately, Irene noticed a new spring to Lydia's step, a more carefree air surrounded her now than when she'd first arrived. They had all settled into a comfortable lifestyle, even Winnie, who still remained in Grand Rapids, teetering in her decision to leave.

At the door Irene turned back to look over the tidy classroom once more. No lessons were planned for tomorrow, since there would be games and foot races as well as refreshments supplied by several mothers and teachers. In effect, today had been the last day of school, but the usual sadness was replaced by a smile.

In the hall, she noticed that Clara's door was ajar and the sound of rustling skirts told of her presence within the classroom. Irene brushed aside the feelings of ill-will that had come between them since she'd refused to attend the meetings, and she crossed the hall to say good-bye. There had been little she could do to change the situation, and Clara made no attempt to bridge the gap with understanding. As a result, they had each kept their distance.

But Irene was more than uncomfortable with the way things were between them. Perhaps now, with a beautiful summer stretching langorously before them, they could breach the rift at least in their working relationship.

"Clara?" she called, pushing the door wide.

Clara looked up from her desk, where slates were neatly stacked, mild surprise registering on her face.

Facing her, Irene wondered just what she should say. Inanities about picnics and walks along the river certainly wouldn't be appropriate. Neither would asking about her summer plans, since they both already knew the sort of things Clara had undoubtedly planned.

"The children are excited about school tomorrow," she offered as a beginning.

"For the first time this year," Clara added while she resumed her work at the desk.

"Well, that's understandable. They're young and full of energy."

Looking up, Clara answered, "I suppose so."

"Well, I just wanted to wish you a nice summer. I doubt if we'll get much of an opportunity to speak with one another tomorrow."

With her eyes unreadable, Clara replied, "Thank you."

Suddenly wondering why she'd even tried, Irene said good afternoon and walked from the school.

Watching her go, Clara resisted the urge to call her back, to try once more to explain the mistake she was making spending so much time with that saloon owner-gold miner and who knew what else. He would ruin her life. Clara felt desperate to stop her, to keep her from the harm she knew could befall her, but Irene refused to heed her warnings. Perhaps any day now she would receive word from the inquiries she'd sent out months ago about Ross Hollister. There was no doubt in her mind that he was an unsavory character and totally ill-suited for someone like Irene. She knew it deep in her soul.

Ross plowed a section of ground farthest from the woods, plodding along behind the team of horses he'd bought from a neighboring farmer. Until today, he figured his plans for farming were probably the best-kept secret in Grand Rapids, thanks to Howard and Ben. He hadn't exactly been ready to bear the brunt of loud laughter that would be directed at him if his attempts failed.

Keeping a firm grip on the handles, he guided the plow in as a straight a line as he could. When the first furrow left much to be desired, he set his jaw and proceeded to do better on the second trip. Up and down the field he walked, feeling more satisfaction with each step, inhaling the smell of freshly turned-over earth. There was a sense of belonging that he'd never felt before, a sense of communion not only with his surroundings but with himself. And it was as intoxicating as the finest liquor. He knew he could never go back to who he'd been before.

With the sun setting at his back, he led the team toward the barn, where he unhitched them, rubbed them down, and turned them into the recently fenced pasture. Then he cleaned off the packed dirt from the plow and once more stood back to survey his surroundings.

Tired and sweaty, he looked with longing toward the cabin, wishing he'd had time to repair it before now so he wouldn't have to make the trip into town. Instead, he went to the pump and pumped himself a bucketful for washing off the grime of the day. With a swat at the newly arrived mosquitoes, he saddled his horse and rode into town, promising himself that he would work on the cabin as soon as the field work permitted.

The evening was cool, with just enough breeze along the river to keep most of the mosquitoes at bay. With each movement of the horse, he could feel the muscles that he'd used all day, but he wasn't all that uncomfortable.

Dusk had settled into early darkness as he reached the edge of town and passed the old inn and the bridge, with Irene's house just ahead. Slowing his horse to barely a walk, he thought about stopping in for a visit. The lights in her house said they were all still up. Tempted beyond refusal, he turned the horse down the street beside her home. Dismounting, he tied the animal to the hitching rail at the shed in back.

A cup of coffee in her kitchen would be the perfect ending to his day, he thought with a smile as he knocked on the door.

When it opened, she stood there in silhouette with the light against her back. A light fragrance drifted toward him, and he breathed it in as though it were life-giving.

"Hello," he said, still smiling. "I hope this isn't too late to stop by." Then suddenly he remembered the night he'd waited in the cold until nearly midnight to get her attention, and how they'd skated on the canal with no one to see.

She smiled in return, looking pleased to see him too. "Not at all," she said, stepping back so he could enter.

Inside the warm room, a teakettle on the stove sent a small mist into the air, and the single lamp on the table glowed brightly.

"I was just making some tea for myself and Mother. She's in the parlor with the children. They're discussing the races scheduled for tomorrow."

"Races?" he asked, moving toward the table where she stood.

In the light, she could see him more clearly. His shirt sleeves were rolled to the elbows, baring his forearms that had not only tanned but thickened, just as his shoulders seemed broader. His brown-blond hair had golden highlights brighter than she remembered. And he smelled faintly of horses, leather, and earth.

Glancing down at his soiled shirt, he spoke apologetically, "I should have cleaned up first, but I was riding by and thought I'd just stay a minute." Looking up, he found her staring at him. "Or two, if you weren't busy," he finished.

Surprised at getting caught admiring him, she quickly looked away and moved toward the pantry. "Would you like some coffee? It won't take long to make."

From inside the pantry, she heard him answer, "That sounds great."

Taking a few moments to compose herself, she smoothed her skirts, the sleeves of her dress, and her hair. With one deep breath, eyes closed, she calmed her thudding heart. It had been over two weeks since she'd seen him, and although she'd been busy with school her thoughts had strayed often to him, wondering what he was doing and if he thought about her as much as she thought about him. Now that he was here, looking bigger than life and filling her kitchen with his masculine presence, she couldn't seem to think straight at all. And no wonder, with the way her heart was jumping about in her breast.

Calming herself as best she could, she reached for the jar with the already ground beans that awaited his arrival. She turned to go and bumped into Ross's chest.

"Oh!" she cried.

"Excuse—" he began until their eyes met. He stood with both hands on her upper arms, holding her firmly just inches away with the jar of coffee between them. "I thought maybe you were having trouble reaching something," he said softly.

She shook her head slightly left to right and back again. "I didn't realize I was taking so long." Holding her breath she saw his head dip, felt his lips touch hers, sensed the tension of the moment within him. It lasted only briefly but had the impact of a tidal wave.

When he lifted his face from hers, he stared into the warm depth of her brown eyes and knew his heart was lost, and had been for some time.

With a grip on the coffee jar that should have broken it, she returned his gaze in the tiny, dimly lit pantry. Something new, something that made his blue-gray eyes shine, gazed back at her—the same sort of look she'd imagined any gallant man would give to his lady when he spoke of his love. Suddenly he smiled and leaned down to kiss the tip of her nose.

Before she could respond in any way, the sound of approaching footsteps alerted her to the certain invasion of their privacy.

"We'd better go," she said, inching past him, turning in a circular dance so that she emerged first. As she stepped from the pantry with Ross right behind her, Lydia and Jonathan entered from the dining room with Winnie right behind them.

Jonathan was the first to react. "Ross!"

"Hey, pal."

"I didn't know you were here!"

"Just got here."

Winnie shot them both a look that said she wondered if it were true.

"We're having races at school tomorrow," Jonathan went on. "It's gonna be great. Can you come watch?"

"Well, I've been real busy. I'll have to see." The look of disappointment on the boy's face prompted him to turn the subject to a happier topic. "So school's almost out, huh?"

"Yep, sure is. I'm glad, but Lydia's not."

Ross watched from the corner of his eye as Irene moved about the kitchen pouring water into the coffeepot and setting it on the stove, then stirring up the fire and adding more wood. She had a grace about her that couldn't be hidden no matter how simple the task.

"Why is that?" he responded absently, his attention focused wholly on the woman he'd come to see.

Lydia shrugged, "I suppose it's silly, since I'll get to spend more time with my friends out of school than in school." When she actually thought about it, there was no reason to be so sad. Now she could spend time sitting beneath shade trees reading or even wading in the river. "Do you think we could take a picnic down to the river sometime?"

"Yeah!" Jonathan interrupted. "I remember you said we could, back when I was sick. I almost forgot about it. Can we do that?"

Irene turned from the stove, and her gaze collided with Ross's. She'd felt his eyes on her from the time they'd left the pantry, and with some difficulty she'd managed to avoid meeting them until Jonathan questioned her. Forced then to turn around, she had instinctively let her gaze rest on Ross. For a fleeting moment, her heart stopped—or maybe just skipped a beat, she wasn't sure which.

A small smile appeared at the corners of his mouth, and that mischievous twinkle, which so intrigued her, lit his eyes. "Well, a promise is a promise," he said to her.

Glancing at a very excited Jonathan, who stood on tiptoes holding his breath, she knew he was right.

"Still a little chilly to spend time picnicking along the river," Winnie put in, but nobody seemed to notice.

"When should we plan to go?" Irene asked.

"Hurrah!" Jonathan and Lydia shouted together. "A picnic!"

In the ensuing melee of joy, Irene felt her color rise in anticipation of spending a whole day in Ross's company. She had long since given up pretending she shouldn't be attracted to him. The simple fact was, she was very attracted to him. And there was little doubt left in her mind how he felt about her. In spite of Clara's warnings, she was coming closer every day to falling in love with him. Looking at him now, he hardly resembled a saloon owner with his homespun shirt rolled to his elbows and dirt spots dotting his broad chest. Neither should he resemble a gallant hero, she thought. But he did.

The day dawned with an overcast sky, which kept the busy occupants of the kitchen constantly stepping to a window searching the heavens with a vigilant eye.

"Do you think it will rain?" Lydia asked, her voice sounded as foreboding as the weather looked.

"Probably," Winnie answered, cutting several wedges of pound cake to place in the hamper.

"Well, if it does we'll just postpone it until another day," Irene replied. "There's a whole summer ahead of us for having picnics."

"But I don't want to wait," Lydia said with a note of wistfulness.

"Neither do I," Irene returned. "Let's just hope for the best."

When the cold beef had been sliced, and the bread and cheese were packed, Winnie added napkins and a jar of grape juice. "I think this should do it, don't you, Irene?" she asked, peering into the wicker hamper.

Irene studied the contents, added some glasses, and said, "There. I believe we're all set. Won't you change your mind and join us, Mother?"

"Hardly. I don't have a hankering to go on a soggy picnic and come home soaking wet, thank you. But I hope you have a nice time." And for once she meant it. Somehow, and she wasn't sure exactly when it had happened, her feelings had changed concerning Ross Hollister. Oh, she still didn't like the saloon, and he still wasn't someone to write to her other daughters about, but there was a change in Irene. She seemed happier, more carefree, and Winnie had to credit Ross in part for that. Andrew had not inspired this sort of zest for life that had Irene smiling more often, and now she was less given to serious faces. And what mother didn't want her daughter to be happier than she'd been before? But it was truly a dilemma, she thought, shaking her head. It truly was.

A knock at the back door brought everyone out of their own personal reveries and instantly to action.

"I'll get the blanket!" Lydia called from the parlor.

Winnie closed the lid of the basket and fastened it while Irene opened the door.

"So is everyone ready?" Ross asked as he strode into the room, filling it with his presence.

"Mother refuses to go and get rained on, Jonathan is out digging worms, and Lydia will be right down," Irene said, a little breathlessly. He looked wonderful and literally took her breath away. His eyes were the same color blue as the shirt he wore, which lay comfortably open at the neck but not indiscreetly so. The hard muscles of his forearms were bare, just as they had been the other day, and she had to force herself not to stare at them when he lifted the heavy hamper.

"Feels like a pretty hefty lunch in here," he said, weighing it up and down.

"We did our best," she answered with a smile.

Arriving in the doorway with all the force of a tornado complete with dirt all over his hands and even on his clothing, Jonathan called, "I'm ready!"

Aghast, Winnie pulled the boy inside. "My, my! Just look at you!" Then on second thought, she whisked him outside, brushing dirt from his clothes and hands.

"It doesn't matter. I'm just going to get dirty again anyway," he said in a pleading voice.

"You can't eat a lunch with worm dirt all over you. I declare."

Resigned, he let his shoulders droop while she pumped water and washed him up as though he were a baby, clucking the whole time about dirty worms. A couple of times, he glanced around to see if any of his friends might be watching.

Inside the kitchen, Ross took the opportunity to study Irene as she smiled, watching through the open door and patiently waiting for her mother to finish.

"You look very nice," he said quietly.

Turning to look at him, she replied self-consciously, "Thank you."

"As a matter of fact, you look like spring in that dress." He smiled appreciatively.

She had changed her clothes three times in her indecision over what to wear, then finally decided on the white muslin trimmed with lace and sprigged with yellow and blue flowers because it reminded her of a spring day. It pleased her that he'd made the same connection.

Entering the back door once again, Jonathan looked a little wilted but still full of unleashed energy.

"That's the best we can do without going through a complete change of clothes, for all the good that would do.

He'll probably fall in the river anyway," Winnie said, shaking her head.

"I won't, you'll see. I'll be careful."

"Hmmm. We'll see, is right." Then, as Lydia skipped into the kitchen bearing a blanket, Winnie shooed them all on their way. "If you don't hurry, you'll be rained out before you even get that basket opened."

After they'd loaded everything into the wagon and everyone was seated, they proceeded on the road east of town, following the river as it wound around one bend after another and over hill and meadow. Before they'd gone a mile, the sun peeked out cautiously, then beamed down upon them in full force, adding its benediction to their day.

"Oh, isn't it wonderful?" Irene exclaimed, squinting beneath the brim of her straw hat. "See there, no rain on our picnic."

"Just the way I planned it," Ross said, smiling at her.

Lifting one eyebrow, she replied sassily, "You're going to take credit for this?"

He shrugged. "Why not? It's just one of the surprises I have for you."

She eyed him suspiciously. "And what surprise do you have next?"

"Nothing to worry about. It's as pleasant as the first. You'll just have to be patient."

Tipping her head to one side in agreement, she settled her hands in her lap and enjoyed the scenery of emerging green leaves, sprouting yarrow, and blossoming lilac.

Ross watched as she took in the sights and smells of the countryside, guessing she'd never been this far along the river before. A fragrance lighter than the aromatic lilacs they were passing wafted from her to him, and he inhaled deeply. She looked as cool and fresh as a drink in summertime in spite of the warmth beating down upon them. Beneath the brim of her oversized hat, soft tendrils of brown hair escaped their pins and fluttered lazily in the

281

occasional breeze. Everything about her was utterly feminine.

Turning her head slightly, she caught him staring at her and smiled easily, not the least self-conscious about being watched. This was the most relaxed she'd been with him since the night they'd skated alone under the stars. Suddenly he realized that he was the one who was tense and moved into a more relaxing position with his forearms on his knees.

They passed the road to the farm, where his fields lay planted and the cabin awaited his time for repairs. He had intended to show her what he'd been up to over the past few months, but on the spur of the moment he decided to wait, thinking that perhaps he should put it off until after the picnic.

After an enjoyably long ride, they came upon a stream strewn with large and small rocks before it spilled into the Maumee River. Tall trees shaded the area, giving it a natural, verdant coolness. Dappled sunshine peeked through wherever possible.

"Here we are," Ross said, slowing the horses until they finally halted.

"It's a beautiful place," Irene replied in the quiet hush that was disturbed only by a breeze high overhead ruffling the leaves at the tops of the trees. "Does it have a name?" she asked, wondering why she'd never seen this place before.

"Tontogany."

"Indian. Right?"

He nodded, then smiled mischievously, "Would you like a history lesson?"

Feeling subdued by the tranquil surroundings, she smiled in return, saying, "That's what I'm supposed to say. But school's out, and I think we should forget about lessons of any kind."

Suddenly, they became very aware of the pair in the back of the wagon, who sat staring lazily up at the leafy roof overhead. If not for their presence, Ross would have been inclined to pull Irene into his arms, where the two of them could learn a few lessons about each other.

Irene blushed as though his thoughts had been spoken words. Her own heart was caught up in the cool, green, dreamy world that now separated them from their everyday life while drawing them inexplicably closer to each other.

But the spell was soon broken by Jonathan's voice.

"Can I go see the river?" he asked Irene as he jumped from the back of wagon.

Answering for her, Ross replied over his shoulder, "Sure. Just don't fall in. Remember what Mrs. Barrett said."

"I will!" he called, running toward the water.

"You don't mind, do you?" Ross asked Irene.

"No." Then, "It isn't deep, is it?"

"In some places it's just a shallow, rocky bed. He'll be careful." He climbed down from his side of the wagon and crossed around the back, helped Lydia out, and proceeded around to help Irene. When her feet hit the ground, he found that he didn't want to take his hands from her waist.

"Thank you." Smiling, she reminded him, "The basket?"

Releasing her, he said, "Sure thing," and turned to the wagon once more, scooping up the hamper. With a teasing glint in his summer-blue eyes, he asked, "Your mother didn't pack rocks to discourage me, did she?"

Laughing, she replied, "No. Although she does believe that most men can be tempted by good food, so I suppose it's possible that they can likely be discouraged by the lack of good food."

Grasping her by the elbow and leading her toward the bank of the stream, he said, "I'll keep that in mind."

When they reached the spot where Lydia was spreading the blanket, Ross set the hamper down.

"Isn't this the prettiest place?" Lydia asked, speaking to no one in particular. "Could we do a little exploring?"

Glancing around, Ross said, "I think we'd better save that for after lunch, or we'll have to share it with some four-legged company."

"Oh, I didn't think of that," Lydia said. "I can wait. I'll see if Jonathan's hungry yet." And she was off in search of her brother.

Bending to pick a white, triple-petaled trillium, Irene said, "You've been so good to the children. I've meant to thank you, but I never . . ." She shrugged lightly. "I guess I've just let the opportunities pass. Until now." Smiling, her face showed more than the gratitude she felt. "Thank you."

Kneeling down, then stretching out on the blanket with his hands stacked behind his head, he looked up at her. "You don't have to thank me. I do things because I like to, not because I have to or for any other reason."

Twirling the flower by the stem, she replied, "But you think I do."

Hesitating to spoil the day by saying that he did think so, he simply said, "It's your life, Irene. You don't have to answer to me for anything."

"That's not the impression you gave me last winter," she remarked softly, sitting on the blanket only an arm's length away from him.

"I spoke out of place."

"Maybe." She picked at the large-veined leaf. "But it made me think about myself. That's not an easy thing to do when you're not used to it."

He watched her take tiny pieces off the edges of the leaf until it looked as though an insect had taken bites from it. Slowly her fingers devoured the leaf until it was nothing more than a bare stem.

"I realized that I'd been allowing others to make decisions for me and I resented it, although I did nothing to correct them." She stripped the leaf stem from the main stem and began working on the second leaf. "Until a few months ago, when I told Clara I wouldn't be coming to the meetings any more."

"That must have stirred her up some."

"Still does."

"I see."

Her fingers took a few nibbling bites from the leaf. "She's angry with me but she'll adjust. Eventually."

"You hope."

Nodding, she replied sincerely, "Yes, I do. It isn't comfortable having anyone angry with you." Glancing at him, she asked, "Or doesn't it bother you?"

"Of course it does. But I guess it depends on why they're angry."

"I suppose earned anger is the hardest to bear. Unearned anger just causes resentment."

Her words caught at him. He thought about the years in prison and the anger and resentment that had eaten at him just the way her fingers had eaten at the leaves she'd held. But then he'd been released, and his freedom was like salve to a wound. Freedom to spend his days as he wished, with the people he liked, doing the things that pleased him. And it pleased him to be on this picnic with her along the banks of a river where he'd spent his boyhood.

"Resentment and anger are dangerous and hard to live with," he replied. "I think Clara had been living with those long before you or I met her."

"I suppose you're right."

"There's little either of us can do about that," he said.

She kept silent as she thought about the anger and resentment she'd harbored toward Andrew for so long. No doubt he had deserved her anger, but the resentment was hers alone. And she could see how resentment led to bitterness, as it had in Clara's life.

Sitting with Ross as she was now, feeling the glow of happiness surround her, she realized that she no longer held any resentment for the past. And she found herself

285

wanting to tell him everything about herself, including Andrew's rejection of her.

Casting aside the stem she'd stripped bare, she met his gaze levelly. "Did Howard ever mention to you that I was once engaged to be married?"

"Yes."

"And did he also tell you that I left Andrew standing in the church while I turned and ran?"

Surprised that she was offering this information, Ross shaded his eyes from a patch of sunlight and stared at her, unanswering.

"Well, I did. It was the hardest thing I've ever done." She smoothed her skirt over her ankle, then went on. "Everyone thought Andrew was the most charming, eligible bachelor within fifty miles. They also thought I was a very lucky woman. So did I until two weeks before the wedding."

Ross watched for a sign in her lovely features that might register regret, but she remained composed and undaunted as she continued her story.

"We'd spent a lot of time and money buying the house and furnishing it. We wanted everything to be perfect." She hesitated a moment, wondering if she should tell the whole story. With a slight lift of her hand, she added, "My money. But nobody knows that. Not even Mother. He said that when he got on his feet again, he'd make it up to me and replace my inheritance. I believed him, heart and soul." Her gaze dropped from his down to her hand where it rested in her lap. Then she drew in a deep breath and released it on the word, "So . . . When I walked into the house to check on the dining room furniture that had been delivered, I heard voices upstairs and went to investigate."

Irene lifted her eyes to Ross's. "He wasn't alone." She shifted her position, uncomfortable with the intensity of his stare. "Of course I ran. And of course he chased me. He apologized over and over, saying that men had these . . . urges and didn't subject nice women to them."

She felt the flush of color on her cheeks but went on. "I believed him when he promised it would never happen again."

From everything he'd heard about Andrew, none of this surprised Ross. But how could any man want another woman when he was promised to this one?

"But deep in my heart," she said, "I knew I could never live with that kind of betrayal. He couldn't have loved me as much as he said he did."

Ross reached for her hand, running his thumb over her soft palm. "I'm glad you didn't marry him."

"Everyone thought I was a fool," she said softly. "I couldn't tell them the truth, because then they would have known that it was he who had rejected me."

In one swift sure motion, Ross sat up, grasping her by the shoulders. "He was the fool," he said earnestly. "The biggest damn fool I've ever heard of."

The sound of feet crashing through the underbrush accompanied by shrieks and laughter drew a halt to their conversation. Ross regretted the lost opportunity to tell her of his own deep feelings for her, even to share his own bitter past.

"Stop!" shrieked Lydia, who was laughing so hard she could barely stay on her feet. "Make him stop!" She ran between the two on the blanket, dropping in exhaustion near Irene, covering her head.

Jonathan stopped within inches of the edge of the blanket, a long, wet worm dangling from his fingers. "She tried to push me in."

"I did not," Lydia said out of breath and not all convincing.

"You did too!" Jonathan leaned threateningly over the blanket toward her.

"That's enough, Jonathan," Irene said. "Lydia, did you?"

"Well, not really." She grinned impishly. "He just thought I was going to."

"You were!" Turning to Irene, he said, "She wanted me

to get into trouble with Mrs. Barrett."

"Boy, you sure would have, too," she retorted, laughing.

He flung the worm onto her dress. With a screech, she scraped it off, but her hilarity didn't stop.

Ross picked up the worm, handed it to Jonathan, and brushed off the blanket. "Are you two even yet?" he asked. "Because if you are, maybe we can eat."

Dropping onto the blanket on his knees, Jonathan replied, "Yeah, I guess so." He tossed the worm out into the grass.

Smiling, Lydia nodded.

Irene looked on, warmed by the easy comraderie between the four of them. Ross's easy way with handling a simple squabble, the children's acceptance of these two adults as the authorities in their young lives, would give any stranger the impression that they were a family.

"Good. I'm eager to find out just what's in that basket. And I hope it isn't rocks," he said with a smile aimed at Irene.

With each of them sitting either Indian-style or side-style, a napkin full of beef, bread, cheese, and cake lay on their laps. Ross poured the grape juice into their glasses with a slight raise of his eyebrows at the rich-colored liquid. "Your mother packed this?" he asked in disbelief, smelling the contents.

Grinning, she answered, "It's grape juice. I made it myself."

"Then I'm sure it's safe."

After they'd feasted and drunk their fill, Irene and Lydia packed the leftovers in the hamper, shook the napkins, and insisted on a walk.

Groaning with regret at having to rise from his comfortable place on the blanket, Ross got to his feet. "Come on, pal," he said to Jonathan. "The ladies want a little adventure."

"Me, too." And Jonathan jumped up and led the way.

After stowing the hamper and blanket safely in the

wagon, the rest of them followed.

Down to the stream they walked in single file with Ross taking last place. Not that he minded. The sway of Irene's skirts was definitely worth it. He enjoyed watching the easy way she dipped to avoid catching low branches on the brim of her hat and the way she tipped and turned her shoulders to navigate narrow passages between bushes.

When they reached the banks of the stream, she turned to him.

"Why, it's so shallow and the rocks are so flat, you could walk across."

"Want to?" he asked.

"You first," she countered.

With a shrug, he stepped around her and onto the first rock, then turned to see if she was following. She wasn't. He took two more rocks and turned again.

"Not afraid, are you?" he asked.

Wide-eyed, she laid a finger on her breast and said, "Me?"

"Go on, Miss Barrett," Lydia coaxed, anxious to see her teacher have some fun.

Bravely, Irene stepped onto the first rock, then the second.

Ross was halfway across when he turned again, only this time he found her carefully following him. Smiling to himself, he took another step but slipped on the mossy edge and lost his footing. With a shout of surprise, he splashed into the cold, knee-deep creek.

"Oh! Oh, Ross! Are you all right?" Irene maneuvered with as much haste as she dared in her attempt to reach him.

Sitting like a turned-over crab, Ross raised his hand to her.

Without thinking about anything but helping him, she grasped his extended hand only to be whisked off her feet and into the cold creek on top of him. With a quick roll, he submersed all but her head, dislodging her wide-brimmed hat, which then floated downstream. The shock of the cold water whooshed the air from her lungs through her open lips.

"Ooohh!" she cried, struggling for breath and composure but finding neither.

Instantly, his warm lips settled on hers as his arms held her tightly to his chest. The thin fabric of her dress became as a second skin, enabling him a contact that previously had been denied. Raising them both to a sitting position, he continued to hold her to him, pulling her across his lap. When the kiss ended, she stared at him in disbelief.

"If you wanted to kiss me, wouldn't it have been easier to just step behind a tree out of view?" she asked, a smile playing at the corners of her mouth.

He glanced down at the front of her wet dress. "I don't think so."

Shrieks of glee floated to them from the dry bank, where Lydia and Jonathan jumped up and down in delight.

"Well, they didn't seem to mind it a bit. But then, neither did I," he added with a grin, holding her close.

She didn't much like being soaked to the skin in a dress that now left little to the imagination, but there was something to be said for spontaneity, and this had certainly been spontaneous. Her smile broadened and a bubble of laughter escaped. In answer, he chuckled.

"I imagine we look pretty ridiculous sitting here in the middle of the water like this," she said.

He looked at her dark hair, now sodden and coming out of its pins, and thought she was more beautiful than ever. Rivulets of water ran down her cheeks and neck and finally disappeared into the lace of her collar.

"I've ruined your dress," he said, but he knew he'd gladly buy her two to replace it.

"It's all right," she said, thinking she'd get another one just like it so she could remember this day forever.

Sliding her off his lap, he stood and pulled her to her feet.

"I guess we'll just forget the rocks, huh?" he asked.

She nodded and he helped her through the water to where Lydia happily reached out to take her hand.

"Oh, Miss Barrett, look at you!"

"Was it fun?" Jonathan asked.

Ross leaned toward Irene and whispered, "More than he'll know."

She gave him a light jab in the ribs before clasping her arms around herself to keep warm as much as to hide herself.

When they reached the wagon Ross took the blanket from the back and draped it around her shoulders. Then, scooping her up in his arms, he lifted her into the wagon.

On the road home, Ross looked over to where she sat huddled beneath the blanket; the only visible part of her dress was clinging to her knees. At her feet a puddle of water formed and grew. Now that they were on their way back to town, he felt more than a little regret for acting so childishly.

"I'm sorry for pulling you in like that. I guess I just wasn't thinking."

Smiling, with her face lifted to the sun, she replied, "Do I look like I want you to be sorry for me?"

Relieved, he returned her smile. No, she didn't look at all sorry. She looked great.

Jonathan poked his head between them, asking in a hushed voice, "Are you gonna get in trouble for falling in?"

Reaching her hand from inside the blanket, she tousled his hair. "Absolutely not. We were only having fun. Right? Why should we get into trouble for having fun?"

"Yeah," he answered, sitting down once more but still feeling thankful it wasn't him who had fallen in.

Ross leaned toward her and whispered, "That excuse could come back to haunt you when he's fifteen."

She laughed. "Or sooner."

Looking like a damsel who had just been rescued from a sinking ship, Irene glanced at the man whom she now considered her gallant hero. He hadn't exactly rescued her from the water at all—far from it—but he had captured her heart by saving her from herself, teaching her to trust, and showing her what life could be like. In fact, he had slowly unfolded the drama of life as it should be, and she welcomed it.

Chapter Twenty-one

Laughter gaily filled the air as the wagon approached the back of her house. In spite of their heavy, sodden clothing, both Irene and Ross felt buoyed by the day and undeniably closer. The sound of his deep throaty laugh brought a smile to her own face, and she was sorry that their afternoon had to end so quickly.

"Whoa," Ross called softly to the horses, and they came to a halt along the edge of her yard. "Don't move," he said to Irene. "I'll help you out." He jumped out and walked around to her side, his boots squeaking soggily.

Trying to disentangle her legs from her skirts took a little time, but at last she was able to step over the side. He grasped her by the waist and lifted her down. On the ground, face to face with the blanket still covering her shoulders, they openly stared into each other's eyes.

"Believe it or not, I really did have a wonderful time," she said.

"Me, too."

"Would you like to come in?" she asked, wishing to prolong their time together.

He glanced down at his own soaked clothing. "No. I'd better get changed. Maybe later. If that's all right."

She nodded.

Suddenly they became aware of the silence that had replaced the silly antics of Lydia and Jonathan. Turning to see what had sobered them, Irene and Ross found Clara Wilson and Superintendent Walker rounding the side of the house.

"Uh, oh," said Lydia.

Ross dropped one hand from Irene's waist but allowed the other to stay protectively at her back. He waited for the stiffness to enter her spine, but it didn't. She seemed calm and in control.

With brisk, no-nonsense steps, the older pair approached. Clara's eyes danced with fire and brimstone, while Mr. Walker's were cold and militant.

"So," Clara began, "how fitting that we should appear at this moment."

Indeed, Irene thought. The confrontation almost seemed planned, not to mention inevitable. She kept her silence, refusing to make an excuse or give any sign of wrong-doing.

In a clipped but loud voice, Mr. Walker spoke to Irene, ignoring Ross. "Miss Barrett. I don't believe I need to remind you of the code of ethics by which we hired you. Or do I?" His eyes roamed over her wet clothing and the blanket in disgust.

Irene stood her ground, saying nothing and forcing herself not to flinch under his terrible scrutiny. She knew perfectly well that the hiring and firing was at his discretion even though the board must vote. They would take him at his word and accept his suggestions.

"Your behavior has been far above reproach until lately. And today—" He paused. "Well, words fail me."

Unable to stand quietly by and allow Irene to take the brunt of their criticism, Ross stepped forward. "Wait a minute. You haven't even given her a chance. Don't you think there might be a reasonable explanation?" He was sick to death of their unbending, hypocritical attitudes. And he was sick of their treating him as though he was cow manure on their shoes.

"Reasonable?" Mr. Walker repeated, his eyebrows raised in disbelief. "What could be reasonable about a woman who consistently keeps the company of saloon owners? Especially when she's been warned by her superiors. And not only that, she goes out at all hours of the night, too. Now, here she is soaked to the . . . skin. I hardly think any of this is reasonable, Mr. Hollister."

With her chin level, Irene spoke, "I prefer that you talk directly to me, Mr. Walker, not about me as though I'm not even present."

"Oh, there's no doubt that you're present," he replied. "No doubt about that at all. Unfortunately."

Ross set his jaw in order to keep from punching the man. He had to remind himself that that was what had gotten him into trouble the last time, and he had no intention of repeating that mistake. Even so, he would not allow them to treat her with such disrespect.

"Guilty until proven innocent? Is that your motto?" he said acidly.

"Speaking of guilty," Clara began, "I'd say you're somewhat of an expert on the subject. Wouldn't you, Mr. Hollister? Or do you just have an aversion to the truth?"

He sensed a change in Irene's position, a shift of a foot, a tightening of the fingers she had clamped to the blanket. Suddenly, he knew they had defeated him—and her. If only he'd explained everything to her before now, before they'd exposed his past in the bright light of their scrutiny and opened the closed book of his own mistakes for her to see. Why hadn't he told her when they were alone, when he could have explained?

"Murder, wasn't it, Mr. Hollister? You murdered a man over a woman in a saloon brawl." Clara focused all of her energy and dislike on this man who seemed so intent on destroying Irene's life. Well, not if she could prevent it.

Ross remained quiet, condemned once more, but this time the pain was infinitely worse. The woman he loved stood beside him and doubted him; he could feel it. Slowly, she turned to look at him, waiting, waiting for him to deny this awful accusation. But he could not.

For Irene, time had slowed until it actually felt as though it stood still. Then, suddenly, it seemed to move backward, transporting her to an earlier scene, five years ago, when the man she'd loved stood before her, revealed by the awful truth of his actions.

But now, as she stared at this apparently gentle man beside her, who had brought laughter, adventure, and especially love into her life, she wondered how could she have so willingly accepted him into her heart without really knowing him.

Seeing the distrust in her eyes, Ross dropped his hand from her waist. What a fool he'd been to ignore the importance of telling her the truth. But then, it probably wouldn't have made any difference. She was a woman who lived her life according to a set of rules, who cared what others thought, while he was a drifter, a murderer, who cared little for the opinions of others. He had come here to make a new life for himself and found everything he wanted. But had he known it would end like this, he never would have come at all.

Without a word, he turned away and walked to the wagon, where he lifted the hamper out. He crossed the yard, set it on the back steps, then returned to the wagon. Nobody said a word. Climbing aboard, he set his jaw and drove away.

"Don't let him go," Jonathan whispered, standing beside Irene.

But she couldn't stop him. She couldn't ignore the voice in her head that kept repeating: You don't know him and he didn't even trust you enough to tell you the truth.

Mr. Walker cleared his throat. "Well, I can see that you

are at least repentant of your association with the man. But I'm afraid it's come too late. Apparently, you are not of strong enough character to withstand the attentions of such a man, and so I'm going to recommend to the board that your contract not be renewed next year. I admit I'm sorry it's come to this. You were a fine teacher."

The words struck Irene just as the sound of thunder bombarded her eardrums. The sun still shone brightly in contrast to the brewing storm heading their way, but that was of little consequence compared to the dark clouds overshadowing her heart and the storm brewing within her breast.

"You're firing me?" she asked in disbelief. "Because I do not do as I'm told?"

"Because you have a moral obligation to your students and to the community," Mr. Walker said sternly, as though he were speaking to a naughty child.

"No. That's not it at all," Irene returned heatedly. "I've been told how to think, how to act, and practically what to say until now. It's all right to dress in men's clothing and enter saloons if you intend destruction. It's all right to speak to saloon owners if you place a curse upon their lives—"

"As they have placed upon ours, Irene," Clara interrupted.

"It's all right to judge men according to their past, point out their mistakes regardless of whether they've paid for them or not." By now she was nearly shouting, but she wasn't sure if it was because of the two who stood before her, or Ross, who had by his silence denied her his trust. "But it's not all right to think, do, or say as one pleases if it is in opposition to your views!"

"I tried to warn you," Clara said, "but you wouldn't listen. I told you he was about devil's work and apparently in more ways than one."

Her supercilious attitude for once grated on Irene's nerves until she felt like shaking the older woman.

"Did he pay for his crime?" Irene shot back, trying to hold her voice under control.

"Does it matter? He committed it, and that's the important thing to remember." Then, seeing that the younger woman might be taking his side in the matter, she added, "Did he bother to tell you about this?" When Irene didn't answer, she went on, "I thought not."

Clara hadn't wanted to hurt Irene so publicly. She would rather things hadn't turned out this way, but Irene was young and resilient, with her whole life ahead of her. It was better that she know the truth now than when it was too late.

Throughout the encounter their voices had risen enough to draw attention from Winnie, who had opened the back door to shake rugs. At first she'd thought Ross would handle it, but when he drove away she became concerned. Dropping the rugs absently on the ground, she made her way toward the group, becoming more irritated as she approached. They could not talk to her daughter using that tone of voice in broad daylight, where all the neighbors could listen! This had gone far enough.

Marching up to the threesome, Winnie said curtly, "Good afternoon." Then, eyeing her daughter's wet clothing, she went on, "If you'll excuse us, Irene needs to get out of these clothes before she catches her death. I'm sure you wouldn't want to be responsible for that."

"Of course not," replied Mr. Walker. "We were just leaving." He tipped his hat, and the two departed.

But Irene noticed that before they turned to go, Clara hesitated as though there was more she wanted to say or ask, then apparently decided against it.

Winnie immediately herded the children ahead out of earshot, while she protectively ushered Irene toward the house.

"And just what was that all about?"

"I've been fired," she replied evenly.

"Fired! They can't do that! Who does that Clara Wilson

think she is anyway? I'll have a talk with her and tell her to mind her own business for once and for all." Shaking her head in disgust as they entered the kitchen, she repeated, "Fired! Hmph!"

"I'm going up to change, Mother. I need some time alone."

With concern on her face, Winnie nodded her head, watching her daughter go. Turning to Lydia, she prodded, "Do you know what this is all about?"

Biting her lip, Lydia nodded.

"Well?"

"Mrs. Wilson said Ross killed a man over a saloon woman and went to prison."

"Have mercy!" Winnie exclaimed. Suddenly winded, she dropped into a chair. Murder? She would never have guessed it. Was it true? Looking toward the doorway where her daughter had departed the room, she thought, poor Irene.

Ross left the horses and wagon at the livery, then stalked down the street, his expression matching the thunderclouds overhead. Brimming anger didn't allow him to see others who walked the boarded walks, and those that passed gave him wide berth, not even thinking to speak a pleasantry to him.

He clenched his fists and forged ahead, his tightened jaw muscles keeping his teeth clamped like a vise. All the while his mind berated the superintendent and Clara Wilson, but mostly he berated himself.

He shouldn't have kept the truth from Irene; he shouldn't have let himself get so close to her. And first and foremost, he should never have fallen in love with her. But it was too late for that; he already had.

With one hand he shoved the saloon door wide and strode through the nearly empty building. He paid no heed to those who stared at him, but went up the back stairs to his room. Slamming the door behind him, he pulled his

299

soggy boots from his feet, shrugged out of his clammy clothes, and swore as his toe snagged a sliver. Damn saloon! Damn town! Damn women!

Plucking the offender from his skin, he ignored the drop of blood and pulled on another pair of socks before he finished dressing. How did he ever let himself get into this fix in the first place? He paused, buttoning his shirt. Because he let his heart rule his better judgment and because he wanted to leave the past behind. He'd thought he could when he got the opportunity to start over. Then he met Irene and wanted more than anything to forget what had happened those years ago, and he'd believed he had that right. After all, he'd paid for what he'd done.

Pulling on a pair of dry boots, he crossed the floor, then aimlessly turned around and crossed it again. Feeling too confined in the small room, he headed for the outdoors once more, this time opting for the less public back door of the saloon. With no thought as to his destination, he followed the ribbon of canal toward the dam.

He marched along the banks unmindful of the threatening storm until he stood within feet of the powerful surge of water that flowed over the dam. The sound filled his head with a steady, whooshing roar but it could not drown out his thoughts.

She had doubted him. She had believed Clara's words and all the implications they carried. Without benefit of explanation, he had been condemned again.

The wind increased and the first raindrops pelted his face, but he ignored them as his thoughts carried him back to that day more than five years ago. Once more he heard the shot ring out as he involuntarily jumped, saw the man's eyes stare blankly into his, while cold fear gripped his guts. And all the while, a woman cried hysterically in the background. He had never killed a man before, and as the realization overwhelmed him, damp perspiration formed in his armpits and along his brow.

A clap of thunder brought him back to the present, his face wet with rain.

Should he explain everything to Irene and hope she would understand? And if she listened at all, would she then treat him with cold indifference or even disdain? He didn't know. Even a compassionate woman like Irene would have trouble forgiving murder.

In her bedroom, Irene numbly removed the clothes that had begun to dry on her body. With little awareness of what she was doing, her mind jolted over the cold words that Clara had spoken, while outside the thunder rolled and the lightning snapped and she felt the house shake with the reverberations of it.

Rolling her stockings from her legs, she paused.

Murder.

How could he have actually taken another man's life? Had she totally misjudged him?

With her damp clothing strewn across the back of a chair, she pulled her wrapper around her nakedness, trying to draw some warmth from the cotton. Sitting on the bed, she felt the thunder rock the house once more.

Unable to let go of them, her mind played back memories of last fall, when he had taken them on their adventure. Surely a man who would take a woman and two children on a picnic, sharing, entrusting them with a part of his past, could not be capable of cold-blooded murder? And the time he'd taken her skating at midnight, holding her warmly, then kissing her passionately. Surely this was not a man so devoid of feeling that he ruthlessly took another's life?

Gripping the edge of the bed, she felt the heaviness in her stomach and knew the awful truth. He had murdered someone and been convicted. His silence told everything. And now there was no use trying to deny it.

She lay down upon the quilt and pulled the edge of it around her, letting the tears of disappointment flow. Not

301

only had her heart betrayed her by letting her fall in love with him, but Ross had betrayed her by not confiding in her. She had trusted him, but he had not trusted her. He had not given her honesty.

What was it the Reverend had said the day she was to have married Andrew? . . . Two people united in their goals and purposes, in their beliefs and, especially, in their honesty and devotion to one another . . . that was love.

She had fooled herself this time just as she had before. Ross could not possibly love her, or he would have been honest with her. She had bared her soul to him while he had withheld his own from her.

The click of the door drew her attention as a fracture of light entered the darkened room.

"Miss Barrett? Are you awake?" Lydia asked softly.

Hesitating for a moment, she replied, "Yes, come in."

Lydia slipped into the room and closed the door behind her. She placed the lamp she carried on the bedside table beside the unlit one and smiled tentatively down at her teacher, who had become so much more than a teacher to her.

"We missed you at supper. Are you hungry?"

"No."

Pulling a chair up to the bed, Lydia sat on the edge, her thumbs fidgeting. Neither spoke for a few minutes.

"I don't believe what Mrs. Wilson said. Neither does Mrs. Barrett. She says the idea is preposterous and absolutely absurd."

Under different circumstances, Irene would have smiled at her mother's about-face. Wasn't it just like Winnie to champion Ross when the odds were completely against him?

"Ross would never hurt another person on purpose," Lydia went on. "That was wicked of Mrs. Wilson to say such mean things. And especially just to hurt you."

Irene reached out to lay her hand on Lydia's. The touch was reassuring to both of them. "I know," she replied.

"She just wants to keep you away from each other, but it isn't any of her business!"

"I know that, too."

"You aren't going to let her, are you? I mean, keep Ross away?"

But Irene couldn't reply. Not yet.

"You can't let her win!" Lydia declared with soft vehemence. "She's just a wicked old woman who can't love anybody and doesn't want anyone else to be loved. I mean, she doesn't even want you to love me and Jonathan." Immediately she halted, having said the words that were really in her heart without intentionally doing so. She loved this woman who had taken them in and cared for them as though they were her own children. But more than that, she had taken them to her heart—at least Lydia hoped she had. Nobody had done that since her mother died.

Irene's hand still held Lydia's, and now she clasped it tightly.

"Of course I love you. Both of you. Nothing Clara says could stop me."

Tears of happiness and relief filled Lydia's eyes. The words were magical, transporting her to a higher plane of security. She jumped off her chair and launched herself into Irene's arms. As she lay on the bed, curled into a ball, Irene smoothed the damp hair from the girl's face.

"There, there," she soothed. "Everything's going to be all right. You and Jonathan will be living with me from now until you're all grown up. Nothing anybody says will stop that from happening."

"I love you, Miss Barrett. I don't ever want to leave."

"We won't even consider it," Irene said.

Lydia lay thinking that it was almost to good to be true and certainly more than she'd ever expected that night last fall when they'd wandered into the first unlocked door. How fortunate for them that it had been Miss Barrett's house, and not Mrs. Wilson's!

"Why is Mrs. Wilson so mean? And what did Ross ever do to her?"

"I don't understand Clara exactly. And Ross . . . Well, I don't know."

Lydia turned to stare at Irene. "You don't believe her, do you?"

Irene kept silent.

"Just because he didn't defend himself doesn't mean it's true. And besides, I'll bet lots of people get killed in the West for all kinds of different reasons and maybe some of them deserve it. It isn't fair not to give him a chance to explain."

"He's had months to tell me about it."

"Are you going to be mad at him forever for not telling you?" Lydia asked, thinking about her own digressions from the truth. Not only had she told Irene those simple lies, but she had destroyed her mail, coming and going. She held her breath waiting for the answer.

"It's a betrayal of trust. That's hard to forgive," Irene replied with sadness in her voice.

With a pain in her stomach and dread in her heart, Lydia said, "I suppose." Rising from the bed, she said, "I guess I'd better get ready for bed." She leaned to kiss Irene's cheek and whispered, "Good night."

"Good night, dear."

Taking the lamp with her, Lydia walked the short distance to her own room while apprehension overwhelmed all the other good feelings inside her. She told herself to concentrate only on the good things, and the bad things would take care of themselves.

She hoped.

Clara sat on the straight-backed chair in her room, staring out the rain-streaked window. She clutched one hand to the other in a moment of fear, then defiance took root. She had dealt the winning blow and seen it hit its mark when Ross Hollister rode away without a word. It was a victory, but not a long-lived one, she was sure. Oh, there was no mistaking the disappointment and disillusion on Irene's face, but she knew the nature of women because she knew herself.

How many times had she forgiven the man she'd loved? Countless. And how many times had he let her down? Countless. She could save Irene from that emotional torture, and she would. Somehow.

Rising from her seat, she made her way through the waning light. Before long it would be supper time, even though the early darkness brought on by the storm made it seem more like bedtime. And she wished it was. With a tired sigh, she made her way down the stairs, each step an effort that cost her an extra breath. At the bottom of the steps, she rested a moment before going into the kitchen.

Even though she wasn't really hungry, she knew she should eat. Slowly, she moved about the unadorned room, deciding on cold fare for her meal.

When she'd finished, she put away the few dishes she'd dirtied and returned to her room. Although it wasn't her nature to lie down during any time of the day, she was far too tired to resist. After a little rest, she would feel more like her old self. It was simply the altercation she'd had with Irene and Mr. Hollister that had worn her out. She was getting too old for this kind of worry. She assured herself that it was nothing more than that.

After removing her shoes and stockings, she lay down. But behind her closed eyes she continued conjuring up Irene's face and the life that lay before her unless something happened to change the outcome. She must think of a way to do that. Somehow she must think of something that would rid this town of Ross Hollister, thus saving Irene's future. With a deeply indrawn breath, she contemplated many alternatives.

Chapter Twenty-two

When the mid-morning train arrived, all the children within running distance were there to greet it. Freshly relieved of their school duties, they raced happily alongside the passenger cars as they slowly came through the bridge, then around the curve to the depot. Jonathan and Lydia, caught up in the carefree excitement of the others, were among these dozen or so children.

After it came to a stop, they stood with quiet interest in a small group which resembled a welcoming committee, waiting to see who might emerge. Within several minutes, a lone woman stepped down from the car onto the platform. She smiled at the group, then went to speak to the man who sold tickets, cleaned up, and generally took care of the depot. The group followed.

As the woman set down her valise, the children circled her. After smiling over her shoulder at them, she spoke through the window.

"Excuse me, but could you tell me how to get to Miss Irene Barrett's house?"

"Sure thing. Just follow back along the tracks—" He stopped, spying Lydia and Jonathan in the group behind the woman. "Well, her children are here, so they can take you right to her front door."

A cold numbness spread throughout Lydia's body as realization dawned. This must be Aunt Sarah!

Sarah Jefferson Blakely turned toward the children after thanking the gentleman, her eyes resting on a young girl who stood half a head taller than the others. Her face had a stricken look, as though something unnatural had just happened or was about to.

"Are you Lydia?" she asked.

Filled with dread, Lydia nodded while continuing to stare dumbfounded at the woman who represented the worst of her nightmares. Beside her, she felt Jonathan sidle up and slip his hand into hers.

"And you must be Jonathan," Sarah added with a smile.

Jonathan refused to answer. Something was terribly wrong. Lydia was afraid. He figured that must mean this woman had come to take them away. Nothing had gone right since they'd come back from the picnic and Mrs. Wilson had said terrible things about Ross. Even Miss Barrett didn't act like herself—and just as bad, Ross never came by. He clutched Lydia's hand tightly.

"Could I trouble the two of you to take me to Miss Barrett's?"

"Yes, ma'am," Lydia replied, her voice small.

Sarah picked up her valise and waited for them to lead the way. As they walked along, she asked, "Do you know who I am?" She was sure that they did by the looks on their faces.

"Yes, ma'am," Lydia replied, her expression downcast. "Aunt Sarah."

"That's right. I haven't seen you since you were a babe in your mother's arms." To Jonathan, she said, "And this is the first time we've met."

He could only stare at her, wondering if his life was to

be upset once more, if he was to be handed off to this stranger. Stunned, he realized that it was true. Until this moment, he'd thought Miss Barrett liked him; he'd certainly liked her almost as good as his ma. But apparently she hadn't felt the same about them. And what would his chances be of seeing Ross again? Probably none. Hurt and anger welled up within him until he thought he'd burst from the pressure.

Seeing him shy away from her, Sarah said comfortingly, "We'll have some time to get to know one another." She wanted to brush back the hair from his forehead, but she knew any advance would be unwelcome. He so reminded her of her own William that her heart became homesick for the children she'd left behind.

They walked in silence for most of the way except for the occasional question that Sarah asked about the town, the school, and their friends. But the two accompanying her volunteered nothing.

At last they stopped before the picket fence, and Sarah smiled approvingly at the large house and the neatly clipped yard where flowers bloomed in gay colors.

"What a lovely home!" she exclaimed.

Both Lydia and Jonathan looked at it with renewed appreciation. It was indeed a lovely home, one that neither of them wanted to leave. Struggling with an intense desire to cry, Jonathan could stand it no longer and took off at a dead run toward the bridge and the mill on the other side.

"What—? Is he all right?" Sarah asked, concerned. "I didn't mean to upset him."

Lydia didn't call him back; she understood his need to be alone.

"He likes to go off by himself sometimes."

"Oh." Sarah watched as Jonathan's arms and legs pumped and churned up dust, putting distance between them.

Reluctantly, Lydia pushed open the gate and led the way to the door. If only there were some way to delay this meeting forever. Not only was she about to lose her new found home but when Miss Barrett learned of the lies she'd told and the destruction of her mail . . . well, Lydia knew quite clearly how she would view such things. A betrayal of trust was unforgivable.

Inside she found Winnie mending a basket of socks, her head cocked to one side, frowning over the tiny stitches she made.

"We have company," Lydia said.

Glancing up Winnie stared in surprise then quickly put away her mending as though embarrassed at getting caught at performing such a menial task. "Please come in, won't you?"

Sarah set down her valise and pulled off her gloves, extending her hand. "Thank you. You must be Miss Barrett."

"Actually, I'm Mrs. Barrett, Irene's mother." Still puzzled she studied the younger woman.

"Nice to meet you."

Glancing around at the stylish furnishings, Sarah smiled, pleased with what she saw. "Your daughter's home is very lovely."

"Thank you," Irene replied as she came through the doorway from the back of the house.

"Hello," Sarah said as she once again extended her hand in greeting. "I'm the children's aunt, Sarah Blakely. I'm sorry about arriving later than I told you in my letter. I hope this won't be inconvenient for you." Her words trailed off as she saw the same puzzled expression cross Irene's face that had earlier crossed her mother's. "You did get my letters, didn't you?"

Irene stared in dumbfounded surprise. This was the woman she'd sought so many months before when she was looking for a home for the children, a home with their own family members. But this attractive, middle-aged woman was a stranger in spite of the fact that she was a relative. Everything within Irene rebelled against the idea of sending the children away with a perfect stranger.

During those same months, she'd come to love Jonathan and Lydia as her own. There were so many things she had learned about them; things this woman would in turn learn. Like using Jonathan's favorite color, red, when knitting his scarves and mittens. It was the only way he could be coaxed to wear them. And he loved any kind of cookies and cakes but cared little for pies. The cowlick at the back of his head would respond to nothing and had become an endearing part of his personality as it bounced when he ran. And Lydia. Dear, tenderhearted, and oh-so-mature Lydia. A child and yet a friend, warm, loving, but a long way from being carefree. Her heart swelled near to breaking at the thought of losing them.

"Letters?" Irene repeated vacantly.

"Yes." Sarah glanced with appeal at each of the women. "I mailed several over the winter, and in one of them I explained that I wouldn't be able to arrive before the second week in May. I guess the mail isn't as reliable as I'd expected."

Irene pulled herself together, trying to regain her bearings and her hospitality. "Please, come in and sit down where we can talk more comfortably. You must be tired after your trip."

Winnie offered to make tea and escaped to the kitchen to brew it where she could be alone for a few minutes to take in this unexpected turn of events. The impact was startling. She hadn't realized how attached she'd become to the two little orphans until their imminent departure stared her in the face. She was afraid she wouldn't be able to hold her emotions in check if she stayed in the parlor another minute.

"I guess I've rather surprised you," Sarah said apologetically.

Still trying to compose herself, Irene replied, "I have to admit that I had given up. We all had."

"I received your letter before Thanksgiving. It took some

time to locate me, since I've remarried after my first husband's death. I suppose it's fortunate that I received it at all."

Lydia sat on the edge of her chair, wishing she were somewhere else but too afraid to leave. A great sadness enveloped her as she realized that Aunt Sarah hadn't come this far just to say hello. There would be no more running, no more lies. A quiet acceptance that life was to be endured, not enjoyed, suddenly came over her and she couldn't shake it off, couldn't rebel against it the way Jonathan had. And as she watched the two women decide her destiny, her only regret was that she hadn't destroyed every single letter before it had been mailed.

Feeling uncomfortable about discussing the children when she'd only just arrived, Sarah chose the subject of her present family.

"We've lived near Buffalo for two years now, but some of my family still lives in the same community where I lived before. I guess that's how they found me. Of course, with a family as large as ours, it would be hard not to find us," she said with a smile.

At that moment Winnie arrived with a tray of teacups and a teapot, from which she poured each of them a cup.

"You have children?" Irene asked, wondering how Jonathan would adjust to the idea.

"Yes. I have four of my own, ages eight to fifteen, and Carl has four of his own, ages twelve to seventeen."

"Eight children!" Winnie interjected. Jonathan and Lydia would get lost in the crowd, she feared.

Sarah nodded happily. "We're quite a family."

There was undoubtedly plenty of love to spare, by the look on Sarah's face, Irene thought.

"That sounds like a lot of cooking and mending to me," Winnie said.

"The twins, Molly and Sally, are a great help. I don't know what I'll do when the time comes for them to marry."

"I hope for your sake that your husband is a farmer,"

Winnie said, sipping her tea thoughtfully.

Sarah laughed. "No, he isn't. But we do keep a rather large garden."

Irene sat holding her teacup, not at all interested in drinking from it. "You'll want some time to get acquainted with the children, so of course you'll stay with us. You can put your things in the bedroom at the top of stairs. Lydia can sleep in my room, and Jonathan won't mind moving his cot into the hallway."

"Oh, I wouldn't dream of imposing further. I've already appeared unannounced and—"

"Through no fault of your own. We absolutely won't hear of the children's aunt staying anywhere but here." Irene couldn't help but like Sarah in spite of her reason for being there. After all, she herself had invited her, and although her arrival was costing Irene pain, she insisted that Sarah be treated as a guest.

As Lydia listened to the pleasant talk going on between the women, her tension increased. With each word they spoke, she felt sure her previous actions would be exposed, and the longer they spent together, the likelihood of that happening increased. It would be hard enough to leave without having Miss Barrett's disapproval between them. That would be more than she could bear. And yet she wanted nothing but the truth between them—truth, understanding and love. Like a force within her, she choked back the desire to confess and make everything right once more. But telling wouldn't make things right. Nothing could ever make things right again.

Andrew swung down from the train and onto the platform carrying only a valise. Five years, he thought as he looked around at the placid little town, and a very long five years at that.

Walking ahead of him was a woman surrounded by a group of children, none of whom he recognized, but then he only barely gave them any notice. With decisive steps he passed them as he strode purposefully down the hill.

Chapter Twenty-three

Winnie hurried into town right after the noon meal. After Sarah Blakely had gone upstairs to rest, Irene had excused herself as well, and Lydia had hightailed it like a nervous doe, leaving the house quiet enough to drive even the mice away.

As she walked along, she mentally went over her list of things to purchase at Howard's mercantile, all the while keeping an eye out for Jonathan. It wasn't uncommon for him to skip a meal if he was fishing with a friend, but she had a suspicion there was more to it than that.

She stepped inside the open doorway and made her way toward the sewing notions. Behind the counter stood Emma, quite large now, sorting through a tin of buttons.

"Hello, Emma," Winnie said.

"Oh, hello, Mrs. Barrett. What can I do for you this beautiful spring day?"

"Well, I'd like some more of that red yarn. And let me see your colored thread." She wanted to embroider some nice linen handkerchiefs for Lydia with her name on them.

She wouldn't have either of the children going off without something to remember her by. Suddenly she had to clear her throat.

"How is Irene?" Emma asked. "I've been wanting to get up there to see her, but"—she patted her stomach—"I rarely venture farther than the house or the store these days."

"Irene is well." At least, as well as could be expected, she added to herself.

"Then she hasn't heard?"

"Heard what?"

"Andrew's back. This morning."

Winnie nearly dropped the red yarn she was fingering. "He is?"

Emma nodded. "He was in to see Howard this morning, which was quite a shock for Howard. He certainly never expected to see a penny of the money Andrew had borrowed from him over five years ago. But he paid it all back."

Dumbfounded, Winnie couldn't seem to find her tongue.

"I suspect he'll be pretty busy going up and down Front Street if he intends to pay back all the money he'd ever borrowed. But I suppose that remains to be seen." Emma pushed aside the tin of buttons as she tried to lean across the counter. "Howard said most people never understood where Andrew ever got the money to build that big house or buy all that furniture. But of course, you probably knew all about that." She paused a moment to gauge Winnie's reaction. When there was none, she continued. "I guess Irene just believed in him so much that she didn't even question using her money. Naturally, when Andrew confessed his sins, so to speak, Howard was quite surprised. Truth to tell, I was shocked speechless."

Winnie had the presence of mind not to allow her mouth to hang open in astonishment, but just barely.

"Well," Emma went on, "all I've got to say is, thank the good Lord that Irene had sense enough not to marry him.

And leaving him standing at the altar was certainly what he deserved."

Unable to gather her wits about her, Winnie decided she'd best take her leave. "Yes. Uh, I guess I'll be going. . . . " She turned to leave.

"Ahem. That will be two dollars."

"Oh, of course." She dug in her purse for the proper coins and paid for her merchandise.

"Tell Irene hello for me," Emma said.

With no more than a slight wave of her hand, Winnie hurried out the door and dashed up the street.

Irene had used her inheritance to cover up Andrew's shortcomings. And all these years, Winnie had been berating her daughter for passing up the most wonderful man a woman could want! Posh! What an old fool she was for not being able to see the truth. As for Andrew—well, he was a smooth-talking, good-for-nothing dandy! And if he knew what was good for him, he'd not darken her daughter's doorstep any too soon. Now that she had the facts straight, she would send him merrily—or maybe not so merrily—on his way.

Ross had wrestled with his thoughts all morning, thoughts about Irene, his past, and even his future. And this wasn't the only morning he'd struggled with them. He'd barely gotten a wink of sleep for several nights, not since that fateful day of the picnic.

Securing a chain to the small stump for removal, he figured his disposition was suitable for the job at hand. Standing beside the horse, he coaxed the animal to ease into the tension, pulling, pulling until the stump slid free of the ground. His own muscles strained with the urge to help.

He had gained little in his attempts to come to a conclusion about his situation with Irene. Physical labor relieved the need to do something but accomplished nothing in his search for answers.

Once more his mind traveled over the alternatives. He could try to explain the truth by telling the whole story and letting her decide. But he'd seen the expression on her face, felt her distancing herself from him. Hadn't she already decided? Perhaps he should leave town and go back to mining. No, he would rather stay and torture himself with being close to her even though she would never be his. The torture could only be worse if he never saw her at all. So what choice did he really have? Even though it was undoubtedly too late for explanations, he guessed he'd never know for sure unless he tried. Having made that decision, he put his mind and muscle into finishing the work he'd begun. On his way back to the saloon, he'd stop at Irene's and talk with her—that was, if she'd even allow him in the door.

Andrew waited in the late afternoon sunshine for Irene to answer her back door. He'd hoped to talk with her privately; there was so much to say.

When she finally opened the door, he could only stare. She was even more beautiful than he remembered.

"Hello, Irene."

"Hello, Andrew." She stepped outside, closing the door behind her. "Mother told me you were in town."

He smiled, remembering Winnie Barrett. "How is she?"

She nodded. "Unchanged, I'd say."

"And you?"

Irene studied him. There was something different about the way he watched her, about the way he waited for her to speak. It was almost as though he really cared.

"I'm well."

"You look—" He stopped. Then he looked down at his feet with an embarrassed grin on his face before glancing up again. "I was about to say, you look as lovely as ever. But I don't want you to get the wrong idea. I didn't come here just to flatter you. I'm a changed man, Irene."

She held her silence.

"I came to apologize. And to thank you."

With a quizzical frown, she waited for him to go on.

"To apologize for my behavior and the hurt I caused you. And to thank you for setting us free. Both of us." He paused, then gently took her hand. "You were right not to marry me." He turned her hand over, then clasped it warmly between both of his. "I won't say my pride wasn't wounded. It was. But I learned a lesson that's served me well."

Seeing him like this, earnest and honest, she realized that she harbored no ill will toward him. As a matter of fact, she felt nothing at all. Somewhere along the line she'd left the pain and hurt of his betrayal behind. How had that happened? she wondered. Then Ross's face came to her, and she knew it was because of her love for him that she had released that long-ago love for Andrew. Perhaps she'd never really loved him at all.

"My life has changed and for the better. I hope it has for you, too." He let her hand go. "I'm getting married next month." He smiled. "This time it's for real."

"Congratulations," she replied, and she meant it. If he was releasing her from the past, then she could release him.

"I only came back to make things right with the folks in town. I'll be leaving in the morning. But I had to see you and tell you how I felt." Quickly, he leaned toward her and kissed her cheek.

The myriad of feelings that swarmed over her had nothing to do with what might have been. There were no regrets for the way it all turned out. It would have been wrong for them to marry. She'd known it then, and he knew it now. She was glad to be able to put this part of her life in a proper perspective. It was truly over for both of them.

Ross halted the horses alongside the bridge, feeling like a Peeping Tom although it was broad daylight.

"Whoa," he called softly as he caught sight of Irene with a stranger in the back yard. Then the hair on the back of his neck rose when he saw the stranger kiss her. His first thought was that the man looked a lot like what he suspected Andrew must look like. The thought didn't set well, and he knew instinctively that he was right.

Andrew was back in town. But why? And what could he have to say to Irene that she would be willing to listen to?

Icicles of fear coursed through his veins in spite of the warmth of the day. Whatever it was that had brought Andrew to Grand Rapids couldn't have come at a worse time. The scene he was witnessing told him that the former fiance wanted his old position back, and he, Ross, had just left that area wide open. Anger rose within him at the unfairness of it all.

With a shake of the reins, he slapped the backs of the horses and set them in motion.

As if she'd felt his eyes on her, Irene turned to catch him staring her way. She stood waiting, and he was not going to pass up the opportunity to talk with her, whether Andrew was there or not. He pulled the team around to the shed and climbed down.

The smoke from the chimney told him they were preparing supper. How many times before had he stopped by and been invited to stay? And what would his reception be this time? He whacked his dusty hat against his thigh. Only one way to find out, he told himself.

Irene's heart skipped a beat at the sight of him. It was good to see him again, so very good to see him, and they did need to talk. But her thoughts were incoherent, and she hardly knew where to begin. Andrew's visit had triggered a landslide of emotions, all of them freed at once.

Unable to ignore what he had witnessed, Ross skipped the amenities and asked straightforwardly, with only a glance for the other man, "An old friend?"

She nodded. "Ross, this is Andrew."

His body stiffened. He was right. What else was he right

about? That maybe Andrew wanted her back and she figured he was a better choice than himself?

"He just came to say good-bye." She kept smiling, staring up into those summer-blue eyes and seeing the concern he felt over Andrew's visit.

Andrew offered his hand. "Hello," he said, smiling.

Ross stared at it, not moving, unwilling to give this man even a modicum of friendliness until he knew for sure what he was up to.

The moment became awkward.

With an apologetic shake of his head, Andrew withdrew his hand. "I guess my reputation has preceded me," he said.

Ross's silence, as well as his stiff bearing, said that it had.

"If it's of any value to you, I've already given my apologies to Irene," Andrew went on. Turning to Irene, he said, "Well, I've got a few more calls to make, then I'll be on my way."

"Thank you for stopping," Irene replied sincerely.

He nodded, gave a small salute, and placed his hat upon his head before turning away.

When he had rounded the corner, she reached out and laid her hand on Ross's arm. "I'm glad you came by. I've been wanting to talk to you."

"About him?" he replied, his voice unyielding.

"No," she answered. "I'm sorry for doubting you," she replied softly. She needed to say more, but she had to take her time and sort through her thoughts before she spoke. "It was simply an old hurt that got in the way. I reacted without thinking. I let the pain of the past take over." She shook her head as though to erase her words. "I mean the fear of that pain. It had little to do with you and everything to do with me. Do you understand?"

His first impulse was to pull her into his arms and tell her how much he loved her, and wanted her, and to hell with Andrew. But he held his peace, sensing her need to speak first, so he settled for simply laying his hand on top of her small one.

With her gaze unwavering, she said, "When a person withholds forgiveness for a past mistake, it grows and festers until the whole body becomes ill. So I'm asking you to forgive me for not trusting in the love I have for you."

This time he did pull her into his arms, savoring the feel of her soft woman's body, the smell of her sweet hair, and the knowledge that she did indeed love him. He buried his face in the tender spot of her neck and shoulder.

"I love you, Irene Barrett. And I'm the one who should be asking you to forgive me."

Warmed through and through, Irene clasped him to her. This was where she belonged. She'd known for some time, but she'd fought it, struggled with it, until, at last, she welcomed it with her heart and soul.

Lifting his head, he met her gaze. "I want to tell you about it now."

She laid a finger on his lips. "Only if you want to."

He nodded, taking a deep breath before plunging in.

"I was in a saloon playing poker when one of the girls who worked there walked by and the fellow across from me grabbed her by the wrist. She sort of screamed and tried to hit him. Little did I know he was the sheriff's son when I told him to let her go. In no uncertain words, he told me where to go. Then, for spite, he twisted her arm until a bone cracked, and that's when I jumped him.

"When we fell to the floor, we rolled around trying to get the other one pinned. Somehow he grabbed my gun. I tried to take it, but it went off. He was killed."

Wide-eyed, Irene stared at him. "That isn't murder! How could they send you to prison for self-defense?"

"He was the sheriff's son, and I was just passing through."

"It was self-defense. In more ways than one." He was a kind and compassionate man, and that was what had gotten him into this trouble.

"No, it was my anger. I killed a man."

She reached a hand toward him, remorse filling her for believing the worst, for not giving him a chance to explain, and for being guilty of the very thing she'd accused him of: betrayal. She loved him with all her heart and yet she'd betrayed that love by not trusting him to be honest with her.

"I love you," she said softly, trying to erase his pain with her words.

He shrugged. "It's over now. I did my time instead of hanging, thanks to the saloon girl, who testified." He gave a half smile and a slight shake of his head, then spoke as if to himself, "I suspected that some of the jurors knew her personally and believed her. Otherwise . . ."

Irene stayed close, leaning against him, her hands upon his chest as a cool breeze off the river brought with it a scent of lilacs.

"I love you, Irene Barrett," he said again into the depths of her hair. "I guess I have since the night you ran your heel into my toe."

She raised her head and gazed into his beautiful blue eyes. "I love you, too, Ross Hollister," she returned. Then, with a puzzled frown, she asked, "Is that the reason you were so against me being in the saloon? Because of what happened to that woman?"

He kissed the tip of her nose. "Partly. And because a saloon is no place for a woman."

"Or a man, for that matter."

With a slight nod of his head and another kiss on her nose, he said, "I agree."

Surprised, she leaned away from him to get a better look at his face. "You do?"

"Yep. That's why I traded it to Howard."

"Howard!"

"It wasn't easy, but I did it."

With a sly grin, she replied, "Emma must be devastated! No wonder I haven't seen her for so long."

"She doesn't know. If she did, I suspect the whole town would."

Irene laughed softly. "You're right. Clara has always counted on Emma."

"Hmmm. I thought so."

She nestled her head beneath his chin, relishing the steady sound of his heart beneath her ear.

"So you made a trade. And what did you get for your part of this trade?" she asked.

"I don't think I'll tell you just yet."

Lifting her head, she asked, "And why not?"

"I think I'll just show you. As a matter of fact, that's what I'd planned the day of the picnic, but you had to go and fall in the water and pull me in too," he teased.

"Wait a minute," she defended herself. "I believe—"

She didn't get the opportunity to finish. His lips, warm and inviting, came to rest gently on hers, suffusing her entire body with a happy glow.

When at last it ended, she went on, "I believe I like that very much."

"I can't tell you how glad I am to hear that," he said, nibbling her ear.

"Hmmm. I like that, too."

He followed the line of her neck, and her head tilted to give him better access.

"That, too," she said a little breathlessly, beginning to wilt around the knees.

At that moment the back door opened, but neither of them was in a position to notice.

Lydia watched while the two people she cared so much about embraced and kissed in the plain light of day. She hated to interrupt them, but her concern over Jonathan's disappearance forced to her to get their attention.

"Ahem!" She cleared her throat as loudly as she could. "Excuse me," she said. Stepping away from the door, she pulled it closed.

Jumping guiltily away from Ross, Irene pressed two fingers to her swollen lips as if to hide them from view. Ross kept his arm around her waist, drawing her close to his side, unwilling to relinquish his hold on her for even a minute.

"I hate to bother you," Lydia began, "but I'm worried about Jonathan. He never misses two meals in a row."

"She's right," Irene said, worry creeping into her voice too. In her concern over Sarah's arrival and its significance, she'd set aside her concern about Jonathan's whereabouts. But with the evening pressing in, she knew something was wrong or he would be home by now.

"When did you last see him?" Ross asked.

"This morning when we met Aunt Sarah's train. He was pretty upset. I guess he knew we'd have to leave here and go with her."

"Leave here?" Ross asked. "Why?"

Turning to him, Irene answered quietly, "I haven't told you. Last fall I began searching for their Aunt Sarah. Well, she's here now. I thought they'd want to be with their family."

"No!" Lydia rushed toward her. "No, we don't want to leave you. You are our family. I think she's nice, but we don't really even know her and she already has such a big family . . . How would we fit in?" Practically out of breath, she paused, her eyes begging.

"We don't love her. We love you!" Lydia threw herself into Irene's arms. "Please don't send us away."

Irene caught her and held tight. She could never do it, she told herself. She could never allow anyone to take these two from her. Over Lydia's head, Ross's eyes met hers, and she found agreement in them. He would stand with her in this decision.

With her voice unsteady, Irene said, "I would never send you away if you didn't want to go. I want you to stay with me."

"With us," Ross added. Sheepishly he went on, "I didn't intend to say it like this. I wish it was a little more roman-

tic—like a boat ride or a carriage ride in the country."
Then as he gazed long into her eyes, he searched for the
answer he hoped she'd give him. "Will you marry me?" he
asked softly. "All three of you?"

It didn't matter to Irene that they weren't on a boat ride
or in a carriage in the country. The only thing she cared
about was that he'd asked her to spend her life with him.

"Yes," she said, her voice barely capable of whispering.
She raised one hand to lay it on his unshaven cheek.

Careful not to squeeze the girl between them, he leaned
down and kissed Irene, trying to put all of his feelings into
that one touch. But he could not. Not if he kissed her for
a hundred years.

Jonathan sulked along the banks of the Miami and Erie
Canal. He'd tried sneaking aboard one of the canal boats,
only to be caught by the captain. And wouldn't luck have
it that it turned out to be the same mean captain who had
thrown them off last fall. Kicking a stone, Jonathan wondered how a boy was supposed to run away if he didn't
have any way to travel. Without Lydia, he was afraid to go
on foot, since his days of hunting with Ross had taught
him that there was plenty to be afraid of.

He walked away from the canal toward the river, looking out across to the town of Grand Rapids and the backside of the saloon. If ever he needed a friend, it was now.
But would Ross still be his friend? He'd heard the things
Mrs. Wilson had said, and he knew that Miss Barrett's feelings for Ross had changed. Maybe Ross wouldn't want
him hanging around anymore since Miss Barrett didn't
like him now. Whatever Ross had done, it wouldn't matter
one bit to him. They were friends. Or at least they had
been.

He made his way toward the railroad bridge and found
a large rock to sit on. He wasn't exactly hidden, but nobody
seemed to pay much attention to him so he guessed this
would do until he could make a decision.

Glancing overhead, he studied the bridge. He could probably follow it until . . . until what? Until he found a home the way he and Lydia had done the night they walked into Miss Barrett's house? No, that was a long, scary trip, and he would never attempt it without Lydia. He was smart enough to know that.

If only he had a friend.

Once more he stared across the river toward the saloon.

It was his only chance. Maybe if Ross was as mad at Miss Barrett as she was at Ross, he wouldn't tell on him. He would sneak inside the storage room until after the saloon closed, then he'd find Ross and beg him to take him out West, where a man and a boy could run away and never be found. And of course, they would take Lydia, too.

It was his only chance.

Clara cleared the dishes from her supper table. Thank goodness her energy had returned; she would need it to accomplish her plans.

With an anxious eye on the setting sun, she washed the dishes, all the while her mind rationalizing the need for this drastic step she was about to take. She had no intention of harming any one personally. That would be wrong. But to destroy that which causes destruction and thereby rid the town of one blot on society would not be wrong. And it only stood to reason that if the saloon were gone, then Ross Hollister would have to leave. It was the only solution.

She dried her hands on her apron before slipping it over her head and onto the peg near the door. It was time to gather the things she would need: a hooded black cloak that was too warm for this time of year but would hide her well, and a box of matches. Simple measures for a simple plan. What could go wrong?

Folding the cloak over her arm with the matches hidden in the folds, she left the house by way of the back door. Dusk had settled upon the town nestled so carefully against the bend in the river. With the drone of mosquitoes accompanying her, she made her way along the side streets and alleys. When she reached Front Street, she slipped unseen between two buildings, donned her cloak, and proceeded toward the side-cut canal. As she approached the back of the row of establishments, she cautiously checked to see if any loiterers hung about. She found only a few barges tied up at their moorings with their captains nearby. With darkness just descending, she wondered if perhaps she'd been too hasty in allowing her eagerness to bring her so early. She would have a long wait before the saloon closed. But if she waited too long, she might run into someone leaving the saloon who would recognize her, and although she would take great pride in this deed, she could not risk being seen.

She walked along close to the buildings with her hood pulled up, shielding her face. Her steps slowed as she neared the saloon, and her hand faltered when she reached for the door. Perhaps she should walk on by until she had the complete cover of darkness to protect her.

Continuing on toward the dam, her steps slow and measured, she watched the last rays of sun ebb from the sky in a brilliant display of colors. Life should be like that, she thought, beautiful and without tarnish. As she turned around and headed back, she decided that tonight she would do her part to see to it that at least one tarnished blot would be removed from her town.

Jonathan sat quietly on an empty bench behind a row of kegs, his eyes adjusting to the pitch dark as well as a cat's. He was sure he wouldn't be seen if Ben had to come in for another keg. So when the door opened, he wasn't startled. He moved his head in order to see between the small barrels, but instead of finding Ben moving through the doorway with a light in his hand, he saw the figure of a cloaked woman. He strained his eyes trying to make out who it was, but it wasn't until she put down her hood just as she closed the door that he realized Mrs. Wilson had joined him. He heard the strike of a match before it flared, exposing the firm jaw and stubborn face of the woman he disliked so much.

What was she doing here? he wondered. And how would he ever get past her to go find Ross? Hardly daring to breathe, he held as still as a mouse being stalked by a cat. If she knew he was here, he would be returned to Miss Barrett immediately; then he would be taken away to live with another stranger. He clamped his lips tight and decided to wait until she left. But why was she sitting in the damp, dark storage room of the saloon?

Irene sat at the table beside Ross. Lydia, Winnie, and Sarah sat with them, worry etched on their faces as well. Supper had been served and eaten in the hopes that Jonathan would show up as he always did, his anger overcome by his hunger. But not tonight.

"This is my fault," Sarah said. "He was afraid I was coming to take him away from here, when in fact I wasn't. I should have said so immediately."

All heads swung her way.

"You weren't?" Lydia blurted out. "But I—"

Sarah shook her head and reached a comforting hand toward Lydia. "I just wanted to see for myself that you were well taken care of." She smiled at Irene. "And I can certainly see that's true. I'm afraid I was feeling guilty about not being able to take you in. What with eight children of our own, we're fairly packed to the eaves. Not that we aren't happy—we are. But I just didn't know where I would put two more. So Carl agreed that the least I could do was to come and visit. And I hope you'll come visit us, too."

A round of sighs, some audible, some inaudible, came from those who listened. Irene squeezed Ross's hand beneath the table, where he held it tenderly, and their eyes met with the unspoken words of love that they would save

327

until after Jonathan was home again, safe and sound.

Relieved, Lydia got up to hug her aunt. "Thank you. We would love to visit with your family." Sitting once more, she felt the familiar heaviness in her heart over the lies hiding there. "I have a confession to make," she said in a small voice. "I . . . I never mailed the letters you wrote to Aunt Sarah and I tore up the ones she sent to you." Raising her head, she waited for the disappointment to show on Miss Barrett's face.

Irene blinked in surprise. She would never have suspected, but then again, Lydia was just the kind of girl who needed to be in control of her life, especially when it was out of control. She would do what she had to do in order to survive, just the way she had when she and Jonathan ran away from an orphanage before finding their way here. At least those were her suspicions, and now she felt sure they were true.

"I'm glad you told me," Irene replied with a small smile of her own. "It restores my faith in the U.S. postal system."

Lydia smiled in return, thankful for the understanding she read in Irene's eyes. Everything was working out better than she'd ever believed possible. Ross was with them once more, Aunt Sarah wouldn't be taking them away, and Lydia hadn't lost favor in their eyes. If only Jonathan knew about all this good news, he would be as happy as she.

Ross pushed back his chair. "We've waited long enough. I'm going to the mill and look for him around the canal."

"I'll go to the schoolyard," Lydia said, "that's where I always go when I need to think. Then I'll see if he went to any of his friends' homes."

Irene rose from her chair, too. "I can—"

Placing a hand on each of her shoulders, Ross said, "You can stay here in case he comes back. He'll need to know you're here for him."

Nodding, Irene acquiesced. He was right. And she wanted to be there for him, to hold him tight and reassure him that she'd always be there.

"I'll whip up a batch of oat-and-raisin cookies," Winnie said, always rising to a crisis with fresh-baked food.

"I'll help," Sarah offered, needing something to do.

Ross kissed Irene's cheek. "I'll check back here every so often."

Again she nodded, feeling helpless.

The evening wore on, long and tedious, while the cookies cooled until they became cold. The fire went out in the stove, but nobody thought to keep it going. Their thoughts were reserved for worrying over Jonathan.

Ross and Lydia had both come back twice without Jonathan or any news of him. The last time Lydia came through the door, Irene insisted she was not to go out again.

Around ten o'clock, Ross showed up with Howard, Ben—who had closed up the saloon--and a few others from town.

"We're going to have to get as many men as we can. It's hard telling how far he might have gone. He might have even gone to the old cabin," Ross said, worry tightening his face. He shouldn't have waited so long, but he hadn't really believed Jonathan would leave. He'd questioned the captains along the canal and was assured that a young boy had indeed tried to stow away on a couple of barges but had been caught. Perhaps he'd succeeded on another; then there would be no telling where he might be. He mentally kicked himself for a fool.

After two more hours of fruitless searching, all of the men converged on Irene's house simultaneously as if of the same mind.

"I'll say one thing," Ben volunteered. "He sure is one smart boy to out-fox ten grown men."

Everyone nodded their agreement, feeling a sad defeat. Only the sound of shuffling, tired feet filled the otherwise silent kitchen.

Then the heart-sinking clang of the firebell resounded through the night as someone frantically pulled the clapper to and fro. Suddenly alert, every man's head jerked up with fears of their own homes in danger. One after another, they rushed from Irene's back door, pouring out like smoke from an overheated chimney. The sky over the town glowed with the flames that engulfed one building and threatened several others.

With the speed that only fear can produce, they ran down the hill in the direction of the fire. Lagging behind them were Irene, Winnie, Lydia, and Sarah. All hands would be needed; no man or woman would be turned away.

When they reached Front Street, they knew without a doubt that it was the Broken Keg that had burst into flames. The crowd outside hadn't waited to begin dousing the building with water, and there among them was Andrew. But their efforts seemed useless. The old timbers were easily and greedily consumed.

"Is anybody in there?" Ross shouted to the first man he met.

"I don't think so," came the response.

Irene caught sight of Emma standing across the street in front of the mercantile. She stood staring with frightened eyes at the sight before her.

"You shouldn't be out here," Irene said to her, trying to usher her away.

"I thought I heard someone. In there. Just before the firebell sounded."

Chapter Twenty-four

Fear ground itself against the walls of Irene's stomach. "There's someone in there?"

Emma nodded. "I think so. I'm not sure. Maybe I imagined it."

Turning away, Irene ran to find Ross. They had given up trying to save the saloon and were concentrating on keeping the other buildings from catching fire.

She clutched his arm, shouting above the voices surrounding them and the raging fire before them. "Ross! Emma thinks someone is in there!"

He stared at her, disbelieving, then turned toward the burning saloon. Could Jonathan be in there? Panic rose in his chest as he watched the orange and red flames engulf the entire front of the building. It would be impossible to survive in an inferno like that. And there was no human way to get in through the front door. But maybe the back, he thought as he took off at a run, skirting the fire.

"Ross! Wait!"

But he couldn't wait. If Jonathan was in there, it might

already be too late. He had no time to lose.

When he finally made his way to the back, he found heavy smoke pouring through the cracks around the door. Wet, he thought, he needed something wet. The canal. Without wasting a second, he tore off his jacket, dipped it in the canal, and then used it as a shield. Quickly, he kicked the door open and called, "Jonathan!"

Inside the little entry way he could see nothing but billowing black and gray smoke.

"Jonathan!" he called again, trying not to choke as he inhaled.

He kicked open the interior door to the saloon, and a flash of fire snapped at him like the head of a dragon before it receded.

"Jonathan!" he yelled, but his words only came back in his face with the scorching heat.

He took one step ahead, then stumbled. Catching himself, he stared down at a dark form on the floor. A timber somewhere gave way and fell, sending a shower of sparks into the already burning room. Quickly, he knelt and rolled over the inert form of Clara Wilson.

Then he heard it, or thought he did. He glanced around but could see nothing. Still, he couldn't be sure. A strange tingle of fear spiraled down his spine. He had to get her out and then search for Jonathan.

With one hand behind her head and the other beneath her knees, he lifted her weighted body and turned to flee. Just as he reached the door, another timber cracked like thunder and fell. With one backward glance, he rushed from the inferno into the cool night, taking great choking breaths of air into his burning lungs.

He carried her a safe distance from the saloon and laid her down. Momentarily, her eyes opened and she smiled.

"Thaddeus, it's you," she cried, her voice raspy from the smoke. "I knew you'd come. I knew you'd come."

Irene appeared around the corner, running toward him. "Is Jonathan in there?" Then she saw Clara and knelt beside her. "Clara? Oh, Clara, what were you doing in there?"

Immediately Ross was on his feet. "Stay here. I'm going back in. I think I heard someone else." He couldn't tell her it might be Jonathan—not yet, not until he knew for sure.

He entered the door once more, but decided not to go into the main part of the saloon. That left two other doors: the one to the upstairs and the one to the storage room. The upstairs was no longer in existence, the fire having eaten most of it. He turned to the storage room and pushed on the door, but it wouldn't budge. He pounded on it with both fists, then yelled through the wood barrier.

"Jonathan! Are you in there?"

He waited for an answer but heard nothing. With all his might, he rammed his shoulder against the door, once, twice and once again. Panic choked him worse than the roiling smoke as he viciously kicked the door and alternately thrust his shoulder against it until, finally, the boards gave way in splintering pieces.

Inside the small room that once had been cool and damp but now was hot and suffocating, he stumbled around, calling as he went.

Then he heard it, a small weeping voice. "Ross. I'm here."

He groped through the dark until his fingers found clothing first, then a sweaty, overheated forehead.

"Come here, son," he said, gathering the limp boy into his arms.

Coughing and sputtering, he carried Jonathan into the welcome cool, damp air of the night. He hurried along the bank of the canal to the place he'd taken Clara, where Irene and several others waited. Kneeling down, he laid the boy on the grass.

Irene and Lydia crowded close, crying with happiness that they'd found him.

"Is he . . . is he all right?" Lydia asked through her sobs, sitting on the ground and cradling his head in her lap.

In a desperate attempt to find out, Irene gently tugged

at Jonathan's shirt, checking for burns.

"He was . . ." Ross could only say a few words at a time since the need to cough was so great. "He was . . . in the . . . storage room."

Glancing up into the crowd, Irene called, "Somebody bring the doctor." To Ross she said, "Sh-h-h. Don't try to talk. Lie here next to Jonathan and rest."

But he continued to sit up, watching as she looked Jonathan over. "How's Clara?" he asked, before breaking into a spasm of coughing.

Her hands stilled as she looked him in the eye. "Gone. You did the best you could."

The snapping and crackling of the fire filled the night as it cast an unearthly glow on the faces watching it. With a crashing blow, the remainder of the roof and upstairs caved in, while a crescendo of live sparks erupted from the center.

"Why did she do it?" he asked. "It wasn't worth her life."

Shaking her head, Irene replied, "I don't know."

In the distance they could hear Winnie's stern voice, "Step aside, please, let the doctor through. Please, we need to get through. Thank you. One side, please. Thank you."

Within seconds, Doctor Stephens was at their side. He checked for Clara's pulse, but the sad expression on his face told them he'd found none. Then he turned to Jonathan while they all continued to look on anxiously.

"He appears to have escaped burns. Thank God. But his lungs . . . Well, it isn't much wonder with all the smoke he's inhaled. But I think he's going to be all right with the proper rest. He'll probably have a sore throat and chest for a while. We'll give him something soothing for that."

He glanced at Ross, but Ross waved him away. "I'm all right, really." He coughed for a moment, then gave in, saying, "I guess I'll take some of that . . . soothing stuff, too."

The doctor nodded his head. "Just what I like, a cooperative patient."

A quiet calm settled over the people as they watched

helplessly as the fire consumed the saloon like so many sticks in a fireplace. They stood in small groups or alone, saying nothing. Word of Clara's death and Jonathan's safety had spread to all, and feelings were a mixture of sadness over the passing of one and gladness over the safety of the other. The fire would continue to burn, then smolder on into the night, so watchmen were appointed to keep an eye on it in case a wind should arise and spread the burning embers to other structures. Eventually, the crowd began dispersing.

Ross picked up Jonathan and carried him toward Irene's house. Winnie and Sarah had gone ahead to make preparations for washing up the tired, smoke-stained boy. Irene and Lydia stayed at Ross's side, not wanting to be separated from either of them.

A kind of melancholy happiness overwhelmed Irene—a contentment for the way things had turned out, yet a sadness for the end of a part of her life. So much had changed in only one day. No, she thought, not one day but a series of days. She'd lost her job as a teacher of many children but had gained two of her own to nurture. She'd thought she'd lost Ross and his love only to find a richer, deeper love full of confidence and trust. When all was said and done, she'd gained much more than she had ever lost, much more than she'd ever dreamed possible.

Ross awoke on the small cot with a cramp in his neck. His throat hurt as though he'd swallowed a hot porcupine, and his chest felt as if he'd been hugged by a grizzly. He couldn't even moan out loud for the pain it would undoubtedly cause, so he lay without moving, just staring at the ceiling in Irene's parlor.

She had insisted that he had no choice but to accept her offer of hospitality, since his own sleeping quarters had gone up in smoke. When he'd hesitated, she'd teased him about his worrying what the neighbors might think. To dispel that idea, he had quickly accepted her invitation.

Now, rolling to his side, he pushed himself to a sitting position, both hands braced on the edge of the cot. The need to cough overwhelmed him, but he choked it back.

"Good morning," Irene said softly from behind him.

He turned and smiled. So far smiling was the only thing that didn't hurt.

"Hmm. Can't talk?" she asked.

He shrugged.

"Not sure, huh?"

He nodded.

"Well, come into the kitchen. Mother is waiting to give you some of the doctor's medicine."

He grimaced but obediently followed.

Winnie stood ready to administer the proper dosage by spoonfuls. He opened his mouth determined to take it like a man.

"The doctor said this would fix you right up," Winnie said, stuffing the man-sized spoon into his mouth. "One should do."

He swallowed, unable to prevent a flinching reaction. Instantly he relaxed as the concoction slid nicely down his throat, soothing as it went just as the doc had promised.

"Thanks," he croaked.

Breakfast consisted of eggs, bacon, and fresh bread with butter, for everyone but him. He got a bowl of thickened gruel laced with molasses. He smiled politely and ate it like a man.

Lydia sat across from him, chattering happily about anything and everything, barely giving the others a chance to speak.

"So when is the wedding?" she asked.

"Wedding? What wedding?" Winnie stared from Lydia to Ross to Irene. "Is there going to be a wedding?"

"Mother, you've repeated yourself three times."

"Don't dodge the issue, Irene. Is there?"

Irene sipped her tea and smiled conspiratorially at Ross.

"Now, listen here, young woman. I demand to know—"

She stopped immediately when Irene turned a blank stare on her. So she amended her sentence. "I would appreciate a little advance notice, if it isn't too much trouble. After all, there will be plenty of things to—"

Once more Irene stared blankly at her.

"All right," Winnie acquiesced. "It's your wedding. But am I at least invited?"

Smiling graciously, Irene said, "Of course you are. We'll let you know when we decide."

"Well, I hope you know that it takes time—" She shifted her glance to the food on her plate. "Never mind."

A round of soft laughter filled the room.

"How is Jonathan?" Ross asked, his voice half normal.

"Sleeping," Irene replied. "We woke him several times during the night to give him the same medicine you took."

"We also explained that he'd be living here and not going home with me," Sarah offered. "I think that helped him sleep a little easier too."

Irene reached her hand toward Sarah. "Please don't be offended."

"Oh, I'm not. In time he'll get to know me, and we'll be great friends. I'm anxious for him to meet William."

"I can't wait to meet the twins," Lydia said.

As the happy chatter continued, Ross reached beneath the table to grasp Irene's hand and tug it. When she glanced up at him, he tipped his head slightly toward the back door. Repressing a smile, she rose from her seat, asking to be excused. Then he did the same.

Outside in the bright morning sunshine, she stood waiting for him. Smiling unabashedly, she walked into his open arms.

"Good morning, Mr. Ross Hollister."

"Hello, Miss Barrett-soon-to-be-Mrs. Hollister."

"Are you going to kiss me?" she asked.

"What? With all the neighbors watching?" he quipped.

"They may as well get used to it." She stretched on tiptoe

and pressed her lips against his. "This doesn't embarrass you, does it?"

"Not in the least," he said, pulling her flush against him and kissing her soundly.

"I could get used to this."

"So could I," he said while nuzzling her neck.

"Maybe we should get married before this goes, you know, much further."

"Good idea." He nibbled her on the ear. "Is today all right?"

She pushed him away. "Today!"

"Okay. Tomorrow then."

Laughing, she replied, "I thought maybe next month."

"Uh-huh. Too long."

"Two weeks?"

He considered that for a moment. "All right. But under protest only." Tipping her chin up, he asked, "What about a honeymoon?"

Smiling, she replied, "That would be nice, but . . ."

"We'll go to Colorado and we'll take the kids. I'll wrap up my business with Jeff."

"The gold mine?"

He nodded.

"It sounds wonderful. Won't the children love it!"

"I suppose it wouldn't really be a honeymoon with the kids along—"

"We'll do just fine." She spoke softly, staring into the depths of his smokey blue eyes. "Shall we go inside now and tell the others?"

"In a minute."

Then he gathered her close and kissed her in the most tender fashion, making her heart leap. Only a gallant hero could do something like that, she told herself.

"Two weeks! Irene, you'll be the death of me yet."

"Two weeks is enough. We want a simple ceremony in the backyard—"

"Backyard!"

"—where the roses are just beginning to bloom."

"And we'll have the smell of the outhouse in competition."

That was an exaggeration considering the layout of her garden and buildings, and Irene knew it.

"Why not the church?"

"I won't have anyone making comparisons between this wedding and the other one."

"What about a dress?" Winnie asked, almost fearful to hear the answer.

"I have plenty of dresses."

"I mean a white satin-and-lace one like your sisters wore."

"There isn't time to order the material and have it sewn. One of my other dresses will be just fine."

"Hmph!"

And so the subject was settled. A lovely arbor would serve as an altar while nature itself would be the chapel. A few close friends would be invited, and afterward there would be refreshments of cake and fruit punch.

"Where will you be staying?" Winnie asked.

"I don't know. Ross said he has that all taken care of."

"Well, at least it won't be above a saloon."

Ross pounded the last nail home, then sat back on his heels to survey the roof.

"Well, the roof is finished and guaranteed not to leak," he called down to Ben and Howard.

"And you've got a new front door, and all the window panes have been replaced," Howard called back.

Climbing down the ladder, Ross smiled and said, "What more could we ask for?"

Ben stuck his head around the door from inside, a mischievous smile on his face. "A bed maybe?"

Ross grinned but said nothing.

"Well, it's pretty sound on the outside, but there's still a lot of work to do inside," Howard commented, stepping through the doorway.

Ben looked up the stone chimney. "Is it okay? The nights are still kinda chilly, you know."

"I'll test it out when I clean up all this." He swung his hand with the hammer still in it to encompass the whole interior of the one-room cabin. He would tear down the old loft and sweep it clean before scrubbing it. He had purchased another bed, which should arrive from Toledo in another week, as well as linens of very good quality. Howard carried a fine selection of small rugs that would suffice. Other than that, there wasn't anything else they needed.

"You plan on living here long?" Ben asked, looking around the small cabin.

Ross shook his head. "She doesn't even know it's mine."

"Not much room here for youngun's," Ben added skeptically.

Ross agreed. "We'll be staying in town at her house until we can get a house built out here. That is, if she wants to."

Their future lay before them unmapped, ready to be explored together. There were so many things to talk about and decide, so many things to plan. And they had a whole lifetime ahead to do it in.

Chapter Twenty-five

Irene stood alone in her upstairs bedroom. The bright morning sun sent its dappled light through the leaves of the trees outside her window. With a nervous sigh, she placed her hand on her stomach to still the butterflies within.

No need to be nervous, she told herself. Wasn't she marrying the man she'd been waiting for all of her life? Hadn't she dreamed about him during the day as well as the night? Yes, she certainly had, and with that acknowledgment the butterflies disappeared.

Walking to the wardrobe, she removed the pale yellow satin gown she'd never worn. The simple yet elegant dress had struck her fancy on a shopping spree, but she'd lacked the appropriate occasion to wear it. Until now.

She slipped it on, over the bustle and petticoat trimmed with pristine lace. She had applied the French lace herself. Something old and something new.

After buttoning the front of the dress clear up to the soft, simple collar, she patted her hair in place. Curls framed her face while a thick braid coiled attractively at the nape of her neck.

With one last look in the mirror, she topped off the outfit with a hat of pure confection. Wide-brimmed, to shield her from the sun, it was decorated with gathers of white organza and laced with yellow flowers.

Giving herself a quarter turn, she smiled, pleased with what she saw, and hoping that Ross would like it too. At that thought, the butterflies sprung to life once more.

With him uppermost in her mind, she crossed the room and made her way down the narrow stairway. The sound of his warm laughter reached her through the open windows, and she paused to listen as he greeted their guests in the garden.

You're a lucky woman, Irene Barrett, she told herself again as she stepped into the parlor, where the minister waited with her mother and Lydia.

"You're so beautiful!" Lydia cried. "I'd like to hug you, but I don't want to wrinkle your dress."

"It would be well worth it," Irene said, smiling and drawing her close.

"Everyone's here," Lydia went on excitedly. "Even Emma and the baby. She's such a darling! Wait till you see her."

"Where's Jonathan?" Irene asked, fighting down the panic that so easily arose whenever he disappeared.

"He's been with Ross since early this morning," Winnie said, beaming with pride at her daughter. "And wait until you see him!"

"Are we ready to begin, Miss Barrett?" asked the reverend, who stood patiently by waiting for his chance to speak.

"Yes, I guess we are." The butterflies returned.

They went over the procedures and everyone departed, except Winnie who stood before her daughter with her eyes glistening and her chin quivering.

"I just want to say . . . you're a wise and beautiful

woman, Irene. And today I'm more proud than ever that you're my daughter." Then she caught her in a fierce hug, holding her tight, unconcerned about wrinkles on either of them.

"I love you, too, Mother," Irene responded, her voice hushed with emotion.

Releasing her daughter, Winnie stepped back and brushed Irene's tears away with a handkerchief. "I guess I'll be leaving for Cincinnati in a day or so. You know, it's a wonder Janie hasn't had that baby yet." Then, with pretended briskness, she shooed Irene through the house to the back door.

But Irene hesitated in the doorway, surveying the small crowd, until she found her children and Ross. He was dressed in a dark suit and tie, carrying a brand-new hat. Standing nearby was Jonathan, also dressed in a dark suit and tie and wearing a brand new hat. Once more she felt the awe and wonder of fulfillment spread over her as she gazed with happiness at her new family.

Ross glowed inside like a million suns when he spotted her in the doorway. As she walked across the yard toward him, Lydia stepped into her path and handed her a bouquet of flowers. Bending, she kissed the girl's cheek, then proceeded toward him to where he stood in front of the arbor. Within seconds she was at his side.

Irene turned toward Ross, nearly unaware of those who watched, and clasped his hand lovingly in hers. They were united in their purposes, their goals, their beliefs, and especially their honesty and devotion. These, she pledged silently, would be the foundation of their marriage.

An abundance of blossoming roses surrounded them, filling the air with the heady scent of spring's perfume, while overhead the birds added their own chorus of love to the moment.

Then the reverend began speaking the familiar words,

although now they seemed brand new, and each promised to love and keep the other.

Then it was over and she was in his arms, returning his kiss with a promise of her own. This is how it would be forever, he thought, the two of them together.

Congratulations were given and accepted. Cake and punch were served and eaten. And all of it was like a blur of time and place and people. Warm sunshine beamed down upon them, adding a special brightness to Irene's face, and Ross thought she had never looked more beautiful.

As the afternoon wound down and the guests began leaving, a carriage pulled up to the backyard. A young driver hopped out, then ambled toward Ross. He gave the boy a coin, clapped him on the back, and went in search of Winnie.

"Did you fix us a hamper?" he asked when he found her in the kitchen.

She produced the familiar basket and set it on the table. "It's heavy. Irene's good dishes and silver are in there." In a lowered voice, she added, "I found a bottle of sherry wine in the pantry."

With a wink of appreciation, he kissed her cheek. "You're a sweetheart."

She flapped her hands at him. "Oh, go on with you." But inside she was pleased beyond measure.

Outside, he found Irene with Emma, cooing and laughing at the baby. When he took Irene's elbow, Emma eyed the hamper in his hand and colored profusely. Making her apologies, she went in search of Howard, leaving the two of them alone.

"Now it's our turn to go," Ross whispered.

"But our guests . . ."

"Those who are left will be well taken care of by your mother. Besides, we're going on a picnic." He hefted the basket for her to see.

"A picnic?" she asked, laughing. "Where?"

"That's a surprise," he answered, grasping her by the elbow and escorting her toward the waiting buggy.

Lydia and Jonathan had spied their leave-taking and called out cheerful farewells. The others, including Winnie, came through the kitchen doorway to wave and wish them well.

As they rode along the river road, Ross kept his gaze trained on Irene until she blushed and had to look away; then, unable to resist, she looked back again. They smiled at each other, enjoying the pleasant ride and especially each other's company.

"Did I tell you that you're the most beautiful woman I've ever seen?" he asked.

As she tilted her head to see him better, her large hat angled in a very becoming way. "How is a woman supposed to answer a question like that?" she replied softly, her lips teasing a smile.

"I don't know." He grinned. "I guess maybe just your smile is enough."

A companionable silence drew them closer, although each was thinking separate thoughts about what lay ahead.

When they approached the turn-off toward the cabin, Ross felt a new apprehension. Maybe he'd made a mistake thinking the cabin was a good idea for their first night together. It was so rustic, so bare, and nothing at all like she was used to. As the horse ambled toward their destination, he almost changed his mind.

Alert to her surroundings, Irene sat a little forward, looking expectant. "This is the way to your little cabin."

Too late now to turn around, he nodded, deciding that after the picnic they would go back and get a room at the inn. He pulled into the clearing where the cabin and barn stood in good repair and the fields beyond lay planted in hopes of a bountiful harvest.

"Why . . . it looks as if someone lives here!" She stared

at the stacked woodpiles, the fences, and the neatly cleared barnyard. "Didn't you say Howard owns this? I can't imagine . . ."

"He did. It's ours now." With quiet trepidation, he waited for her reaction, wondering what he'd do if she was displeased.

Surprised, she repeated his words, "It's ours?"

"Whoa," he said softly, pulling the horse to a halt. Then he climbed down and circled the carriage to her side.

"Do you have animals? Oh, Jonathan and Lydia will be so pleased! How did you manage to keep this a secret?"

A wave of relief flowed over him as he caught the excitement in her voice.

With a grin, he answered, "We didn't tell Emma."

She laughed and the sound filled his head like soft music. Lifting her down, he set her feet on the ground until her toes nearly touched his. With his hands still on her waist, he held her close until the brim of her hat grazed his forehead.

He leaned toward her. "Mrs. Ross Hollister," he said just before he brushed her lips with his own.

"Mmmm. I like the sound of that."

"So do I." He stepped back slightly. "Would you like to see the cabin?"

"Very much."

Careful not to catch her dress on any brambles that had escaped his blade, he ushered her toward the newly renovated building.

"A new door," she said, approvingly. "And window panes, too."

Before he opened the door, he stood between her and it. "I tried to make it more presentable, but I'm not sure—" He stopped. "I mean, it's still just a rough cabin."

She reached up with her hand and placed her fingers over his lips to silence him. "Anywhere you are, that's where I want to be."

With those words, the last remaining tension went out

of him, and he stepped aside to allow her to enter.

The first thing she saw was the fireplace, its hearth neatly swept and a stack of dried wood waiting nearby. Off to the side and beneath a window sat a table with two plain chairs. And opposite the fireplace, occupying the greatest share of the room, was a large four-poster bed covered with a colorful quilt which brightened the otherwise darkened space. Beside the bed was a stand holding a glass filled with a variety of wildflowers he had picked just for her. And everywhere there were rugs to warm the pine floors.

"It's lovely." Turning toward him, she placed her hands on his chest. "Let's don't ever tear it down. I love it just the way it is."

Suddenly his heart expanded until he didn't think it would be able to hold all that he felt for her. Grasping her lightly by the shoulders, he pulled her to him as he lowered his head. Her sweet fragrance was nothing compared to the taste of her mouth. With tenderness giving way to the needs of passion, his arms encircled her but the straw hat she wore proved to be an undeniable nuisance, so reluctantly he released her.

"I guess I should take out the pins," she offered, reaching up to remove them. Then he slid the hat from her head, tossing it onto a rug.

"That's much better," he said as his fingers plied the confining coil of hair at her nape until finally its thickness fell about her shoulders. Gently, he lifted a handful to his face, savoring the texture and the scent before brushing it back out of his way. Then his gaze swept over her face until it rested lower, where her quickened pulse beat visibly above the top button of her dress. With deliberate care he worked the first one free.

She in turn tugged at his tie. "Shouldn't we bring in the basket?"

He heard the breathless catch in her voice, and his fingers stopped at the fourth button. Slowly, he peeled back the gown and dropped a kiss on her now bare shoulder. "Later," he replied.

Closing her eyes, she reveled in the ripple of emotion that cascaded through her as she allowed him to slip the soft yellow satin from her body.

"What if the horse goes back to the livery?" she asked, barely aware that she spoke of ordinary things when such extraordinary things were happening in the center of her being.

"I guess," he said, stopping to nibble at the swell of her breast above her chemise, "we'll just have to stay here until somebody finds us."

"Mmmm." She lifted her arms to circle his neck. "That could take a while."

Pulling her flush against him, he replied with great sincerity, "I hope so."

Her responding smile became lost as his mouth melded with hers, bringing a sweet warmth that suffused her entirely. Any thoughts of what she ought to do next seemed pointless under the circumstances. Her body definitely had a will of its own, and she was, quite simply, at the mercy of these new emotions. As his kiss deepened, she was drawn, body, mind and soul, into another awareness, and suddenly the outside world fell away. They were free to explore, to touch and be touched, to give and to receive.

She felt his work-roughened hands caress her body as he unbuttoned, unlaced, and removed the rest of her clothing. Setting her slightly away from him, he removed his own clothes. Standing now, with their bodies touching, she reached up to trace the outline of his jaw.

"Ross Hollister, I love you," she said softly.

He lifted her into his arms and laid her on the bed, stretching his frame alongside her and pulling her soft curves into the contours of his hard ones. The heat of his skin was like a match to her own.

"Remember the day I pulled you into the stream?"

She nodded, her muscles feeling too fluid for even a smile.

"I had an idea then how you would look." He ran one fingertip lightly over the crest of her breast, and she gasped. "I was right."

Her eyes slid closed in anticipation of what was to come next. Not in her wildest fantasies had she believed it could be like this. So bold, so free, so full of loving.

"Irene, open your eyes. I want us to do this together, not separately in our own worlds."

She opened her eyes and smiled. "We'll never be separate again. No matter what."

He leaned over her then, covering her with his body, touching her with his lips, caressing her with his hands. A fiery tremor built inside her, rising until it engulfed her and encompassed both of them. Passion, all-consuming, bore them to a new height as she welcomed him into her body. They moved with it, flowed with it, soaring higher and higher until ultimately they succumbed to wave after wave of ecstasy, pure and explosive.

"Irene," he whispered into the curve of her neck where his breath caused a delicious tingling in her skin. It wasn't a question, so she didn't answer. She knew he was simply saying her name aloud in order to bring some reality to a moment that seemed unbelievable.

"Ross," she whispered back, expecting no reply.

He shifted his weight slightly so as not to burden her. For several long minutes they held each other, savoring the experience, enjoying the gift that each had just received. This was just the beginning of such moments, and that knowledge alone made it more precious.

At long last, he rolled back, taking her with him until they lay face to face. Irene kissed his chin, and he in turn kissed the tip of her nose. She snuggled against him, entwining her legs with his, filled with an uncontrollable joy.

With his arms wrapped securely around her, he cradled her head against his shoulder.

"What do you think about building a house out here?" he asked.

"I wouldn't want to live anywhere else," she replied, snuggling closer.

Smiling, he added, "There's plenty of room for children."

"Jonathan will love it. And so will Lydia."

"And what about more children?" he asked, tipping her chin up so he could look into her eyes.

"I imagine that isn't going to be a problem," she replied with a mischievous grin.

Outside the cabin, the horse nickered softly.

"I suppose I'd better unharness him. He must think we're trying to torture him with all that fresh grass that he can't reach." Reluctantly, he rose from the bed, depositing a lingering kiss on her lips.

"Can't he wait just little longer?" she asked, refusing to release her hold on his neck. "After all, we have some important planning to do." She gave a tug and he fell onto the bed, his lips just a whisper away.

"On second thought," he replied, scooping her into his arms. "Maybe he can wait . . ."

SPECIAL SNEAK PREVIEW FOLLOWS!

Madeline Baker writing as Amanda Ashley

Cursed by the darkness, he searches through the ages for the redeeming light, the one woman who can save him. An angel of purity and light, she fears the handsome stranger whose eyes promise endless ecstasy even while his mouth whispers dark secrets. They are two people longing for fulfillment, yearning for a love like no other. Alone, they will face a desolate destiny. Together, they will share undying passion, defy eternity, and embrace the night.

Don't miss *Embrace The Night!* Available now at bookstores and newsstands everywhere.

He walked the streets for hours after he left the orphanage, his thoughts filled with Sara, her fragile beauty, her sweet innocence, her unwavering trust. She had accepted him into her life without question, and the knowledge cut him to the quick. He did not like deceiving her, hiding the dark secret of what he was, nor did he like to think about how badly she would be hurt when his nighttime visits ceased, as they surely must.

He had loved her from the moment he first saw her, but always from a distance, worshiping her as the moon might worship the sun, basking in her heat, her light, but wisely staying away lest he be burned.

And foolishly, he had strayed too close. He had soothed her tears, held her in his arms, and now he was paying the price. He was burning, like a moth drawn to a flame. Burning with need. With desire. With an unholy lust, not for her body, but for the very essence of her life.

It sickened him that he should want her that way, that he could even consider such a despicable thing. And yet he could think of little else. Ah, to hold her in his arms, to feel his body become one with hers as he drank of her sweetness. . . .

For a moment, he closed his eyes and let himself imagine it, and then he swore a long vile oath filled with pain and longing.

Hands clenched, he turned down a dark street, his self-anger turning to loathing, and the loathing to rage. He felt the need to kill, to strike out, to make someone else suffer as he was suffering.

Pity the poor mortal who next crossed his path, he thought. Then he gave himself over to the hunger pounding through him.

She woke covered with perspiration, Gabriel's name on her lips. Shivering, she drew the covers up to her chin.

It had only been a dream. Only a dream.

She spoke the words aloud, finding comfort in the sound of her own voice. A distant bell chimed the hour. Four o'clock.

Gradually, her breathing returned to normal. Only a dream, she said again, but it had been so real. She had felt the cold breath of the night, smelled the rank odor of fear rising from the body of the faceless man cowering in the shadows. She had sensed a deep anger, a wild uncontrollable evil personified by a being in a flowing black cloak. Even now, she could feel his anguish, his loneliness, the alienation that cut him off from the rest of humanity.

It had all been so clear in the dream, but now it made no sense. No sense at all.

With a slight shake of her head, she snuggled deeper under the covers and closed her eyes.

It was just a dream, nothing more.

Sunk in the depths of despair, Gabriel prowled the deserted abbey. What had happened to his self-control? Not for centuries had he taken enough blood to kill, only enough to assuage the pain of the hunger, to ease his unholy thirst.

A low groan rose in his throat. Sara had happened. He wanted her and he couldn't have her. Somehow, his desire and his frustration had gotten tangled up with his lust for blood.

It couldn't happen again. It had taken him centuries to learn to control the hunger, to give himself the illusion that he was more man than monster.

Had he been able, he would have prayed for forgiveness, but he had forfeited the right to divine intervention long ago.

Where will we go tonight?"

Gabriel stared at her. She'd been waiting for him again, clothed in her new dress, her eyes bright with anticipation. Her goodness drew him, soothed him, calmed his dark side even as her beauty, her innocence, teased his desire.

He stared at the pulse throbbing in her throat. "Go?"

Sara nodded.

With an effort, he lifted his gaze to her face. "Where would you like to go?"

"I don't suppose you have a horse?"

"A horse?"

"I've always wanted to ride."

He bowed from the waist. "Whatever you wish, milady," he said. "I'll not be gone long."

It was like having found a magic wand, Sara mused as she waited for him to return. She had only to voice her desire, and he produced it.

Twenty minutes later, she was seated before him on a prancing black stallion. It was a beautiful animal, tall and muscular, with a flowing mane and tail.

She leaned forward to stroke the stallion's neck. His coat felt like velvet beneath her hand. "What's his name?"

"Necromancer," Gabriel replied, pride and affection evident in his tone.

"Necromancer? What does it mean?"

"One who communicates with the spirits of the dead."

Sara glanced at him over her shoulder. "That seems an odd name for a horse."

"Odd, perhaps," Gabriel replied cryptically, "but fitting."

"Fitting? In what way?"

"Do you want to ride, Sara, or spend the night asking foolish questions?"

She pouted prettily for a moment and then grinned at him. "Ride!"

A word from Gabriel and they were cantering through the dark night, heading into the countryside.

"Faster," Sara urged.

"You're not afraid?"

"Not with you."

"You should be afraid, Sara Jayne," he muttered under his breath, "especially with me."

He squeezed the stallion's flanks with his knees and the horse shot forward, his powerful hooves skimming across the ground.

Sara shrieked with delight as they raced through the darkness. This was power, she thought, the surging body of the horse, the man's strong arm wrapped securely around her waist. The wind whipped through her hair, stinging her cheeks and making her eyes water, but she only threw back her head and laughed.

"Faster!" she cried, reveling in the sense of freedom that surged within her.

Hedges and trees and sleeping farmhouses passed by in a blur. Once, they jumped a four-foot hedge, and she felt as if she were flying. Sounds and scents blended together: the chirping of crickets, the bark of a dog, the smell of damp earth and lathered horseflesh, and over all the touch of Gabriel's breath upon her cheek, the steadying strength of his arm around her waist.

Gabriel let the horse run until the animal's sides were heaving and covered with foamy lather, and then he drew back on the reins, gently but firmly, and the stallion slowed, then stopped.

"That was wonderful!" Sara exclaimed.

She turned to face him, and in the bright light of the moon, he saw that her cheeks were flushed, her lips parted, her eyes shining like the sun.

How beautiful she was! His Sara, so full of life. What cruel fate had decreed that she should be bound to a wheelchair? She was a vivacious girl on the brink of womanhood. She should be clothed in silks and satins, surrounded by gallant young men.

Dismounting, he lifted her from the back of the horse. Carrying her across the damp grass, he sat down on a large boulder, settling her in his lap.

"Thank you, Gabriel," she murmured.

"It was my pleasure, milady."

"Hardly that," she replied with a saucy grin. "I'm sure ladies don't ride pell-mell through the dark astride a big black devil horse."

"No," he said, his gray eyes glinting with amusement, "they don't."

"Have you known many ladies?"

"A few." He stroked her cheek with his forefinger, his touch as light as thistledown.

"And were they accomplished and beautiful?"

Gabriel nodded. "But none so beautiful as you."

She basked in his words, in the silent affirmation she read in his eyes.

"Who are you, Gabriel?" she asked, her voice soft and dreamy. "Are you man or magician?"

"Neither."

"But still my angel?"

"Always, *cara*."

With a sigh, she rested her head against his shoulder and closed her eyes. How wonderful, to sit here in the dark of night with his arms around her. She could almost forget that she was crippled. Almost.

She lost all track of time as she sat there, secure in his arms. She heard the chirp of crickets, the sighing of the wind through the trees, the pounding of Gabriel's heart beneath her cheek.

Her breath caught in her throat as she felt the touch of his hand in her hair and then the brush of his lips.

Abruptly, he stood up. Before she quite knew what was happening, she was on the horse's back and Gabriel was swinging up behind her. He moved with the lithe grace of a cat vaulting a fence.

She sensed a change in him, a tension she didn't understand. A moment later, his arm was locked around her waist and they were riding through the night.

She leaned back against him, braced against the solid wall of his chest. She felt his arm tighten around her, felt his breath on her cheek.

Pleasure surged through her at his touch and she placed her hand over his forearm, drawing his arm more securely around her, tacitly telling him that she enjoyed his nearness.

She thought she heard a gasp, as if he was in pain, but she shook the notion aside, telling herself it was probably just the wind crying through the trees.

Too soon, they were back at the orphanage.

"You'll come tomorrow?" she asked as he settled her in her bed, covering her as if she were a child.

"Tomorrow," he promised. "Sleep well, *cara*."

"Dream of me," she murmured.

With a nod, he turned away. Dream of her, he thought. If only he could!

"Where would you like to go tonight?" Gabriel asked the following evening.

"I don't care, so long as it's with you."

Moments later, he was carrying her along a pathway in the park across from the orphanage.

Sara marveled that he held her so effortlessly, that it felt so right to be carried in his arms. She rested her head on his shoulder, content. A faint breeze played hide and seek with the leaves of the trees. A lover's moon hung low in the sky. The air was fragrant with night blooming flowers, but it was Gabriel's scent that rose all around her—warm and musky, reminiscent of aged wine and expensive cologne.

He moved lightly along the pathway, his footsteps making hardly a sound. When they came to a stone bench near a quiet pool, he sat down, placing her on the bench beside him.

It was a lovely place, a fairy place. Elegant ferns, tall and lacy, grew in wild profusion near the pool. In the distance, she heard the questioning hoot of an owl.

"What did you do all day?" she asked, turning to look at him.

Gabriel shrugged. "Nothing to speak of. And you?"

"I read to the children. Sister Mary Josepha has been giving me more and more responsibility."

"And does that make you happy?"

"Yes. I've grown very fond of my little charges. They so need to be loved. To be touched. I had never realized how important it was, to be held, until—" A faint flush stained her cheeks. "Until you held me. There's such comfort in the touch of a human hand."

Gabriel grunted softly. Human, indeed, he thought bleakly.

Sara smiled. "They seem to like me, the children. I don't know why."

But he knew why. She had so much love to give, and no outlet for it.

"I hate to think of all the time I wasted wallowing in self-pity," Sara remarked. "I spent so much time sitting in my room, sulking because I couldn't walk, when I could have been helping the children, loving them." She glanced up at Gabriel. "They're so easy to love."

"So are you." He had not meant to speak the words

aloud, but they slipped out. "I mean, it must be easy for the children to love you. You have so much to give."

She smiled, but it was a sad kind of smile. "Perhaps that's because no one else wants it."

"Sara—"

"It's all right. Maybe that's why I was put here, to comfort the little lost lambs that no one else wants."

I want you. The words thundered in his mind, in his heart, in his soul.

Abruptly, he stood up and moved away from the bench. He couldn't sit beside her, feel her warmth, hear the blood humming in her veins, sense the sadness dragging at her heart, and not touch her, take her.

He stared into the depths of the dark pool, the water as black as the emptiness of his soul. He'd been alone for so long, yearning for someone who would share his life, needing someone to see him for what he was and love him anyway.

A low groan rose in his throat as the centuries of loneliness wrapped around him.

"Gabriel?" Her voice called out to him, soft, warm, caring.

With a cry, he whirled around and knelt at her feet. Hesitantly, he took her hands in his.

"Sara, can you pretend I'm one of the children? Can you hold me, and comfort me, just for tonight?"

"I don't understand."

"Don't ask questions, *cara*. Please just hold me. Touch me."

She gazed down at him, into the fathomless depths of his dark gray eyes, and the loneliness she saw there pierced her heart. Tears stung her eyes as she reached for him.

He buried his face in her lap, ashamed of the need that he could no longer deny. And then he felt her hand stroke his hair, light as a summer breeze. Ah, the touch of a human hand, warm, fragile, pulsing with life.

Time ceased to have meaning as he knelt there, his head cradled in her lap, her hand moving in his hair, caressing his nape, feathering across his cheek. No wonder the children loved her. There was tranquility in her touch, serenity in her hand. A sense of peace settled over him, stilling his hunger. He felt the tension drain out of him, to be replaced with a nearly forgotten sense of calm. It was a feeling as close to forgiveness as he would ever know.

After a time, he lifted his head. Slightly embarrassed, he gazed up at her, but there was no censure in her eyes, no disdain, only a wealth of understanding.

"Why are you so alone, my angel?" she asked quietly.

"I have always been alone," he replied, and even now, when he was nearer to peace of spirit than he had been for centuries, he was aware of the vast gulf that separated him, not only from Sara, but from all of humanity as well.

Gently, she cupped his cheek with her hand. "Is there no one to love you then?"

"No one."

"I would love you, Gabriel."

"No!"

Stricken by the force of his denial, she let her hand fall into her lap. "Is the thought of my love so revolting?"

"No, don't ever think that." He sat back on his heels, wishing that he could sit at her feet forever, that he could spend the rest of his existence worshiping her beauty, the generosity of her spirit. "I'm not worthy of you, *cara*. I would not have you waste your love on me."

"Why, Gabriel? What have you done that you feel unworthy of love?"

Filled with the guilt of a thousand lifetimes, he closed his eyes and his mind filled with an image of blood. Rivers of blood. Oceans of death. Centuries of killing, of bloodletting. Damned. The Dark Gift had given him eternal life—and eternal damnation.

Thinking to frighten her away, he let her look deep into his eyes, knowing that what she saw within his soul would

361

speak more eloquently than words.

He clenched his hands, waiting for the compassion in her eyes to turn to revulsion. But it didn't happen.

She gazed down at his upturned face for an endless moment, and then he felt the touch of her hand in his hair.

"My poor angel," she whispered. "Can't you tell me what it is that haunts you so?"

He shook his head, unable to speak past the lump in his throat.

"Gabriel." His name, nothing more, and then she leaned forward and kissed him.

It was no more than a feathering of her lips across his, but it exploded through him like concentrated sunlight. Hotter than a midsummer day, brighter than lightning, it burned through him and for a moment he felt whole again. Clean again.

Humbled to the core of his being, he bowed his head so she couldn't see his tears.

"I will love you, Gabriel," she said, still stroking his hair. "I can't help myself."

"Sara—"

"You don't have to love me back," she said quickly. "I just wanted you to know that you're not alone anymore."

A long shuddering sigh coursed through him, and then he took her hands in his, holding them tightly, feeling the heat of her blood, the pulse of her heart. Gently, he kissed her fingertips, and then, gaining his feet, he swung her into his arms.

"It's late," he said, his voice thick with the tide of emotions roiling within him. "We should go before you catch a chill."

"You're not angry?"

"No, *cara*."

How could he be angry with her? She was light and life, hope and innocence. He was tempted to fall to his knees and beg her forgiveness for his whole miserable existence.

But he couldn't burden her with the knowledge of what

he was. He couldn't tarnish her love with the truth.

It was near dawn when they reached the orphanage. Once he had her settled in bed, he knelt beside her. "Thank you, Sara."

She turned on her side, a slight smile lifting the corners of her mouth as she took his hand in hers. "For what?"

"For your sweetness. For your words of love. I'll treasure them always."

"Gabriel." The smile faded from her lips. "You're not trying to tell me good-bye, are you?"

He stared down at their joined hands: hers small and pale and fragile, pulsing with the energy of life; his large and cold, indelibly stained with blood and death.

If he had a shred of honor left, he would tell her good-bye and never see her again.

But then, even when he had been a mortal man, he'd always had trouble doing the honorable thing when it conflicted with something he wanted. And he wanted—no, needed—Sara. Needed her as he'd never needed anything else in his accursed life. And perhaps, in a way, she needed him. And even if it wasn't so, it eased his conscience to think it true.

"Gabriel?"

"No, *cara*, I'm not planning to tell you good-bye. Not now. Not ever."

The sweet relief in her eyes stabbed him to the heart. And he, cold, selfish monster that he was, was glad of it. Right or wrong, he couldn't let her go.

"Till tomorrow then?" she said, smiling once more.

"Till tomorrow, *cara mia*," he murmured. And for all the tomorrows of your life.

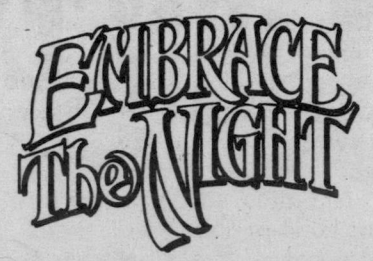

JAUNCEY

Melody Morgan

"A lovely romance." —*Romantic Times*

After inheriting property in Laramie, Wyoming, Jauncey Taylor makes big plans for the future—until she discovers her inheritance is a bordello. Then she chases off former customer Matt Dawson, even as she wonders what ecstasy she could taste in his kiss. But Jauncey won't find out until she makes an honest man of the rugged cowpoke—and turns the bawdy house into a house of love.

_51992-5 $4.99 US/$5.99 CAN

DANCE of the FLAME

ELAINE BARBIERI

**Elaine Barbieri's romances are
"powerful...fascinating...storytelling at its best!"**
—*Romantic Times*

Exiled to a barren wasteland, Sera will do anything to regain the kingdom that is her birthright. But the hard-eyed warrior she saves from death is the last companion she wants for the long journey to her homeland.

To the world he is known as Death's Shadow—as much a beast of battle as the mighty warhorse he rides. But to the flame-haired healer, his forceful arms offer a warm haven, and he swears his throbbing strength will bring her nothing but pleasure.

Sera and Tolin hold in their hands the fate of two feuding houses with an ancient history of bloodshed and betrayal. But no matter what the age-old prophecy foretells, the sparks between them will not be denied, even if their fiery union consumes them both.

_3793-9 $5.99 US/$6.99 CAN